VENGEANCE:

AN OAK GROVE SUSPENSE

Happy Reading!!

BY

REESE STEPHENS

Printed in the United States of America

First Printing, 2016

ISBN 978-0-9981134-1-8 (ebook)
ISBN 978-0-9981134-0-1 (paperback)

WINYAN PRESS LLC

Tampa, Florida

Copyright © 2016 Winyan Press, LLC

Cover Art © Alex Marin

DEDICATION

To my husband. I've put you through way more than you deserve, but you've stuck around. So, you're either one of the good ones, or just as crazy as I am. Either way, I'm totally in love with you. Thank you for being you.

I love you, Schmoopy!

PREFACE

I think in everyone's life there comes a time when you have to choose what direction your life will take. Sometimes that direction is laid out easily by things out of our control, but sometimes we have to decide our direction. The first time I chose a direction in my life was by trusting Christ as my savior; I was nine when I went to my dad and asked him about heaven. He stopped everything he was doing, sat down with me, and told me the story of Jesus. I'd heard it in church a hundred times, but it wasn't until that moment that I realized how real he was and that he'd died for me. He came to Earth and died on the cross for me! How amazing is that? Since accepting Christ as my savior, I have continued to pray and ask God for direction and guidance. Sometimes it's hard, and not everyone agrees with my choices, but I have to follow the path I believe God is taking me on.

When my husband and I moved away from our family in 2007, we felt it was what God wanted for our lives. I believe that with all my heart. We had peace, a job, a house, everything laid out in a nice little package. Once we moved and got settled in, we started to talk about children. We decided that since we knew we couldn't have kids of our own, we'd already dealt with that heartbreak and were ready to move past it, that we'd help those who didn't have the love of a parent or anyone to really care for them.

We went through the process of becoming foster parents and about six months later had our first placement, then, shortly after, our second. We loved those two little girls as if they were our own. They were with us for over two years, and it really looked like we'd get to adopt them. Then we found out that our first placement would be going back to her bio family. Then a few days later we found out that the second girl, who we thought for sure would be ours forever, was going to live with a family who adopted her half-brother four years earlier. Within five days both girls were gone.

We were devastated. Our children were gone and there was absolutely nothing we could do about it. We knew going into foster care that it was a possibility, but, until that moment, we never thought about that outcome. We just loved those girls and wanted them forever, but that wasn't God's plan. He had something else in mind for us and them. It was hard for me to accept. It sent me into a depression, which I had never experienced in my life. I couldn't get out of bed. I couldn't leave my house. I could barely do anything, not even the things I'd once enjoyed. I felt anxious, alone, and scared. I felt out of control and, honestly, I felt unwanted. I was angry at myself, my family, God. I couldn't believe that this could happen after having prayed and trusted Him completely that he'd give us the desire of our hearts.

I was bitter. I was mean. I couldn't see past my situation. I stopped going to church. I didn't read my Bible. I didn't talk to the few friends I had, or my family. I barely talked to my husband. It was a dark time in my life. I never thought I'd see the light.

Then one day I received a call from the DHHR. They had a little girl who needed a home. She would most likely be back with her mother in six months or so. I thought, sure, I can go into this, no expectations. I needed a reason to function. I needed something to push me to get out of bed. So, I said yes. I don't even remember if I talked to my husband about it or not. She came, and surprisingly, she was just what I needed. She was the wildest child I'd ever met. She was funny and full of personality. She wouldn't obey anything I said, or anyone else for that matter. She was a mess! But you know what? I needed that mess. I needed someone to get my mind off of losing my girls. It worked. She helped me start to heal a little bit. I still had a hard time getting out of bed or leaving my house, I had a lot of anxiety, but my heart felt a little lighter.

After a few months, I got another call asking if I'd take two more kids. They were already in foster care with a family who couldn't keep them any longer. Termination of parental rights was set, and they wanted them to be moved to a family who could adopt them. I did talk to my husband this time. The worker wanted to gradually introduce them to us and then transfer them. We liked that, for two reasons: one, it gave the kids a little time to get to know us before staying with us, and two, it gave us time to get to know them. We wanted to go into this with an open mind. We didn't want any surprises. Well, God had other plans. About two or three days later, the foster mom called me to say I had to take them the next day or they'd have to go to a different home, because they just couldn't keep them any longer. Their situation was changing so quickly, they had to make other arrangements for the kids.

So the first time I met them was the next day. I met the foster mom at the school so I could be added to the forms and be able to pick them up the next day. Once everything was set, they brought her to me. For a long time I couldn't describe how I felt the first time I laid eyes on my daughter, but now that I've given birth, I know. It was that instant love you have the first time you hold your baby in your arms. I knew. I knew this little bubbly silly girl was mine. There was no question in my mind. She was perfect. The moment I saw her walking down the hall to me with the biggest smile on her face. I knew. Then she hugged me and said, "You're my new mommy." That was that. There was no going back. I tell her all the time that I prayed for a green eyed, brown haired little girl and that's exactly what I got. God gave me the perfect child. She wasn't a baby like I'd envisioned, but that didn't matter. She was mine and she was perfect.

We went home and I got to have that feeling all over again when the foster mom took my son out of his car seat and handed him to me. He was just as perfect. He was exactly what I'd prayed for, a boy with blue eyes and brown hair. He couldn't say much, and he looked at me like I was crazy, but it didn't matter, I knew he was mine. I instantly fell in love with him. We got all their stuff in our living-room and the foster family left. The kids started to cry a little bit; I wrapped my arms around them and just held them. My daughter asked me if she could stay forever, and even though I shouldn't have, I promised she could. I meant that. I had an unexplainable peace that they'd always be with us. That they'd truly be ours one day.

Things weren't completely smooth in their adoption. Those things never are. We had some minor setbacks and delays, but they worked themselves out. I still had issues leaving my house, because depression isn't something you can turn on and off. It's something you have to fight, but things were getting better. We went back to church, not as faithful, but we were trying to get closer to God, to do what we thought He'd want us to do.

We were finally able to adopt the kids after two years. Things were great. Everything seemed to be going smoothly. My depression and anxiety had lessened considerably. I only had slight fits of anxiety in public. I was totally happy and content with my family and our church. I'd even found a passion for creative writing. I'd met some people who had kids the same ages as mine. I had friends close by. I was becoming more active. I was finally starting to feel a little like I had years before all the heartache started, before I knew I couldn't have children.

I couldn't find anything in my life at that point that I was unhappy about. Then, right after my daughter's ninth birthday, my son started telling everyone, even complete strangers, that I had a baby in my belly. At first I just laughed and told him I didn't, but he didn't stop. If you know him, you know if he gets something in his mind, he's not going to give up until he gets what he wants. I honestly tried really hard to not let it bother me, but it did. I knew it wasn't a possibility, and I couldn't help but be a little sad.

We'd been married almost ten years and had gone through countless infertility treatments. I wasn't taking any medication at that time. I wasn't even thinking about a baby. I loved my little family of four. A girl and a boy. It was perfect. It was just what I asked God for. But on May 6th, right before Mother's Day in 2013, I found out that I was pregnant. My son was right! I did have a baby in my belly. To say I was shocked would be an understatement. It was in no way an easy pregnancy, but the result of having a baby was the icing on the cake. Our little family is complete and perfect. It's more than I'd ever hoped or prayed for.

God truly answers prayers. It's not always in the time we want it to happen, but it happens in his perfect timing. That's something I've had to learn over the years, and I'll probably have to be reminded of it again.

All my life I wanted to be a wife and a mother. I thought it would be the easiest thing the world. But God had other plans for me. He knew if I had a baby when I originally wanted one that I wouldn't have adopted. I truly believe that my kids were made just for my husband and me. God used another woman's body to give them life, but Him giving them to me, gave me life when I needed it the most. He gave me purpose and direction when I had none. Most people look at foster/adoptive parents as saving kids in need, but those kids saved me. I'll never stop thanking God for allowing me to be their mother, for letting me give birth to my youngest daughter. He's truly and completely answered every prayer request I've ever asked for. I'm so thankful that my parents taught me the value and power of prayer.

I know, without a doubt, that if these things hadn't happened in my life as they have, that if even one little choice had been different, that I wouldn't be where I am right now. I wouldn't be fulfilling one of my dreams of becoming a published author.

There are so many people I'd like to thank for helping me on this journey; I almost don't want to mention names, in case I forget one. But I feel they deserve the recognition. To Sam, for always being there for me and believing in me. Carrie, for reading everything I send you, and telling me how much you loved it, even when its crap. Jessica, for our late night chats, and all your encouragement/butt-kicking. Ange, Tiff, and Chris for editing everything I've given you over the years, even when I'm sure you wanted to tell me I was hopeless when it came to grammar. I've learned more than I can explain from you guys. Dee, you'll always be my "Hero". To my new friends Jessica and Heather, you guys have been awesome, and came into my life just when I needed you. Tawa, who has helped me every step of the way with this book. You've truly become a great friend. Alex, for your awesome cover work. To Leanne for editing all my grammar mistakes, bless you! To Amanda for proofreading this story. Winyan Press, for giving me this awesome opportunity and for believing in me. To my readers past and present. I wouldn't be here if it wasn't for each and every one of you. I don't know if this little glimpse into my life will help anyone, but it has certainly helped my heart to be able to share it with you.

ACKNOWLEDGEMENT

Winyan Press, LLC would like to acknowledge the following individuals for their contributions on <u>Vengeance: An Oak Grove Suspense.</u>

Leeanne Lemaster, copy editor

Alex Marin, Graphic Artist/Illustrator

Amanda Rash, proof reader

Tawa Witko, developmental editor

TABLE OF CONTENTS

DEDICATION..3

PREFACE..4

ACKNOWLEDGEMENT...9

CHAPTER ONE..13

CHAPTER TWO..30

CHAPTER THREE..45

CHAPTER FOUR...57

CHAPTER FIVE...74

CHAPTER SIX..86

CHAPTER SEVEN...103

CHAPTER EIGHT...118

CHAPTER NINE..138

CHAPTER TEN...158

CHAPTER ELEVEN..180

CHAPTER TWELVE..200

CHAPTER THIRTEEN..216

CHAPTER FOURTEEN..225

CHAPTER FIFTEEN...235

CHAPTER SIXTEEN 246

CHAPTER SEVENTEEN 255

CHAPTER EIGHTEEN 268

CHAPTER NINETEEN 282

CHAPTER TWENTY 293

CHAPTER TWENTY-ONE 305

CHAPTER TWENTY-TWO 317

CHAPTER TWENTY-THREE 329

CHAPTER TWENTY-FOUR 340

EPILOGUE.. 349

AUTHOR NOTE.. 355

ABOUT THE AUTHOR... 356

CONTACT INFORMATION 357

PROLOGUE

As humans, we grow, evolve, and simply change. Everything that happens to us alters our outlook on the world, and the choices we make. Even the people we surround ourselves with make a humongous impact on our lives. Although, some choices are not our own and there's nothing we can do to change how our lives are forever affected by these events. One choice, just one decision, started a chain of events that forever changed the course of my life.

CHAPTER ONE

Shayla

I stand in my shower pondering all the ways my life has changed since my parents' death when I was thirteen. How would things be different for me if my parents hadn't been killed, if I hadn't ended up pregnant at fifteen, or if I hadn't had to raise my son alone? How different would things be if his dad would have been there for us? What if I hadn't married a man who was already married? That last one is still a sore subject for me. But none of these things were in my power to control or change. Not that I'd want to change anything ... okay, I would change marrying a married man. The rest, though it's a nice idea to have one's parents, I couldn't change it and still be sure I'd have my son. I love my son more than words and I've made something out of myself in spite of everything I've gone through in my life. What doesn't kill us makes us stronger they say, and I believe it. I'm definitely a stronger person because of my experiences. Even if those experiences were due to others' choices for my life.

I haven't squandered the gifts and privileges that the Thorns (my adoptive parents) and my birth-parents' trust-fund gave me. I'm sure *trust-fund* sucked all sympathy for me out of your mind, but it wasn't an extreme amount. It was enough to get me through college, buy myself a car, and my first house. Plus, the Thorns helped with my son and anything else that came up. They went above and beyond as I became a doctor and got my life started in our new home. They even supported my decision to marry my husband, even though they weren't pleased.

The latter was entirely my choice and it was the wrong one. He was a fellow resident and things were easy with him. I thought he was the forever my son and I needed, but I was terribly wrong. He seemed like a good man. Everyone (minus my parents) loved him, but two weeks ago, I found out that his business trips were really just to see his other wife. He handed me "divorce" papers, giving me everything. In exchange, I was to never contact him or his real wife, whom he had married the day they graduated high school, making our marriage a

---

complete farce. Angrily, I signed the papers and threw them back at the lawyer before storming out of his office.

My son, Dylan, was devastated. Todd had been the only father he knew. He didn't even have the decency to tell him goodbye. Instead, he left a note telling Dylan he was sorry. I can forgive a lot of things, but that isn't one of them. A pounding on the bathroom door startles me back to the present.

"Mom! The movers are here!" Dylan shouts.

That would be my current life choice. One I'm not sure is the best, but at least I'll be back home. I'll have the Thorns around for support. Plus, Dylan's dad (his biological one) wants to get to know him. I'm probably more nervous about that than Dylan, but only because it's Ryan, the love of my life. I shake thoughts of him from my mind as I quickly finish up my morning routine and head out to instruct the movers what must go. It doesn't take them long to clear out the already packed boxes, and by ten in the morning, we're ready to make the six hour trip home. We ride in almost complete silence for the better part of two hours before Dylan says anything.

"Is Ryan going to be there tonight?" Dylan asks.

I quickly glance over at him. He seems nervous. "Um, I asked him not to be."

"Why?"

"I just thought it would be better if we could get settled in before we have to deal with him."

Dylan turns in his seat. "What's that mean?"

I run my hand through my hair. "Nothing bad. I just haven't seen him in almost sixteen years."

"Oh." He pauses then asks, "Do you still love him?"

I scrunch my nose. Not that it's unexpected for a kid to want to know about his parents, but it's so complicated. Ryan and I had decided it would be best to not tell Dylan about our phone calls. He knows that I've talked to him, of course, just not the extent or frequency. I wanted to be sure Ryan was really committed to having a son and everything that entails and that he wasn't just feeling entitled because he contributed DNA. Especially, since a lot of his reasoning was that he wanted to get to know me again with the added caveat that we should work through our issues. Our issues have nothing to do with him knowing his son. But, I agreed, because I honestly believed Dylan would be better off in the dark for now. Why get his hopes up if Ryan turns out to be a jerk about the whole thing?

"Mom?" Dylan asks, drawing me out of my thoughts.

"I don't know," I finally say. "People change, Dyl. I love a part of him, the part that gave me you."

"That's grownup speak for, 'Yes, I pine for him.' or whatever those romance novels say." He laughs. I swat him playfully.

"I have no clue what they say, but no, it's not *adult speak* for anything. It's just the truth. I'm not the same person I was when I was fifteen and I'm sure he isn't either."

"He sounds like a total douchebag to leave his pregnant underage girlfriend to join the military."

"First, watch your mouth. Second, he didn't know anything about you until a year ago."

Dylan scoffs. "Why didn't he step up then?"

I exhale. I know he's not a little kid, but there's so much he just wouldn't understand. I don't even understand it myself. This bond that Ryan and I had. I can feel it simmering under the surface, and I know if I let it, it will consume me again. I just need time to sort through my feelings without giving a blow by blow to my son. I let out an exasperated sigh and try to be as honest as I possibly can.

"Because he was in the middle of moving across country to care for his mom and he didn't find out about you in the best of ways, so he was a little rattled."

"Yeah, you've told me that already." I can tell by his tone that he's not happy with my answer.

"Yes, but you keep asking. Dylan, there's really not much to it. He broke up with me and joined the Marines. I found out I was pregnant after he left. I tried contacting him and couldn't reach him. Then a year ago some girl we knew from high school told him I had been pregnant and had a little boy who she thought the Thorns kept."

"So he went to Maw and Pops?"

"Yeah, and they told him the truth; that I'd tried contacting him. He knew that was true, because he was the one rejecting my calls."

"Why would he do that?"

"The one time he answered, he basically told me he was an adult and didn't have time for childish games anymore and I should stop calling him because he was with someone else. He hung up and I never tried again."

"Jerk."

I hate that Dylan is forming a low opinion of his father, but I can't lie to him either. Ryan hurt me deeply.

"Yep, but in his defense, he had no clue about you."

"But you knew each other your whole life; your parents had been best friends. Weren't they supposed to take you when your parents died?" my son asks. I can hear a tinge of anger in his voice.

I inhale a deep breath and explain to him again, "Yes, that's true. I later found out that they'd had a huge falling out and had planned to change their will so that the Thorns would take me. That's why it took them so long to get me. They only had a handwritten letter that my dad had started. They had to go through foster classes and be approved, since the change wasn't put in place."

"That took over two years?"

"Yeah, because at first they tried fighting to get me with the letter, but I got lost in the shuffle of things and they couldn't find my file. The system is so bogged down that things just happen, but luckily I went to them right before I found out I was pregnant. I have no clue what would have happened to you if I'd been in a group home." I shudder at the thought.

"Was your adoption finalized before you knew?" Dylan asks.

I shake my head. "No, not until June, right before I had you."

"Right. So, Maw and Pop adopted you, you had me, then went to college and became a big time surgeon."

I laugh. "Yeah, exactly." There was so much in between those things, but that was the perfect summary for a teenager.

We're about an hour from our new, old home when the phone rings. I groan when I see that it's Ryan. "It's your dad, you want me to answer?"

"Go ahead, but do hands free."

I roll my eyes at my protective offspring, but do as he asks. Nosy kid. "Hello," I answer.

"Hey, you almost here?"

"About an hour out."

"Awesome. Listen, I know you don't want me there, but I'd really like to have dinner with you guys tonight."

"Ry …"

"I know what you said, Shayla! You've kept me from my son for fifteen years and I will not miss another day of his life. You owe me this much. It's just pizza." Sighing, I look at my son, who looks almost hopeful. I'm about to answer when Ryan continues. "Unless Dylan doesn't want to meet me tonight, I'll be there."

I gesture for Dylan to answer. He clears his throat and says, "Uh.

Yeah, that'd be great."

"I'm on speaker?" Ryan says with an edge of anger.

"Duh, you called me while I'm driving."

He huffs. "Right, sorry. It's good to hear your voice, Dylan. I can't wait to finally meet you."

"Me too," Dylan replies.

I've spoken to Ryan a handful of times since he called me that first time. That initial conversation was full of anger and accusations, but eventually we called a truce. The rest of our conversations were ... nice, for lack of a better word. He filled me in on a few things about his past, and I about mine. We never talked about our break up other than both agreeing we wished things had been different. It's crazy that those little interactions have stirred up feelings in me that I don't know what to do with. I miss Ryan; that much I do know, but there's a hopeful longing inside of me that things between us might work out this time. I'm not sure how I'll react to him when I see him. I know I want to be careful, and take things slowly, but it's hard to tell my heart to do that. I'm scared we'll move too fast, and not only will I get hurt, but Dylan will as well. That alone makes me so anxious that I feel sick.

Dylan and I are quiet the rest of the ride until we get about a mile from the house. "Um, we're almost there. You sure this is okay? If you don't want to meet like this, I'll call him."

"No, it's fine. I want to meet him." I nod in agreement, hoping this isn't the wrong choice for my son.

We arrive at my childhood home not long after. My heart thuds a rapid rhythm in my chest as I see Ryan standing on the porch steps. He looks so ... good.

"Dang, that's him?" Dylan asks.

I can't help but giggle. "Yep, that's your dad."

"Awesome. I hope he can teach me how to build muscle like that. Wonder if he'd take me to get a tatt."

"No!" I yell, looking at him with wide, surprised eyes. He throws his head back and laughs.

"You're so easy, Mom."

I smack his arm. "You snot."

He continues to laugh as he gets out of the car. Taking a deep breath, I reach for the door handle, only to let go when the door is pulled open by Ryan.

"Long time, no see," he greets me with an easy bright smile. The one I remember so well, the one his son also has.

"Yeah, I guess it is." My smile is involuntary.

This easy nature is one of the things I fell in love with when we were kids. He's like gravity; he's always pulled me in. Suddenly, and without warning, he pulls me into a tight hug. My arms hang limply at my sides.

"I've missed you," he whispers into my hair. I exhale softly, closing my eyes to keep my tears at bay. Just as quickly as the hug starts, it ends and he says, "Introduce me to our boy."

I pull back and wipe my eyes before turning to our son. "Dylan, this is your dad, Ryan."

"Hey," Dylan says quietly.

He sticks out his hand into the customary first meeting handshake. Ryan, who is a hugger by nature, swats his hand away and pulls him into a full bear hug. Dylan squeaks in surprise, but accepts the hug from his dad and returns it. My heart melts at the sight of it.

"I'm so glad you're here. We have a lot to talk about, but first, I want to introduce you to Luigi's famous pizza!" He slaps Dylan on the back and pulls him towards the house.

I can already tell that Dylan is being sucked in by Ryan's charm, but I guess that can only be a good thing. Gail Thorn, or Maw as Dylan calls her, stands on her porch next door and waves hello with a big smile. I return her smile and wave.

"I'll come over soon."

"Take your time, darling. Get reacquainted. We'll be here." I nod and hurry up the stairs. By the time I get inside, the guys have filled their plates and have started to eat.

"Just alike. No manners." I tease. They both give identical snorts.

"So I get my awesomeness from my dad," Dylan says with a cheese-pizza-filled grin. I shove him playfully by the shoulder.

"You get your nastiness from your dad."

"Hey, I resemble that remark!" Ryan defends with the same pizza-filled grin. I knew they looked similar but seeing them together, it's remarkable. Dylan is a younger Ryan.

"You're ridiculous as always, I see," I tell him.

"Always," he agrees. "So, Dylan, you excited about going to school where your parents went?"

Dylan rolls his eyes. "I'm pretty sure all schools are the same. I do want to try out for football though."

"Well, you're in luck. I happen to be one of the coaches." He winks.

I look at him. "Really? I thought you were a police detective."

He nods and wipes his mouth. "I am, but the school lost their coach over the summer and asked me if I'd help out."

"Is Principal Dillard still there?" I ask.

"Nope, he retired last year, but his daughter took over. You remember Amber, right?" I grimace. We were almost enemies because of Ryan. Well, because Ryan dated me. "She's not so bad anymore. She's married with a couple of kids."

"That's good."

Ryan laughs at me. "You sound barely convinced. It won't be as bad as you think."

I give him a look to show my disbelief. "I'm sure there's gossip. The town isn't that big."

Ryan nods as he grabs his third piece of pizza. "Of course. A town this small wouldn't be what it is without gossip. I'm sure if I'd come back sooner, I'd have known right away that you'd had my kid," he says this almost playfully, but I can tell there's some hurt too.

"I'm …" Ryan holds up a hand to stop me.

"I'm not over it, but I understand, mostly. It's in the past and I'm ready to move on. All I'm saying is this town thrives off of the latest juicy news." I know he's right so I don't argue.

"Where have you been if you weren't around here?" Dylan asks. He knows his dad was in the military, but neither of us know much else.

"I was in the Marines for four years. Then I worked in DC with the FBI. I came home a year ago to help my mom, who had cancer, but she's doing a lot better now. She's in remission. I hadn't been back here in sixteen years before then."

"What do you do now?" Dylan asks.

"I'm a detective with the police department. There's not a lot happening in this tiny town, so I often work with a few of the surrounding cities or sometimes fill in as a Deputy Sheriff."

"You like it?"

I watch as father and son talk and my heart aches for them both, for time lost. Even though I didn't intentionally choose to separate them, I had done just that. My choice caused this, but Ryan's choice to not speak to me also played a part. I can understand his guilt and anger, but I can also understand moving forward. After talking for a few hours, Dylan glances at me.

"Do you mind if I crash?"

I know he's exhausted; neither of us has been sleeping well. I nod my head, standing. "Of course not. I'll help you get settled."

Ryan stands as well. "I'll work on the mess."

I nod and mouth, "thank you." I lead Dylan to his room, which is up the stairs and the first bedroom on the left. Gail has already fixed it up for him, though I'm sure he still needs to personalize it. His bed and furniture were delivered a few days ago so he can shower and jump right in.

"What'd you think?"

"I like him," Dylan says immediately.

I smile. I'd meant his room, but I'm glad he and Ryan hit it off so well. "That's good."

"You think he likes me?" He seems so much like my little boy, I want to hug him tightly, but I know he won't like an emotional mom moment.

"Of course he does. You're awesome, what's not to like?" I tease.

He smiles. "I hope he sticks around."

"He will. Everything will be okay, baby." I smooth my hand through his hair like I've done many times throughout his life.

"I hope so. I'm really tired. I think I'll just crash, okay?"

"Whatever you want. Tomorrow, we'll have to help unload the moving truck, but after that we'll just take it easy and start unpacking the next day."

"Sounds good. Night, Mom. I love you," Dylan says, hugging me.

I squeeze him tightly, making him chuckle, then stand on my tiptoes to kiss my over six-foot-tall son on the cheek. I pause for a moment as I step out of the room, not looking forward to going back downstairs and having what I'm sure will be an awkward conversation with Ryan. When I reach the kitchen, I stop and stare at the man before me. He is so much different from the boy who left me. He's grown a few inches taller, making him closer to six-three and he's bulked out. Not like a body builder, but very fit and lightly tanned, with visible muscles. His slightly wavy, almost black hair is longer than I've ever seen it. It's now hanging down to his shoulders. I can see bits of tattoos peeking out of his tight, black t-shirt, and his blue jeans are faded and worn but fit him so perfectly. He's absolutely as breathtaking now as he was when I was fifteen. At that time in my life, I thought the world revolved around him.

"See something you like?" he asks, startling me out of my thoughts.

I clear my throat. "Yep," I answer honestly.

"What's that?" he asks with a quirked eyebrow.

"The walls. I like the paint color Gail chose."

He guffaws. "Yeah, right. You're still a horrible liar. I saw you checking me out." He flexes his muscles, to which I roll my eyes.

"So why ask then?"

Chuckling, he walks over, stopping directly in front of me, and giving me a sexy smile. His hand lifts and moves a piece of my hair behind my ear, causing my breathing to hitch.

"I still affect you," he whispers leaning into me. "You still very much affect me." He presses a kiss to my temple. "Beautiful," he murmurs.

My eyes close as I try to reign in my emotions. It's ridiculous for him to affect me all these years later, especially with the hurt we've both caused each other. He must sense my distress, because he gathers me into his arms and holds me tightly.

"It's going to be okay, sweetheart. I'm not going anywhere this time. I swear."

I clutch his shirt in my hands as the dam breaks. He lifts me off the ground, carrying me into the living room and settling us both on the sofa.

"I needed you and you wouldn't listen," I sob, letting every bit of pain I'd felt all those years ago surface. "I had to raise him on my own."

"I know. You'll never understand the depth of guilt and regret I feel. I hate myself for turning you away. For how I spoke to you the day you called."

I pull away and sit beside him on the sofa, instead of on his lap. I brush my hair out of my face and twist it into a messy bun before letting my hands fall to my lap to pick at the invisible lint on my pants.

"I'd never hated anyone until that day. You were so cruel. I swore I'd never forgive you, but when I held Dylan in my arms, that all went away. I was so thankful you'd given me him, even if I was too young to really care for him properly. I swore that day that I'd never let him down. I'd finish school and go to college. I'd be a doctor just like my dad. If it wasn't for the Thorns taking me in when they had, none of that would have happened."

He squeezes my hand. "I'm grateful for them and what they did for you both. I'll never hurt you like that again."

"Don't promise me that. You don't know me and I don't know you. We haven't seen each other since we were basically kids."

"I can tell you're still the same loving and sweet girl you were then. Sure, you've grown up and matured, but under that armor of adulthood, you're still the scared little girl who would climb into my bedroom window and let me hold her all night."

He leans forward and presses his lips to mine. I resist for about half a second before I give into the passion of my first love. My hands move to his hair and pull him closer. He winds his arms around my back and shoulders, holding me tightly. I haven't had a kiss this passionate, this exciting, or this full of meaning since the day he broke up with me. Only this time, it isn't a goodbye.

A bang causes us to break apart and look to our left. Dylan stands there with his mouth gaped open and his eyes wide. He stutters a few times, but gets out a rushed, "Sorry, I didn't mean to bother you."

I try in vain to right myself. "What's wrong?" I ask him.

"Nothing. I was thirsty and couldn't sleep."

I jump up. "I'll get you a bottle of water."

I hurry into the kitchen, leaving father and son alone. Leaning heavily on the counter in front of the sink, I mentally scold myself. What was I thinking letting Ryan get to me like that? I swore to myself long ago to never get involved with him again. Things would never be off the table for us, ever. I see that now. I grab a water bottle and fill it with filtered water and ice. I head back into the den, but stop when I hear voices, not wanting to intrude. Okay, okay, I was eavesdropping.

"Sorry you had to see that," Ryan says.

Dylan snorts. "What, you molesting my mom?"

"I was not molesting her. I was kissing her. There's a huge difference," Ryan tells him with a bit of anger in his voice.

"Yeah, like it's not rape for a nineteen year old to have sex with a fifteen year old."

I knew he couldn't be as accepting as he had seemed to be. I step out and stare at the two of them for a moment before shifting my look solely to Dylan.

"Okay, that's enough. He did not rape me. He was eighteen when you were conceived."

Dylan sputters and shrugs his shoulders. I know it's not much of a concession. He takes the water bottle from me and then storms up the stairs to his room, slamming his door. I turn to Ryan.

"I have never said anything like that to him. Ever."

"Don't worry about it. If he was with an eighteen or nineteen year old, I could see myself having issues with it. We probably shouldn't have been dating, but we were and he's the result. I'll deal with whatever anger he needs to get out."

I sit down on the couch right in front of him as he sits on the coffee table. "You never raped me."

"I know," he tells me, looking me in the eyes. I see his regret.

"You're not quite three years older than me. It might have been different if you were ten years older, but almost three is nothing, really."

We are quiet for a long while before I look up to him and see his eyes water as he stares at me. I can see so much on his face right now that I have to fight the urge to pull him towards me.

"I loved you so much. I never wanted to leave you. My dad convinced me that it was the best thing for you. I had no idea you were pregnant. Then when you called me, he told me you were just trying to get me back and I had to stay strong because you were so young. He said that since the state was involved with you, they'd arrest me for statutory rape or something. Even that Simon guy said something similar. I'm so sorry. I should have…"

My eyes tear up as I give in and pull him into my arms, holding him tightly. I'd always thought it was strange the way he was acting, but I never thought it was because of his parents, or Simon for that matter. I thought Simon understood.

"Your dad knew I was pregnant when I called you," I confess.

He pulls back. "What?"

I clear my throat. "I called you at home first, but he wouldn't let me talk, so I went to your house. Your dad answered the door. I told him I needed to talk to you, or at least write you a letter, that it was important. I didn't expect you to take me back, I just had to tell you something. He said it wasn't a good idea and refused to give me your address. I begged him, and finally confessed that I needed to tell you I was pregnant. I told him that I didn't expect anything out of you or them, but I thought you should know." Ryan sat for a long time just staring at me. I grew uncomfortable under his gaze. "I'm sorry." I blurt out.

"Why didn't you tell me this before?" He shakes his head. "I don't understand why he'd do that. Unless, he thought I'd get into trouble. What exactly did he say to you?"

I decide to only answer his first question, because I honestly don't want to relive the latter questions. "Because you wouldn't listen to me. The first time you called was horrible and then after you calmed down, you only wanted to talk to Dylan."

He nods agreeing. "And my dad, what did he say, Shay?"

I look down for a moment and steady myself. "Your dad told me not to tell anyone because you could go to jail." He lifts my chin so that I'm looking at him. "Then he told me to keep my legs closed from now on. I'm paraphrasing, because there was some really harsh language in there that doesn't need to be repeated."

Ryan makes a really disgusted noise before standing. "I need to go," he growls as he heads to the door.

I grab his arm. "Hey, it was almost sixteen years ago. Just let it go, please." When he still doesn't move, I say, "For Dylan."

He slowly turns towards me, taking my hand from his arm and holding it in his. "Shayla, my dad died two years ago."

I gasp. "Oh, I'm so sorry. I had no idea. I shouldn't have told you."

He waves me off. "It's fine. I just need to process all this. I have no doubt he said that to you. He's said several things to me over the years that I didn't understand, but now it all makes sense. I need some time to think. I'll see you tomorrow."

I nod. "Okay. Drive carefully."

"I don't need to drive. I live next door." He chuckles. I look at him confused. "I bought the old Brammer house a year ago. That's when I found out about Dylan. Sarah Davidson was the real estate agent. She mentioned you and you being pregnant. She had no idea the baby was mine, but I marched right over to the Thorns and asked them. They didn't want to talk to me, but after I saw his picture, there was no denying it."

I knew he'd gone to them, but I didn't know the circumstances. "Why didn't you tell me when we talked?"

"I didn't want you to change your mind about moving here." He had me there. I definitely would have reconsidered.

"You want to see my house?"

"Yeah, but maybe tomorrow. I'm beat and you need to process, remember?"

"You're right. Plus, if you came over I wouldn't let you leave." He chuckles.

"I'm sure that would make our angry son so happy."

He frowns, all teasing gone. "I really hate that he thinks that about me."

I shake my head. "I don't think he does. He's just angry. He has a lot of pent-up feelings. I mean, the only man he's ever known as a father cut all ties to him. He basically lied to him most of his life. Then he finds out about you. It doesn't take a genius to figure out the age difference thing."

"Right, we'll talk. Hopefully, he won't hate me forever."

"He doesn't hate you."

"What about you?"

I smile sadly. "I could never hate you, Ryan. We'll work something out."

He gives my hand a squeeze. "I love you, Shay. Always have and always will."

I can tell by the look in his eyes that he's totally serious. I believe him, but I can't tell him I've always loved him. It may be true, but I need to guard my heart a little while longer.

CHAPTER TWO

Shayla

I wake up early the next morning. It's still dark out, but I can't seem to fall back to sleep, so I head to the kitchen for some coffee and a piece of leftover pizza. I feel like death warmed over. Unfortunately, it's not a feeling I'm unaccustomed to. This is often the feeling I get after pulling double shifts at the hospital. Thankfully, my new position is mostly days with only a few on-call nights.

I take my very nutritious breakfast to the window seat in the den and stare out to my backyard. It's hard not to think of my parents when I see my old tree house. My dad spent a month of weekends building the thing. It's survived well through the years, but Pop recently hired a treehouse expert to make sure it was stable enough for an adult. He also turned it into a mini man-cave for Dylan. He has no clue. I'm actually pretty excited to show him later today.

I'm not sure how long I sit thinking about all the times my parents, Ryan, and I played in this backyard; even Ryan's parents and siblings were here all the time. Our house was always full and loud. No one would have guessed I was an only child. I may not have had a ton of friends from school, but I had plenty from my parents' friends who mostly had kids around my age. I never felt deprived or like I was missing out. I loved my life and my parents. I had everything a kid could ever want or need. It was perfect and I want that for Dylan. I'm startled when I hear a throat clear behind me.

"Morning," Dylan says, his voice thick with sleep.

He looks like he's had a rough night. I open my arms to him and just like he did as a little boy, he curls up beside me, wrapping his arms around my waist, letting me cuddle him.

"Don't tell anyone," he mutters.

I giggle. "I won't ruin your street cred." I kiss his forehead. "It doesn't matter how old you are, sometimes you just need your mom. I know I sure do."

"I'm glad I still have you. I feel like a jerk for saying that to Ryan. I was just so angry. I mean, I'm not a kid anymore. I know about rape. Sometimes it happens on dates."

"I assure you that he did not rape me. We were very much in love. I was sad and lonely, but I loved him, and I chose to give him my virginity."

"Gross," he mumbles, making me laugh.

"I'm just being straight with you, babe."

He sighs and tightens his hold on me. "I don't think I could handle it if I was a product of … that. My friend from school, Jenni, was, and she said she felt guilty, and even though her mom and stepdad loved her, she had a hard time connecting with her mom."

"I'm sorry that happened to her mom, but it's never the child's fault. Please believe me; you were not created out of trauma."

"I do." He sits up to face me. "I was worried that's why you wouldn't tell anyone who my dad was."

"I didn't tell anyone because I knew he was eighteen and I was a minor. I didn't want him to be in trouble and even though we dated when he was a minor, it wouldn't have mattered. My parents were gone and I was in the system. I had no adult to say they approved of us. Things were different back then."

"That was probably smart then." He takes my cold coffee from me, smiling. "I'll get you more. Did Maw bring over those homemade pop-tarts she was talking about?" His hopeful grin is adorable and very reminiscent of his father at his age.

"Yep, in the fridge, or there's cold pizza."

"No way. I need the tarts!" He takes off running to the kitchen.

Shaking my head, I follow. I turn the corner to see him already popping them into the toaster. "You know, I've told you your entire life, since learning to walk, to stop running in the house."

He smiles big. "Sorry."

"Sure, sure. Your dad is coming over in about an hour," I tell him as I look at the clock.

He grimaces. "How bad does he hate me?"

"He doesn't. He was upset that you thought that, but it's understandable. You should probably apologize for yelling at him though." He nods but says nothing. I don't dwell. "Registration for school starts at noon. You excited?"

"Not really. I do want to try out for football though. Did Ryan tell you when tryouts were?"

"Saturday, I think."

"Do you think we can find my cleats and gear before then?"

I nod, taking a sip of my fresh coffee. "I labeled the box. The movers were supposed to put the boxes in each room."

He groans. "I have so many boxes."

I laugh. "Probably more than I do."

We chat for a few minutes as we eat, then head to our rooms to get ready for registration. It doesn't take me long to get ready, and by the time I'm heading down the stairs, the doorbell is ringing. I open it with a smile when I see Ryan standing there. He's wearing a pair of navy basketball pants and a white polo with the school's eagle logo in the corner.

"So you're coach today and not Detective Jacobs?"

"Yep, though I'm going into the station after registration. Is our boy ready?" He kisses my cheek as he enters the house.

"Probably. Want something to eat or drink?"

"Nah, I have a coffee in the truck."

"Hey, Ryan," Dylan says as he enters the kitchen. He's wearing faded jeans and a vintage t-shirt with converse sneakers. I smile at him. "What?"

"Nothing, it's just surprising to me how little styles change. Your dad wore something like that when he was in high school."

"I still wear stuff like that," Ryan chuckles.

Dylan looks down at himself. "Maybe I should change."

"Don't be like that." I laugh and hand him the shirt he'd asked me to press earlier this morning.

After Dylan gets his shirt on and I've gathered my things, we head out to Ryan's truck. The drive to the school is fairly uneventful. We pull up about twenty minutes later. It's strange to me how little it's changed.

"I'll go with you to the office, but then I have to go to the gym," Ryan explains as he helps me out of his truck. He's always been a gentleman.

"What exactly do you do here?" Dylan asks his dad.

"I'm one of the temporary assistant football coaches until they find a replacement. Then I'll probably just fill in and help out."

"What happened to the last one?" I ask.

Ryan chuckles humorlessly. "He was caught with the head cheerleader. She was eighteen, but that doesn't really matter to the school board."

"I'd say not. That's awful."

"Pretty much. So, after he was fired, they asked me to fill in. I'd been helping out before it all went down, so it was an easy transition."

"You played in school?" Dylan asked.

Ryan stops by the school's trophy case and points to a picture of him next to a huge trophy. "Yep, we won state that year. We've only won state twice since."

"That's cool. My old team won state a few times. We even had a few students go to the Little League World Series in baseball."

"That's awesome. I'm proud of you, son." Ryan clapped Dylan on the back, making his son smile broadly. "You okay?" Ryan asks me as he runs a hand down my arm.

I nod. "Yeah, it's kind of surreal. I mean, not much has changed. Some updates, but basically I feel like I'm right back where I was."

"I know what you mean. I felt that way when I first came back." He opens the office door for us.

"Well, as I live and breathe. Look who the wind blew in!" Jeanie Montgomery yells as I walk through the door.

"Hi, Jeanie."

"I didn't believe Gail when she said you were coming home. Good to see you, sis." She hugs me tightly. Jeanie is one of Gail's best friends. I wouldn't be surprised if she knows every facet of my life.

"It's true. I'm back."

"And this must be Dylan. I feel like I'm in 1994 again. You're a spitting image of Ryan at your age."

"If it's my age, then you'd have to be back in 1992," Ryan smirks. She slaps him playfully.

"Shut up, you fool." She turns to address Dylan. "I'm Vice Principal Montgomery. Don't believe a thing these two have to say about me." She sticks her hand out to Dylan. "Welcome to our school."

"Thanks."

We chat for a few more minutes, then Ryan excuses himself to the gym and Dylan and I headed off to find his classes and meet his teachers. The day is full of familiar faces, some I wish I could permanently forget, but others are a nice surprise. By the end of the day, Dylan's met a few of the guys from the football team and is excited about trying out Saturday morning.

Dylan and I head over to the gym to meet up with Ryan. On entering the gym, we find him in a heated conversation with a woman. I recognize her as Dylan's English teacher. She looks over to us a few times as she argues with Ryan. I wish I could hear their conversation or at least read lips. The sight in general makes me nervous, though I have no idea why. I have no claim to Ryan.

"Enough," I hear Ryan yell, his hands go to his hair, pulling roughly. He looks like he's about to lose his cool. He turns from her and heads over to Dylan and me.

"This isn't over, Ryan!" she yells after him.

He rolls his eyes and groans. "Ready to go?" he asks us cheerily. No sign of his previously expressed frustrations.

"What was that all about?" I ask.

"I'll tell you later. How about we go get some lunch? There's a new place that serves Thai food not far from here. It's pretty good.

"Okay, but I need to get home soon. I have work tomorrow."

He frowns. "I didn't think you started for a few weeks?"

"Officially, I don't. But they want me to fill out some paperwork and talk to a few people."

"Who's staying with Dylan?" Ryan asks.

Dylan chuckles and replies, "I'm fifteen, Dad. I can stay by myself."

Ryan just stares at our son. He'd yet to call him Dad. Dylan looks confused back and forth between his dad and me.

"What? Did I do something wrong? Why are you guys staring at me?"

Ryan shakes his head. "You called me Dad."

Dylan blushes. "Oh, uh … sorry. I didn't reali …" Ryan waves him off.

"Don't apologize. I want you to call me Dad. It just took me by surprise. I like it, really."

"Okay. I can stay by myself," he says, going back to the previous topic.

Ryan nods. "If you want, but I don't have to be at work until four. I thought maybe we could hang out. Do you like to fish or golf?"

"Golf? I haven't been in months. I was in First Tee when I was little."

"Cool, I'll set up a tee time."

"Mom, do you know where my clubs are?"

The acceptance they have for each other is heartwarming, though I worry about Dylan blowing up again. It's to be expected really. I think he wants to let his dad in, but teenagers are fickle creatures.

"Yeah, they're in the garage. I had the movers unpack that already."

"Awesome. So you think you can get a tee time, Dad?"

Ryan beams at his son. "Of course."

He pulls out his phone and calls immediately, setting it up for nine A.M. The rest of the day we spend eating, laughing, and just being a family; it's probably the most fun I've had in years. It's not that we were an unhappy family with my ex-husband, but this is different. I feel a sense of belonging here; I just hope it isn't premature. I worry that Ryan will decide this isn't what he wants.

"You look happy," I say as I sit down on the sofa after refilling our coffee cups.

Dylan is out in his man-cave, which he totally flipped over. He ran straight over to the Thorns looking for Pop, but he was still on his fishing trip. I can see the two of them hanging out in there for days.

"I am." Ryan turns towards me. "He called me Dad. I didn't think I'd ever hear that from him."

"He just needed to feel comfortable, and wanted. Todd has really done a number on him. I mean, he's always known Todd wasn't his biological father and, until last year, he was a good dad. He was at all his games and practiced with him. He really was the perfect parent." I hate feeling like I'm sticking up for my ex, but it was true. Todd was a great dad.

"If he'd been married since high school, how'd he stick around for you guys?"

"What I was told was that they were married right after high school graduation at the courthouse. They didn't tell anyone. He still went away to college, but the stress of a long distance relationship, plus college, was too much, so they broke up. He said he thought she'd filed years ago, when we had no issues getting a marriage license. Then, I guess sometime in the past couple of years while on one of his real business trips, he found out she hadn't filed. He hadn't bothered going back to his hometown before he had that conference, because his parents had moved closer to be with him. He started going to conferences two years ago, different areas never the same places."

I pause and shake my head. I was so blind and stupid. What wife doesn't realize the frequency of her husband's business trips? I glance at Ryan and I can almost tell he's thinking it too. With a sigh, I continue this uncomfortable tale.

"He is in a different field than me. I never questioned anything. I was glad he was continuing his education. Then last year, he got offered a job in Utah. That's where he grew up and she lives ... he lives now. He talked about us moving with him, but I was under contract. My contract was up this past summer and the plan was that

I'd move there before school started. However, a few months ago, he came home from his trip and told me our marriage was never valid because he was already married. He took everything in his personal bank account and a few things from the house. Other than that, I got the rest. Oh, and get this, during the year he's spent on business trips, they had a baby."

I can't blame Todd for wanting to be with his kid, but he certainly could have told me a lot sooner. Cheating is cheating even if, technically, he was cheating on her with me. The whole mess is ridiculous. I'm distracted when Ryan squeezes my knee.

"I'm sorry. You didn't deserve that. He's a moron."

Smiling, I say, "I know he is. His other wife knows all about me. I'm trying hard not to be bitter, but it's difficult."

"I don't doubt it. I think you're handling it well."

"Yeah, now, but the day I found out, I sent Dylan to his friend's house. I then burned everything that was Todd's and a few things he'd bought me, including our wedding pictures."

"Good. You should have an outlet."

"I wouldn't say I'm over it, but it did help." I giggle, thinking about the pyre I had in my back yard. The neighbor called the city on me.

"What'd you do with my stuff when I left?" he asks cautiously.

I frown, staring down into my almost empty coffee. "You really want to know?" He nods. "Okay, but don't think less of me."

"Never."

Sighing, I shift on the couch so I can see him better. "At first, I kept everything. I cried for days. I only had two pictures of us and a few things you'd bought me. I kept them on my person. I stared at your picture for hours, sobbing. I've never felt so alone in my life, even when I lost my parents."

His face is pained, and rightfully so. I'm not so vindictive that I want him to hurt, but I do want him to realize how hard his leaving was and how it affected me. He turns away from me and rests his head on the back of the sofa with his eyes closed. I continue, and even though my eyes tear up, I hold it together. This is the past, I've moved on. At least that's what I keep telling myself.

"You know before you left I'd been moved to the final group home. I kept everything with me, of course, but I was taken from the group home the day I came to the Thorns, without being allowed to get my stuff. They said they'd send it to me, but I only had one picture with me and the necklace you'd given me for my birthday the year before my parents died. I never took it off. Eventually, the picture was ruined. So, I had nothing left other than the locket you bought me. I kept it on, until I married Todd."

I never told Todd the significance of the locket. It felt too personal, even to share with my husband. We sit in silence for several long moments before he abruptly sits up and pulls me into his arms.

"I'm so sorry. You'll never know how much I hate myself for what I did to you."

He hugs me tightly, kissing my head, face, and eventually making his way to my lips. His kiss starts out slow and soft but ends in deep passionate kisses that leave us both breathless. He sits back, letting me go as he scrubs his face.

"I shouldn't have done that," he mumbles.

"I didn't push you away." I probably should have. I'm not ready for a relationship right now, especially with Ryan. There's still too much to talk about between us, but this pull I feel to him is so unreal. I'm not sure how long I can keep my feelings at bay.

He grabs my hands. "I won't leave you again. I swear."

I want to believe him, I really do, however, my faith in men right now is at an all-time low. "I don't know if I'm ready for an exclusive relationship right now. Besides, what about the English teacher?"

He looks confused for a moment, then recognition lights his eyes. "That's Lydia. We dated for a few months last school year. I broke up with her, she's too clingy. I couldn't handle a relationship at that time anyway. My mind was wrapped up with you and Dylan, and honestly we didn't really get along very well. It wouldn't have worked. What you saw today was her trying to get me back and me completely refusing."

"Are you sure?"

"Totally. Shay, you're who I've always wanted." He leans in to kiss me again, but this time I pull back before he can. He nods in understanding.

"Why do I always walk in when you're sucking face?" Dylan grumbles, rubbing his eyes.

"We didn't ... I mean weren't," Ryan blurts out.

I laugh. "Stop being a snoop. I thought you were in bed?"

"Oh, the kid's in bed, so the parents get to make out?"

"Exactly," Ryan says with a huge smile, recovering from his outburst with cockiness. Typical Ryan. I shove him, laughing.

"Yuck," Dylan gags.

I can't help my smile. "What do you need, Dyl-pickle?"

He glares at me. "I told you not to use that name in front of anyone."

"I didn't. Parents don't count. It's our right." I wink.

"Whatever. I have a headache and can't sleep."

I frown, standing, I grab a pin light and give him a brief scan, at which he huffs and grumbles. "I have oils in my purse. Use the one labeled migraine." He nods and heads into the kitchen.

"Oils?" Ryan asks.

I nod. "Yeah, I know I'm a doctor, but I like natural remedies before medications. I don't like pumping our bodies with synthetic, if natural will work. We use a lot of essential oils."

"Oh, that makes sense, I guess. Will that help him?"

"It normally does. He only gets them when he's stressed. All this mess has him on edge."

Ryan runs his hand through his hair. "I don't think I'm helping the situation either."

"Don't worry about me, Dad. I want Mom happy and I haven't seen her as happy as she's been the past couple of days in my whole life. It's not you." Dylan kisses my cheek, then heads back upstairs with his water and rollerball bottle of essential oils.

"If I'm hindering anything, I'll give you both space, but I can't stay away for long."

I grab his face in my hands and stare into his eyes. "Please don't leave. I can't stand the thought of you giving us space."

I feel the tears forming in my eyes. It is irrational, we haven't seen each other in almost sixteen years, but I can't fathom the thought of losing him again. All my feelings and desires rushed back into me the moment I laid eyes on him. Not to mention what Dylan would think if he gave us space. He's been through so much lately.

"Oh, baby. I'm not leaving you guys. I meant what I said, I can't stay away long, but if you need a couple of days to process, I'm willing to give them to you. We've been through a lot. I know we've talked a lot about what happened. I, for one, don't blame you for any of it anymore. You were a scared little girl, believing a man who you called uncle most of your life. I believed him too. I shouldn't have. I can't hold any of this against you. I made poor choices and I listened to the wrong people."

I shake my head and answer with an emphatic, "No! This isn't all your fault. We both listened to people we shouldn't have. We tried to protect each other. I've never blamed you. I blamed your dad, and yes,

I hated you for a little bit, but like I said, that went out the window the moment I held our son in my arms."

Irrational as it may be, for once I am going with my heart. I am going to see where this goes. Though, I'll try to set a reasonable pace, my head and heart doesn't always agree on what a reasonable pace is.

We talk until our eyes won't stay open, getting out every hurt and fear we've had. We end up falling asleep together on the sofa. I wake to the sound of crunching. Slowly, I open one eye to see my son sitting on the coffee table facing me, a crunchy granola bar in his hand and smirk on his face.

"Morning," he chirps.

I rub my eyes and stare at him. "Morning. What are you doing?"

He shrugs. "Just eating breakfast."

He waves his granola at me. Just then a loud grumble alerts me to the fact that I'm not alone on the couch and I am, in fact, lying on Ryan's lap. I sit up quickly. Dylan chuckles and gives me an all too familiar smirk. Snorting a laugh, I grab a throw pillow and smack him with it.

"You know who you remind me of right now?"

"Who?" Dylan asks, still chomping away.

"Your father." Dylan's smile widens.

Ryan wakes up abruptly with my movement, shakes his head with said smirk on his face. "Looking in a mirror, I tell ya."

"Really?" Dylan asks.

Ryan nods as he readjusts himself to sit up better on the couch. "Yeah, you could be my twin. I'll find some pictures for you."

"That'd be cool. You think your parents would want to meet me?" he asks, making him seem so much younger than his short fifteen years.

Running a hand through his hair, Ryan says, "Of course. It's just my mom now, but she'd love to meet you. So would your aunt and uncles."

"Yeah?"

"Of course. I'll set something up for this weekend. Maybe Sunday. Do you have to work?" he asks me.

"No, I don't actually start until a week from Monday. I'm on days, and then on call twice a week," I explain.

"Oh, that's awesome. I thought you'd be gone a lot." He gives me a wink.

"She's always worked that schedule since I was little," Dylan explains.

"Speaking of schedules, what time is it?" I ask, looking around for my phone.

Dylan pulls his out of his pocket. "Seven-thirty. I have to leave in about an hour for football."

"I have to be at work soon," Ryan says, standing.

I look up at him, not wanting him to leave yet. I know it's ridiculous, but it's been so nice reconnecting.

"Can you stay for breakfast?"

"Yeah, you need help?"

"No, I'll handle it."

"Do I have time to run home and shower really quick?" he asks as we walk into the kitchen.

I nod. "Yeah, I'm going to put bacon in the oven then run for a quick shower myself."

"Perfect. I'll be back in fifteen minutes." He gives me a quick kiss to the cheek then runs out the side door to the neighboring house.

"You're in love with him aren't you?"

I turn to my son. "I've always loved him. He gave me you."

"Yeah, but I've never seen you look at a guy like you look at him. Even with Todd." He's way too perceptive for a fifteen year old.

I don't say anything as I set the oven and place the tray of bacon inside. "I love your dad. I don't know if we'll start a relationship or not. We shouldn't have kissed and I'm sorry you saw that. More than anything, I don't want you to be hurt again. I know he's your dad, but my first priority is always you."

"Sometimes it's okay to make yourself happy, Mom."

He kisses my cheek before heading to the den to watch T.V. I wipe the tears from my eyes, caused by my ever so sweet little boy.

CHAPTER THREE

Shayla

After a super-fast shower, I blow dry the front and top of my hair and let the rest air-dry. I grab a pair of jeans, a t-shirt, a pair of Chuck Taylor's, and then head down to the kitchen. I'm just cracking an egg into the skillet when Ryan enters the back door. I can't help but stare. He's wearing dark jeans, a white dress shirt with a skinny black tie, and a black leather jacket. He looks … badass, for lack of a better word. Well, hot…he looks hot. He knows he's getting to me, because the smirk on his face is absolutely ridiculous. It's the one his son had donned less than an hour before.

"You look beautiful," he says, kissing my cheek.

"Thanks. You clean up well. You look … good."

He laughs and wipes the side of my mouth, like there's really drool there. "Yeah, I can tell you like how I look."

I swat him with a kitchen towel. "Conceited much?"

He shrugs as he grabs an apple, taking a huge bite. "Nah, I'm just confident."

"If you say so, Mr. Detective."

We chat and tease a little more before Dylan enters the kitchen and takes a seat on the window bench at the table. I pass him a plate of bacon, eggs, and toast.

"Thanks, Mom."

"You're welcome, sweetheart. Do you want cashew or almond milk?"

"Do we have chocolate cashew?"

"Yep." I get him a glass.

"Cashew?" Ryan asks.

I chuckle. He has a lot to learn about my healthy ways. "Yeah, we still drink whole milk, but only on occasion, and if it's organic and minimally processed."

"You're a hippie in disguise, aren't you?" Ryan laughs.

"Naturalist, actually." I wink.

He guffaws. "Whatever, weirdo." I roll my eyes at him as I place his food down in front of him. He digs in. "What're your plans for today?"

"Unpacking, and taking Dyl to football," I tell him, sitting down with my own plate of food.

"I'll drop him off. It's on my way. I can probably pick him up today too. My schedule is pretty flexible."

"Okay, that would help. I need to run a few errands, so that will make it easier for me."

Ryan winks. "That's what I'm here for, babe." I smile as I shake my head at him.

"I thought you helped coach?" Dylan asks.

Ryan wipes his mouth then says, "Yeah, I do. But mostly as a fill in at games. I will probably pop by at some point."

"Cool."

"When are you off? I'll cook dinner," I ask.

Ryan pulls out his phone and then says, "I should be done around five, unless I get a case. It's pretty slow around here. I'm the only detective, but a lot of times I fill other roles. Sometimes I help out neighboring precincts."

"Why do they have a detective if they don't need one?" Dylan asks.

Ryan holds up a finger to indicate to wait while he chews. "Normally, they just use uniformed cops, they serve both roles, but I'm actually just waiting for the chief to retire. I'm taking over when he's done. I kind of just do my own thing. I fill in a lot for the chief. He has two more months before he can retire. He's not in the best of health."

"So why not just retire early?" I ask.

"Stubbornness." Ryan chuckles. "You want to meet for lunch?"

"Sure." I hand Dylan his water bottle and kiss his cheek goodbye.

"I'll be in the car so you can be gross," Dylan says as he walks out the side door to Ryan's house.

"Gross is fun," Ryan says, chuckling as he leans in for a kiss.

~*~

Later that morning, I'm finishing unpacking in the living room when there's a knock at the front door. I open it with a smile on my face.

"Hey, Mama!"

She wraps me in one of her motherly hugs. She may not be the woman who gave birth to me, but Gail Thorn loves me like she did.

"How are you, sweet girl?"

"Good. Really good."

"I'm glad to hear it. I brought baby boy a banana cake. I made it with your recipe so it's nice and healthy."

I chuckle. "Thanks, he'll love it." I take the cake into the kitchen. "When will Pop be home?"

"Oh, they should be back tomorrow."

I shake my head, laughing. His fishing trips are more about

drinking beer and gossiping than about the fish.

"Where are you headed today?" I ask.

"Crochet circle at church."

"You mean gossip circle. Make sure they don't gossip about me," I tell her. I'm only half kidding.

"You know they will, but it will only be good things. How are Dylan and Ryan getting along?" she asks as she sits down on the sofa.

"Great. They are so much alike it's scary. It makes me feel even worse about keeping them apart for so long."

"It couldn't be helped. You tried."

"I know, but I should've just blurted it out on the phone or something."

Gail rubs my arm soothingly. "You did everything you could. At least they have each other now."

"That's true, I guess."

"Everything happens for a reason, sweetheart. Don't beat yourself up about the past, just try to move forward." I nod in understanding. She is right, I know that. "I hate to run, but I need to be at the church in twenty minutes. This weekend, you guys should come over."

"Ryan wants to take Dylan to meet his family."

"Oh, well you do that. We'll be seeing you guys a lot anyway."

"Why don't you come over Monday night?"

"How about you come to me. You've moved and unpacked, let mama take care of you. I really need to run."

"Have fun gossiping. I'll see you Monday." I giggle.

She smiles. I love the twinkle in her eyes. She lives for the latest juicy gossip, but at the same time, I know if they bring me up in a negative light, she'll be the first to put them in their places.

"You know I will. Dave Johnson was spotted with Helen Zhar. You know that will be the talk of the morning."

"I'm sure it will be. Love you," I tell her, still chuckling with her.

She kisses my cheek, returns my love, and then heads back to her neighboring house. I'm lost in the unpacking again when my phone rings. I smile when I see Ryan's number. A few weeks ago, his number caused me panic. He was trying to reconcile the news of having an almost grown son and, as expected, he wasn't handling it well. He definitely wasn't happy with me then.

"Hey," I say as I take a seat on my bed.

"Hey, you. How's the unpacking?"

"Good. I finished the living room and kitchen. I started on the den, but got distracted by my bedroom."

"Ah, bedrooms can do that." His voice drops in tone. He might be sixteen years older, but it's the same voice he used when we dated. It got me every time. Seems to be no different now. "But I wasn't calling about bedroom activities, I was calling to see if you wanted to meet me for lunch? If you're too busy, though, I understand."

"I can do that. I have all week to finish. The movers really did most of it already, I don't have a ton left."

"Great. I'll be there in ten. Is that enough time?"

"Yeah, as long as you don't mind me wearing what I had on at breakfast."

He chuckles. "Well, I would like to see you in less, but for lunch at the diner, it's great."

"Oh stop it! I'll be ready, but I need to get off the phone."

"Okay, I'll see you soon."

"The side door is open," I tell him quickly, hoping he's not disconnected.

"Not safe, babe." I can see the scowl on his face in my mind. I smile.

"You'll be here in less than ten. I'll be fine."

"I need a key."

"Fine, we can stop by Hadley's."

"Seriously?" He asks at my mention of the local hardware store.

"Yes! Your son lives here. You'll need to have access."

He hums. "Yeah, that's why."

I laugh. "Exactly why. He might accidentally lock himself out, and Maw and Pop may not be at home. Now, let me go so I can freshen up."

"I like you sweaty and dirty."

"Oh my God! I'm hanging up now."

I hear his laughter as I end the call. My face warms with blush, but I shake it off. I don't have time for fantasies right now. By the time I'm exiting my bedroom, he's coming through the side door in the kitchen. He looks incredible. He's lost his jacket as the weather has warmed, and rolled up his long sleeves, tattoos exposed, and others peeking from under his sleeve. His hair is more tousled than this morning, like he's been a little stressed through the day and had his hands in it often.

"See something you like?" He asks, noticing my stare. He flexes his muscles.

"You said that earlier. I think you're a touch conceited." I can't help the grin that spreads on my face. I run my hands up his tattooed arms until they wrap around his neck. "You've aged well. You were hot in high school, all the girls thought so, but now you're just so much more. I can't stop staring at you," I answer, going with my heart instead of my head.

He smirks at me before leaning forward and pulling me tightly against him, taking my breath away with a searing kiss. Pulling back with a sigh, he rests his forehead to mine.

"We should go before something happens we're not ready for."

I nod, agreeing. "How can I feel this way after sixteen years, after everything we put each other through?"

He hugs me tightly. "I don't know, but I feel it too. I was serious when I said I'd missed you through the years. I tried to move on, but in the few relationships I've had, I just couldn't get you out of my head."

"When you say things like that, it makes me incredibly sad. I feel so guilty." I turn from him and grab my jacket and purse.

He runs his fingers down my arm to my hand and twines our fingers. "Don't. I could have talked to you. I wanted to, but I let my dad get in my head. I had choices, but I let someone else make them, thinking it wouldn't be my fault. It was wrong. I loved you with my whole being. I should have never let you go. I lost not only you, but my son too. I won't make that mistake again."

I blink away the tears building in my eyes and clear my throat. We don't have the time we need for this conversation. "We should go. You have to be back to work soon." He nods, tugs my hand, and leads me outside. "I didn't know you had a squad car?"

"Loaner. Mine's being serviced." He opens the passenger door for me to get in.

"They don't care if you have a civilian in your car?"

"Nah, but I could cuff you and make you sit in the back if you'd like."

I guffaw. "Ah, no. I'll be just fine up front."

"Suit yourself." He smirks. "Is the diner okay?" He asks as he buckles his seatbelt.

"Yeah, I haven't been there since I've been back. Does Ray still run it?" I ask, thinking of the man who was in his early fifties when I moved away.

"No, his son, Ray Jr., took over. They use the same recipes. He worked there for a long time before. It hasn't changed much. He has put a few new things on the menu though."

"Sounds great."

We hold hands and chat about Dylan on our way. It only takes about ten minutes to arrive. He kisses the back of the hand he's holding before telling me to stay put while he gets my door. He has always opened my door. When I was young I thought it was silly, but now I think he's incredibly romantic. Gentlemen are hard to find nowadays. It's another thing about him that our son has missed out on. Guilt flares once more. He helps me out of the car and leads me into the diner with his hand on the small of my back.

The diner is exactly like I remember. Red and white décor, pictures of the greats through time scattered all over the walls, an old juke box in the corner as before, but also a new version alongside the older one. There are touches of new, but mostly it's remained the same. It's comforting.

"Hey there, detective. Usual?" A very endowed blonde girl asks as she pours another customer's coffee.

"Yeah, but she'll need a menu."

The woman then notices me. Her eyes travel down to our joined hands and scowls. *I guess Ryan still has a fan club.* He motions for me to sit in a booth then slides in beside me. He lays his arm on the back of the bench and turns towards me.

"This okay?"

"Yeah. I take it you come here a lot."

He smiles cockily. "Yeah. You jealous of Tracy?"

I roll my eyes. "No, but she's clearly not happy about you holding my hand."

"Nah, she's harmless. We went out once, but she's not my type." I don't know if I like knowing that he's been with her. It makes me insanely uncomfortable, especially since she's our waitress.

"What if she spits in my food? She looks like she's trying to blow my head off with her mind," I whisper as I look at Tracy, who's shooting daggers my way.

"I didn't sleep with her. We went on one date, to the movie in the park. She spent most of that time talking to the guy beside us, who she went home with later that night."

"Well, that's rude." I shake my head. "I don't understand how anyone could not want to be with you."

"You're biased, though. Maybe I make a horrible boyfriend."

"I doubt it. You were a great boyfriend."

"No, a great boyfriend wouldn't have broken up with the girl he loved unconditionally."

"You did what you thought was the best. Let's not dwell in the past. We have a fresh start. Let's just start over."

"Okay, sounds perfect." He gives me a quick peck to the lips as Tracy arrives with my menu and a cup of coffee for Ryan. "Tracy, this is my girlfriend, and mother of my son, Shayla. Shay, this is Tracy. Best waitress *Ray's* has."

"Nice to meet you," I tell her.

"Girlfriend? Didn't you just move to town yesterday?" she asks me.

"Actually, I moved here on Thursday." I figure she's questioning Ryan's declaration.

She rolls her eyes. "So you move here two days ago and you've already snagged the town's hottest bachelor?" She mumbles. "You must be giving it up." Ryan hears her.

"Listen, Tracy. Not that it's any of your business, but I've known Shayla since we were kids. We have a fifteen-year-old son together. This isn't new, this has always been." Tracy looks offended as she turns and storms off. "Sorry. I don't know what her problem is. We can go somewhere else."

"I don't want to cause you problems. We can stay."

"It's not causing me any problems. She'll get over it. She doesn't have a say in what I do. I literally see her once a day, in here; I order and leave."

"She obviously thinks she has some sort of claim to you."

"Nope. You're the only one I want to claim me." He winks and kisses my lips softly.

I sigh. "We need to talk about the girlfriend proclamation. I told you I wasn't ready for a relationship right now."

A clang breaks us out of our bubble. Ryan turns, eyebrows scrunched together with an unsatisfied look on his face. "Tracy, I'm not sure what's going on, but I think we need to have Melody as our waitress."

"Whatever," Tracy snaps as she rolls her eyes.

A few moments later, Melody comes to the table and apologizes for Tracy, takes our order, and doesn't stare at Ryan like he's a piece of meat. Our lunch is smooth from that point forward. We talk mostly about Dylan and how he did at tryouts. They went well, but I knew he'd do well. He's as good as his dad, if not better, when it comes to sports. We also talk about my schedule at the hospital and clinic, we don't, however, mention anything about our relationship.

"So, you don't stay at the hospital all day?" he asks, taking a big bite of his sandwich.

I take a drink to clear my throat before answering. "No, well sort of. The clinic is right off the hospital in the medical complex. I do consultations there, but mostly I do emergency surgeries."

"So you work in the ER?"

"Yeah, but only when they need a possible surgery. I stay in the OR wing."

"What days do you do consultations?"

I pull out my phone to view my schedule. "I'll print this out for the fridge at the house and you can have a copy if you want. I'm basically working four twelve hour days, though at times it turns into sixteen hour days or longer. I'm on call once a week, on one of my working days. I have three days a week off, unless I need to fill in for someone. It's a pretty set schedule."

"Do you have days that are just in the clinic?"

"Yes, unless I have a patient in the hospital or emergencies. I do surgeries on Monday, Wednesday, and Thursdays and again if there's an emergency. Tuesdays and Thursdays are clinic days. I work my clinic schedule on Thursdays around my surgeries that day. I have off Friday to Sunday. On occasion I might have to work a weekend."

"That seems like a pretty good schedule."

"It was one of my stipulations on taking the job. I didn't want to miss any of Dylan's games."

"You're a good mom."

I blush at his compliment. We've never addressed me being a mother directly. I mean, we both know, we've just never talked about what it has been like for me being a single mother.

"Thanks. I think you'll be a good dad. You've been great with him so far."

He doesn't say anything for a few moments, then looks up with a glisten in his eyes. "I hope so." I squeeze his hand in assurance.

We leave the diner and head back to my house. "Thanks for lunch. Will you be done in time for dinner with us?"

"Yeah, Dylan is going to ride home with Tyler from down the street. I meant to tell you earlier."

"Is he on the team?"

"Yeah. You might not remember his parents, they were in my grade. Sam and Julie Winters. I think Julie's maiden name was Porter.

"Is she Debbie Porter's older sister?"

"Cousin, but yeah, that's her. They're good friends of mine. Tyler's a good kid. He's a year older than Dyl."

The silence stretches in the car, it's a bit uncomfortable. I want to say so much, but know it's not the time for anything I could bring up. I settle with, "I should let you get back to work."

"Yeah, I should check in."

"Thanks for lunch."

He kisses the back of my hand. "Of course. I love spending time with you. It's like no time has passed, but at the same time, it's like an eternity. We have so much to learn about each other."

"Yes, we do. Be safe, I'll see you at six for dinner."

"Sounds good, Shay." He leans over and kisses me. I can't help wrapping my fingers in his dark wavy hair and pulling him closer to me. "Keep that up and I won't be going back to work." He winks as I giggle at him. I feel like that love sick girl from so long ago. It's a nice change for my heart.

"Bye," I whisper as I jump out of the car and head up to my house. I stop on the steps to wave and blow him a kiss. He returns it before backing out and heading down the street.

CHAPTER FOUR

Ryan

A year ago, if you would've told me I'd be dropping Shayla off after a lunch date, I would've laughed in your face. A year ago, I hated her. I was too consumed with anger and guilt to see anything good in my life. Anger with myself, my dad, heck, even my mom, took over my life, and everything else was not important enough for me to give a second thought. I couldn't believe they'd keep something like this from me. In my mind, Shayla was the enemy. I was dead set on getting my kid no matter what it cost me. I wanted to hurt her for the hurt she'd caused me. Remembering that first phone call now, well, let's just say it makes me feel like total scum.

I angrily pace back and forth in my childhood bedroom. I had come home to interview for the chief of police position. A position I would have never taken if it hadn't been for my mom. She was sick, cancer, and even though my brothers and sister were close, most of them have kids and families. They tried to take care of her, but I could tell it wore on them. I loved my job with the FBI, but I couldn't keep it and help at the same time. This was the only reason I came back to this backwards town. I hated this place so much when I left at eighteen. I haven't come back here since. My parents always flew to me. I didn't even come back for my dad's funeral. I was on a case, undercover. No excuse, I guess, but that's the one I used. He was my dad and I loved him, but we didn't get along. Everyone knew that. So, here I am back in the town I hate, looking at the house next door to the house Shayla lived in until her parents died. I had no idea when the realtor told me about the perfect house for me, that it was the one beside her old one.

The house was perfect. It was one of the smaller houses on the block, three bedrooms. Everything I needed. It was at the end of the street, woods surrounded the back and one side. I could purchase the wooded lot too. It was really perfect. That was until that dumb, gossipy tramp, Sarah Davidson opened her mouth and told me I was a father and my son was fourteen years old. Fourteen! In her defense, she had no clue what she'd just done. She never mentioned me as the father. I didn't say another word to her though. I just stormed out of the house and straight to the Thorns.

"Ryan?" Mr. Thorn addresses me.

"You knew?"

Sighing, he pulls the door open and waves me in. "Gail, Ryan Jacobs is here."

"Oh dear," Gail mutters as she comes around the corner.

Looking around the room, I notice pictures of Shayla growing up, then of a little boy. I grab the one closest to me. There's no denying he's mine. He has the same black hair, bright blue eyes with the annoying ring of navy around the outer edge that I have. He even has a dimple in his left cheek as I do. My legs feel as if they're about to give, so I collapse onto the chair nearest me. I look up to them with angry tears burning my eyes. How could she do this to me? I thought she loved me.

"Ryan," Mrs. Thorn starts, but I interrupt.

Shaking my head angrily, I ask, "Why would she do this to me? I thought she loved me."

"Oh, sweetheart. She did love you and she tried so hard to find you. We would've helped her, but she refused to tell us who the father was. We, of course, suspected you, but she was in the system so long, and some of that time we didn't see her. We didn't want to do anything to jeopardize her placement with us. It was wrong, I know, but we only did what we thought was best for her and Dylan."

"Dylan?"

"Your son," she answered kindly.

Tears spill down my checks. I've never in my life felt so many emotions at once. Hurt, anger, joy, confusion, and a slew of others I can't even begin to pinpoint.

"How long have you known?" I ask after I've collected myself.

"Since she graduated from med school, so about six years. She only told us then because Dylan had asked about his dad."

"I don't understand why she wouldn't have tried to find me. I mean, I get while she was in the system, but she would've been out by the time he was two or when you guys adopted her, right?"

"I think you need to ask her that. She would never tell us what happened. But please know, she did what she thought was best. It killed her not to tell you. I would find her rocking him and crying her little eyes out. It was heartbreaking to watch."

I shake my head and halfheartedly chuckle. "Shay was always the stubborn one."

Mrs. Thorn laughs. "Oh, that is definitely true and that son of yours gets that from her too."

I smile knowing a little about him helps. "Can I keep this?" I ask motioning to the picture in my hand.

"Of course. Would you like Shayla's number? She's told us several times if you ever showed up to give it to you if you wanted it."

"Please. I don't know if I'll call. I need to get this …" I trail off not knowing what to say.

Mr. Thorn squeezes my shoulder. "We understand, son. Take your time. We won't mention it to her. You both need to work through this on your own."

I'm shocked he'd do that for me. "Thank you."

Nine months pass and I never call. Well, I dial her number a few times, but I never push send. Then one day, I don't know what made me do it, but I push send and she answers.

"Hello?" Shayla answers. I'm frozen. I can't respond. "Hello? This is Doctor Thorn; do you need help?"

"Dr. Thorn?" I say. She's a doctor. She made it, just like I knew she would.

"Yes, this is she. May I help you?"

I don't know what brings on my anger, but I lash out. "Yeah, you can tell me why I was never told I was a father!" I yell.

"Oh, no! Ryan?"

"Of course, it's Ryan." I mock her with as much disdain I can muster. "This is the lowest thing anyone could ever do. I never thought you'd be capable of something so evil, Shayla. You let me go for the past fifteen years, totally unaware. How could you do that?"

There is silence, then, "Excuse me. I'll be in my office, but only get me if there's an emergency. This is important." I hear walking and a door shutting. "Ryan?"

"I'm here." I'm breathing heavily, my adrenaline pumping wildly.

"I'm so sorry. I can't even tell you how sorry. I tried, in the beginning, to contact you." Her voice shakes as she speaks.

I've scared her. Good. I know she had tried; I ignored her calls but she still should have tried harder to get a hold of me. She shouldn't have given up so easily.

"That's why you kept calling?"

"Yes."

My anger starts to deflate, but is still very much present. "It wasn't because you wanted me back?"

"No ... I mean, I did, but I accepted you didn't want me. I just wanted you to know about your son."

I snort. Didn't want her. If only she knew how wrong that was ... is ... was. I'm so confused right now.

"Dylan?"

"Yes, Dylan James Thorn."

"James?" My middle name as well as her birth father's name.

"Yes."

Something about knowing that I'm represented in his name causes the rest of the anger to fall away. I'm still upset, but I've had nine months to process, to accept. I honestly wasted those months. I should have gone straight to her, but she was married and Dylan was happy. Even though, at first, I wanted to rip him away from her, I couldn't do that. My siblings and mother made sure I didn't do anything rash or stupid. I step out on my back porch and stare at the treehouse in the backyard of Shayla's old home. A couple of kids, a boy and girl were playing, screaming, and chasing each other. They remind me of a more innocent time.

"The treehouse?" I ask, as the memory of us hits me.

"What?"

"It had to have been in the treehouse. That was the first time."

"Yeah, I mean, there was only twice, but I figured the first. The math works."

"Sorry I yelled."

"Don't be. I deserve it."

I shake my head. She's always taken the blame, even when we were kids. "Don't do that. We're both at fault. It's overwhelming." We're both silent as the minute's tick by. It's uncomfortable at best. When I can't take it anymore, I ask, "Does he know about me?"

"Yes. Gail sent me a yearbook so I could show him a picture. It's black and white, but it's all I have."

I nod. We had tons of pictures, but they're all at my mom's.

"I want to talk to him."

"Okay, let me talk to him and I'll see what he wants to do."

I snort, anger flaring again. "How about you let me talk to my son, because I have that right. You didn't list me as the father, but I have blood right to him. I'm sure any judge would agree."

"You'll not take my son from me," she snarls.

"I'll do whatever it takes to get to know *my* child. You took what wasn't just yours."

"I didn't say you couldn't talk to him. I said I'd let him decide. He's not a child. He's fourteen."

A knock on my car window startles me out of my thoughts. I was so horrible to Shay. I don't know how she forgave me, but by the next phone call, I'd calmed down and we talked. She told me about her divorce and moving home. I decided to wait to talk to Dylan. I wanted to be sure I was calm. I didn't want him to hate me if I was caught off guard and said something out of anger. I look up at my knocker and smile.

"Son, what are you doing?"

"You've been sitting in the car for over thirty minutes. I thought you were practicing with us today. The guys are getting restless. He pointed back to the field."

"Sorry. Just thinking. Actually, I have to head to the station; I just stopped by to check on you. Is Matthews not here?"

"No, he's here. He just thought you needed something. I'm still okay to ride with Ty, right?"

"Yeah, yeah. I told your mom. She said dinner's at six."

"Okay. I'll be back. Practice is over at four."

"Good. I'll come to Monday's practice. I have some paperwork to finish so I better get going."

He nods. "You sure you're okay? Mom's okay?"

I smile. "We're both fine, buddy. I'm just a little distracted, that's all."

"Okay. I'll see you at home then."

I nod, smiling, before backing out of the parking spot and heading to the station. I still can't believe that I'm where I am now, my son in my life, Shay in my life again. I hate myself for not getting my act together sooner, but I'm going to make up for that. If it's the last thing I do.

~*~

I've been working in my office for about an hour when May, my assistant, pokes her head around the corner.

"You have a phone call on line three. A Special Agent Marsh?"

I smile and nod. "Yeah, thanks. Shut the door, please." She does as I ask and I pick up the phone. "Harry! How's it going, man?"

"Same as always. I finally popped the question to my girl."

"No kidding! Man, congrats. That's awesome."

"Thanks. It's going to be crazy big. You should come. How's life in Podunk?"

I laugh. "Ah, it's not bad. Now anyway. At first, it was miserable. My mom was sick, finding out I have a teenaged son, finding a house. It's been crazy."

"Whoa, now. Back that up. You have a teenaged son?"

"Yeah. Nothing like finding out something like that through your realtor."

"Shayla?" He asks, his voice still shocked.

I clear my throat. It's not that I don't want to talk about Dylan and Shayla, but a part of me wants to keep them for myself, but he is my best friend and I haven't spoken to him in over a year. He'd been on a case when I left and other than the quick email on a case I'd been on, we hadn't had time to chat.

"Yeah."

"What in the world? I just can't comprehend why she wouldn't tell you."

Sighing, I tell him, "She tried to tell me. I was too stubborn to listen. Then my dad and her social worker had her scared to death. She thought I'd go to jail if she told, which could have been possible. I had turned eighteen when we had sex the first time. And cliché as it is, she got pregnant from that."

"Wow. I can't imagine. I bet you were pissed at her."

"Yeah, I went through a big angry phase. I hated her for a while, but then we really talked. I don't blame her for what happened. She was trying to protect me and our son. I wish I'd come home during the past years, but that was my choice."

"She's lived there this whole time?"

"No, she lived up north about six hours from here. She moved back after her scum of an ex broke her heart."

"How'd your parents not know?"

I snort in disgust. I still haven't forgiven my father. "My dad did know. He scared the crap out of Shay so she never told a soul. Made it seem like it was a boy in one of the homes she was in. Her adoptive parents figured it out, but she didn't confirm it until a few years ago. There's no denying he's mine. The boy is my twin." I laugh.

"That's awesome. Congrats, Papa," he laughs.

I smile. "Yeah, man. It's been great. I never thought of myself as a father, but hearing him call me dad, it's been ... life changing really."

"I bet. Hey, I hate to ruin all this happy talk, but I called with some info for you."

"Hit me," I tell him sitting back in my chair ready for whatever he throws at me.

I hear shuffling papers and his throat clearing before he says, "You remember Jason Mathis?"

"Of course, The Fox Killer."

"He's been released."

I fly up out of my seat in shock, almost knocking my coffee over. "What do you mean he's been released? Tell me you're lying. He killed ten people! Ten, Marsh! And that's only the ones we found. Who knows how many there truly are."

"I know, I know. One of the witnesses recanted her statement. Somehow, they came up with undeniable proof she was lying. She's in jail for falsifying. It's messed up. They're still trying to pin him with what's left, but she was a major witness. The whole case is being reevaluated. He was held as long as possible, but his release was ordered."

I let out a huge breath. I have no clue what to think. This guy was no joke. It took me over two years to take him down. There's no way that my biggest case could have had some technicality that would throw the evidence into question. This whole thing reeks of an inside job.

"This is huge," I finally say.

"It is, but that's not all. He left an origami fox on his bunk."

My heart sinks. That's his calling card. He left it with his victim as a clue before he'd kill his next victim. I almost don't want to ask, knowing the implications of the answer but I do anyway.

"What was in it?"

"A hair. Forensics ran it, but there's nothing in the data base. We have nothing to go on. We've got uniforms on him, watching, but he's being citizen of the year."

"Keep me posted."

"I will. He was ordered to stay put and check in with a parole officer, not that that will stop him if he wants to leave."

"Right, I'll do what I can, but I don't know what good I'll be."

"They have your testimony, but you might have to come back in once the case is back in court."

"Yeah, anything. I have to get going. I'm meeting Shay and Dylan for dinner."

"You guys back together already?" he asks with a chuckle.

I can't help smiling. "Nah, but it's only a matter of time. She wants me. I can tell."

He guffaws. "Oh, there we go with your Rico Sauvé ways."

I laugh with him. "Nah, it's not like that. I love her. Always have. I'm tired of messing around. We messed up as kids, we wasted sixteen years without each other, I'm done. I want her and Dylan."

"I get it. That's awesome. I'm happy for you."

"Thanks. And thanks for calling. Keep me in the loop."

"I will. Later, Jacobs."

"Later, Marsh."

I shake my head, trying to wrap my head around the news that Mathis is out. Jason Mathis was my biggest case. I was undercover in the Mathis Crime Organization for almost a year. That was what I was doing when my dad died. We had so much evidence, it should've been impossible to turn over. Something is very wrong here. My initial thoughts are that it's an inside job, that some official is pulling what should be un-pull-able strings. I slam my hand down on my desk. I have a sinking feeling he'll be coming for me. He sees me as his nemesis. I don't think he can find me, but I'll be damned if I let him get to me or my family. I grab my things and head out of the office, ignoring the wave May gives me as I pass her.

My mind is everywhere as I travel to Shay's. I can't even process what would happen if Mathis came after me. Shayla and Dylan are my priority now. I won't let anything happen to them. When I finally arrive at Shayla's, she calls out to me to just take a seat, that dinner is almost ready.

"Will do," I say as I do what she tells me.

I'm happy that dinner is a simple affair, but a happy one. I want more days like this with them; this natural day-to-day conversation has already lightened my mind and put Mathis' release on the back burner for now. This is what I never knew I needed, my family.

~*~

Sunday comes quicker than I would have imagined. It's afternoon as I watch my son pace back and forth in the living room while we wait for Shayla to finish getting ready. We are set to head over to my grandma Penny's house. The whole family will be there, well, all that can be at least. Dylan seems uneasy about something, but I can't imagine what he would be nervous about.

"Son, you're wearing a hole in the floor."

He stops and turns towards me. "Sorry. I'm just worried. What if they don't like me?"

I snort. "They love you already."

"How's that even possible. They've never met me." He finally sits down in the chair across from me.

"You've talked to my mom on the phone, you know she's head over heels for you."

This, of course, is an understatement. Sure, my mom has other grandkids, but Dylan is the oldest. She's seen him over the years and always suspected he was mine, but every time she brought it up to my dad he shut her down quickly. She was relieved to know she wasn't crazy and that Dylan did indeed look like me, because he was mine. It caused a big rift between my mom and Gail's relationship, but it's now on the mend. She understood this was my father's doing and she wasn't unaccustomed to his poor choices.

"Yeah, on the phone, but what if I'm not good enough in person?"

I tilt my head to the side and stare at him for a second, before standing to my feet and kneeling in front of him. I rest my hand on his shoulder so he's looking straight at me.

"Dylan, my family isn't Todd. They aren't going to turn you away or think anything other than how lucky they are to have you with them. I feel the same. I know we've only known each other a short time, but you are my son and I love you. Nothing could ever change that. It was instant the moment I saw your picture at the Thorns."

"But I wasn't good enough for T ..."

I stop him. "Todd is a jackass. He didn't know what a good thing he had. And you know what? I'm glad. If he hadn't screwed up, I wouldn't be here right now with you."

I pull him into a hug. I feel him sighing in relief and his tears soaking my shirt. He's needed to do this, to get out his true fear. Todd made him feel unwanted. Oh, but this boy is so wanted and so needed, he has no idea. I wasn't lying when I said it was instant. The very moment I looked at that picture, I loved him. I may have been angry, but never with him. He's not done a thing wrong in this situation. I rub his back soothingly, holding him tightly, trying to comfort him the best I can. To make up for all the times I should've been there but wasn't.

"Hey, what's going on? What happened?" Shayla asks, sitting on the arm of the chair. Dylan sits back and pulls her to him. She's halfway in his lap and in the chair. She squeaks at the suddenness. "Oh, baby, what's wrong?"

"I'm scared."

"Of what, Dyl?"

"Of not being good enough for the Jacobs'." He sits back, wiping his eyes. I grab some tissues from the table and hand them to him.

"You are a Jacobs and you are good enough. That was never the issue. Trust me," Shayla says.

He leans his head back on the chair and rubs his eyes. "I need to know why you did it. Why you didn't tell them about me?"

I look at Shay and she looks at me. She moves back to the arm of the chair so she can see him better. I can see she is debating, running through possible responses and then she looks resolved as she starts speaking.

"I was in foster care when your dad and I started dating. He's older than me, not that it's wrong, it's fine. We could date, but we couldn't be intimate. He could've gotten into big trouble, even though the Thorns were adopting me, and the worker didn't know I was pregnant until it was finalized. I begged them not to tell. I didn't show until really late in my pregnancy and I wore baggy clothes. Simon, my caseworker, he didn't know until you were two. He sought me out. He tried then to get me to tell him who your dad was, but I told him it wasn't his business anymore. He knew it was your dad, accused him. He wanted me to press charges. Plus …"

I stop her. I turn to Dylan. "Your grandpa, my dad, he scared your mom. That's why as soon as she graduated, you guys moved away."

"That's why Maw and Pop came to stay with us so much? You didn't want to come back here?" Dylan asks.

"I was so afraid that even though I was over eighteen, they'd still find a way to press charges. I knew your dad was in the military and I just imagined all these terrible things happening to him. I couldn't bring myself to admit to anyone that he was your dad until you asked when you were nine. I knew then I had to, but I made Maw and Pop promise not to tell anyone until I could reach your dad." She took a huge breath, then looked over at me. I can see tears in her eyes. "I've never told anyone this, but I called your dad," she says to me, then turns to Dylan, "your grandpa, shortly after your birthday that year, and told him you were curious. I told him I understood he didn't want Ryan to know and that was fine, I was engaged, and I didn't want anything. I just thought you should at least know your dad. He told me

Ryan couldn't be reached and if I tried to call him again or contact Ryan, he'd press charges for harassment. I should have kept trying, but I didn't want to cause problems."

I stare at her for a long while. I'm not sure why she never mentioned any of this, but then again, she didn't tell me about my dad's involvement until we saw each other. She's always trying to protect me, crazy girl. She looks at me concerned.

"I'm not mad at you. I'm upset with my dad more than I can explain, but he's not here anymore. I'd like to put all this behind us and move forward. A lot of mistakes were made, but they were made in the effort to protect those we love. Let's just vow from this point forward, that the three of us are a team, even if we aren't dating, Shayla. The three of us talk about everything, no secrets."

They both agree. I pull them into a family hug. That's what we are, no matter what. The drive to my mom's is full of happy chatter. I tell Dylan a few silly stories about his mom, teasing her. She laughs, but for the most part, lets us talk. I squeeze her hand as I pull into the drive of my family home. I know there's nothing for her to worry about, but I can tell she's nervous.

"Oh, my goodness!" My mom squeals from the porch steps. She pulls Shayla and Dylan into her arms.

I chuckle. "Let them breathe, Mom."

"Sorry, I just … oh, look at you. You look more like your dad in person." She pats Dylan's face. "Come in. My manners are out the window. Have a seat. I'll get us something to drink."

"I've got it, Mom," my sister, Alaina, says, setting a tray of drinking glasses with a pitcher of iced tea on the coffee table. "Hi, I'm your Aunt Alaina, but everyone calls me Laney."

She smiles at Dylan and then looks at Shay. She and Shayla used to be friends, not like Shay and I were, but they're the same age and had several classes together in school.

"Shay," she greets her with a warm smile.

"Hey, Laney."

It doesn't take long for us to get settled in or for my mom to drag out the photo albums from my youth. There's tons of Shayla as well. The fear I'd seen in Dylan's eyes on the ride over is replaced with laughter and contentment. The easy acceptance of my mom and sister has done that for him.

I look over to Shay. She's been quiet most of the time. She's answered questions and laughed, but I can tell she's a bit distant. As Dylan is looking at pictures from right around the time he was conceived, she excuses herself to the bathroom. She's gone so long, that I go to check on her.

"Shay?" I say, knocking on the door.

"Sorry, be out in a minute."

I can tell she's been crying. I twist the knob, finding it unlocked. I slowly push it open, giving her a chance to deny me. She doesn't. I find her sitting on the side of the bathtub, tissue in hand.

"Hey, what's wrong?" I ask, kneeling down in front of her.

"I'm a horrible person. I kept him from his family."

Frowning, I push her hair back so I can see her face. "You're not horrible. We both made mistakes. You can't shoulder all the blame."

"You should hate me. I kept your son from you, your mom, and your whole family. I was selfish."

"You were scared, that's not being selfish. You thought something horrible would happen to me, so you protected me. That's not being selfish." I snort and shake my head. "If anyone's at fault, it's me. If I wasn't so hardheaded and would have let you talk when you called, I would have known. I don't know what would have happened, but it would have been worth it."

"Not if you were in jail or labeled a sex offender. That's what would have happened. Even if you didn't go to jail, you'd be considered a sex offender because you were eighteen and I was fifteen. That wouldn't be worth it. You couldn't see him right now. You'd have lost your job and any chance of being what you want. At least, now you have him in your life. I just wish that I would have found you sooner. I'm so sorry."

I wipe the tears from her face. "We've apologized enough. Let's place the blame where it belongs, on my dad and that stupid social worker, Simon. We have forgiven each other; we've agreed to move forward. Right?" She nods. "Then come back out there with me and visit with my family. I know they may not say it, but they missed you."

"Yeah, okay. When will your brothers be here?"

"Nathan had to work, and Paul is on a business trip, but we'll meet up with them when we can. Paul's wife is going to bring the boys down to meet Dylan and watch his first game."

"Good. They're about the same age right?"

"Yeah, Sam is fourteen and Danny is about to turn thirteen."

"Good, he needs cousins. He'll like that," she says, wiping under her eyes.

I kiss her forehead, then help her up. I squeeze her tightly and she returns my embrace with a chuckle. God, I have missed her. I won't let anything get in the way of us being a family.

"I love the sound of your laughter. Now, let's go hang with my family."

CHAPTER FIVE

Ryan

"Hey, bud. We're going to be late," I say, lightly popping Dylan's leg that's hanging out of the covers.

He groans. "Five more minutes."

I laugh. "You've had fifteen minutes. We have to leave in ten. Up! Don't make me go drill sergeant."

He sits up, flopping the covers down to his lap and glares at me. "I change my mind. I want Mom to take me."

A giggle from behind me makes me smile. I turn to see Shayla dressed to kill in a black knee length pencil skirt with a silky looking blouse, her blonde hair pulled half way up in some sort of twist. It shows off her long neck. She's absolutely killing me right now. I wish I could do what I'd like, but I promised last night to respect her boundaries. However, I haven't agreed not to push those limits.

"Sorry, Dyl-pickle. You're on your own. Your lunch is packed. I also put some drinks in the cooler for you two for practice."

"Traitor," Dylan grumbles. I ignore him as I walk to Shayla.

"Morning, sweetheart." I kiss her cheek. Perfectly within the realm of her rules, but the hand resting low on her hip is pushing me towards the edge of getting slapped. Not that I care.

I hear the hitch in her voice before she says, "Ry" breathily. Her hand rests on my chest, ready to push me away, but before she can, a pillow hits my back with excessive force.

"Out! Be gross anywhere else, just not in my room," Dylan says, aiming another pillow my way. I pick up the pillow from the floor and toss it back to his bed.

"No grossness here," I tease, holding my hands up in surrender, laughing. Shayla grabs my arm, pulling me from the room.

"Love you, Dyl," she says, closing the door. He mumbles in return. "Poor baby."

"He'll get over it because I don't plan on giving up on us anytime soon."

"I don't expect you to give up. I don't want you to. I'm not trying to be complicated, Ryan. I just don't want to rush."

I walk backwards as we enter the kitchen so I can see her. "Way I see it, Shay, we've wasted enough time already. I don't want another minute without you."

She blushes. "When you say stuff like that, it's impossible for me to say no to you. It's not that I don't want us. I just don't want to do anything we'll regret or that will hurt Dylan."

I take her hand and pull her to me. "I get that. I'm not going anywhere. I'm with you wherever you go. I lost you once, I won't do it again. I'm going to kiss you now. On that sweet mouth of yours," I tell her, watching for rejection. Every time has killed me, but I understand. This time though, she leans up on her tiptoes, wraps her arms around my neck, and kisses me before I can move. I smile as I kiss her. "Knew I'd wear you down."

She laughs and slaps me. "You're so arrogant. I'm not worn down, but I'll admit my feelings for you are just as strong as they always were. A kiss, a simple kiss like we just shared, is okay on occasion, but I can't go farther yet."

I nod. "I get it. I do. I'll wait. You're worth waiting for, Shayla." I pull her close again and kiss her. It's sweet, soft, and slow. See, I can follow rules.

"Ryan!" she squeals as my hand dips down to her butt.

All right, maybe I can't be good, but she's laughing so I know she's not angry with me. I give her the crooked grin I know she loves as I gather the supplies she's prepared for Dylan and I.

~*~

"I said run!" I yell into the megaphone as the football team makes their laps around the field. Half of them are barely moving.

"They were just as pitiful yesterday. We'll never beat Central at this rate," Trent Mathews, the other assistant coach, says.

"Titans, get your butts moving!" I shout again, bringing my drill sergeant voice out a little more.

We make them run for another ten minutes, then I about kill them with drills. By the end of practice, the boys are barely moving.

"A few more weeks of this and they'll be ready for that game," I tell Mathews.

"Heck, yeah. It's not until September fifteenth. They'll be in good shape by then. Hey, did you hear they have a candidate for coach?"

"No, who?"

Mathews snorts. "Some ex-football player. I don't think he's very well-known because he was hurt his first year. His name is Grant Hamby. I've never heard of him. Have you?"

I shake my head. "Nope, can't say that I have. Maybe that's what this team needs though." He nods in agreement, but doesn't say more.

I wrap my arm around my tired son. "Good job, Dylan."

He glares at me. "You're evil. The guys all hate me now." I throw my head back, laughing loudly. He weakly shoves me.

"A few more weeks of this and you'll be just fine. You're not that out of shape."

He snorts. "I'm nowhere near as fit as you."

"Yeah, but I was in the Marines and FBI. I trained for years, still do. You'll get there. I can help if you want."

"Heck yeah." He immediately perks up.

"I have all the equipment we need at my house. You're welcome anytime, even if I'm not home."

"Seriously?" he asks surprised.

I nod. "Of course. You're my son. I know you don't live with me, but consider the house yours. I have a spare room that we can fix up for you. You can stay over anytime."

"What about tonight?" he asks.

I'm a little taken aback so I sputter. "S... sure, yeah. If your mom doesn't mind."

"I'll ask her. I just thought it'd be easier, since practice is at six in the morning."

I nod, he's probably right. I'm just worried about what Shayla will say. I mean, he's my kid too. But I'm not sure she's ready for this step. They've only been back a couple of weeks.

I drop Dylan off at home and head into the station. I have a ton of paperwork to file and a few things to check out in the next county over. Apparently, there's been a string of break-ins. The local police have no leads and they've asked that I come and help out. I'm about half way through my paperwork when Shayla calls my cell.

"Hey, babe."

"Hi. So … uh, Dylan called me. He asked if he could stay with you tonight."

"Oh, yeah. He mentioned that in the car. Are you okay with that?"

She sighs. I brace myself for the worst. "Can I be honest with you?"

"Always."

"I'm nervous about it. I mean, I know he'll be safe. That's not the issue. It's just, it's always been me. Now, he has you, and I'm happy, but a part of me feels like I'm losing him. That's silly, I know."

"It's not silly. I'm not going to take him away from you. You know that, right?"

"I know."

"When I said I wanted custody of him, I was angry. I didn't mean that. I mean, yeah I want to be responsible for him as any dad should, but I won't take him from you. I want to help you raise him. You're not alone anymore."

"Dr. Thorn, line four. Dr. Thorn, line four." The intercom blares loudly enough that I can hear it through the phone.

"You need to go. We can finish this later. But know this, if you aren't comfortable, we can wait. He doesn't have to stay at my house."

"He can stay. It'll be fine. I do need to go though."

"All right, baby. See you later."

We say our goodbyes and hang up. I understand her fears. I'm not gonna lie either, I do want custody of Dylan, but I want it when Shayla and I are married and we change both their names to Jacobs. I want to share everything with her.

~*~

I walk around the glass that litters the floor of the jewelry store in Riverton Park. It's only ten minutes from my neighborhood in Oak Grove. There's been four break-ins in the past two weeks in towns surrounding Oak Grove. The older officers tell me this is the first time something this big has happened in the area. Granted, big to them is four break-ins, but it's still serious. Last night, two men were injured. Thankfully, not seriously.

"Whatcha think, Chief?" Officer Mills asks.

I turn to him and chuckle. He's probably been on the force since my dad was a kid.

"I'm not chief yet, but from the looks of this, it's intentional. Things are just too clean ... planned. Look at this," I tell him, pointing to the long glass jewelry counter. "This is smashed, but nothing's missing. If I were going to go to the trouble of breaking it, I would have taken something. This is just smashed."

"Could it have been forgotten when the two men came in?" Mills asks.

"According to the footage on the surveillance camera, John and Mark were here when the perp was over here." I point to another counter on the other side of the store. "See, right here is where they smashed the glass, but it didn't break completely. They fired their guns and fled." I pause, looking around. "What's missing?"

"Michaels, where's the missing items list?" Mills calls to his colleague.

Michaels looks through some papers, then pulls out one for Mills. Mills looks it over for a few minutes then says, "There are some very specific items missing."

"Specific, like what exactly?"

"There's a wedding band set in size six, a necklace, earrings, and a watch. Why would they only steal those things, but smash up the rest of the shop?"

"I'm not sure, but it gives us a starting point. I'd like to check in with the other robberies and compare," I explain.

"Let me know if you find a connection. I'd say your area is next. It's the only one in the surrounding towns not hit."

"Exactly, if I can find a pattern I might be able to catch these guys."

"I hope you can, Ryan."

Mills shakes my hand and hands me the file he has on the two robberies that happened in his district. I leave the crime scene to Officer Mills and his officers, and then stop by the other two stations to pick up copies of their files before heading back to my office to examine all the material.

"Your mom called," May tells me as I pass her desk.

"Thanks, I'll call her back." I put my stuff down and pick up my phone.

It rings a few times before she answers. "Hello?"

"Hey, Mom. Just calling you back."

"Oh, good. I wanted to see if you and Shayla would mind Dylan spending the night Saturday. The boys will be here. I thought they'd have fun getting to know each other. I'll take them to church with me on Sunday, then you two can come to dinner."

"Sounds good, I'll talk to Shayla."

"Okay, dear. How are things going with her?"

"Okay. We're taking our time. Doing things right this time, you know?"

"That's probably best, sweetie."

"That's what Shayla says." I laugh.

Mom giggles. We chat a few more minutes, but I tell her I have work to do so we end the call. I love my mom, more than I have words, but the woman will talk your ear off if you let her. Finally, I sit down at my desk and start looking over the break-in files. There's no pattern in regards to places hit. The first was a home, only the TV was taken. Second was a furniture store, a sofa and two chairs were taken. Third was a gas station where they stole food and money. Fourth was the jewelry store. The only connection I see so far is with the first three. It seems like the offenders are getting a place together, home or hide out maybe. Or they could be totally unrelated. The jewelry store seems unrelated, but still odd that they only stole a few items. I glance at the clock and sigh. I'm no closer to an answer than I was two hours ago. So, I pack up and head home. It's been a long day and I just want to relax.

I don't even bother going to my house. I head straight to Shayla's and use my key to let myself in.

"Hey, Dad!" Dylan calls, looking over his shoulder to me as he watches TV.

"Hey, bud."

I kick my shoes off and hang my gun holster and gun on the coat rack. I go to the kitchen and grab the awesome iced-tea that Shayla made. This stuff doesn't even have sugar in it, but it's somehow sweet and so good. I crave it. I plop down on the sofa beside my son.

"What're you watching?"

"Tyler gave me a copy of the game against Central last year. These guys are awesome. I don't know how we're going to beat them. Our guys can't seem to work together."

I chuckle. "I know. Tomorrow you're really going to hate me. We're going to start working on team work and communication."

He groans. "What kind of crap are you going to make us do?"

"You'll just have to wait and see. I can't be giving you an advantage. What time does your mom get home?"

He shoves me, making me laugh. "She said six. Maw and Pop want us to come over for dinner, you coming?"

"Oh, yeah. I forgot she told me about that. She called me about you spending the night."

"Yeah, it made her nervous. I don't know why. It's not like I wouldn't be fine. I mean you're ex-Marine and FBI, and the local cop. No one will mess with me."

"I don't think that's the problem. I think it's more my fault. I don't know if I've told you this, but when I first started talking to your mom again, I was angry. I threatened to take you from her. It was stupid. I would've never gone through with it, but it was out there and even though I took it back, it still bothers her. It bothers me. I'd never do something that cruel. I think her fear is you'll want to live there instead of here."

"No way. I'd never do that to her. She needs me here." I smile at my son's protectiveness. He looks thoughtful for a while, then says, "After you two get married, will we live here or there?"

I choke on my sweet tea. "Dyl, uh, your mom and I aren't even officially dating. I don't think marriage will come anytime soon, if at all. It's not something we've even thought about."

"Why not? I mean, you guys love each other. You were together as kids, I'm proof. Does it bother you she was married before?"

I shake my head. Sometimes kids, even fifteen year olds, have a totally skewed view of the world. Not that they are always wrong. They just see the world from a completely different view. At times, that's refreshing.

"I love your mom. I've had other relationships, but no one like her. I'd marry her today if she'd let me. It doesn't matter to me that she was married. It was fake anyway."

"Todd is an idiot," Dylan grumbles. I nod, agreeing.

We sit in silence for about ten minutes, watching the game. I can see a lot of areas my guys need to work on. Two more weeks isn't a long time to get them conditioned, but we'll do the best we can.

"Hello?" Shayla calls as she enters the house. I turn to see her wearing a pair of blue scrubs and a white doctor's coat.

"Hello, Dr. Thorn," I say as I stand to greet her. I hug and kiss her forehead. "Rough day?"

She shakes her head. "Not rough, just strange. I'm going to grab a quick shower before we head to Maw's." Leaning over the backside of the couch, she gives Dylan a kiss on the head, then darts down the hall to her bedroom.

~*~

I lean back in my chair and groan. "I forgot what a good cook you are, Gail." I pat my belly as I smile at Shayla.

"Thank you, Ryan. Did you save room for dessert? I made pie."

"Apple?" Dylan beams at his grandmother.

She chuckles. "Of course."

I sit up, looking as eager as my son. "Oh, boy," Shayla laughs. "I see where he gets his obsession for sweets."

"Heck yeah. Apple pie is my favorite," I say, rubbing my hands together greedily.

We eat, mostly in silence, once the pie is set in front of us, but as we finish up Shayla says, "Mama, do you remember that guy I went on a date with in college, Trevor Daniels? He was really intense and had us married off after the first date?"

Gail nods. "Yes, I seem to remember you saying something about him. What brought that up?"

"Well, he's been on vacation, so I just saw him today. A nurse told me he's worked there less than a year. All the nurses swoon over him and talk about how handsome and sweet he is, but I can't shake this weird feeling I get around him."

"Does he make you uncomfortable?" I ask her.

"No, not uncomfortable really … I did catch him staring at me, but I think he was trying to remember who I was. When I introduced myself, he seemed to remember. I guess we'll see how it goes."

"Let me know if he gives you any trouble. I'll come in there with guns blazing." I wink, making her giggle. Which is what I want, but I'll murder the guy in his sleep if he messes with my Shay.

"I'm sure it'll be fine. I think my uncomfortableness was just a remnant of before. He seems different now."

"I hope so. I want you safe, always," I tell her, squeezing her hand, and bringing it to my lips for a kiss.

After we say our goodbyes to the Thorns, the three of us head back across the yard to my house. Dylan, who seems to be a little pumped up, is doing backflips as his mom and I walk hand in hand. I snort.

"I wish I still had that energy."

"Seriously! He wore me out when he was younger. He's always had tons of energy," Shayla says with a laugh.

"I'm pretty sure I was like that. Must be a boy thing."

"I think so. That's what people always told me. He always got into trouble in elementary school. I had him tested for everything you can imagine. Technically, he's ADHD, but that's so over diagnosed. He's just an active kid. I've never treated him for it, he does well in school and now he's rarely what I'd call hyper. This," she points at our flailing son, "is sugar. He rarely has refined sugar, so when he does, he's off the wall for a while."

I laugh loudly. "That's the real reason you're a health nut."

She chuckles. "Busted."

"I'm getting my stuff," Dylan calls as he runs into his and Shayla's home. Shay and I stay out on the porch.

I smile as I look up at her. She's standing on the first step, making her almost my height. "We used to stand just like this when we were kids; you were always trying to be taller."

"Nah, I was just thinking about what it would be like to kiss you."

I grin. "Were you? Well, I can show you if you'd like." She shrugs nonchalantly. "If you're not interested, I'll just go home." I turn to leave, but she grabs me and presses her lips to mine. We've not kissed often enough for me, but times like this make it worth the wait.

"Gag! You guys should seriously consider getting a room." Dylan pauses. "Nope, on second thought, a room would be worse. You should just stop kissing in front of me."

I grab him and pull him into a headlock, giving him a nuggie. He tries to get out of my grip, but fails miserably. I let him up and he shoves me, laughing.

"One day, probably soon, you'll have a girl and you'll want to kiss her. It won't be so gross then."

"Yeah, I'm a teenager. That's what we do. You guys are old."

"Old! I'll show you old." Shayla yells, chasing after him.

He takes off, laughing. I follow, trying to block him in. He's laughing and dodging us, even throwing his bag at us at one point. Finally, Shayla catches a hold of his shirt and it's over. We're all in a pile on the ground, laughing hysterically. I grab my phone and take our first family selfie. This right here is the best feeling in the world. I'd do anything for these two people, even give up my life for them.

CHAPTER SIX

Shayla

Yawning and stretching, I make my way into my kitchen. Last night was the first night Dylan stayed with his dad. I wasn't worried about his safety, but I have to admit I am little worried about him wanting to stay permanently with Ryan. I know Ryan wouldn't do that to me, but it's always a fear I've had as Dylan grew up. Plus, Ryan had said as much when he was angry with me. I stop short at the kitchen door and laugh.

"I thought the whole point of you guys staying over there was to make for an easier morning?"

Ryan shrugs. "What can I say, we missed you."

He gives me a wink, then waves his fingers at me to hold his hand. I do and he pulls me onto his lap. It's pushing the boundaries I've set, but I can't seem to find it in me to care. The man has my heart.

"Missed me, huh? I think you're just too lazy to make your own breakfast." I kiss his cheek, then stand to search out our meal. I keep it simple and have them eating within ten minutes.

"What're your plans for today?" Ryan asks, as he finishes off the last bit of his sausage.

"Just work. I have a couple of surgeries scheduled. Hopefully, I won't have to stay over, but it's a big possibility. My last surgery is at three-thirty."

"I don't think I'll make it to dinner tonight anyway, my schedule is packed. After practice I have to go to neighboring areas about these break-ins," Ryan explains.

"Any leads?" I ask.

He shakes his head. "No. I think it's a couple of punks trying to see what they can get away with, but they're being smart. I haven't found any fingerprints or identifying evidence."

I squeeze his hand. "You'll find them. What about you, Dylan?"

"After football, Pop is picking me up. He said we'd get lunch, then he'd drop me off at Grandma Penny's to spend the night," Dylan answers.

"Oh, that's right. I forgot that was this weekend. You'll have a great time. I always loved going to Aunt Penny's as a kid."

Dylan snorts. "Yeah, because your boyfriend lived there."

I chuckle. "No, smarty-pants. We've known each other our whole lives, our parents were best friends."

"I know, I'm just picking on you. I need to grab something out of my room before we leave." Dylan darts up the stairs, leaving Ryan and I alone.

"Morning kiss?" he asks. I give him a raised eyebrow. He never behaves. He holds his hands up in surrender. "I'll be good. I'll keep my hands on the table if you'd prefer."

I smile. "You don't have to be extreme. I like it when you touch me, that's the problem." He pulls me to him so I'm standing between his legs.

"It wouldn't be a problem if you'd just let go and follow your heart."

He kisses my shirt covered stomach. Even though it's on the silk of my night gown, it still sends chills down my spine. I run my fingers through his hair. As if it will lessen the blow I'm giving him.

"I want to follow my heart, but I have to be smart and protect my son ... my heart."

He sighs, pulling me down to his lap. "I love you, Shay. I will wait for you. I don't know what I can do differently to prove to you that I'm not going anywhere. I've wasted enough time without you."

"You have me."

He kisses me long and slow. It's wonderful, but I want more. I move to sit astride him. We both groan as he pulls me closer to him. His hand moves to the back of my head and the other tightens around my waist as he deepens the kiss. I can barely breathe when we finally pull apart.

"Don't hurt me," I whisper, giving in to the need I have to be his.

"Never," he whispers back before pressing his lips to mine again. Of course our moment of bliss is completely destroyed by our always poorly timed son.

"Ugh. I need brain bleach! Not only do I have to see the two of you kiss, but you're in his lap. You're a mom!" Dylan says in disgust, but I see the smile he's hiding. He's absolutely thrilled we're trying to work on our relationship. He'd have us married today if he could.

I smooth my hair back, trying to hide my embarrassment. He's never seen me like this, not that we were doing anything major. I just can't even remember doing anything in front of him other than a quick peck on the lips with Todd. I feel like the teenage girl I was. The girl who wasn't able to control herself with Ryan.

"Sorry. You guys have a good day. I love you." I kiss Dylan's cheek and hightail it to my room.

"I'm just kidding, Mom," I hear Dylan call as I shut my bedroom door.

I lean my head against it, trying to control my emotions. I shouldn't be embarrassed, but I so am. We were pretty intense into that kiss and there may have been a small amount of grinding. I groan and bang my head on the door again. I blow out an exasperated breath and turn to gather my clothes for the day. I'm about to enter the bathroom when there's a light knock on my bedroom door. I pull it open to see Ryan.

"Hey, we're heading out. I wanted to be sure you were okay. Dylan feels bad for embarrassing you."

"I'm fine. I just get so carried away with you."

He gives me a cocky smirk. "That's a bad thing?" He pulls me into his arms and kisses my neck.

My breathing picks up. This man totally wrecks my brain. "No … no, it's not bad. Unless our son is in the room."

"He's fifteen, he knows about the birds and bees." He goes in to kiss me again, but I shove him away, laughing.

"Yes, I know. I had the sex talk with our son, but he doesn't need to see it in action. I don't mind the kissing, as long as we keep it PG."

He pouts. "Fun ruiner."

I turn to head back to my bathroom, giggling at this silly man. "I'm sure you'll still find your fun. You do like to push the rules." I squeal as he runs up behind me and lifts me up by the waist, tickling me.

"Rules are meant to be broken, sweetheart. Haven't you heard that?"

Out of breath, I pant, "Yes, but you're a parent now."

"Right, I make the rules," he argues. I roll my eyes.

"I need to shower. Go take our son to practice." I shove him playfully towards the door. He can't wipe the smug smile off his face.

"I love you, baby. Have a good day at work. Call me if you need me. Especially if that Trevor guy bothers you." Ryan kisses me quickly.

"I'll be fine. Don't worry. Have fun torturing the children with exercise."

I always feel bad not returning his love. It's not that I don't. I do love him. I've always loved him, but the fear of being hurt by him again is too strong. By the time I'm out of the shower and dressed, the guys are gone. Dylan, my sweet, sweet boy, left me an apology note. I hate that he feels guilty. I grab my phone and shoot him a quick text to let him know I'm okay and I love him.

~*~

I've been at the hospital for a couple of weeks now and I like it. It's much smaller than my previous hospital, which is a good thing. I feel like I can spend more time with my patients and, with the exception of emergencies, it's not nearly as hectic as the other hospitals where I've worked.

"Morning, Dr. Thorn," a deep voice says.

I don't know what it is about this man, but he makes the hairs on the back of my neck stand at attention. Don't get me wrong, he's handsome, even more so than he was when we were in college. His dark brown hair is short, smoothed in a look of years gone by, but it suits him. His eyes are a deep interesting shade of brown. He's fit and he's ... well, he's just pretty. But he absolutely and totally creeps me out! I fix my scowl to a friendly smile and turn to face Dr. Trevor Daniels.

"Good morning, Dr. Daniels. How are you today?" I ask, not that I really care, but I do try to be friendly.

I pull the keys to my office out of my purse and begin to open the door, but fumble and drop them. Before I have the chance to grab them, a large hand swoops them up. His fingers graze the inside of my wrist in an almost sensual way. I pull back immediately as a shiver courses through my body.

I'm almost positive he takes my reaction the wrong way, because he leans in a little too close as he says, "Careful now" and opens the door for me. "See you soon, Shayla." He winks at me.

I grimace as I shut the door, not saying anything else to the man. Was he flirting?

I soon forget about Dr. Creepy and go about my day. It's actually a busy one, full of surgeries and a few patients later in my day. I'm checking up on my last patient of the day, when my cell rings. I notice it's my son, so I excuse myself from the room to take his call.

"Hello?"

"Mom, Maw and Pop's house was broken into," Dylan says in a rush.

"What?" I ask, not really comprehending what he's said.

"Let me have the phone." I hear muffled sounds then Ryan comes on. "Hey, Shay. Can you get off work early?"

"What's going on, Ryan? Are my parents okay?" I ask, starting to really worry. Trevor, aka Dr. Creepy, walks up as I'm speaking and just stands there watching me.

"They're fine. But we're going to need you to come over. The thieves broke into your old room. Gail and Tom aren't sure what was taken. It's a mess in there though."

"My old room? Why would anyone want something from there?"

"I don't know. Can you come?" Ryan asks.

I nod. "Yes, yes, of course. I'll be there soon." I hang up and turn to Trevor. This is probably a horrible idea, but I ask anyway. "Hey, would you mind taking over my patient? He's the last one on my shift. My parents house was broken into and the police need me to come over there." I look at him pleadingly.

He nods, giving me a warm smile. This one is far less creepy than before. "I'd be happy to help you. I'll take care of him, don't worry. I hope everything is okay."

"Thank you! He just needs his incision checked; I've already done everything else. Thank you again, this is very nice of you. I'll return the favor one day," I say and instantly regret it as his warm normal looking smile turns into a sinister creepy one that almost makes his brown eyes look black.

He gives my upper arm a squeeze then trails his hand down to mine, taking the file. He winks. "I know you will."

I don't have time to process Trevor's possible meaning to his almost menacing sounding words. I push it to the back of my mind as I hurry down the hall, away from him and to my office. I quickly gather my things and head out of the hospital. I see Ryan pull up to the entrance as I'm darting through the front doors.

"What're you doing here?" I ask.

"I was worried you'd be too upset to drive. Hop in." I nod, and do as he says, because he's right.

"What happened? They're okay?" I ask after we're settled in the car.

My heart is pounding way too quickly. The very thought of something happening to them is sickening. I try to take several deep, calming breaths, but the panic is still rising. Ryan grabs my hand and brings it to his lips, pressing it with a soft kiss.

"Sweetheart, look at me." I do and he says, "Your parents are fine. They weren't home."

I nod and take a few more deep breaths, wiping a few stray tears from my eyes. "Nothing can happen to them. I can't lose more parents. I know one day it'll happen, but …" I trail off not knowing what else to say.

"I know. I understand. Losing Hannah and James was hard on you. I was there, but, baby, you haven't lost Gail and Tom. I swear to you, they are fine. They weren't home," he says again.

I look over at him, sniffling and wiping my eyes again. "Really? They're okay?"

"Yeah, baby. They're just fine. I promise you." He leans over as he stops at the traffic light to give me a quick kiss. "You okay, now?"

I nod. "Yeah. Sorry for being so emotional."

He snorts. "You don't have to apologize. It's a natural response to a scary situation." I just nod, but say nothing else. I'm too worried.

As soon as he has the car parked in the driveway of my house, I'm out and running across the yard to the home of my adoptive parents. "Mom, Dad!" I yell as I enter the front door.

"We're here!" Gail says as they round the corner. I'm in her arms immediately. "We're okay, sweet girl," she coos in my ear.

"Hey, now. We're just fine, honey," Tom says as he wraps his arm around me, kissing my forehead.

"I know. I was just so worried." I've managed to calm my nerves now that I've seen them. "They didn't take anything except from my room?" I ask.

"We don't know if they took anything from there either, but it's a mess. They've dusted for finger prints, but we weren't able to tell if there was anything missing," Gail explains.

"Here, babe. Wear these."

Ryan hands me a pair of blue latex gloves. I slip them on quickly and follow him up the stairs to the room where I spent the last part of my childhood.

"Wow, they really did tear it up," I whisper.

The fact that whoever broke in destroyed my room bothers me more than it should, but this room means a lot to me. It's where I brought Dylan after he was born. Where I lived until I went off to college and made a life of my own. The only place I felt safe for so long. Now, it's completely trashed.

"Were they looking for something?" I ask, moving things around to see if I can figure out what, if anything, is missing.

"Appears that way. Is there anything gone?" Ryan asks.

I look around a little more. "It's hard to remember what was in here, but from what I can tell, my yearbook and some pictures." I point to my bulletin board with bare spots. "The freaking bedding." I'm so confused. This stuff is so insignificant. Why would anyone care about it?

"Shay," I turn to Ryan and he points to a jewelry box on my old dresser.

I gasp. "No, please no," I groan as I walk over. I can feel my eyes burning. "They took my locket. The one you gave me, Ryan. Why would they want that? It's probably not worth anything. It was old and tarnished." I can't contain my tears any longer. That was the only thing I had left from my time with him.

He hugs me. "I don't know, baby. Do you see anything else?" he asks as he rubs my back.

"I didn't have a ton left in here …" I trail off as I notice they took a box of my pictures. "Why would they want this stuff?" I practically yell, growing angrier by the minute.

"Do you think someone is after her, Ryan?" Tom, my adoptive father, asks. That does seem reasonable, but why would they come here?

"I don't know. Nothing strange has happened to her before now. She's not been harassed or anything. Have you?" Ryan directs towards me.

I shake my head. "No. Never. Why would they break in here and not my house?"

Ryan says nothing as he shakes his head. After a pregnant pause, he says, "I think I should stay with you for a while. Just to be sure." I start to protest but he raises his hand. "I'll sleep on the couch or in the guest room. I'd just feel safer knowing the two of you are okay."

"I think it's unnecessary, but for Dylan's sake, I'll agree."

He rolls his eyes and laughs. "Dylan's sake, huh? You are just as important and precious to me, baby."

He smooths the hair back from my face and kisses me sweetly. I wrap my arms around him and squeeze him tightly. I can't help but hold on to this man. There's no more walls or denying what he means to me. He's it for me. He always has been.

"Let me stay," he insists. I just nod and kiss him.

~*~

"Have everything you need?" I ask as I lean inside the guest bedroom of my house where Ryan is unpacking his bag.

"No, but I can't have what I need right now," he responds, giving me a smirk.

I roll my eyes. "And what exactly is it that you need and can't have?"

He drops his bag onto the dresser and stalks over to me. "You, of course." He pulls me close to him as he kisses me deeply.

"Still gross!" Dylan yells from down the hall.

I giggle as I pull away. "He can't even see us," I say.

"That's a boy for you. Seriously, I have everything I need. Thanks for letting me stay. I feel better being here with you guys, knowing you're safe."

"I'm glad you are here too." I move to sit on the bench at the foot of his bed. "This whole thing has me really spooked."

He follows me and wraps his arm around my shoulders. "I'll find them. But in the meantime, I'm going to have a car patrol the neighborhood for a while. I can drive you to and from work too, if you'd like."

I shake my head. "No, that's not necessary. Well, tomorrow it is, since my car is there, but no one has actually shown interest in me. I'll be fine."

He stares at me for a few long seconds, then says, "They don't have to approach you to be after you, Shayla. This could be serious. The break-ins in the past few weeks have been random and odd, but they're likely connected. I don't want to discount this one."

"I'm not saying don't investigate. I'm just saying you don't have to follow me around."

"For now, but the second I feel you are in danger, you better believe I'll have someone on you twenty-four-seven."

I roll my eyes. I love that he wants to be protective of me, but I honestly feel it's unnecessary. I've been in town less than a month, why would anyone be after me, they don't even know me.

The rest of my week goes by quickly with no issues, thankfully. The break in rocked me more than I let on to anyone. I'm a worrier by nature and I have been worrying non-stop about my family. I've also become a little paranoid. I feel like someone is always watching me. And speaking of someone watching me ...

"Dr. Daniels, may I help you?" I ask, as he stares at me from behind the nurses station as I note my patient's chart.

He smiles. I think he means it to be flirty, but it comes across even creepier than usual. "Go on a date with me," he says.

I'm taken aback for a moment while I process his words. It wasn't a question. It was more like a demand. "Uh ... sorry. I'm seeing someone."

He looks almost angry. "You've been here less than a month."

"Yes, but I'm still seeing someone," I explain slowly, like I'm talking to a small child.

He narrows his eyes. "Who?"

"I don't really think that's any of your business," I snap. Suddenly, I'm feeling very protective of Ryan.

He stalks over to me and invades my personal space. "Because there is no one. Are we doing this again?"

I back up, but my back hits the wall. I move to the side and head to my office, but as I reach for the door, his hand shoots out and stops me. He leans in close, my heart speeds up considerably. I feel frozen and panicked.

"What are you talking about?"

"You know exactly what I'm talking about. You did the same thing to me in college."

"I assure you, I have no clue to what you are referring." I try to be strong, but I'm failing miserably.

"I'll tell you to what I am referring. In college, you flirted with me just as you do now. You'd bat those pretty blue eyes at me, say sweet things, and then say no when I'd ask you out."

"I went out with you. It didn't work," I remind him.

He glares. "It didn't work because of your inability to do as you're told."

I just stare at him. He's crazy. He leans in again and is just about ready to say something in my ear. My heart begins to race. I feel trapped, suddenly unsure what to do.

"Shayla!"

We both jump and he takes a step back. A furious Ryan is charging down the hall, dressed in his full uniform. It's the first time I've seen him dressed this way and I can't deny the affect it's having on me.

"Ryan," I say, relieved. Ryan continues to stalk towards us, anger burning on his face.

"What's going on?" he asks me.

"Nothing," I say immediately.

He turns toward Trevor and glares. "She's mine," he says, pointing to me.

He grips my upper arm and practically shoves me into my office without another word to Trevor. The door slamming shut makes me jump yet again. I've never in my life seen Ryan this angry. He takes a few deep calming breaths before he speaks.

"Shay, I'm going to ask you this once."

"Okay," I nod.

"Did he kiss you?"

"What?"

His question shocks me. I then realize he's not angry with me at all, he's angry with Trevor. As much as I'd like to throw Dr. Pain-in-my-butt Daniels under the bus, I don't want to lie.

"No, that was Trevor Daniels. The guy I told you about. The one I went on one date with in college. If he had kissed me I would have kneed him in his happy place!"

I can see the anger falling from his face as he tries, but fails, to hide his laughter. He covers his mouth with his hand as he says, "Happy place?"

He starts laughing out right. I can't help but join him as the uneasiness and tension of what happened with Trevor starts to wash away. He pulls me into his arms and I feel better already. He gently kisses the top of my head.

"You're adorable."

"You're not mad?" I ask.

"Oh, I'm mad all right, but not at you. I'm sorry I acted that way towards you. That wasn't right." He pauses and his demeanor changes again. "I don't care what you say, something isn't right with that guy. If he tries anything like that again, you call me. Understand?" He barks out like a command.

"Yes, sir," I bark back which makes him smile.

"You're so feisty. I like that," he says, pulling me to him for a kiss.

I roll my eyes. He watches me for a moment. "Seriously, are you okay?"

"Yeah, I'm fine. Let's go watch our boy win his first football game," I tell him, grabbing my jacket and purse.

Ryan throws his head back and guffaws. "I love that boy, but the team sucks. It might be a while before they get their first win."

I shove him. "Be nice. They're just kids. You're supposed to be the proud supportive parent."

"I am. I actually can't wait to see him play. I've missed out on so much. Sharing this with him … it just feels awesome."

It makes me sad every time he says something like that. I know he doesn't mean anything towards me by it, but it still gets to me all the same. He notices the change in my attitude and immediately knows what's wrong. He pulls me into his side and kisses my temple.

"Not your fault."

I just nod. There's no reason to hash it all out again. We're moving on and he and Dylan are together now. That's all that matters. By the time we get to the school, the crowd has started to gather. It's not packed yet, but it's close. Central is probably the Titans biggest rival. It's gone on for generations. When Ryan was on the varsity team, they beat Central at the State Championships for the first time in the history of the team. The Titans haven't won a championship against them since. Dylan swears he'll change that by the time he's on varsity. I believe he can, because he's the greatest player I've ever seen. Not that I'm biased or anything.

"Babe, I want you to meet the new head coach Grant Hamby. Grant, this is Dylan's mom Shayla." We shake hands.

"Nice to meet ya. Dylan is a great player," Grant says in a thick southern accent.

"Nice to meet you too. Thanks. He loves football. Just like his dad," I say, squeezing Ryan's arm.

"I'd say he gets that talent from him. I've heard some stories about you the past couple of weeks," Grant tells him. I swear Mr. Tough Guy Ryan blushes.

"Yeah, he's a good player. I hope you were able to whip those boys into shape. Last time I helped out, they were terrible."

Grant smiles broadly, showing off a perfect set of white teeth. "I think you'll be surprised."

Ryan and I head to the stands to find a seat. I'm able to see Dylan briefly before he kisses my cheek and runs off to the locker room. My boy is never ashamed to kiss his mama in public. I hope he never changes. We find a seat in the middle front. I can see everything perfectly.

"You warm?" Ryan asks as we sit on the bleachers.

"Yep. I have a blanket in my bag if I get too cold. Are you upset about not coaching anymore?"

He shakes his head. "No, not really. With everything going on at work, I wouldn't have time anyway. I was able to help out last week on my day off. They pretty much hate when I coach because I make them run." He laughs.

"Mean man," I tease. "But I think Dylan likes it when you coach." He's mentioned it a few times.

"I'll help him out at home. I think one on one will be better anyway. Some father-son bonding time." He can't wipe the smile off his face. He's such a good dad already. A total natural.

"You're probably right. He's head over heels for you. He gets it honestly though," I say with a wink. Ryan smiles back at me, placing an arm around my waist, and giving me a soft kiss.

"Lucky me," he says. We chat for a few more minutes and I pull out two thermoses, one coffee and one hot chocolate. "You think of everything."

"That I do. It's the mom in me." One of the cheerleaders trots over to the fifty-yard line beside Principal Amber Dillard and Vice Principal Jeanie Montgomery.

"Thank you all for joining us for the first game of the season. We're looking forward to a great one this year. Let's hear it for the Titans!" Amber yells. The crowd goes wild. She calls everyone to order, then says, "Singing our national anthem is ninth grader, Faith Gibson."

Everyone stands and places their hands over their hearts as Faith begins to sing. I'm totally blown away by the voice on this little girl. She does an amazing job and the crowd goes crazy as soon as the last note is over. She does a huge bow, waves, and runs off the field. The football team gives her high five as she joins her fellow cheerleaders.

"Wow," Ryan breaths. "That was incredible."

"Completely, that is a hard song."

They introduce all the players, Ryan and I cheer extra loud for Dylan, who shakes his head as he falls into his place. The game moves quickly. The players are doing great. We're up by fourteen points when Ryan stands up.

"Come on, Ref. Are you blind?" He yells and sits back down grumbling.

"Uh, what happened?"

He looks at me in disbelief. "You didn't see that?" I shake my head no. "Dylan threw to the receiver, it was an incomplete pass because of interference. The ref should have called a penalty."

"Okay," I say. I don't understand anything he's said. I watch my son play, but I'm mostly clueless about football.

"This ref needs freaking glasses," Ryan mumbles.

The game seems to be growing really intense when suddenly the linebacker hits Dylan near the sideline, causing Dylan to slide into a cheerleader. He hits her legs and she falls completely on top of him.

I'm on my feet, ready to grab my bag and run to my baby. Just as I'm about to make my move, Ryan grabs my arm.

"He's fine, look."

I turn my eyes to the direction he's pointing and see my son, helmet off, smiling at the girl on top of him. She bends down, kissing him quickly before hopping off of him and holding out her hand to help him up. He takes her hand and jumps to his feet, pulling her hand to his mouth for a kiss. She giggles. My son, the charmer he is, blows her a kiss as he runs back onto the field.

"Seems our boy has a little girlfriend," Ryan says proudly.

"I don't like it," I mutter. I don't like it one bit.

CHAPTER SEVEN
Shayla

Dylan was on cloud nine for days after the win against Central. I was proud of him. Ryan was so excited. As soon as the winning touchdown was scored, he jumped down from the bleachers and ran on to the field with the team. Dinner that night with the team was loud, to say the least, but I didn't mind one bit. I even warmed up to the idea that my baby had a girlfriend. They'd met at Aunt Penny's church when he'd stayed the weekend with her and his cousins. She was also the girl who sang the Anthem at the game. Faith is a sweet girl, but I'll be putting some rules into play for my son. Just in case.

"Morning, Dyl-pickle," I greet my son, kissing his head as I pass him in the kitchen.

He's pouring a bowl of cereal for breakfast. It's already October and close to Halloween. Dylan will be going to his first alone group party for the holiday. I'm a little nervous, but Ryan assures me that he'll be fine. Faith's parents, who are the music directors at Aunt Penny's church, are chaperoning as the party will be at their house. So, I'm trusting Ryan on this one.

"Morning," he grumbles with a mouth full of cereal.

"Chew, swallow, then speak," I remind him.

He swallows, then says, "Sorry. I didn't sleep well last night. I'm tired."

"Do you feel bad?" I ask.

He shakes his head. "No, I just couldn't sleep. I was talking to Faith last night, I just couldn't shut my brain off." I smile. I totally understand. I was the same way with Ryan, still am sometimes.

"That's pretty normal, I think," I tell him.

He nods. "She's really sweet. I think I'm going to go to church with her on Sunday. Is that okay?"

"Of course it is. I went to that church most of my childhood."

"Do you care if I go to her house on Sunday after church?"

I look at him for a long moment, then quirk a smile. "You really like her then, huh?" He nods. "Just be careful. I know how tempting things can be."

He clears his throat and sits up straighter. "Mom, I mean this with the most respect possible, but I'm not you or Dad. I'm not going to make those mistakes. I'm not going to have sex with her. We're too young. We've kissed, but that's all."

"I'm glad you've thought about everything. That's very mature to have already thought about what you want from your relationship. I would say I wish I had been so smart, but if I had been, you wouldn't be here. So for me, I'm glad things happened like they did."

"I get that. I'm glad you were a dumb kid too," Dylan says with a huge smile. I smack his arm with a dishtowel as I laugh with him.

"Why don't we go out for dinner tonight, just the two of us?" I ask.

He takes his dishes to the sink before answering with, "Yeah, that'd be great. Can we go to that new place, on Beaker? Tyler says it's awesome. I think it's called Max's Pizza."

I nod. "Yeah, it is. I noticed it was open last week. I'll get you after football and we'll go."

"Okay, let Grandma Penny know." He kisses my cheek then heads out the door to Tyler's house for his ride to school.

"I will. Have a good day." I watch him cross the street to Tyler's house, then finish getting myself ready for work.

~*~

"Morning, Dr. Thorn," a nurse, Missy Anders, greets me as I breeze into the hospital.

"Hey, Missy. How are you this morning?"

"Oh, fine. I'm headed home after a twenty-four," she answers with a yawn.

"Oh, wow. Poor girl. I hope you get some rest."

She thanks me and I continue on my way to the OR wing. I grab a few patient files and head to my office to review them. I have clinic today, so I won't be in the hospital much other than to check my post-surgery patients, which is why I'm here right now.

I'm startled when a coffee appears in my vision. "Ryan, you scared me," I say, looking up into his handsome face.

"Sorry. I missed you this morning. I thought I'd stop by on my way in," he explains.

"I missed you too. You know you can come over for breakfast anytime you want."

"It's okay. I slept in today. I wanted an excuse to see you, so I brought coffee," he says.

I stand from my desk and walk around to him, wrapping my arms around him and pressing my lips to his. "Thank you. That was very sweet."

"You're very welcome. I like this," he says fingering the collar of my purple silk blouse.

"Thanks. It's some fancy brand. I should probably burn it because Todd bought it, but it's one of my favorite shirts."

"Well, we can forget he bought it. I bet I can give you a new memory to go with this blouse," he says, his voice dropping in tone as he descends to my neck, kissing along my collarbone. He pops the first two buttons before I stop him.

"Ryan, I can't … oh, we can't." I step back.

He drops his hands to his side and sighs. "Sorry. I just get so carried away with you."

"Me too. Don't be sorry." I kiss him softly to help lessen his guilt. He's such a good man. I want everything with him, just not in my office at work.

"I should get going. I'll be out of the office most of the day, but I'll have my cell if you need me. I'll probably be late and not make dinner."

"I can't do dinner anyway. I have a hot date," I tell him. His face falls and I giggle. "He's about your height and has your smile."

He smiles. "Ah, taking the boy out? That's good. I was about to lay down the law," he says with puffed chest and fists balled at his hips. You can see his gun under his leather jacket. He might look intimidating to anyone else. I find him and his jealousy adorable.

"Oh, you were, were you? What would that law be, Officer?"

He takes a step forward and pulls me flush to him. His face comes within centimeters of mine as he whispers, "You're mine. No one else's." He kisses me deeply. We jump when someone knocks on my door. "We're always being interrupted," he grumbles as he pulls away from me.

I giggle. "Well, maybe you should stop attacking me when we aren't truly alone," I recommend.

He grunts. "Fat chance with your rules." At that I burst out laughing as I open the door, but my laughing stops as I see Trevor on the other side.

"You working today, Dr. Thorn?" Trevor asks tersely.

I try to discretely straighten my blouse, and clearing my throat I say, "Of course I am, but I'm not on the clock right now. Can I help you?"

"Just making sure you're all right. You're normally at the nurse's station by now." He looks behind me and says, "But now I see why.

You have patients to see, Dr. Thorn. Playtime is over." He turns and storms off before I can utter a word.

"Is he your boss?" Ryan asks. His face is pure fury.

I shrug. "He's OR chief, so I guess … sort of. I really should get to work. I have to be at the clinic soon."

Ryan is still not looking very happy, but he nods in understanding, He kisses me one last time before he heads out the door. Just then, I remember about Dylan and call after him.

"Ryan?" He stops and turns to me. "Do you mind calling your mom and letting her know that I'll get Dyl from school."

"Yeah, babe. Be careful. I love you." He blows me a kiss before continuing on his way. I watch him for a long moment before turning towards the nurse's station.

~*~

My day passes pretty quickly once I get going. There are plenty of patients to see and things to do. I'm almost ready to get Dylan when an emergency surgery is called. I call Penny to let her know the change of plans. She assures me she'll take care of Dylan. Not that I had any doubt. I send him a text to let him know we'll go tomorrow instead. I don't wait for his reply before I'm off to get ready for surgery.

I swing by my locker to change for surgery. When I round the corner, I notice a piece of paper is sticking out of the vent. I pull it out to see my name scrawled on the front. Inside it says, *'Your beauty is timeless. When I look at you I can't help but stare. You stun me.'* It's not signed, but I can imagine Ryan doing this. It makes me smile. He's so sweet. He must have stopped by here on his way out this morning. I'll have to thank him when I get home.

I hurry and change my clothes then head to the OR to scrub up. I'm at the sink washing my hands and arms when Trevor comes storming into the room. He comes as close to me as possible without actually touching me, but I can feel his hot breath on my neck. A surge of fear runs down my spine.

"Next time you decide to suck face with some man in your office, you might want to be sure the blinds are closed." He steps back a little as a nurse enters. "It was highly unprofessional, Dr. Thorn. I suggest you take that under advisement for the future," he says a little too loudly.

I'm so angry. How dare he say anything to me? He may be the chief of this OR, but he has no say in what goes on in my office.

"I wasn't being unprofessional. I wasn't on the clock," I tell him.

I don't say a thing about Ryan. He's none of Trevor's business. I don't know why he's so angry about it anyway.

"Clock or not, you're a representative of this hospital. I'm not sure what the policy was where you last worked, but here you aren't to have unauthorized guests in the physicians hallway. Don't let it happen again. Am I clear?" he barks.

"Crystal. Excuse me, I have a patient to save."

I wish I could stand up to him, but I don't. I just want away from him as quickly as possible. The man is crazy and making me nervous. I rush into position, check my surroundings and ask the nurse for a scalpel. My hand trembles as I hold it out for her to place the instrument in my hand.

"Are you okay, Dr. Thorn?" she asks.

I nod and shake my hands out and take a calming breath. "I'm okay. Scalpel."

She hands it to me and I go to work. I put Trevor and his nonsense behind me for the time being. I'll have to deal with it later, and as much as I might not like Ryan's reaction, I think he needs to know what's going on. I take another steadying breath and begin my procedure.

~*~

I lay my head down on my desk with a little thud. I'm so tired. The surgery went well and my patient will be just fine. But now that it's over and I can settle down, I'm crashing hard. I know it probably wouldn't be like this if Trevor hadn't yelled at me earlier. I have a hard time handling yelling, especially when it's directed at me. I think it's likely a left over from my time in the group homes. Even though that was sixteen years ago, it still makes my heart race. Sometimes, like today, I come close to having a panic attack. If he hadn't dropped it I would have had one.

"Knock, knock," the devil himself says as he taps on my open door. I should have shut the stupid thing! "Great job in there. I think that's the fastest I've ever seen someone complete an appendectomy."

"Um … thanks. Was there something you needed?" I ask, confused by his sudden mood change.

"Nope, just wanted to tell you that you did great. Get out of here. You're off the clock now. Enjoy your day off tomorrow." He smiles brightly then scampers down the hall.

I sit, staring after him. He was so furious with me less than an hour ago, now he's acting as if nothing happened. Maybe he's manic. I shake all thoughts of that freaky man out of my head and get my stuff together. At least he was right about the fact that I'm finished for today and tomorrow is my day off. I plan to go shopping with Gail and then take my son to dinner. I'd let him skip school if he didn't have a test and practice.

I stop by my locker, having forgotten to get my regular clothes after I left the OR and I find another note. Maybe Ryan came by while I was in surgery. This one says, *'Perfect pairs are rare indeed, but I found mine in you. I can't wait to start our forever.'* I can't help but smile. He's so sweet. He is perfect for me. Hopefully, I'll get to see him tonight and thank him. I could call him, but he said he'd be really busy today. I don't want to bother him. It can wait.

My house is dark when I get home. Though, I pretty much expected it would be. Dylan decided to stay over at Penny's and Ryan texted to say he wouldn't be home until late tonight. So what's a girl to do when she's all alone? A bubble bath and a sparkly drink sounds perfect to me.

I can't remember the last time I was able to soak in the tub. Between work, moving, and Dylan's activities, I just haven't taken the time for myself. I'm taking extra time tonight. I need to relax after the stress of work today. Sinking into the hot, bubbly water is the best feeling in the world. My whole body goes limp with relief.

My mind drifts from thought to thought. No matter how hard I try, I can't get Trevor out of my head. I don't understand him. In college he was nice, kind of shy, but he was relentless about asking me out. I said no at first because my schedule was so busy, plus I had Dylan. I wasn't over Ryan either. I was still daydreaming constantly about him showing up at my apartment. I didn't think dating was fair to me or any guy I might go out with. So I said no. Trevor seemed fine with each rejection, he never gave up though. I'd say we were tentative friends, at best. Then one night, when I was feeling lonely and vulnerable, I said yes.

The date itself was okay. We went to eat at a nice little Italian restaurant and then took a walk on the boardwalk near the river. We held hands and talked about our lives, college, Dylan, and even Ryan. It was nice. It was perfect, until the end of the date. He dropped me off at home, but before he said goodnight, he told me he could see us getting married, giving Dylan siblings. He talked about homes, cars, boats, and careers. It was too much for me. I told him so, but he wouldn't listen. Then, and I don't know why I never remembered this before now, as he was getting ready to leave he said, *'You'll always be mine.'* I almost missed it, and when I asked him to clarify, he said something completely different. I avoided him for weeks after that and by the fall, I was dating Todd. I never really spoke to Trevor again, even though I saw him often.

I must have dozed off in the tub because the loud banging of my bathroom door against the wall startles me so badly I scream and knock my glass to the floor, shattering it and spilling the red liquid all over my white tiles. I scramble to cover myself with my towel as I pull my knees to my chest.

"Shayla!" Ryan shouts.

He barrels through the door and I'm sort of surprised by what I see. He's completely disheveled, shirt half untucked, hair pulled back in a very messy bun, several strands have fallen out and his eyes are a mix of worry and relief. He's to me in seconds, pulling me into his arms. Water splashes all over him and the floor. I'm so shocked that I don't say anything for several long minutes. I don't speak until I notice he's shaking.

"Ryan, what's wrong?" I can feel the growing panic. "Is Dylan okay?" I ask as my stomach drops to my feet.

"He's okay," he mumbles.

He lifts my naked wet towel covered body out of the tub and walks us to my bed and sits us down. He grabs a blanket from the bench at the foot of my bed and wraps me in it before pulling my face to his, kissing me with so much desperation it scares me. I pull back, breathing sharply. He doesn't stop kissing me, he just continues down to my neck.

"Ryan, please tell me what's wrong. You're scaring me."

I try to push him back, but he won't budge. He just shakes his head, and keeps kissing me lower and lower. I give up and enjoy. It's not until he gets to my breast that I come back to my senses.

"Stop, please," I beg. Not that I want him to stop, but we can't do this when he's in this state. "Ryan, stop."

He moves his forehead to my neck, resting it there. After several deep breaths he says, "There was a body found not far from the hospital matching your description. I couldn't get you on the phone or at the hospital. I came straight here. I had to know." He squeezes me tighter. "I can't lose you."

I tighten my hold on him and run my fingers through his hair, soothing him. "I'm here. It wasn't me. I'm sorry I didn't hear the phone. I fell asleep. Why didn't you know she wasn't me?" I ask, hesitantly.

He sits up and looks at me several moments, like he's searching my face for something, then he cradles my face in his hands and kisses me sweetly. All the worry and panic seems to be gone.

"She was beaten so badly, her face was unrecognizable. Shay, she could've been your twin. Same blonde hair, body size, and shape. I lost it. I yelled at the chief and took off to find you."

"Oh, baby. I'm so sorry. That poor girl."

I hug him again, trying to soothe him as best I can. He pushes us back in the bed so we're lying side by side. It's not until then that I register I'm naked. I pull the blanket around me tighter and he chuckles.

"I've already seen it all." He bops my nose with his finger.

I smile, grabbing and biting his finger. "That wasn't fair."

He shrugs. "Maybe not, but it doesn't change the fact."

I get up from the bed to get clothes. If he keeps looking at me like that, things will happen that I'm not ready for yet.

"Spoilsport," he grumbles as I enter my closet.

"Patience is a virtue, Ryan James."

"Don't middle name me. I have patience. The patience of a saint." His voice is closer. I turn to see him leaning against the closet doorframe.

"Do you mind? I'm not finished." I say, trying to cover myself, even though it's pointless.

"I don't mind at all. Those are pretty," he says, gesturing to my lacy hot pink bra and panties.

I blush. "Thanks." I reach for my shirt, but he whisks it away.

My heart beat speeds. I'm not afraid of him … quite the opposite, I want him badly, but now isn't the time. He drops my shirt to the floor and drops to his knees in front of me. I have no idea what he's going to do, but I know I won't have the will power to stop him.

"Thank you," he says, leaning forward and kissing my faded stretch marks from our son. He traces each one, kissing it with an almost reverence. "God, you're beautiful."

He looks up at me, his eyes full of love. I kneel down with him and kiss him with everything I have. Never has one action ever made me feel so beautiful, loved, or wanted. Oh, how I love this man. I can't contain it anymore; I don't know why I tried.

"I love you so much, Ryan." Tears spring into my eyes. "I'm sorry it took me so long to say." I kiss him again.

"Don't be sorry. I understand why, but say it again." He smiles happily.

"I love you," I repeat.

He peppers my face with kisses as he says he loves me over and over again. "Let's get out of this closet before we do something we're not ready for," he tells me. I notice then, that we've ended up lying on the floor with him perched on top of me. It would be easy to give in, but he's right, we're not ready.

~*~

"Hey, sweet girl," Gail says as I enter her kitchen.

I greet her with a hug and kiss. "Morning, Mom."

Her smile could light a dark sky. In the past, I didn't refer to her often as Mom. I've mostly called her Maw, or Ma, because that's what Dylan calls her, but since the break in I've realized that they are my parents. It doesn't mean Hannah and James aren't, but they can't be here. Gail and Tom have been my parents for a long time and have done more than I could even express. They deserve to be called Mom and Dad. So, at thirty-one, I'm finally giving them the title they've deserved for so long.

"You ready for a day of shopping?" she asks excitedly. It's the one thing we do not share. She loves shopping and I tolerate it.

I groan. "As I'll ever be."

She laughs. "I don't understand you. You love clothes and shoes, but you hate shopping for them."

"I don't mind shopping online, but then I end up sending stuff back. So I guess it's a necessary evil," I explain poorly.

She hands me a travel coffee mug with a smile. "You're ridiculous. You know that?"

"Oh, I think you've told me that a few times." I chuckle. "Let's get the torture started. I have a date tonight," I tell her.

She quirks an eyebrow. "So, things are going well with Ryan?"

"Yes, but I mean Dylan. I was supposed to take him out yesterday, but I had an emergency surgery. We're going today instead."

"I think that's great. You used to do that a lot when he was little."

I nod in agreement. We did. I took him out weekly, if possible, to where ever he wanted to go. We would talk about whatever was on his mind. Sometimes it was video games or toys; sometimes it was troubles he was having in school or about his dad. The last was always hard for me, but I tried to be as honest as possible.

"I've not taken him out as often as I'd like. The older he gets, the harder it's been."

"He's a busy boy. He told me about his little girlfriend," she says.

I groan. "It's too soon. I know Ryan and I dated when I was around Dylan's age, but I also gave birth to Dylan at sixteen. We obviously did things we weren't ready for. Our son is the result of that. I just don't want that for him. No matter how smart he's being, things happen in the heat of the moment."

"You're right, but he's fifteen. You can give him rules. I know we tried to give you rules, but it was hard since you were gone from us for so long. We probably shouldn't have left you alone with Ryan, but I was afraid to make you angry. I didn't want you to change your mind about staying with us."

"I still would've stayed with you. I wanted that more than I can explain. I know we've talked about it a lot, but the homes I was in, they weren't … they didn't feel like home. I only felt at home with you guys."

She squeezes my hand with a happy grin. "You were our dream come true. I know I've told you that before, but we tried for so long to have a child. Moving to that house and watching you grow up. It was enough for me. I was devastated when your parents died. I lost my best friends … my sister. Your mom was so important to me. Even if we weren't blood, she was my sister. I still miss her. When they said we couldn't have you until we did all this paperwork and classes, I was crushed. I was so afraid we'd lose you, especially after it took so long for them to actually give you to us." Gail pauses, overwhelmed with emotion. It doesn't matter how often we talk about that time in our lives, we both end up emotional.

I stop the car and pull her into my arms. "Oh, Mom. You have me and I'm home now. No one can take me from you," I tell her.

"I know. You and Dylan mean the world to us. I know he's our grandchild, but we helped you raise him. He's filled just as many holes in my life that you have. And once you and Ryan get back together, I expect more little Dylan's. Of course, girls would be great too." Her tears dry up and a smile graces her beautiful face.

I throw my head back and laugh. "You and Ryan both, the man can't keep his hands to himself. We're so not ready for more than what we have now though. But I know I'll marry him. There's not a question in my mind that he's it for me. I just want him to be sure I'm it for him."

"I think he's sure, sweetie. It's not like he left because he wanted to. His stubborn father basically gave him no other choice."

"I know, but still, sixteen years is a long time."

She nods. "Oh, I know. I think you're being smart. Just don't let your head overrule your heart."

"I'll try not to."

~*~

"Sorry about yesterday," I tell Dylan as he slides into the passenger seat of my SUV.

I had dropped Gail off at home after our mega-shopping excursion. It was actually a lot more fun than I expected, and I got some really beautiful clothes and lingerie. She insisted that I buy them; stating it would help in my endeavor to give her more grandbabies. I had rolled my eyes at her for that one.

"It's okay. You were saving lives." He stares at his phone distractedly.

"You think we could have an evening that is cellphone free?" I ask.

He looks over at me, giving me his father's grin. "Sorry. You know Faith asked me over on Sunday after church, but Grandma Penny said we're having a family dinner. Maw and Pop are coming too. You think it'd be okay if I invite her?"

"That's right. I forgot about that. You'll need to ask your dad and Grandma Penny, but it's all right with me," I tell him.

He nods. "Ya know, things were much easier when I just had to ask you."

"Would you rather we go back to that?" I tease.

He shakes his head. "No way, having a real dad is great. I mean Todd had his moments, but it was hard to connect with him. He liked football, but that was about all we had in common. He tried for a while, but mostly his idea of spending time together was watching TV."

"He always made it seem like you guys did all kinds of things," I tell him. Todd always had a list of things they'd be doing. I guess I never followed up close enough. Doesn't matter now, I'm just glad he's out of our lives.

"Eh, don't sweat it, Mom. Things are great now. Dad actually does stuff with me and even though he's been really busy lately, he's taken time to at least check in with me or send me random texts. Things are ten times better now than they were."

"I'm glad. I want you happy, kid." I tell him.

He turns to me. "I am. I don't know why you hated this town. I think it's pretty awesome."

"Fifteen and pregnant," I say.

"Oh, right. Sorry about that." He chuckles.

I smile at him. "It turned out all right in the end. You're right, this town isn't so bad."

We make it to the restaurant and he happily bounces inside. It's an arcade themed pizzeria, so he's in heaven. It isn't long before a few kids from school come join him. I know we won't be having any more time to talk until we're back in the car, but I'm all right with that. I love seeing him having fun.

CHAPTER EIGHT

Ryan

I can't stop staring at the pictures lying on my desk. The woman's beaten and lifeless body sends a cold chill through me and straight to my heart. She looks so much like my Shay that it hurts. It physically hurts, which is nuts. I've seen many dead bodies in my life, and while they are always hard, none have been as hard as this. This one ... it's too much. I keep thinking if I stare at it long enough, I can set my mind at ease. This woman is not Shay, so why is this driving me crazy? I slap the file closed and run my hand nervously through my hair. The phone ringing is a relief. I need a distraction from this.

"Hey, Dyl. What's going on?"

"Hey, Dad. You busy?" he asks.

"Never too busy for you. What's up?"

"Well, on Sunday, Faith wanted me to come over, but Grandma Penny is having a family dinner after church. Would you mind if Faith came with us?"

I'm a little shocked. I mean he's asked me before for things, but just small stuff. He's never asked for my approval to do something he wants to do.

"Sure, I don't see anything wrong with her coming over."

"Thanks. Mom said I had to clear it with you and Grandma first," he explains.

"I'm sure your grandma won't mind either."

"Great, I can't wait to tell her. Crap, she just left for her candy striper shift at the hospital. Oh well, I'll tell her later." His rambling makes me smile. I really need some time with my boy.

"Hey, are you busy today after school?"

"Not after practice; it's over at four today." I hear some chatter on the other end and a bell ringing. I forgot he's at school.

"Why don't you come over around six? We'll eat, I'm thinking subs, and maybe play some video games."

I tap my pencil on my desk as I stare at the closed file. Talking to Dylan is helping, but that file is still taunting me. I've got to see Shayla, it's the only way to clear my mind.

"That sounds great. Mom's working late tonight, she said she was covering for an ER doctor."

I frown. I hate when she has to work over.

"Okay. Thanks for telling me. I'll let you get back to class. Love you," I tell him.

"Love you. Bye."

He hangs up. It's ridiculous that hearing my teenage son tell me he loves me makes me so happy. I stare at my phone for a few more minutes and check my social media. I didn't bother with this stuff while in the FBI, but Dylan insisted on setting me up with different accounts. I generally don't bother with it most of the time, but right now, it's a welcome distraction. I check out Shayla's page and see she's posted a picture of her and Dylan.

"My two favorite people. Love you guys!" I post as a comment.

She responds back almost immediately. "We love you, stud."

I shake my head. She's been trying to find me a nickname. She's randomly called me different names, but thinks none of them really fit me. Her silliness is one thing that I love about her. I dial her number.

"Hey, stud," she says. I can hear the grin in her voice.

I laugh. "Stud, huh?"

"Yeah, I like it. What're you doing? I thought you were busy on that case today."

Taking a deep breath, I begin, "I am. I've gone over the case files ten times, if not more, this morning. I'm going to head out to the scene again later. I needed to hear your voice. I'm not going to lie, babe. This stuff is getting to me. She looks so much like you."

"It's just a coincidence."

I nod even though she can't see me. I pray she's right. "I hope so. Can I see you?"

She doesn't respond right away, but I hear voices through the line, so I know she's still there. She does this often when someone needs her attention. It's a little annoying, but I understand. She has an important job.

"Uh, okay. Sure." There's another pause. "That was weird."

"What?" I ask curiously.

"Well, this guy just delivered a small package here for you."

I jump to my feet. "Don't open it."

"Of course I won't. It's for you," she responds.

I grab my leather coat, keys, and head out of my office.

"May, I'll be out the rest of the day. Call if you need me." I don't wait for her response as I run to my car.

"Ryan, what's wrong?"

"Shayla, listen to me. I want you to go to a nurses station or somewhere where there are a lot of people. Don't leave that spot until I get there. Understand?"

"You're scaring me, Ryan." I can hear her movement over the line.

"I know. I'm sorry. Just leave the box and go to the nurses station. I'll be right there. Don't be scared. I'm just taking precautions. There's no reason why someone would need to deliver a package for me to you."

I'm in my car, lights on, and speeding to the hospital, trying to quell the panic rising within me.

"I'm at the nurses station."

"Which one?"

"The one on my floor."

I fly into the parking lot and park in the drop off zone. I toss my keys to a candy striper. "Park my car. I'll get the keys from the desk when I leave," I bark out.

"Okay," the girl responds, her voice is shaky.

"I'm a cop," I tell her, flashing my badge as I get to the elevators a good twenty feet from her.

"I know. I'm dating your son, but I can't drive."

I laugh. "Faith, just find someone to park it. I have an emergency. Okay?"

"I will, Officer Jacobs."

I dart into the elevator. The thing is going incredibly slow. I'm sure my bouncing is annoying the other passengers, but I can't stop myself. I have to get to Shayla. I should've taken the stairs. I'm the first one out as soon as the doors open. I'm running to her. I can see her worrying her lip from here.

"Shay," I say as I scoop her up in my arms. "You okay?"

"Yes, I'm just worried about you."

She runs her fingers through my hair. It's nice, but I can't be distracted by that now. I pull her hands into mine.

"Where is the box?"

"In my office, but I'm not allowed to have unauthorized visitors back there." She sighs.

I don't care what policy is. This is a police matter. I shake my head.

"That doesn't matter. Take me to it."

She turns to a nurse. "Julie, I'm taking Officer Jacobs to my office. He needs to ... check something out. Page me if you need me."

"The box?" she asks. Shayla nods.

I turn to Julie. "Did you see who delivered it?"

"He was one of those local delivery guys. Not one of the big name places, just a hired courier. I've seen him around here before. I don't think he'd knowingly do anything wrong. He mostly delivers flowers and food," she explains.

"Thanks, Julie." I turn back to Shay and take her hand. "Come on, babe."

We walk hand in hand to her office. "Do you really think this is necessary?" she asks.

"I don't want to take any chances where you're involved." I pull her to a stop and take her face in my hands. "You're everything to me."

I kiss her with desperation. Nothing can happen to her; I just got her back. I'll do anything I can to protect her. She nods and then points towards her desk.

"It's over there."

The box is maybe three inches tall and wide. A perfect cube. No markings of any kind. Not even a name. I pull a blue glove out of my pocket and slip it on. Then I pick the box up, noting that it weighs nothing. There's no sound. I don't think it is explosive, that's not 'The Fox's' M.O. I open it. Then I drop it with a string of curses flying out of my mouth. After I compose myself, I pick the thing back up and shove it in my pocket. Hurrying to Shayla, I grab her upper arm and drag her from the office and down the hall.

"You're staying with me the rest of the day. Tell someone to cover for you."

"Ryan, I can't just leave. I have a surgery at four."

"Is it vital? I mean, can it wait or can someone else do it?"

We stop back at the nurses station.

"I suppose it can wait a day, but I've already seen the patient this morning so they're expecting me."

"Shayla, baby, this is important. Please, get someone to cover for you," I plead.

Trevor Daniels appears behind her, too close for my comfort. "Cover for what?" he asks, glaring at me.

"Hello, I'm Detective Jacobs with the Oak Grove police. I need Dr. Thorn to come to the station with me. There was suspicious activity in her office this morning."

"She has surgery. This can't wait until after work, Detective?" I don't miss the way he spits out detective, like it's beneath him.

"Afraid not."

"Fine," he fires back angrily and then turns to Shayla. "You'll make up the hours you've missed. I'll take your surgeries today." He storms off in the opposite direction.

"Wow, he's ..."

"A jackass," Julie supplies. We all laugh. "Seriously, he looks like a god, but acts like the devil, and not in a good way either." She winks.

~*~

Once we're in the car, I breathe a small sigh of relief, but my panic is far from receded. If anything, it's grown. I'm trying to keep a lid on my feelings, but the thought of *him* being so close to her has me unnerved. I don't want her out of my sight.

"You going to tell me what's going on?" Shayla asks. I shake my head no. "You can't force me to leave work and not explain yourself, Ryan."

I look at her for a long moment. "I'll tell you later. First, I need to get Dylan."

A surge of panic swells. What if *he* goes after my mom, the Thorns? What if he's the one who broke into the Thorns house? It doesn't make sense, but, it's a possibility. Though, breaking and entering isn't really his style, but I can't rule out anything.

"Why? He's at school, I'm sure he's fine. He shouldn't miss," Shayla says.

I run my hand through my hair in frustration. "He's my son, too. I want to pick him up!" I snap. She visibly flinches back in her seat. "I'm sorry. I shouldn't have shouted. Can you just trust me on this?" She nods, but offers nothing back. I look over to see tears glistening in her eyes. "I'm sorry, Shay." I grab her hand and squeeze. "I didn't mean to yell. I'm stressed, like really stressed. I've never felt anything like this before. I just need to see him with my own eyes. I'm sure he's fine. I just need to see him. He can stay at school."

She wipes her eyes. "Is he in danger? Are we in danger?"

"I don't know, babe. I hope not. I've got some things to check out. I just can't do it without you being near me. I need to see you," I try to explain, but I feel crazy in doing so.

"Maybe we should get Dylan," she mutters softly.

I shake my head. "No, you're right. He's safe at school. I'll have one of the guys get him after school and bring him to the station. I just need to talk to him first."

As soon as we arrive at the school, I'm out of the car and helping Shayla out.

"I look horrible," she says, wiping under her eyes.

I smile softly. "You look beautiful, sweetheart. I'm so sorry I scared you."

"It's okay. Stop apologizing. Let's go see our son."

We head to the office and speak to the receptionist. It takes about five minutes for Dylan to arrive.

"Hey, what's up?" he asks as he sees us. His face becomes concerned when he sees his mom's red eyes. He kneels down in front of her chair and takes her hands in his. "Mom, are you okay? Did something happen to Pop or Maw?"

"Oh, no, nothing like that. I'm okay," she tells him, trying to smile.

"I upset her. She'll be okay. I just want to talk to you for a few minutes." I turn to the receptionist. "Do you have somewhere private we can talk?" She points to an empty office off to the side of the entrance, labeled Conference Room.

"What's going on?" Dylan asks. He helps his mom into a chair and stands protectively between her and me with his arms crossed over his chest. "Why did you make her cry?"

I stare at him, exasperated. I'm not handling this well at all. "I didn't mean to," I finally say.

At the same time, Shayla says, "Dylan, it's alright. It's not his fault."

He turns sharply to her. "I'm not listening to you protect another man. I don't care if it is my father!"

Shay and I speak in unison again. She says, "Dylan!" While I say, "What is he talking about?"

Shayla puts her hands on either side of Dylan's face. He looks at her with a childlike pleading, mixed with protectiveness. "Dylan, I'm not protecting your dad. If you'd let him explain, we'd both understand. I don't know what's going on either."

"Fine." He faces me with a stern expression. I see myself, as well as my father in him. It's a little scary.

"Can we sit?"

He nods and we sit at the table with the two of them on one side and me on the other. I reach out a hand to both, Shayla immediately grabs mine, but Dylan moves slowly. Once his hand is in mine, I squeeze it gently.

"I love you both, more than I can even put into words.

Dylan shoots up out of his seat. His hands grip his hair tightly. "Oh, crap. You're freaking leaving, aren't you? I knew it was too good to be true!"

I can't help the chuckle that leaves my mouth. Not that anything about this is funny, but the kid is adorable. He reminds me of his mother when she's angry.

"Son, I'm not going anywhere. Please, sit back down and listen." He does, so I continue. "Thank you. When I worked for the FBI, I was undercover on a lot of assignments. Some of those were with very dangerous people. My last case, before I moved here, was to gather evidence against a mob boss named Jason Mathis. Mathis was a beast to take down. It took me almost two years. I didn't speak to my family at all during that time. I missed my dad's funeral. It was a tough time for me, but in the end, I put him behind bars. However, a few weeks ago, I learned he was released when a key witness recanted her testimony. I don't have all the details, but he's out. He's supposed to be under watch until the new hearing, but this morning someone delivered this to your mom."

I pull the box out of my coat pocket and sit it on the table. I take a deep breath and open it, setting the small figure on top of the box. Dylan throws his head back and laughs. I chuckle with him, but not out of humor, more from ridiculousness.

"So an origami fox has caused you to lose your mind?" Shayla asks, a smirk on her sexy lips.

"Seriously, Dad. It's not a bomb," Dylan jokes.

I know it's silly, but this is serious. I slam my hand down on the table as I stand to lean over towards them. They both jump and sit back in their chairs. The laughter is gone.

"This may be a stupid folded piece of paper to you, but to me it's how he marks his victims. Every murder this guy has ever committed, he's left a fox on the dead body. Dead, Dylan." I hold it out to him. "He sent this to your mother!"

Dylan's face pales as he stutters, "H … he's after Mom?"

"I don't know. The delivery person said it was for me. So, he might just be letting me know he's here. I'm not taking any chances. I'm keeping your mom with me today. I want you to stay here. Don't go to practice. I'll have an officer pick you up about thirty minutes early today. He'll bring you to the station."

"If I don't practice today, then I can't play in the game this weekend," Dylan panics.

Rethinking, I say, "I'll just have a uniform here and he'll bring you to me when you're finished. Okay?" Dylan nods. "I don't want you telling this to anyone, and if anyone comes to you with something for me, you run. You understand?"

"Yeah, Dad."

"I mean it. Don't try to be a hero. Keep yourself safe. Understand me?" He nods again. I know he might be scared, but I need him to understand how important this is. "The murder the other night, you heard about it?"

"Yeah. Near the hospital," Dylan responds.

"The girl who was killed looked just like your mom. I'm not trying to scare you, but I want you to know how serious this is. You're not a little kid anymore. I think you can handle this. I need you to be extra careful. If this guy is after me, then he'll stop at nothing to get to me. Please, keep yourself safe."

"I promise."

The bell rings, covering Dylan's words, but there's no question that he understands how serious this is. He stands to leave, hugging his mom tightly, whispering in her ear. He hugs me with more force than I expect, but I return his hug and kiss his forehead.

"I love you, Dylan. I'll fix this." He shakes his head, but doesn't say anything before darting out the door to class. "You okay?" I ask Shayla. She's been so quiet through all of this.

She takes my hand. "I'll be okay. Let's get to the station."

We're silent the whole way in. I lead her into my office and shut the door, telling her to sit wherever she'd like. She chooses the black leather sofa. I sit beside her and brush her hair from her face. "Are you all right?"

"Not really, but I will be. Today … was just draining. It's not over either."

"Yes, that's true. I need to call my buddy with the FBI."

I press a kiss to her lips, then walk over to my desk to find his number. I grab my office phone and dial.

"Marsh," he answers in a clipped tone.

"It's Jacobs," I reply.

He lets out a deep breath. "He's there, isn't he?"

I shake my head, growing angry as curses fly from my mouth. "How could this happen, Marsh? Did you guys just open up the door and let him get away?" I snap.

"Honestly, I don't think anyone here even knows that he's gone. I had this gut feeling he was going to come for you. Hold on," he tells me. Then he barks orders at someone about checking on Mathis. "I'll have confirmation in about thirty. Tell me what's going on."

I rub my forehead as I recount the body we found and the fox that was left at Shayla's office. By the time I'm done, he's the one cursing and yelling at his assistant to get him on the first plane out. He's coming here. I knew he would. He's the most loyal man I know. We've had each other's back since our time in the sandbox. It doesn't take more than fifteen minutes to confirm that Mathis is gone and that one of Mathis' men was staying in the house, posing as him. How that slipped by the local guys, I'll never know. Rookie mistake for sure.

"He'll be here in the morning," I tell Shay.

"What will he do?" she asks.

I scrub my face with my hands. My stress level is through the roof. Glancing up, I motion Shay to me. She looks so afraid. I hate that. Especially, since I know I'm the reason for it. It kills me that I'm causing her to hurt again.

"I'm sorry," I tell her as I pull her down on my lap.

Running her fingers through my hair, she says, "Oh, baby. This isn't your fault. You can't help what someone else choses to do. We've talked about that. Everyone's choices are their own."

"No, it's not my choice, but he wouldn't be after you if it weren't for me. He promised he'd come for me and mine. I just didn't think it was possible with him in jail. I'm a fool."

"How did he know it was you who betrayed him?" She continues to run her fingers through my hair, massaging my scalp and neck. It feels incredible.

"At first, I was only reporting to my handler, because I was undercover." I take a quick breath and look up at her. "I was getting antsy though. I wanted out, but what I was getting was really valuable and I was close to taking down the whole family. So, they wanted me to stay undercover for as long as possible." I chuckle humorlessly at my own stupidity. "I don't know, I got careless and was discovered. The agency pulled me out as soon as they could, but Mathis still found out I was the traitor in the organization. I ended up testifying in court, which was necessary, but also furthered Mathis' hate for me. It's one of the main reasons I moved back here. I needed to get out of the area. And, my God! I just never … imagined he would get released. He was convicted of ten murders and several miscellaneous drug charges." I breathe out quickly and shake my head. "There's got to be something going on in the system. Maybe a corrupt judge."

"Will the FBI open an investigation?" Shayla asks.

"Possibly. I hope they will. Finding a corrupt official is a touchy thing. There are a lot of loopholes we'd have to go through. I mean, they would have go through."

"You miss it, don't you?"

I shrug. "Sometimes I do. I miss the excitement and the challenge, but I'd quit all over again to be with you and Dylan. I don't regret my decision at all."

"I worry you will."

"Never. I'll never regret being able to get you and my son back," I say, kissing her. I pull back after a few minutes. "I know you're not going to like this, but I think I want to call in a few favors and have someone guarding you and Dylan." I brace myself for the worst but she just smiles.

"If you think that's best."

"You're not going to fight me?" I raise my eyebrow in surprise.

She's always been a pretty passive person, except when it comes to me. She'll rip me apart in two-seconds flat if she doesn't like what I have to say.

"No. You're only doing what you think is best. I don't like it, but I won't fight you. I don't know how that will work at the hospital, but to and from home would probably be enough."

We sit quietly for a few minutes, both overwhelmed with the situation we find ourselves in. At least I am, and knowing Shay the way I do, I'd say she's doing the same.

"Ryan, are these the crime photos?" she suddenly asks, sitting forward on my lap.

"Crap. I'm sorry. You shouldn't have to see those."

I move forward to grab the photos, but her hand shoots out to stop me. I look up at her in question, but her eyes are trained on something. She stretches out her arm and plucks one of the photos with the girl's body and some of the surrounding area.

"Does this look like a fox to you?"

She points to an area by a tree surrounded with dead leaves. I grab my magnifying glass and turn my desk lamp on.

"It's him," I say gravely. "I knew it was him. Shayla, this means he's most definitely after you. You're exactly his type."

I stand up and almost dump her on the floor, but she moves quickly enough. I run my hands roughly through my hair. It was one thing to think he might be here and after her, but this … this is confirmation.

"Why would he do that?" she asks.

"Do what?" I stop to turn to her.

She picks up the picture. She has a look that's a cross between panicked and somewhat curious. "Hide it? I mean, you said it was always his thing. To let everyone know it was him. Why hide it this time?"

She has a point. I consider that for a few moments, then say, "Maybe he wasn't ready to let me know he was here. Maybe he can't stop himself from leaving his calling card."

"That would make sense. It's probably a compulsion. He can't function without doing what he feels will finish the job."

"Exactly! The profiler for the FBI said he was OCD. Do you want to see the photos?" I ask her, pointing to the others on my desk.

"Yeah, if you don't mind."

I grab the pictures just as she pulls out a pair of glasses from her purse and puts them on. I freeze as I hold the pictures out to her. She easily just went from being a ten on the hotness scale to a fifteen! This woman leaves me speechless and stupid.

She cocks her head to the side. "What?"

I clear my throat. "Uh, you just look really hot in glasses. I'm having some pretty inappropriate fantasies."

She laughs loudly. "Oh, Ryan. I see not much has changed since high school, your mind is still in that gutter." I grin crookedly at her. She's not wrong.

She takes the photos and sits down at my desk. She then proceeds to study them and I can't help the pride that swells inside me. She's always been so astute. I tuck a piece of stray hair behind her ear and kiss her temple.

"I can't help it. You're gorgeous. I want you so bad, baby. You just can't understand."

She looks up at me over the top of her frames. My head rolls back with a groan. I stumble backwards towards my sofa and dramatically flop down with my hands over my heart. She's killing me.

"I want you too, Ryan. I'm serious though, it's not happening in our workplaces or my closet." She gives me the stern face she gives Dylan, which causes me to laugh and her to giggle. "Shut up, I'm working here."

I grab my football and lie back on my couch again, tossing it up in the air and catching it as she studies the pictures. I do this often when I'm trying to figure out a plan or solve a case. It keeps me focused and helps me think. I can use all the help I can get with her in those distractingly sexy glasses!

"Ry, what was the cause of death?" Shayla asks. I look over to see her staring at the picture.

"We assumed strangulation because of the marks on her neck. I can pull the autopsy report. It should be back." I jump up and go to my computer to see if the file is there.

"Is strangulation Mathis' M.O.?"

I type as I speak. "No, he was pretty direct with a shot to the head, but he would abuse his victim. Never sexually, just... brutally. This girl was beaten badly, the worse I've seen from Mathis"

I finally get the report up and show it to her. She purses her lips as she reads over the document. I can see the wheels turning in that pretty head of hers. She looks over to me and then to the picture.

"Do you have any of his past case files?"

Curious, I nod before going over to my locked file cabinet. "These are copies. I shouldn't be showing you this, but we'll just call you a consultant on this case."

"Of course," she says with a smile. "I'll help with anything I can."

She studies the files I've handed her for a few minutes, then says, "Ry, I'm not saying this new one wasn't done by him, but there's so much damage right here," she points to the back of the skull. "It's almost too much," she notices my confused look and shrugs. "You know, like he was trying to hide his M.O. or maybe it's someone trying to throw you off. Like a copycat."

"How would someone else know about my cases? They aren't exactly public knowledge." It's not that I totally disagree with her, but the idea seems farfetched. "I don't know. There are really good hackers out there. It's possible, but I don't think it's a copycat."

"Do you think I could examine the body? I know the report says blunt force trauma, but they could have missed a bullet with all this damage and rust debris. If we could find a bullet hole, then we'd know it was him. Maybe not one-hundred percent, but we'd have something more to go on."

I look at her a little shocked. "You'd want to do that? I mean she's so similar to you."

She looks at me mournfully. "Baby, she's not me. Yes, it's disturbing that she looks similar to me, but I want to find this guy and put this girl's family at ease, if only a little bit."

"You're amazing." I kiss her.

She chuckles, pushing me away. "Okay, stud. Let's get going before things go too far."

It takes us less than ten minutes to get downtown to the city morgue. We have no problems getting back to see the girl. Shayla expertly dons the blue latex gloves. She steps up to the body, reverently pulling back the sheet that covers her. Gone is the silly fun loving girl I love so much, in her place is Dr. Thorn. She's in her element, talking to the pathologist about the body and the damage sustained. She's not at all queasy. I wish I could say the same. I still hold on to the fact that this death is harder for me because she looks so much like Shayla. She examines the face and head. I shudder as I watch. The damage to this girl is sickening. There's not one area that isn't destroyed.

"Ryan," Shayla says as she feels around behind the girl's neck. I look up and she continues. "There's a small hole here at the base of the skull. It feels circular. Would you like to feel it?" she asks.

Not really, I think to myself, but I grab the proffered gloves and slip them on my hand. It's not that I haven't done something like this before, but well … I've said it before, this girl looks too much like Shay. I put my hand where directed and she's right, it's circular and my first thought is that it feels like a bullet hole.

"What did the toxicology reports find?" Shayla asks the pathologist, Dr. Mackey. He flips through the file, then looks up to her.

"There was nothing odd about her blood workup. She wasn't drugged. She was a healthy thirty-year-old woman. The weapon was assumed to be a pipe. The wounds are concave with rust residue. But there was no ballistics run for possible gunshot residue. With all the damage, I didn't notice the possibility, but she was in the woods approximately 8-10 hours before she was found. It rained during that time, it's possible a lot of the evidence we could have was washed away," Mackey states.

"True," Shayla agrees. "From what I can tell from this wound at the base of her skull, it could be a bullet wound, but without the proper testing there's no way to confirm that. It's been so long that any residue is likely to be gone, especially with the rain." She turns to me. "We can't prove it's him, but there's a definite possibility."

"Thanks for letting us take up your time, Dr. Mackey." We shake hands and head out to the car.

"I'm not saying anything bad about the team of people who covered this, but there are some holes in their process. When I did my rotation in pathology, we were taught to leave no stone unturned. In cases where there is an unknown weapon or a lot of damage sustained, you check for everything. Sometimes, I think smaller communities like this one forget that because there's not a lot of serious crime. It's sad for the victim and her family."

"It is. I'll have to make sure my team is caught up on procedures. Thanks for helping, Shay. It really was eye opening." I open the car door for her and hurry over to my side. "It's interesting seeing you like that. I mean, last time we were together we were kids, now we're adults with serious careers. Seeing you talk shop with him, kind of blew me away. You're good at what you do."

"I understand completely. Seeing you at work and talking about this case … we're not those naïve kids anymore." She gives my hand a squeeze. "How about we grab Dylan and have a family dinner? I'm starving."

"Sounds like a plan."

When we arrive at the school, Dylan is just heading to the squad car for his ride home. I pull up beside the car and jump out. "Hey, Pete. We can take him. Thanks for keeping an eye out for him," I tell my deputy.

"Sure thing, boss. See you back at the station." He waves as he gets back in his squad car and takes off.

Dylan is already in the backseat when I get back into my car. "Where to?" I ask.

Dylan lifts his head from where he's lain it on the back of the seat and says, "Burgers." He flops his head back again with a groan.

Chuckling, I ask, "Rough practice?"

"Coach Hamby is brutal. We thought you were bad. You've got nothing on him. He made us play against varsity. They kicked our butts, but he said if I keep it up, I'll be starting varsity next year."

"That's awesome, buddy," I tell him. The pride I have in this kid is unreal.

He leans up and rests his chin on Shayla's seat. "You okay, Mom?"

She turns to him with a smile. "Of course, sweetie. It's just been a long day. I'm okay though."

He nods. "So, that guy … he's really after you?"

She pats his cheek. "Let's not worry about that right now. I'd like to have a nice family dinner. No talk of murders or foxes. I just want to enjoy my two favorite men."

"Sure, but I'm still your favorite, right?" Dylan asks her, looking more like a five year old, than fifteen.

She turns further in her seat to see him better. She kisses his forehead. "Of course. You'll always be my number one boy."

Dylan smirks at me. I chuckle. "You're her number one boy, but I'm her number one man," I tease. We pull into the parking space and I grab her and kiss her quickly.

My son growls. "It's not a contest! Get off my mom." He shoves me. Shayla is laughing hysterically as the two of us get into a shoving match. It's not like we can do much in the car.

"Oh, knock it off. I swear I feel like I have two children!"

Shay opens her door and gets out. She's about halfway to the restaurant before Dylan and I reach her, as we've continued to shove and taunt each other. What can I say, I love having a son to goof off with. Having these two in my life is the best thing to have happened to me in a long time.

I'll take family man over single FBI agent any day. I'll never regret coming back home.

CHAPTER NINE

Ryan

Several things seem to happen at once; Shayla gasps, a grey cargo van skids, and before it stops, two huge men jump out and grab Dylan. During our roughhousing, Dylan ended up too far away for me to grab him and protect Shayla. By the time I'm moving into action, Dylan is already in the van. I try to fight off one of the men, but he hits me on the head with the butt of his gun and I go down. I'm not out, but I am disorientated enough that the van is already heading down the street when I begin my pursuit. I don't know who these guys are, but they will not take my son. It's pretty evident that I'm not going to catch them; I'm not fast enough. They're getting away, but I can't let that happen.

"Call for backup! Use my radio," I yell back to Shayla.

I pull my gun out and shoot one of the back tires. The van swerves and skids off the road, hitting a tree head-on. They weren't going fast enough to cause real damage, so the driver jumps out and takes off for the woods. The passenger door flies open and two men jump out and take off running. One heads towards the woods with the driver, but the other guy tries to make a break for it in the opposite direction. I'm able to tackle him to the ground, but he fights back hitting me twice in the ribs and once in the face. I get the upper hand though when I punch him in the face several times in a row, before slamming his skull into the pavement. He's out. I flip him to his stomach and cuff his hands to his feet. Shayla is running to the van during all this. I want to yell at her, but I can't. I jump off the cuffed guy and take off to the van. Dylan is lying there lifeless. I can barely find my voice.

"Is he okay?"

Shayla turns on me, punching me in the chest. I'm not going to lie, it hurt, but I take it, more out of shock than anything else. Is my boy dead? Did I kill him? Finally, I snap out of my stupor and grab her upper arms, squeezing them just enough to stop her.

"Is he okay?" I ask again.

"You could have killed him!" she yells, punching me again.

I give her a shake. "Shayla, is he going to be okay?" She nods, collapsing against my chest. Relief surges through me. "Why isn't he awake?"

"The crash must have made him lose consciousness or the guys did. I looked, but I didn't see any type of drugs. They could have knocked him out though. He has a bump on his head that's bleeding, but it looks like he hit it over there." She points to a bloody spot on the exposed metal side of the van. "I can't really examine him well like this. He needs to go to the hospital. He most likely has a concussion."

I squeeze her tightly. "They'll be here soon." No sooner than the words leave my mouth, does the sound of sirens meet our ears.

Dylan groans, "Mom?"

Shayla is on him in a second, pulling out a pen light and checking him over. "Shh, baby. Just lie still. You probably have a concussion. Did they hit you or do anything to you?" she asks him.

"No, but I kicked the guy in the face," Dylan says proudly, holding out his fist.

I smile and give him a soft fist bump. "I'm proud of you, Son."

He tries to sit up, but Shayla gently pushes him back down. "Mom, I need to sit up."

"Sweetie, the ambulance is almost here. Let them get you to the hospital first, please."

He shakes his head. "I'm fine." He sits up anyway and swings his legs out of the van door. He cradles his head.

"Do you feel nauseated?" Shay asks.

He shakes his head. "No, but my head hurts." She sits beside him and wraps an arm around his shoulders, pulling him to lie against her.

"Hey, I need to go check in with my men. You two okay?" I ask.

Shayla looks up. "Yeah, we'll be fine. The EMT is on his way over here." She points behind me. I nod, kissing both of their heads and then run off to my men, who have the assailant up and heading toward a squad car.

"You okay, boss?" Jessica, my only female officer asks.

"I'm fine. You read him his rights?" I motion my head towards the perp in the back of the squad car.

She hands me his wallet. "We did. His name is Lester Harvey, thirty, of Brantsville."

I nod as I read the same info on his license. I hand it back to her. "Run this. Be sure it's correct. I need to know as much about this guy as you can possibly find."

"Yes, sir!"

I turn to my other deputies and send them to search the woods for clues on where the other assailants could have gone. Then, I head over to Shayla. Dylan is already on the stretcher when I walk back over there.

"Dad, tell them I'm fine and don't need to ride on this thing."

I chuckle at my disgruntled son. "Sorry, bud. You need to be checked out."

He mumbles under his breath. "Fat lot of good having a dad does me." I can't help but guffaw. I know he'll be fine now. He glares at me.

"I'm riding with him," Shayla says, moving to the ambulance.

I give her a quick kiss before muttering, "I'll meet you guys there."

I watch the ambulance pull off and then turn to my deputy. "Take him to the station and put him in interrogation room two. I'll be there after I make sure my son is fine."

"Will do, boss."

Jessica and her partner, Matthew, head off to the station. I give a few instructions to the remaining officers and then head to my car. I walk into the hospital ER twenty minutes later and go straight to the sign-in desk, flashing my badge.

"I need to see my son, Dylan Thorn."

"Oh, you must be Detective Jacobs. Dr. Thorn told us to expect you. I'll buzz you in."

The receptionist leans over and pushes a button on the wall, causing the glass doors to open. I don't waste any time heading through them. The same receptionist peeks out of her little cubicle and nods her head down the hallway.

"Straight back. He's in the last room on the left."

Shayla is talking to Trevor Daniels, the doctor who interrupted us in her office. He is standing really close to her with his hand on her upper arm as he talks. She's much smaller than him so she has to crane her neck up at an uncomfortable looking angle to see him. I don't like the look on his face and I don't like hers much either. I know it's jealousy flaring in my chest, but I can't seem to tamp it down. I think of Dylan, he's the priority right now.

"Shay," I say as I walk up to them. She sighs in relief and is in my arms in a second. The doctor glares at me as I hold her to me. I stick my hand out to him. "Detective Ryan Jacobs."

"Yes, we've meet. I'm Dr. Trevor Daniels." His voice is full of disdain.

I nod. "Right. I think I remember that. How's Dyl?" I ask Shayla, pretty much dismissing Trevor.

She doesn't let me go as she looks up. "He's okay, complaining mostly. He has a slight concussion. He's probably fine to go home, but I've asked for him to stay overnight. You never know what might go wrong. I just keep imagining all these horrible things in my head.

Being a doctor sucks when someone you love is hurt."

I chuckle slightly and kiss the top of her head. "Will he be in this room?"

She shakes her head. "No, they're getting him a bed. That's what he's complaining about. He doesn't want to stay. He can't miss football, but even if he goes home, he can't play for at least a week. Another hit to the head could cause serious damage."

"Let me talk to him."

"Okay, I'll see what's going on with the room."

I kiss her, probably a little too long for public viewing, but today has really rattled me to my core. I'm sure she'll be upset once I tell her what's in store for her and Dylan, but I need to keep them safe until this is settled. I smile at her and take off, forgetting about the wrath of my girlfriend as I enter my son's room.

"Hey, champ," I greet him.

He rolls his eyes. "I'm fine. Please, tell Mom I can go home."

I shake my head. "No can do, bucko. I agree with her. I'd much rather you be here, safe, if something happens. Head injuries are dangerous." He groans and flops back onto his bed, then groans again because he's hurt himself. "Easy, Dylan."

"It doesn't hurt much. It's just like a nagging headache. I guess I should know it's serious since Mom let me take ibuprofen."

"No oils this time?" I ask, chuckling.

He smiles warmly. "Of course there were oils. She put them on me too."

"She loves you."

"I know. I love her, she just worries too much. She used to say it was because I was all she had, but she has you now. I think she worries even more now instead of less."

"Probably," I say with a nod. "My job, even though it's not as dangerous as it was, is still dangerous. Right now, more so with this threat out there. They're obviously after me, but coming for my family was a mistake. I'm not going to let anything happen to you guys. I'll die before it does."

"Don't say that. I just got a dad. I don't want to lose you."

I smile. "I love you, kid. That's just how it goes. Parents will do anything for their kids, even if the kids don't understand it."

I'm struck with images of my father, telling a scared Shayla to stay away. Yeah, what he did was wrong, but he was protecting his son at all costs. My dad never wanted to hurt me. He wanted me safe and protected. The situation with Shayla could've turned out badly, I know that now, he wanted to save me from that fate even if it hurt me. No matter how wrong or misguided he was, he did it because he loved me. I have to respect him for that, because I'd do the same for my son.

"I'd do anything for you and my mom," Dylan says with a yawn.

I smile at my boy and pat his leg. "Can you sleep?"

"Yeah, Mom said I can try." He closes his eyes for a few seconds then pops them wide open. "Dad?"

"I'm here."

His eyes start to close. "I don't like that doctor."

"What doctor?"

"Daniels," he slurs. His eyes stay shut and his head kind of lolls over as he sleeps.

"Neither do I, bud. Neither do I." I kiss his head, then step outside of the door. I pull my cellphone out and dial, not caring about any hospital polices.

"Jessica, get two guys to man my son's room. I want around the clock protection on him." She agrees. I hang up without saying goodbye as I see Shayla enter the hall followed by two nurses.

"Ryan, this is Dana and Nathan. They're going to take Dylan to his room."

"He just went to sleep."

Shayla smiles. "Good. We don't have to wake him. They'll just transport him while he's in the bed."

It doesn't take them long to get Dylan into his room and settled. After about ten minutes of silence, Shayla says, "Hey, you don't have to stay here. You can go down to the station. I know you want to talk to that guy."

I look up from my phone to Dylan, then to her. "I don't want to leave him."

She looks at me with an expression that I think is a mix between love, sadness, and hope. I'm not sure why hope. I mean, I'm all in, but I could be wrong.

"I know. I love that you want to be, but trust me, Dylan will totally understand. You need to catch this guy before he tries something like this again."

"Are you sure?"

"I'm positive. Just be careful."

I kiss her like it's the last time I will see her, though I pray it's not. When I pull away, I'm panting slightly. "I have two guys on this door at all times. Don't leave the hospital, okay?" She nods. I kiss her again.

"Gross," we hear a groggy Dylan mumble.

Chuckling, I stand up and walk over to his bed. I kiss his forehead. "Just remember that the next time I catch you and Faith."

Shayla gasps. "They kissed?"

I nod, laughing. "I'm not talking about the football game peck. I caught him outside the locker room the other day. They were wrapped around each other so tightly I couldn't have gotten a sheet of paper between them." Dylan groans.

"Dylan!" Shayla exclaimed. "We talked about ..."

He cuts her off. "It was just a kiss, Mom. I'm not having sex."

"But ..."

He sits up and cuts her off again. "Mother, I'm not going to have sex yet."

She huffs and crosses her arms across her chest, pouting adorably. We both laugh at her. I lean down and press a kiss to her pouting mouth. "They really were just kissing. He's a smart boy. You've raised him well."

"He's growing up too fast. He should still be in diapers."

"Mom," Dylan groans again.

"I wish he was too, but he's almost sixteen. Things will change, but now I'll be there to help. Love you." I kiss her once more, because I can't help myself.

"Dad, seriously! Get off my mom."

I laugh. "You wouldn't be here if she wasn't so irresistible." I wink. He gags. I love it. Being a parent is pretty awesome. At least, when they aren't getting hurt or almost abducted. That thought sobers me up quickly. "I need to head to the station."

"It's fine, Dad. Catch the bad guys." He holds out his fist for a bump and I oblige.

I quickly maneuver out of the hospital and to my vehicle. I need to talk to the perp and get confirmation of what I believe is going on. When I walk into the station, I see nothing but chaos.

"What's going on?" I ask the girl at the front desk.

"The man they arrested tried to escape. They have it under control now, but two people were hurt." She's barely finished with her sentence when I've taken off towards the interrogation rooms.

"What happened?" I bark.

Jessica answers. "Anderson released his cuff to attach him to the table. The guy lost it, started attacking him. Snyder stepped in, but he fought him off too. Finally we tasered him, he's still out, he's fine though."

"What about Anderson and Snyder?" I ask, looking around for the men.

"They're okay, but we called the EMT's to check them out. Everyone was in a frenzy. Nothing like this happens around here."

I look around at the scene before me. There are four EMT's here with their packs. One EMT is working on the two officers and the other two are checking over the prisoner, who looks to have hit his head at some point in the altercation.

"What info do we have on the perp?" I ask, shaking my head as I redirect to Jessica.

"Just the info I got from his wallet. He's not talking."

I nod. "Great. I need to make some calls. Get me when he's awake."

"Yes, sir."

Jessica turns to head back to whatever she was doing and I slowly head to my office. This place is a freaking mess. The guy must have put up a good fight. I pick up an overturned chair outside of my office door. Thankfully, my office looks untouched. Sitting down at my desk, I take a few minutes to regroup. The day has been exhausting and I know I have hours before I can get back to the hospital. I text Shayla to check in, she says Dylan is back to sleep and all is fine. That eases my mind enough to focus on the work ahead of me. I pick up the phone and dial a familiar number.

"Marsh."

"You here yet?" I ask with a grunt.

He gives a chuckle. "That bad, huh? What's going on? I'll be there by o-nine-hundred."

"Good. Three men tried to take my son this evening."

"What?"

"They grabbed him as we were going into a restaurant. I don't know how they knew we were there other than they must have been following us. I've got two officers on him and Shay right now. Dylan's okay, but I think we're all pretty shaken up."

"No doubt. I'll see if I can bring a couple people with me. Why don't you call the boys in?"

"Yeah, I should ... I'll do that. Thanks for coming out. I know I'll need the help. I have good people here, but this town is so low on crime, they have no idea what to do."

"Don't worry, we'll find who's doing this."

I believe him. If there is one thing I know, it's that my guys will stop at nothing to help me and I'd do the same for any of them. After the call ends, I get to work contacting my brothers from my time in the service, Jonathan Miller, Paul Samson, and Riley Peters. The five of us were inseparable during our term. We all made it back, mostly in one piece, and have kept in touch since. Where Marsh and I went off to join the FBI, they started their own bodyguard/private investigator group. Between Marsh and my connections in the government, they've made a pretty good living for themselves. The five of us worked insanely well together. We always get our mark.

Jessica pokes her head in my office. "Sir, he's awake."

I nod to let her know I've heard her. I stand from my desk and take my jacket off. I want the guy to know I'm loaded. I'm not messing with him. He has no clue who I am or what I'm capable of. I'm at the point where I'll throw the law out the window to get answers and I've not even questioned him yet. No one messes with my family and gets away with it. First, I watch him through the two-way mirror. He looks smug, cocky even. I instantly hate the guy. Lester Harvey, 30, of Brantsville is about to meet my wrath.

"He hasn't said a word," Jessica tells me.

"Did you pull his file?"

She nods and hands it to me. "Petty theft? That's it? How do you go from robbing a person's house to kidnapping so quickly? He was only charged four months ago. This seems off. Did you run his prints?"

"Yes, they match."

I nod. I think there's more to Lester than meets the eye or is on his record. I brace myself to head into the room with the man who tried to take my son. I enter the room silently, walking over to the table and dropping the file on top. I stare at him for a long while. He's pretty big; I'd say at least six-three, two-hundred-fifty pounds of muscle. He definitely does not look like a Lester. I stare him down for about two minutes, trying to ramp up his nerves, but honestly he looks as if he couldn't care less. The guy has been smirking the whole time.

Finally I speak, "Kidnapping ... that's a big leap from petty theft." He says nothing, just stares at me with his head cocked to the side, condescendingly. I continue. "Trying to take a cop's kid is pretty stupid. Did someone put you up to it?" He still stares. He's trying to unnerve me, but it's not working. "Who are you working for, Lester?"

Nothing, no response at all. I stare at him for a long moment, leaning back in my chair. The man watches me, but he seems to be thinking about something else. Maybe I can still get him.

"Kidnapping and assault of an officer can put you away for a long time, you do know that, don't you?"

Still no response from him. I get up and head to the door, my hand turns the knob, I start to turn back, but I can't let this guy get to me. I yank it open letting it slam close. I try to take several deep breaths, but this guy is pissing me off. I go back into the viewing room where Jessica waits.

"Did you find the other two perps?"

"No, they looked for hours. The trail ended in the creek. They must've stayed in there."

I blow out a breath. "I'm going to let him sit for a while. I'll be in my office. Do not un-cuff him."

"Yes, sir."

I watch the guy for a long time. He doesn't really move at all, just rotates his shoulders a few times, but that's it. What's his game? This has to be connected to 'The Fox'. Why else would he be here trying to take my son? I head back to my office and stare at the file on my desk before finally picking up my phone to call Shayla.

"Hey, baby," I say when she answers.

"Hey, how's it going?"

I groan. "He won't talk. How's our boy?"

She giggles. "He's being a big baby. Whining about everything, complaining about how he's fine, then crying because he hurts. I feel bad for him, but honestly, he's trying my patience."

"I'm sorry, sweetheart. I'll be there soon. I'm legally required to let this guy rest for eight hours. I'll be there as soon as I can."

"It's okay. I understand. We'll only be here overnight. He's really okay. He's going to have a headache for a few days but he'll be fine." She sounds like she's trying to convince herself. I hear her sniffle.

"Oh, Shay. It's okay. I have you guys protected. No one will get either of you." My heart breaks for her.

"I know. I'm just tired. I hate seeing him hurt."

I rub my forehead as I rest my elbows on my desk. "I need to try to talk to this guy once more and then I'll be there. I'll bring you dinner."

"Okay. Can you just get us a pizza from Luigi's?"

I smile sadly, because when my healthy doctor is asking for pizza, I know she's having a rough time. "Of course, baby. Love you."

"Love you, too."

I blow her a loud kiss through the phone to hear her giggle, then ready myself to head back to the interrogation room.

"Coffee?" Jessica asks, handing me a cup before I go back into the room with Lester.

"Thanks. I'm heading out after this, but I'll wait to be sure he's in a cell."

She nods, so I head in. I pull out the chair and sit down. I steeple my hands on the table in front of me and stare at him. He's been sitting in here for several hours and is starting to look tired. That's good, maybe he'll crack.

"Who do you work for?"

He sighs, hanging his head. All bravado and cockiness seems to be gone. He looks up at me and says, "I don't know."

"You don't know who you work for?"

"Nope, I've never seen him."

"Why'd you do it?"

Lester shrugs. "He paid me."

"Did you know the target was my kid?"

He says nothing. I ask again, still no response. "It doesn't help you to avoid my questions. Just tell me what I want to know."

"You gonna cut me a deal?"

I pause to think about it for a minute. "I might be able to convince the D.A. to drop the assault against an officer charge."

"What about the kidnapping? I mean, I didn't take him."

I'm getting pissed at his flippant attitude. "You did take him. You'd have gotten away with it too if I hadn't shot out your tires. That was probably the worst planned abduction I've ever witnessed."

"What can I say; I'm not really into taking kids."

"Who paid you to do it?" I try again.

"I don't know."

I stand up quickly, sending the chair skittering across the tilled floor. I lean down on the table, putting my face level with his. "Tell me who you work for!" I yell. He smiles and I lose it. "Tell me his damn name!"

He smiles again. I'm about to hit him when the door flies open. Two of my biggest officers come towards me.

"Chief wants to see you," Marks says.

"Fine. Get me a name!" I yell as I fling the door open and storm off. I head straight to the chief's office.

"Chief?" I say as I enter unannounced.

"Have a seat, Ryan." I plop down. "I think we should remove you from this case. You're too close."

"No, you can't do that! I'm the only detective you have here."

He shakes his head. "Glen can do it."

I snort. "I'm the one training him. He doesn't know what needs to be done."

"Ryan, this isn't a suggestion. You need to take a step back. You're too close."

I shake my head in disbelief and stand. "Fine. Have it your way. I'm taking a leave of absence, effective immediately. My family needs me."

I don't wait for his response. I head straight to my office and grab all my files, shoving them into my bag, and storming out of the precinct. I head straight to the hospital and find Shayla asleep on the small love seat in Dylan's room. I grab one of the thin hospital blankets and drape it over her. She opens her eyes and smiles at me.

"Hey," she says as she sits up. She pats the cushion beside her and I sit down. She wraps herself around me, covering me with the blanket too. "Glad you're here."

I put my arms around her and kiss her head. "Me too. I didn't mean to wake you."

"This is a hospital, there's no rest. I wasn't asleep anyway. I just had my eyes shut."

I chuckle. "You were snoring."

She half heartily smacks my chest. "I do not snore!" I just smile as I shrug my shoulder. I love seeing her smile, even over something so silly.

"Of course not. How's our boy?" I ask, looking over at our sleeping son.

His coloring looks much better than earlier and he is free of tubes coming out of his arms. You wouldn't know anything was wrong except for the bandage on his head. Shayla sits up and looks over at our son.

"He's okay. He's had a pretty horrible headache, but the medicine has helped. He should be completely better in a few days."

"I'm sorry. This is all my fault." I dry scrub my face as I rest my elbows on my knees.

Shayla rubs my back. "This isn't your fault. You didn't tell those guys to take him."

I huff and look up at her. "Shayla, this guy is working for someone who is after me. I'm off the case, so now I won't be able to find out who it is unless I can find the other kidnappers. But I didn't see them; I have nothing to go on."

"Why are you off the case?"

I snort angrily. "Because the decrepit chief, who is way too old to be working, thinks I'm too close and shouldn't be on the case. I could've had that guy talking. He already told me someone hired him. These guys around here don't know how to interrogate anyone. They're backwoods country. I hate this town." By this point, I'm pacing back and forth, and pulling at my hair.

Shayla steps in front of me. "Baby, calm down," she whispers, looking over at Dylan. He's still totally out thanks to the pain meds. I sigh and pull her in my arms. "You'll find them. I doubt very much that you'll be sitting on your butt just because the chief says you're off the case.

"You've got that right. My guys should be here by tomorrow morning. I have to pick them up at the airport. We'll go back to my house and work on a plan. I'll try to get the chief to change his mind. Maybe Marsh, my FBI friend, can persuade the chief to let him take lead on the case."

"Sounds good. I knew you'd figure something out. Sit, let me comb your hair, you've made it a knotted mess." She gives me a gentle shove into the wooden chair. I appease her, even though I don't care about my hair right now.

"Ow," I complain as she takes the rubber band out.

"You're the idiot who used a regular rubber band instead of a hair tie. I might have to chop off this mess."

I jerk away. "You are not cutting my hair."

She giggles. "Shh, you'll wake up my baby. I won't cut it."

"You better not. I love my hair."

She laughs. "See, I told you. You haven't changed, still as conceited as ever."

"You love my hair. You should've seen it when I had to chop it off in the service. I just grew it back a year ago."

"I bet you still looked hot with it short, but you're right, I love your hair longer. I also like this beard you've got going on." She scratches at my face. The beard isn't intentional. I've been busy the past few days and haven't shaved.

I turn to look at her. "You do?"

"Yeah, I like it. Short like this. I mean, I don't know how I'd feel about a Grizzly Adams look, but this is nice." I grab her wrist and kiss her palm.

"I'll see what I can do." I wink.

She pushes me to turn forward. Her smile is huge and her cheeks are pink with blush. She combs through my hair with her fingers and I won't lie, it feels amazing. She then puts it back into a messy bun using a real hair tie. As soon as she's finished, I pull her into my lap and kiss the heck out her. A throat clearing breaks us a part. She jumps up and straightens her clothes. I look over to see Dr. Daniels glaring at us.

"Trevor?" she says.

"Dr. Daniels. I'm here as your son's physician."

"Of course, sorry. Is there something wrong?" she asks, suddenly seeming worried.

"No, I just want to examine him before I sign off on his release." The doctor's voice is sharp and clipped.

Shayla seems to shrink back into herself around him. I don't like it at all. I rub Shayla's back in support, but it seems to anger Daniels. He glares at me before studying Dylan's chart.

"He seems to have had a good night." He turns to Dylan. "Dylan, can you wake up for me?" He says, placing his hand on Dylan's shoulder and nudging him slightly. Groggily, Dylan opens his eyes.

He sits up and stretches. "What?"

"I'm Dr. Daniels; do you know where you are?"

Dylan rubs his eyes and yawns as he speaks, "Yeah. Hospital. I hit my head."

"Good. I'd like to examine you quickly and then we'll get you out of here."

Dylan's face lights up. "Sure. I can't wait to get home."

It takes about an hour for us to get out of there. They sure take their sweet time when they discharge people. Once we're home, Dylan goes upstairs to charge his phone so he can call Faith, leaving Shayla and I in the den alone. I pull her down with me on the couch.

"You should get some sleep," I tell her.

"So should you," she retorts. I nod and lay my head on the back of the sofa. She giggles. "In your bed."

I sit up, turning towards her. "I'm not leaving you guys here alone."

"You can use the guest room," she offers. I'm glad she's not fighting me on this.

"I'll sleep here. I don't want to be upstairs with you down here."

She sighs. "You don't have to do that. I have a security system. No one will get in."

"You could just sleep in her bed, but, ya know ... leave the door open." I turn to see our son standing at the foot of the steps.

"Sounds good to me," I say. Standing, I hold out my hand to

Shayla. "Let's go to bed, baby."

"How does this keep Dylan safe?"

"The systems on and I'll stay in my room," he tells her. "I don't feel that great. I sent coach a text and called Faith. She's coming over after school. Okay?"

"Dylan it's four thirty in the morning," Shayla chastises him. He just shrugs.

I look at Shayla. "We'll leave the door open. I'm a light sleeper. I'll hear if someone tries to break in. The system is set."

"Maybe he should sleep on my chaise," Shayla offered.

Dylan grunts. "Mom, I'm too big for that thing. I just want to sleep in my own bed. I'm tired."

I squeeze her hand. "He'll be fine."

"Okay," she submits. I pull her up from the couch and towards her room.

"You don't have to seem so excited," Dylan grumbles as he heads up the stairs.

I just laugh. I am excited, even though I know we're just sleeping, but to have the love of my life in my arms as I drift off is more than enough for me right now. It's something I've wanted for as long as I can remember.

"You do seem awfully excited," Shay says as she comes out of her bathroom. She's dressed in sweats, but she's still hot and completely adorable. I hold my arms out to her. I've already stripped down to my boxer-briefs and t-shirt and gotten into bed.

"I can't help it. I want to hold you." She smiles warmly, getting into bed and cuddling close to me. I kiss her head. "I love you."

"I love you too. This is nice."

"It is, even if we have to leave the door open."

"Yeah, our son is surprisingly strict."

"He should be. If that door was closed right now, I wouldn't be such a gentleman."

She sighs. "You keep kissing my neck like that and I'll shut the stupid door myself." I growl, capturing her lips with mine. I start to roll her on her back when we're interrupted. Like always.

"Hey, get off my mom. I thought you said you had some kind of super sense?" I reluctantly remove my lips from Shayla's and look up at our son. He's standing there with a smug smile. The little twerp.

"Can we help you?" I ask.

"Just wanted to let you know Faith will be here around noon. She's bringing me lunch."

"How long will she be here?" Shayla asks, sitting up.

"How long can she stay? Her mom's dropping her off. She has an orthodontist appointment this morning, so she doesn't have to go back to school."

"However long her mom wants her to stay is fine. I just need a few hours of sleep." Dylan looks happy with this response.

"Thanks. Night. Love you both!" he calls over his shoulder as he heads back down the hall.

I flop back on the bed, pulling Shayla with me. "Night, beautiful."

"Night, stud." I drift to sleep with a smile on my face. Glad that, at least for now, my family is safe.

CHAPTER TEN

Shayla

I wake up to the sound of tiny clicking noises. I groan as I roll over to see Ryan sitting up on the other side of my bed with reading glasses perched on his cross looking face as he types away on his laptop. He stops to pick up a cup of coffee, he hands it to me without looking at me. His expression never changes, it makes me chuckle.

"What'er you doing?" I ask.

He looks at me, giving me a half smile. "Working on the case. Chief isn't all that computer savvy, he didn't lock me out of the system. I can still pull up all the case files. The guy we arrested hasn't said anything to anyone since I left other than to ask for me."

"You think they'll call you in?"

"No, they told him I was suspended."

I sit up, pausing to take a sip of my coffee, then say, "Uh ... that seems really unprofessional."

He nods. "Completely. They could have used my absence to make him think I was getting my info from someone else, or that they'd caught one of the other kidnappers. They've really screwed the whole thing up. I told the chief they didn't know what they were doing. They're going to ruin the whole investigation. I know, for a fact, that more is going on than just trying to take Dylan. There's someone out to get me. This won't stop."

"You really think it's this Fox guy, Jason Mathis?"

He turns to me with a worried look. "Yeah, I do. Mathis is vindictive to the extreme."

"You think he's behind Dylan's kidnapping?"

"Yeah. I wouldn't put it past him to take my kid to get to me. I don't know how he would know Dylan's mine, but it wouldn't be hard to find out."

"I never told anyone you were his father. I mean, there's no legal record to tie him to you."

"No, but he calls me dad. Even if people don't think he's my biological son, they know we have that relationship. You've only been here a few months, but this is a small town; I wouldn't doubt if everyone knows he's mine."

"That's true. Plus, I don't think Mama has corrected anyone at gossip central either."

Ryan laughs. "Yeah, the crochet club is full of gossips."

"And the reading club, knitting club; oh let's not forget about the fishermen."

We both crack up. Our parents are just as much town gossips as anyone else in this small town. He's right; everyone who lives here knows Dylan is his. There's no doubt.

"I'll catch this guy, baby. I swear." He leans over and kisses me softly.

"I know you will. And … I think Dylan should see a therapist. I know he wasn't really taken, but he might have nightmares or issues about the almost abduction."

"Whatever you think is best, babe. I'm not saying that as a copout for parenting. I really mean it. I trust your judgement on all things medical."

He looks so sincere and slightly vulnerable. I lean forward and kiss him. "Thank you. I trust your judgement with him too. Just because I'm a doctor doesn't mean I know everything. Sometimes, I think my training overshadows what's best. Though, I try really hard not to let that happen."

"You are really good with him. He's a lot more respectful than most of the kids on his team are to their moms. You should be proud." I can't help but blush. I've always doubted my parenting abilities. But Mama always says, that means I'm a good mother. Maybe she's right.

"Where is he anyway?"

"Last I checked, he and Faith were watching a movie in the den." I nod in response as I get out of bed to check on my sweet boy.

I find Dylan and Faith sitting in the den, his arm around her, her head on his shoulder, his right hand in her left. They are incredibly sweet looking. Before he notices me, I grab my camera and take a few quick snap shots. The flash causes Dylan to look up and smile. Faith tries to pull away, but he doesn't let her go. I smile. He's so much like his father.

"Do you guys need anything?" I ask.

"No, Dr. Thorn. I'm okay," Faith answers.

"Dyl?"

He shakes his head. "No, I took an ibuprofen earlier."

"You got it yourself?" I ask. Not that I question his ability, but I'm very paranoid about medications, even over the counter ones. I've seen too many teenagers accidentally overdose.

He shook his head. "No, Dad gave them to me when he checked on us. I took two. I feel fine."

"Well, if your head starts hurting before it's time for the next dose, you can use the pain oils."

He smiles. "I know, Mom." He holds up the bottle of oil. I smile. He's such a good kid. Tears spring in my eyes and I quickly turn away.

Ryan finds me crying in the kitchen. He wraps his arms around me. "Hey, what's this? Why the tears?"

I sniffle a few times, taking the paper towel he offers me. I don't move from his embrace and after drying my eyes a little I say, "He could've been killed. They could have taken him and I never would have seen him again. I can't handle the thought. I'm trying to be strong, but he's my baby. He's been the most consistent person in my life since my parents died. I don't think I'd survive losing him."

He squeezes me tighter to him. "I'll keep him safe, Shay. I'll keep you both safe. I love you too much to lose you now."

"I know you'll try, but you can't be everywhere. You can't control what people choose to do. You'll make yourself crazy trying. But I would really like it if one of us was with him at all times. I have to be back at work tomorrow. Can you stay with him?" I ask, finally finished with my tears.

"I will, but I really think you should stay home too," he tells me sincerely. I can tell he just wants what's best, but I have to work or I'll lose my job.

"I want to, but I can't. I just started. I can't keep taking personal days."

"Then take a leave of absence. Doctors do that."

I sigh. He means well, I know, but that's not how it works. "I haven't been here long enough to build that kind of tenure. I have to work. There's no option. I'll be fine. You can pick me up if that makes you feel better."

"Fine," he says tersely. "I will pick you up and I'll have someone watching you."

I groan. "Ryan ..."

"Don't 'Ryan' me. You are the most important person in my world. You need to be protected. You said you wouldn't fight me."

"I'm not, but I'll be fine. They were after Dylan, not me."

He shakes his head then runs his fingers through his long hair. "If they're after him, they'll be coming for you next. I messed up the plan, they'll regroup. I'm sure we'll be fine for a few more days, but eventually, they'll come again. I know this kind of thing like the back of my hand. It's what I'm trained for." I'm not sure what my face conveys to him, but he changes tactics. "Listen, I know this is weird and you don't want people watching your every move, but the truth is that there is more than likely someone out there right now following you. I'm not trying to scare you, baby. It's just the truth. I have my guys set up at my house right now, but that doesn't mean we aren't being watched."

"Your guys?"

"Yeah, I went and picked them up while you were sleeping," he explains.

I'm a little shocked. "Who watched Dylan?"

"Faith's mom stayed until I got back. Plus, I had one of my officers parked out front." I have nothing to say so I just nod. "Come on, I want you to meet the guys. Then tonight, we're going to my mom's with the Thorns to celebrate Dylan being okay. I told Mom we weren't going to church with her Sunday."

"Why not?"

"I don't want to." He laughs as he pulls me behind him and out of the side door to walk across the yard to his house. There are two huge SUV's sitting in his driveway and a patrol car in my driveway.

"What about Dylan?" I ask, forgetting about his church refusal.

He stops and smiles. "They're fine. We won't take long." He confuses me, one minute we need tons of protection, the next Dylan and Faith are okay inside the house alone.

As Ryan opens the side door, I can hear voices. We walk through the laundry room and kitchen to come out in the den. There's a hubbub of activity going on; three men sit around several monitors. I then notice that on the screen are different images of my house outside and ... inside. I look at him with wide eyes.

"You're watching inside my house?" I ask, my voice almost a yell.

He holds up his hands in surrender as the guys all look at him with different levels of mirth. "Shayla, it's not sinister. It's for safety. There are no cameras inside yours or Dylan's bedrooms, just the main areas and doors. They're for your protection … for our son's protection."

I'm angry, but I'm not exactly sure how to process this information. He did this without my permission. He didn't even mention it. He had over an hour to tell me. I decide I won't show my anger in front of his friends. So, I turn to them and smile.

"Hi, I'm Shayla. Thank you for coming to help."

Ryan seems to sigh in relief, but I hope he doesn't think this is over. "Shay, this is Harrison Marsh. We were partners while I was in the FBI and we served together in the desert."

"It's nice to finally meet you. This guy has talked about you for years," Marsh says as he shakes my hand.

I feel the heat rise up my neck like a school girl. Don't get me wrong, I love Ryan one-hundred percent, but Harrison is ruggedly handsome. He looks like a lumberjack, including his beard. He's all around stylish, just freakishly tall. I look over to Ryan to see his ears pink with embarrassment.

"Yeah, yeah. Anyway, this is Jonathan Miller, Paul Samson, and Riley Peters. We also served together."

"Hi," I say with a little wave.

All three of them are what I imagine the typical military man looks like. They could be the poster boys for the Marines. All of them are tall, built, tattoos peeking out from under the sleeves of their t-shirts, and hair buzzed so short you can't really tell what color their hair is supposed to be.

"So, Jon is going to be guarding you," Ryan says hesitantly. I turn to him quickly. He holds up his hand to stop me from talking. "You asked me to stay with Dylan, I am, but he's going to shadow you. This is serious, Shayla, you need someone with you."

My facade is crumbling fast. "I don't need to be babysat. I know this is serious, but I'm not the one they are after, it's Dylan. Besides he can't come in the hospital with me, so it's a waste of time."

"He'll take you, wait in the parking lot and bring you home."

"No."

I understand Ryan's concern, but there's no way some big military dude is going to go over well at the hospital. I said I wouldn't fight him, but I can't see this working. Anger surges through Ryan.

"It's not up for discussion, Shayla. I'll do whatever it takes to protect my family."

I stare at him for a long moment and then turn on my heels and storm out of his house. I hear a murmuring of voices, but I can't understand what any of them are saying. I honestly don't care. I let the door slam on my way out and I go straight into my house and to my bedroom, slamming that door closed as well. I grab some clothes and head to the shower to get myself ready for work, even though I don't need to go in today. I need to work so I can calm down. I know I'm being irrational, but I hate when someone else decides what's best for me or my son. I had enough of that in my life.

After exiting the shower, I realize I've grabbed a pair of cotton undies with rainbows and clouds on them and a bright purple bra, which I normally reserve for laundry day. Sighing, I step out of my bathroom but instantly freeze, seeing Ryan sitting on my bed looking crestfallen. He looks up at me for a moment before he fights a grin. I huff and put my hands on my hips, I'm not in the mood to deal with him. Nor am I in the mood to care that I'm in my ridiculous underwear. I'm not finished being angry.

"You are adorable," he says after he finishes laughing. He stands and walks over to me. I hold my hand up and take a step back. "Oh, come on, Shayla. I wasn't laughing at you. You remind me of the teenage you. I like these." He runs his finger over the waist band of my underwear.

I can't help but smile. "I'm still angry."

"I know." He steps forward again and I don't stop him. He trails his hands around my hips and up my back until I'm pressed into his solid chest. "Please don't be angry. I just want you safe."

I push against him and he reluctantly lets me go. I turn from him, wiping angry tears from my eyes. I walk into my closet, speaking loud enough for him to hear me.

"It has nothing to do with that. It's about you taking my choice away."

I grab a long sleeve black t-shirt and a pair of black scrub pants. I grab my tennis shoes and walk over to my dresser to grab socks. I sit down on the bed and look over at him as he sits down beside me.

"From the time I was thirteen years old, everyone decided what I would do. My opinion never really mattered. Even in my short marriage, I didn't really have a choice. I mean, I said yes and choose to marry him, but after that, it was always what he wanted, even our divorce. I tried … I tried to not let it get to me, but it does. I can't handle it. I feel out of control."

He squeezes my hand. "I didn't mean to make you feel that way. I didn't think. My number one thought was to keep the two of you safe, no matter what. If it really is Jason Mathis that's after Dylan or you, then I have to go overboard. I have to do everything I can possibly think of; it's not about taking away your choice. You don't know this guy like I do. I lived and worked with him for almost two years and I barely scratched the surface of his evilness. I need you safe."

I nod. "I understand. I'm safe at the hospital. There's always officers on duty there. Just tell them what's going on."

"I will. But you won't be at the hospital all the time. I want Jonathan to drive you."

I huff. Standing up, I lean over and grab my cellphone. "I don't want a chauffeur. I can drive myself." I storm out of the room.

Dylan and Faith are still sitting on the couch in the den. I sit down on the ottoman in front of them. "I need to go to work."

"You and Dad are fighting?" He looks heartbroken.

I shake my head. "We're fine. We just don't agree. It happens. I'm sure you and Faith won't always agree on everything. Don't worry about it. Okay? I'll be home in a few hours. I just need to make up some hours and do some paper work. If you need me, call; I'll keep my cell on. If I have a surgery, I'll give it to someone to answer."

"I'll be fine. Faith will be here until eight and Dad said I can go over to his house after she leaves."

"Okay. Thank you, Faith, for taking care of him today."

She smiles at me. "No problem, Dr. Thorn. I didn't mind at all." She's sweet. They seem good together and, though I hate to admit it, they do remind me a lot of Ryan and me.

"I'll see you guys later." I kiss my son's head and then head out to my car. Jonathan is leaning against the open garage frame. I roll my eyes and whip open my door, jump in, and back out of the driveway, ignoring Ryan as he tries to flag me down. I just catch Jonathan jumping into his car as I reach the stop sign down from my house. I'm not trying to be difficult, but I'm not having a chauffeur.

Once I'm in my office, I feel like I can breathe; I feel in control again. I start doing paperwork. I'm behind from everything that's been happening in the past week, it'll take me hours to get caught up. I'm totally engrossed in my dictation when a loud knock on my door startles me. I'm half expecting it to be Ryan, but it's not. It's Trevor.

"Dr. Thorn," he greets me.

"Dr. Daniels, what can I do for you?"

He smiles and moves aside to reveal a student. I inwardly groan. "I didn't know you'd be in today, but since you are, I'd like for you to take Amelia here under your wing for the day."

"I'd love to, but I'm only getting caught up on my dictation and paper work today."

He smiles again. "Actually, I need you on the floor. Dr. Gwinn had an out of state family emergency, so we'll need to double up on our shifts for a while. I emailed you your new schedule."

I'm instantly annoyed. "Oh, okay. Well, let me finish up the one I'm working on and I'll be out."

He nods, leaving Amelia standing in my doorway. "Is he always so clipped?" she asks as I motion for her to have a seat.

I laugh. "For the most part, yes. I'm actually at a stopping point with my dictation, but I don't want him to think I'm jumping to do his bidding."

Amelia smiles. "I think we'll get along great."

I grin, thinking the same thing. We've not said more than a few words, but I can tell she'll click with me. My phone vibrates on my desk. Looking down, I sigh as I see its Ryan.

"If you need to get that I can wait in the doctor's lounge."

I shake my head. "Nah, it's just a text."

Ryan: Sorry. Can I please pick you up?

Me: Yes

Ryan: Love you

Me: Love you. I'll be done at eight.

"Come on, I'll show you around."

It doesn't take me long to show her everything. She's a very bright girl, and seems to really know her way around the hospital already. We end our tour back at the OR nurses station. Julie hands me a few files on the patients I'm taking over for Dr. Gwinn, but I'll have to look them over later as it looks like I'll be assisting Trevor with a surgery in just a few minutes, much to my chagrin. I quickly read over the surgery patient's chart and point out a few of the notes to Amelia. I'm wrapping up my conversation with her as Trevor enters the O.R.

"Time to scrub up, ladies," he says, smiling. It's odd to see him so happy. He's normally creepy when he smiles, but today he's genuinely nice. If he was like this every day, I might be able to consider him a friend. He's already at the sink scrubbing up by the time Amelia and I get in there. She has already learned how to do this, but I make sure she doesn't miss a step.

"How's Dylan?" Trevor asks.

"He's good. He might be milking his injury a bit. His girlfriend has been at the house most of the day."

Trevor laughs and again it doesn't look or sound creepy, it makes me suspicious, but I shrug it off. I'll take him like this any day over the creepy lurker he's been since I started working here.

"If you have a pretty girl around, things are always better. Let me know if he needs anything. I'll do whatever I can."

He's so genuine it makes me smile. "Thank you, Trevor. That's really … nice of you. I'll let you know."

"You do that." He winks.

The surgery doesn't take long and Trevor isn't as demanding or flat out mean to the staff as he usually is. He actually thanks one of the nurses for anticipating his need. Maybe he has a girlfriend. Poor girl. I don't know what it is, but I'm thankful for it today. After we are finished, I head to my locker to change into clean scrubs. As I get closer to my locker, I notice a small piece of paper sticking out from the locker's vent. I grin, knowing Ryan must have stopped by while I was in surgery. I feel badly for having acted so immature about the whole guard thing; I'll apologize when I see him. I know he only wants to keep me safe. As I open the note, a small origami figure falls to the ground.

To show you my affection, I've given you a gift. It's so magical, just like you and me.

I gasp, staring at the figure lying unassumingly on the ground. I look around quickly but see no one. I quickly grab my things, the letter and the origami figure, and run from the hospital to my car. I don't even bother going back to my office to lock up. I have to get home. I don't see Jonathan as I exit. I'm about to pull out my cellphone to call Ryan, when I see a man standing at the back of my car. I turn to run, but he calls my name making me stop.

"Where are you going?" I breathe a sigh of relief.

"Babe?" Ryan says, his footsteps coming closer. "Hey, what's wrong?" he asks, turning me to face him. Wiping my eyes, he asks, "What happened? Are you hurt?"

I shake my head, and hold out the note and the now squished origami. I can see the panic on his face when he looks back at me.

"I thought it was from you. I thought all of them were from you."

"All of what? You've gotten other origami figures?"

Shaking my head I answer, "No, love notes. The others are in my office."

He grabs my hand and pulls me back into the hospital. When we reach my office, he makes me stand outside the door as he checks it over to make sure no one is in there and then comes back to get me. He grabs my hand and leads me inside with a hard expression on his face.

"Where are they?" he asks.

"In my right hand bottom drawer. There's a box."

He yanks the drawer open and pulls out the little decorative box I'd stowed the notes in. He opens it, snatching the notes out. He quickly reads through them. His face grows angry the more he reads.

"Why didn't you say anything?" he asks, barely containing his temper.

"I thought they were from you. Then with everything happening, I forgot. I was only thinking about Dylan and his safety, not about a note I thought was from you."

His face softens, but I can tell he's still upset. "Let's get back to my house. I need to show this to the guys and try to pull up the hospital CCTV cameras."

"They have them in the locker room?" I'm horrified at the thought.

"No, but in the hallways. We'll find who did this, Shay." He squeezes my hand.

"I know you will. Did you go to your mom's tonight?"

"No, everyone came to my house instead. I wanted to be able to keep an eye on everything. I saved you a plate."

"Thanks."

Our drive to the house is silent. I feel like I should say so much, but I don't know what to say at the same time. All of this is just so confusing.

"Sit tight. I'll get your door," Ryan says as he parks the car in his driveway. I appease him.

He opens the door and leans in to kiss me. "Everything will be okay."

I just nod. I'm tired, stunned, and just confused. I'd like to go home and take a hot bath, but I don't think that will be happening anytime soon. He leads me inside his house and into what he considers command central. It looks like they've acquired even more equipment since I was in here a few hours ago. He walks over to the dining room table where Marsh sits and throws the note and origami creature at him.

"Is this him?"

Marsh looks a little taken aback. He picks up the note, scans it quickly and then turns the origami around in his fingers. "This isn't a fox."

"I know, but its close enough."

Marsh sets it down and picks up an expensive camera. It looks like the kind a medical examiner would use at a crime scene. He takes a photo of the note, origami, and then opens the origami to examine the inside of it.

"If it's not a fox, what is it?" I ask because it looks like a fox to me.

"It's a jackal."

Marsh types on his computer and pulls up a photo of a jackal and a fox side by side. The jackal is sleeker with larger ears, and a little taller than the fox. It has more of a wild dog quality. The fox has a shorter face and ears, and its coat is much fluffier with a different color than the jackal. However, when made of folded paper they do look very similar. Marsh brings out the fox that Ryan received to compare it to. The differences are very clear.

"So it's not The Fox?" I ask.

Marsh shakes his head. "I'm not totally convinced it's not, but I'm also not going to rule out that it's just a coincidence. That perhaps your admirer thought you'd like this."

"How are you going to sit there and say this isn't Mathis? I don't care if it's a fox or a jackal. He's toying with us. He wants to throw us off!" Ryan yells.

"I'm not saying you're wrong, Ry. I'm just saying we can't rule anything out. We have to look at this as any other case. What would you do?" He turns it back to Ryan, making him think objectively.

"Fine. If this were any other case, then I wouldn't rule out the possibility that she has an admirer that has nothing to do with this and just thought she might like it, but these notes … Marsh, these notes are so pointed. If you really read them, look for a meaning. Someone is out to get her and it's not by winning her heart."

One of the guys, whose name I think is Riley Peters, asks, "Where are the other notes?"

Ryan starts to hand them over. Marsh snatches them before Riley can get them. He proceeds to photograph them and then puts each one in a clear plastic evidence bag. He then hands them to Riley who reads them and passes them to the next person.

"We'll send them out in the morning. See if there are any print remnants on them," Marsh says to everyone.

"I agree with Ryan on this," Jonathan inserts. "This really seems linked to the case. I think, if it's not Mathis, it's someone close to him. He knew sending this jackal would get to you, Ryan, and if he didn't know already, he certainly knows now that it has an effect on Shayla too."

"Did you notice anyone watching me or anything suspicious?" I ask.

"No, but we'll be going over all the feeds tonight. We'll find him if there's something to find."

"Anything?" Ryan asks Marsh who has been unfolding the jackal.

"I don't see anything but I'll send it off as well," he responds. "I'd also like to run Shayla's DNA against the hair we found in Mathis' cell."

Ryan pales. "You think it could be Shayla's? I didn't think of that. We should run Dylan's too. Just in case. It'll be good to have them on file regardless." Marsh nods in agreement, but I'm completely lost.

"Why do you need to run my DNA?" I ask.

Ryan runs a hand through his hair. "Remember me telling you that The Fox left an origami in his cell when he was released?" I nod. "Well, what I didn't say, because I didn't see the significance then, is that he left a hair inside."

"But how would it have been mine? I wasn't with you then and you didn't know about Dylan."

"That doesn't mean Mathis didn't," Paul comments.

I look at him in disbelief. "It's impossible, only my parents knew that Dylan was Ryan's until a few months ago. Ryan had no clue either. There's no way this Fox guy could have known."

Paul shakes his head then hands me a journal. "According to this," he points to the book, "Mathis knew more about Ryan than he ever let on. Once he knew Jacobs was FBI, he sent his men to work. They sent him all kinds of info. Mathis left the origami for us to find in his cell. He knew we'd give it to Ryan. It heightens his game. He wants Ryan to know he's after him and will stop at nothing to get him. Correct me if I'm wrong, Ry, but even if you didn't connect with Shayla and you didn't know about Dylan, you'd still do whatever it took to save them."

"Of course I would!" Ryan says without hesitation.

Paul looks back at me. "Mathis knew that. He counted on that. This isn't some fly by the seat of his pants plan. This is calculated. He's going after you."

"You don't know that," I insist.

Ryan stands in front of me with his hands on my shoulders. "Baby, listen to me please. This guy isn't a joke. I've showed you his cases. You've seen what he does to women who look just like you. Please, listen to me."

"I am listening, Ryan. But I can't just stop my life and hide. I have to work. If I lose my job, I have no way of taking care of my son."

"I will take care of both of you and if they don't understand a family emergency, then you shouldn't be working there in the first place. You aren't going back until this is resolved and that's final." His voice is loud, almost yelling, it makes me flinch, but it also makes me angry.

"You're not going to tell me what I can and can't do. This is my life too, I won't hide. I'm safe at work."

Ryan scoffs. "Oh, yeah, you're so safe there, aren't you? How many notes have you gotten? It's only a matter of time before this guy comes for you. He'll come there. I know he will."

I shake my head. "You don't know that. You don't even know if this guy is actually the same person. You have no proof that it's not someone who just has a crush."

"They tried to get Dylan. Why are you being so stubborn? I'm only trying to protect you." Ryan growls grabbing his hair. He looks like he's about to hit something.

"I'm not being stubborn. I can't lose my job."

"But your life is okay?"

I roll my eyes. "I didn't say that."

He grabs me by the shoulders again, giving me a little shake. Not to hurt me, but I assume to get me to pay attention. I am paying attention, but I won't let him boss me around. I've had enough of that to last me a lifetime.

"I won't lose you. Do you understand that?" His face looks so panicked and defeated. I give in just a little.

"I'm not going anywhere. Send Jonathan with me. I'll let him drive me around, but I'm going to work." I turn to leave.

"If you die, I'll never forgive you."

I pause at Ryan's words, but I don't turn around and I don't stop. I throw the door open and run to my house, locking myself in my bathroom. I slide down the door into a heap and cry. I cannot believe he'd say something like that to me. I'm so angry with him. Why can't he understand? I can't lose my job. People count on me ... our son counts on me. I can't hide in fear over something that may or may not happen. Eventually, after I've cried all that I can, I get up and shower. When I'm done, I dress in one of Ryan's t-shirts and climb into my bed.

~*~

I'm almost ready for my day when a soft knock sounds on my bedroom door. I open it to see a sullen looking Ryan standing with his hands in his pockets and head down. He looks up when I say nothing.

"Morning. So, you're going to work then?"

"Yes."

He bobs his head then pulling his hands from his pockets he pushes my door open and steps forward forcing me to take a step back. He closes the door.

"I don't want you going to work. I know I can't stop you, but I'd really like it if you'd trust my judgement on this."

"I'm going to work," I say firmly.

He grunts and shakes his head. "I knew you'd say that. You're so stubborn." He doesn't say anything for a long moment, then reaches up and cups my face. "I'm so angry with you. You're making my job fifty times harder than it needs to be." He kisses me then. It's not like our other kisses. This kiss feels like goodbye. It reminds me of the time he kissed me before he left me. I hold back a sob. "Jonathan will take you to work. I'd like you to carry this." He reaches into his pocket and hands me a can of mace.

I stare at it for a few seconds and then take it from him. "Thank you."

"Watch your back. Try not to go places alone. I know you have to be in your office, but lock the door." I nod. "Jon will wait for you at the door to the parking garage. He'll bring you to and from work. If you feel scared or off about anything, you call him." He takes my phone from my nightstand and programs Jonathan's number. "Dylan isn't going to school. I talked to his teachers and the principal. They think it's part of his recovery. I don't want to cause unneeded gossip. Don't fight me on this. He's my son too."

"I know. I'm not." I mean that. I don't want Dylan anywhere but with Ryan or one of the guys.

"Thanks. I'll see you when you get home."

He turns and leaves. I feel so many emotions right now, none are very good. I totally deserve his cold shoulder. He'll probably dump me and that'll be what I deserve too. Hopefully, after he catches this guy, he'll forgive me. The ride to work is a silent one. Jonathan says nothing the whole way and neither do I. He pulls up outside of the main entrance and stops the car. I open the door and climb out, as I turn to get my bag he speaks.

"Shayla, please call me if you even feel the slightest bit of uncomfortableness or if anything seems strange. I'll do a few drive arounds and come in for lunch. Text me if you want me to grab you something. Ryan said he might come up for lunch."

"Okay. I don't always get a lunch, but I'll let you know." He gives me a curt nod then pulls away as I enter the hospital. I head straight to my office.

"Hey," Amelia says with a little too much pep for this early in the morning.

I smile despite my urge to turn and run back to the SUV. "Morning. Have you been waiting long?" I ask as she stands from sitting on the floor outside of my office.

"Nope. Just about five minutes. Dr. Kill Joy told me I had to wait by your office. You guys don't get many students, do you?"

"I don't think so. I haven't worked here long, but at my old hospital I worked with a lot of interns and students of all levels."

"Oh, maybe that's why he is so insistent on me following you."

"Could be. Come on in. I need to get some files sorted. I start seeing patients at eight."

I'm actually a little relieved that she's here. The guys have me really paranoid about being at work. Hopefully, having a tag-a-long will help me relax. I work on getting a few of my patient's files together, then we set off for my rounds. I only have two post-surgery patients to see and those go smoothly. Then, I head to the clinic to speak with about ten pre-surgery patients. As I told Jonathan, I work through lunch and by four o'clock, I'm ready to check on my one post op patient, who wasn't released yet.

"Mr. Carver, how are you feeling?"

"Ready to get out of here." He sighs heavily. He should have been released two days ago, but he developed a fever and an infection.

"Well, let's see what we can do." I have Amelia take his vitals and give me her opinion on what his course of treatment should be.

"I think he should be able to go home after the intravenous medication is delivered. He hasn't had a fever in almost twenty-four hours and his incision looks well."

"His counts?" I ask.

She checks the chart. "Everything looks good. Nothing is elevated." I nod, checking with her.

"Mr. Carver, I think we can safely release you to go home in about five hours. I'll leave my instructions and you'll need to see your primary care physician in two days."

"Thanks, Doc." I smile and squeeze his hand.

"Dr. Thorn." I turn to see Trevor walking towards me. I wonder which Trevor I'll face today. I haven't seen him most of the day. He grabs my elbow and pulls me away from Amelia.

"Do you mind?" I ask, pulling my arm back.

He smiles at me. "I don't mind at all, but that's not what I came to talk to you about. I need you to stay for about an hour over tonight."

I look at the clock seeing it's already after seven. "I've already stayed an hour over."

"I know, but I'm covering for the E.R. until eight. I need you to see a few of my patients." He hands me a stack of files.

I quirk my eyebrow at him. "A few?"

"There's only five. It won't take you long. You owe me, remember?" I roll my eyes. Of course he'd cash in on a favor.

"Fine, but I'm not staying a minute past eight. I don't care where you are. The on call doctor can handle anything else."

"Thanks. I won't make you regret helping me." He winks then he's gone. He's so mercurial.

I break the news to Amelia and we set to work. She does really well. I think she'll make a fine doctor. I've actually enjoyed my time with her today. By the time eight o' clock comes, we've covered all of Trevor's patients and are both completely exhausted.

I text Jonathan that I'm on my way out and he responds he'll be waiting. I do as Ryan asked and pay attention to my surroundings, but when I step out of the elevator on the bottom of the parking garage I don't see Jonathan. I grab my cell and call him. I hear ringing to my right, so I head in that direction. As I turn the corner, I see Jonathan lying on the ground with a pool of blood around him.

"Jonathan!" I shout, running to him.

I skid to a stop, dropping my purse and briefcase as I kneel at his head. I feel for a pulse, it's there and steady. I grab my phone and call Trevor, but he doesn't answer. I call the hospital, but my phone starts beeping that it's lost its signal. Quickly, I check Jonathan over. He's been shot in the shoulder. It could be potentially fatal, but I don't believe it will be. It looks as though the bullet went straight through. I'm about to grab my bag when he wakes up with a start.

"Run," he breathes.

"No, I need to stop the bleeding. Be still." He grabs my hand.

"Shayla, run, please," he begs.

His eyes are wide as he stares behind me. I start to stand to follow his orders and to at least get him help, when I'm grabbed from behind.

I know immediately I won't get away. I recognize the smell of chloroform as the effects rush through me. The last thing I see is the frightened face of Jonathan.

CHAPTER ELEVEN

Ryan

"Dude! You just killed my guy!" Dylan shouts at Tyler as they play video games on my system in the den.

"Hey! That was an accident. Why'd you do that?" I step around the corner as Dylan and Tyler start a shoving match. Normally I wouldn't say anything, but Dylan still gets dizzy from his head bump.

"Easy, guys," I warn.

"Oh, man. Sorry, Dyl. I forgot," Tyler apologizes.

Dylan waves him off. "I'm fine."

They continue to play and I go back to my work on the CCTV files. So far we've watched about a week's worth of files. We haven't found anyone coming or going from the doctors locker room. Shayla doesn't remember the exact day she received the notes other than the one from yesterday, but aside from doctors and nurses, no one enters that room. This leads us to believe that it's an employee of the hospital that's leaving the notes. My first guess is Dr. Daniels, but without proof I can't do much but keep an eye on him.

"I can't look at this anymore," I tell Marsh and Paul as I stand and head into my kitchen. My eyes are blurry from staring at the computer for so long. I grab a bottle of water from my fridge. I spy the bottle of oil Shay left me for tension and decide to give it a try.

"What's the smile for?" Marsh asks as he leans against the counter across from me.

I hold up the bottle of oil. "Shay is into essential oils. She made this up for me. It's been so long since anyone cared for my well-being and it just reminds me of how lucky I am. I was a complete jerk to her. I knew how she felt about having things decided for her. I should have talked to her and got her more involved."

"Do you think she would have gone along with it?"

"No, but she would have compromised better. Now, she's angry with me." Frowning, I grab my phone and notice it's about ten minutes past the time she should be home. I try her cell, but get no answer.

"Have you heard from Jon?" I ask.

Paul shakes his head as both he and Marsh pull out their cells. "Ry," I turn to see an ashen looking Riley.

"What is it?"

"Jon just called. It was hard to hear him, but he said that someone took Shayla from the parking garage and shot him. We need to get down there."

I stand there, shocked. Mathis moved quicker than I expected. I should have anticipated this. This can't be happening. I can't lose her. My mind starts to flash back to my childhood with her. Coming over to her house, kissing her skinned knee, her parents funeral, holding her tightly, the night she snuck into my room, missing her, leaving her, finding her again. I was always her protector. I'd been there through so much, but when she needed me the most, I wasn't there. When she had Dylan, for the past sixteen years I haven't been there. Now, she's gone, and to top it all off, she thinks I'm angry with her.

"Ryan, snap out of it, man. We've got to get moving," Marsh or Paul says, I can't even tell. My mind is a frozen haze of Shayla.

A hand touches my arm, startling me. I look into the eyes of my son. Mine and Shayla's son. "Dad, you have to help Mom." His voice is soft and terrified. He should be scared. I am.

I snap out of my daze and rub my hand over my face. "I'll find her," I tell him.

"I know. Hurry." I hug my boy to me.

"Riley, stay here with Dylan. Don't leave this house."

"Sir," Riley answers.

"Dad, I want to go." Dylan looks at me pleadingly, but it's not happening.

I shake my head. "No, it's too dangerous. I can't concentrate on finding your mom if I have to worry about you too. Please, just stay here with Riley. Tyler can stay too. I just need to know you're safe."

He sulks, but finally says, "Okay. Please find her."

His eyes begin to tear up and I can't help but to pull him into my arms again. I kiss his head, tell him it'll be okay, that I'll find her, and that I love him. I just hope I'm telling the truth, and I do, in fact, find Shayla. Marsh and Paul are already gearing up. They have their weapons locked and loaded. Paul has gotten our communications together and is working with Riley to be sure everything is a go. I grab my bullet-proof vest and gun harness, putting them on as Dylan watches it all from the edge of the room. I look at him for a few seconds.

"I'll find her."

"I know you will. Just watch your back. I don't want to lose you either." I say nothing as I start to get choked up, but I nod to him so he knows I've heard.

"Let's go," I announce to the guys. It took us about ten minutes to gather what we need, but it's too much time as far as I'm concerned. She'll be long gone by now. Unfortunately, she was probably long gone by the time Jon called it in.

Marsh drives and I take shot-gun. Paul sets up in the back with his laptop. "I've got the tracker up and running. It looks like they were headed down South Street to the lake."

I turn in my seat to see the screen of Paul's laptop. "It stops?" I ask.

"Yeah, it just ends. The signal was strong for a few minutes then it just goes out."

"They threw it in the water," I surmise.

"Most likely. I'm sure Mathis knows you'd put a tracker on her somewhere. They probably dumped all her stuff."

"What about her cell phone?" Marsh asks. He continues to drive swiftly to the hospital. We need to make sure Jon is okay and scan the area for clues. I'm hoping the security cameras caught something.

Riley clicks away on his laptop then says, "Nope, looks like it was disconnected about a mile from the tracker. They either turned it off or smashed it, but that gets us a mile closer." His tone is hopeful and I'm grateful for his optimism. God knows I need some.

"Can you turn it on remotely?" I ask. He nods as his fingers fly over the keyboard. He curses under his breath.

"It's either smashed or the battery is out," Paul answers. I slump against my seat. I have to find her.

We pull into the hospital garage and find Jon sitting on a gurney getting stitched up. "You okay?" I ask.

"It went clean through. They want me to go inside, but I told them no way," Jon tells us. I shake my head at him. Stubborn mule.

"Tell me what happened?" I demand.

Jon sighs and rubs his head. "I was waiting for Shayla in the car. I saw this guy lurking around, so I got out and followed him. He went to a van, about a block down. He talked to two men; they were all dressed in dark clothes, nothing identifying. The van was black with tinted windows. The license plate number is written down in my SUV. I doubt it'll come up though."

"What happened after you followed them?" Marsh asks.

Jon rubs his head again. I can tell he's fatigued. He should get checked out, but I know he won't. "They got in and left the guy. I waited for him to pass me and then I followed him back to the garage. They must've realized I'd followed, because the next thing I know I'm hit in the head and shot. When I came to, Shayla was running to me, but before she could get to me, the van I'd seen in the street pulls up and two of the guys grab her. I think they chloroformed her, she went limp fast, but I tried to fight them off. I'm so sorry, Ryan. I failed you."

"No, you didn't. We'll find her. You did what you could. I shouldn't have had you out here alone. We should've had a camera or something on you at the very least." I was so stupid. I should have never listened to Shayla. Even if I had to go behind her back, it would have been better than what she's facing right now.

Paul comes back over to us, looking grim. "I don't see anything here we can use. The security system was down for a routine check. It's possible that the persons involved have someone inside the hospital helping, it'll be difficult to tell right now."

"Let's get down to the water, where the signal was lost. We might be able to find something there," I tell them.

We help Jon into the back of the car and take off. There's nothing at the marina that we can find at night and the signal from her phone died around the town border. It's really impossible to know where they went from there. There isn't anything else we can do right now so we head back. I want to check on Dylan and maybe regroup a bit. I groan as I flop down on my couch. I feel like a failure.

"Dad?" My eyes burn with tears at the sound of his voice. "Where is she?" he asks, voice wavering.

I sit up and look up at him. "Come here," I say, gesturing for him to join me.

He sits beside me and I wrap my arms around him, letting him cry into my chest. I try to hold it together, but fail at that too. After a while, we eventually stop crying and just sit silently. My arm stays around his shoulders, but he's not curled into me like he was.

"I'll find her," I say softly.

"Is she dead?" he asks, voice cracking with new tears.

I lean forward, putting my elbows on my knees. "I hope not. God, I hope not."

"Boss." I look up to see Jessica from the station standing in front of me. I didn't realize she was even here.

"Jess?"

She smiles softly. "I know this is probably going to get me fired, but I think what the chief is doing is wrong. We needed you there. Those guys don't know what they're doing. They let Harvey go."

I shoot to my feet. "What?" I ask angrily.

She nods. "They let him out this morning. Said Harvey would lead them to the other guys and then they'd catch them both. But they lost Harvey about an hour later."

Curses fly out of my mouth at lightning speed; I pick up the first thing I see and throw it as hard as I can into the wall. "I told him. I told him they didn't know what they were doing. Now, Shayla has to suffer the consequences!"

Jessica pales. This isn't her fault. I know that. She's actually a better detective than the guy the chief asked me to train. She listens and takes instruction.

"I'm so sorry, Ryan." Her voice is devastatingly sad.

"It's not your fault. You did what you could. I just need to figure out what to do now."

"Well, you can start by getting some rest. I took a nap this afternoon, so I'm good to go. Riley and I are going to start mapping out the surrounding areas and see what we can come up with. We'll find her, Ryan. You don't have to do this alone. There are several of us at the station who will help you no matter what. I'm on vacation for the next week. I can do whatever needs to be done."

I squeeze her hand. "Thank you. That really means a lot."

"No thanks needed. You'd do it for me." I nod, because she's right. I would.

"Dyl, let's try to get a little rest. We need to be sharp to find her," I tell my son. He stands and follows me up towards my room. I turn to him to ask what he's doing, but he speaks before I can.

"Can I stay with you?"

He looks lost and scared, like a little boy and not a six-foot-tall teenager. I nod and he follows me into my room. We change for bed. I let him have the bathroom while I get ready. I don't want to sleep long, but I really do need some rest. He comes back in lounge pants and a t-shirt.

"You can have the right," I tell him as I climb into the left side of my king sized bed.

"I'm a wuss," he says with a huff as he sits down on the opposite side of the bed.

I can't help but give him that crooked grin Shayla loves so much. I rub my chest as the thought of her shoots a pain through me. "You're not a wuss. It's okay to need your dad every once in a while. I'm not going to tell anyone you slept in my bed. I'm pretty sure that's one of the things parents do. They let their kids' crash in their beds when times are bad. Honestly, I think I'll sleep better knowing you're right here and you're safe."

"Yeah, okay. But if you ever breathe a word of this to anyone, I'll never forgive you." He gives me a tough glare, which makes me smile again.

I mime zipping my lips. He rolls his eyes as he pulls the covers back and lies down. "I won't tell." I hold out my fist for him to bump and he does. "Night. I love you."

"Love you, too."

We lie in the quiet for a long time. Long enough that I think he should be asleep. Suddenly he rolls over and says, "What will happen to me if she's not okay?"

I copy his position before answering. "I won't let anything bad happen to you. I'll be there for you, but I don't think she's dead. I know this might sound horrible, no it is horrible, but the guy who we believe is behind this, isn't going to hurt her right now. He wants to toy with me. He loves the thrill of making people suffer."

"Making her suffer?"

I grimace. "Possibly, but I don't want to think about that. We're working on this round the clock. Jess and Riley are out there right now putting maps together and getting stuff ready for daylight. We'll do everything we can. I promise."

"I know you will. I'm just scared."

"Me too," I admit.

Eventually we both fall asleep and the next thing I know, Jessica is shaking me awake. "Ryan," she whispers.

I bolt upright. "What?"

"We found something," she says. I throw the covers back and dart out of the room after her, not bothering to change.

"What's going on?" I ask as I enter our make shift headquarters in my den. Riley clears his throat. Everyone is looking grim. I begin to freak out. "Tell me what's going on right now!" I demand.

"There's a body near the pier. It matches Shayla's description," Riley responds hesitantly.

I feel like the earth has opened up and swallowed me whole. This can't be happening. This isn't how he plays the game. He should be contacting me, leaving me a clue, something. He doesn't just kill his victim, especially one who he's using to get to someone else. I spent almost two years with this guy. He's sneaky; hence the name The Fox. He playfully torments his victims and anyone else from whom he seeks a response or reaction. He delights in others suffering. That's what made him the perfect mob boss; it's also what made him so hard to catch. He had the means and know-how to cover his tracks. It wasn't until I infiltrated his organization that we were able to catch him. Whoever let this piece of scum out of prison is going to pay! Shay and Dylan wouldn't have been in any danger if it weren't for that.

"Boss," Jessica says, touching my arm to get my attention.

I blink and few times, coming out of my thoughts. "It's not her," I say solemnly.

"You don't know that for sure," Jonathan says.

But I do know. He won't break from his pattern. He won't hurt Shayla until he has me where he wants me. "Let's go," I command, not bothering to explain myself to my men.

"Are you going to get dressed?" Marsh asks as I grab my gun. I look down at myself and shake my head.

"Yeah," I grumble before heading to my room where my son is still sleeping. Quietly, I grab a pair of jeans and a shirt then go to my bathroom to change.

Dylan is sitting up, yawing and stretching when I come out. "Where are you going? Did you find her?" he asks, jumping out of bed.

I shake my head. "We're going to go investigate something. We'll be back soon."

"Can I go?"

"No, bud. This is serious and highly dangerous. I can't take you. You can stay here with Riley and help with the mapping if you want." He sighs and nods his head. I squeeze his shoulder. "We'll find her. It's going to be okay."

"Stop telling me that," he says angrily as he stalks out of the room.

"Dylan," I call after him.

He wheels around so quickly, I almost run into him. "No! Stop lying to me. That's what you're doing when you say it's going to be okay. You're lying. You have no clue if she's okay. She could be hurt or dying or dead! You don't know!"

"You're right. I don't know. But I do know The Fox. I know how he works. He'll want me to witness whatever it is he's going to do. He's playing the same game he always has. He likes to make people suffer."

"What if it isn't this guy?"

"I have no reason to think it's anyone else. He's sent me clues and messages. I'll take every precaution I can, Dylan. You're just going to have to trust that I know what I'm doing."

"I don't know if I can trust you. You haven't been there my whole life, she has!" He turns and storms out of the house before I can say anything else.

"I'm on him," Paul says as he follows Dylan.

"He's just stressed, that's all. I'm sure he trusts you," Jessica says, trying to comfort me, but it doesn't.

Dylan's right. I haven't been there for him; we have a fledgling relationship. Sure he calls me dad, but I think it's more about wanting to fit in with the other kids his age than because he feels that way towards me. I choose to ignore this situation for now and deal with the death of the girl, who most likely only died because she looked like Shayla. This is all on me.

"Let's go," I command, this time dressed and ready.

I leave Riley and Paul behind with Dylan, as Marsh, Jess, and I head out to the crime scene.

"I knew you'd show up," Chief says exasperated.

"Of course. You can kick me off the force, but I won't stop until Shayla is home safely. This guy isn't the run of the mill kind of bad guy. He's doing this to get at me. You'll never find him." I stare at the chief. I won't back down. Not from this, there's too much at stake.

He grunts irritated. "You have no idea who this person is. There's no proof. I suspended you; now get out of my crime scene before I have you arrested for interference."

I glare at him for a long moment, trying to reign in my temper. "You'll regret this," I say as I turn to storm off.

"You threatening me, Jacobs?" he yells. I give him the finger and keep going.

As my team climbs back into the SUV, I tell Marsh, "Go to the hospital. I want to at least question some people."

"You're not worried this body is Shayla?" Jessica asks.

I dry scrub my face before answering. "Yes, of course I'm worried, but I really don't think it will be. Mathis, The Fox, he wants to get me back for everything I did to him. He won't make this that quick or easy."

"Any idea where he'd take her?"

"No. If we were back east, I'd say yes and give you about a dozen locations. Here, I don't know. I mean, there's lots of forest areas around here. There are plenty of abandoned hunters lodges this time of the year. It could be anywhere in a hundred-mile radius."

"Why don't you drop me off at the house? I'll get Riley to help me get started on a map listing all the hunters cabins or any other type of building, abandoned or not." Jessica types away on her phone as she speaks.

"Yeah, that sounds good. Thanks. I don't know why the chief wouldn't let me train you. You're a much better detective than Nathan."

"Well, when you're chief, just remember that." She beams at me.

I smile back. "I will."

We drop her off and I debate on going in to see Dylan, but opt to leave him be. I need to talk to some of the people she works with before the chief lets them know I'm suspended. Marsh parks on the level that Shayla was taken. I know the likelihood of finding something new is slim, but we search anyway.

"There's nothing here. Let's go see who we can interview," he suggests.

"I know just who I want to speak with first," I say as we head into the main lobby.

We head to the OR area where Shayla would be working if she was here. I absentmindedly rub my chest. Each thought of her makes me hurt. We stop at the nurses station. I recognize Julie, the girl who I spoke to about the anonymous delivery.

"Detective, what can I do for you? Dr. Thorn isn't in today," she says.

"I know. Actually, I'd like to talk to a few of you. Shayla was taken last night on her way home. Were you working?"

She gasps loudly, her hand going over her heart. "Oh, my God. I had no idea. I was off yesterday."

"Do you know who was working last night?" I ask.

She nods and flips through some pages, before handing me a sheet of paper. "This is our schedule. D stands for doctor, N for nurse. It's pretty self-explanatory. I'll help you with finding whomever you need."

"Thanks. I see here that Dr. Daniels was working. Is he here today?"

"Yeah, he came in a few minutes ago. He was late," she explains.

Red flags are flying everywhere. This guy is up to something. I find it hard to believe that his showing up late the day after Shayla was taken to be coincidental.

"Point me to his office."

"I'll take you." She smiles broadly. I remember Shayla telling me Julie was one of the only nurses that couldn't stand the guy. She knocks on his open door. "Dr. Daniels, Detective Jacobs is here to see you."

"He doesn't have an appointment. He can make one," Daniels says without looking up from his computer.

"Sir, he's right here. He needs to speak to you about a case."

Daniels glares at her and then looks over to us. "Come in," he says tersely.

We enter but don't sit down. "Where's Shayla?" I ask immediately.

Marsh smacks my arm. "What my partner means is, have you seen Dr. Thorn?"

"I saw her here, at the hospital, last night."

"Do you know what time?" Marsh continues.

"Why? What's going on?" Daniels asks.

I take several deep breaths. This guy is trying my patience already. He's so smug with a stupid smirk on his face. He thinks we can't touch him. He's dead wrong. If he's involved with this at all, I'll kill him.

"Shayla was taken from the hospital last night. We're looking for clues as to who took her or where she might be."

He looks a little taken aback. "Taken? As in abducted?" I nod. "Wow, um, I have no clue. I saw her yesterday around seven when I went into surgery. I didn't see her after that. She's not scheduled today, so I never thought anything about her not being here." He sounds and looks sincere, but I have my doubts. From what Shayla has said about him, he seems to be good at hiding his true emotions.

"Let us know if you hear anything or remember something else." Marsh hands him his card and shakes his hand.

"Let's check her office," I tell Marsh as we exit Daniels office.

I try the door; it's locked. I pull out my keys and use the spare key she had at her house. I'd grabbed it as I was leaving one day, wanting to plan a surprise for her.

"What are you looking for?"

"I don't know. She gave me the notes. I don't know what else could be in here. I'd like computer access, but I'll have Riley do it. There's too much red tape to go through. The chief would never agree anyway."

"I don't think anything's here," Marsh announces after we'd been searching a good fifteen minutes.

We head back to the nurses station to question a few more people, and as suspected, no one noticed anything off yesterday or this morning. This was planned. The abductor knew she wasn't working today.

"Julie, who knows the schedules?" I ask.

"Just the nurses and doctors, but I guess if someone new were to look, they could find it. I mean, we're short on people during the night. So if one of the nurses was with a patient and another patient needed something, then no one would be at the station."

"What times are there only two people here?" I ask.

"Between two and six. At six, two others come in and then at eight, we're fully staffed. There's between six to eight nurses on the clock during the day. We're not all behind the desk, but between the OR's and patients, we're pretty busy. Normally, the desk has at least one person behind it all day," she explains.

"Thanks. You've been a lot of help. Here's my number. If you remember anything or suspect something, call me," I tell her. She agrees and we leave. We're almost to the SUV when Marsh's cell rings.

"Marsh," he answers. He listens for a few moments and then lets out a curse. "When?" He listens again. "We're on our way. Keep me posted." He hangs up.

"What's going on?"

"Dylan's gone."

I stop walking. "What do you mean gone?"

Marsh runs his hand over his beard. "He ran away. Tyler and Faith are most likely with him. Tom is out looking for them."

"Why did they let Shayla's dad go out alone?" My temper is skyrocketing. "Get me home now." I slam the car door.

We drive home in silence and as soon as the car comes close to a stop, I'm out and running into the house. "You were supposed to be watching him! It was your job to protect him! Why weren't you watching him?" I demand looking at Riley.

"We were. He snuck out. He said he was going to the bathroom. It was taking too long. When we looked, he was gone. Then when we came back, the other two were gone."

"That's …" I can't go on; I'm too angry. "How long has he been gone?"

"About twenty minutes. They took one of the maps we were charting. I think he's going to look for Shayla."

"Which way did Paul and Jess go?" I ask, slightly more calm. This is my fault. I should have talked to him earlier.

"Paul headed into the woods behind your house, Jessica to the street heading east, and Tom took the street heading north." I nod then take off out the door.

"Hey," Marsh calls running to catch up with me. "We'll find him."

"This is just what I need. My girlfriend is taken by a madman who would like nothing more than to kill her and Dylan up and runs off on some misguided mission to save his mom all because he doesn't trust me. I mean, I can't blame him. He barely knows me."

"He knows you. Words are said out of fear that aren't truly meant. He's scared. He probably feels like it's his fault. You saved him, not her. He probably has a lot of guilt that he doesn't know how to process."

I don't really want to hear Marsh and his psychobabble. "Save it. I'm not in the mood to hear any of this right now. My son ran off because he doesn't trust me. I failed at my job. I've been an awful father his whole life. Why stop now?"

"Ry," he starts.

"No, stop." I stop walking and face him. "This isn't helping me find my son. Why don't you head east? I'll go west."

"Fine. Just don't forget who's really to blame in all this. It's Mathis, not you."

"He wouldn't be here if it wasn't for me." I don't let him say anything else. I dart off behind my neighbor's house.

We all search for hours, but come up with nothing. There are no tracks in the woods, so our assumption is they ran down the street to the gas station and possibly hitched a ride with someone, or took off down the road on foot. Either way, they've stayed close to the main road. I'm walking up my porch steps when my cell phone rings.

"Jacobs," I answer without looking at the ID.

"Jacobs," the voice snarls. I know it immediately.

"Mathis."

"Nice of you to remember. Have you enjoyed my presents?" he asks with a cackle. I hurry inside to tell Riley to trace the call.

"Where is she?"

He laughs. "Who?"

"Shayla. Where is she?"

"Now, why would I tell you a thing like that? It would ruin all my fun," he says with a sinister laugh. "I will say though; she is quite exquisite. I've never seen anyone with such … perfect skin. It's not quite golden, but not pale either. You'd think you would have taken better care of her. Well, I suppose I'll have to do that now, won't I?"

"You stupid son of a bitch! Tell me where my wife is right now!" I scream.

He cackles manically. "She's not your wife."

"What?" I ask completely confused.

"Shayla isn't your wife, but that makes things so much more fun for me. You really can't live without her, can you?"

I don't remember saying that, but that's what I want her to be. I've always wanted that. I've totally screwed up yet again. Now he knows exactly how I feel about her. He'll use it to his advantage.

"Where is she?" I ask again, trying to get back to what I want.

"She's safe … for now. She's actually cooking dinner. She's adjusting well to being here. She may like it better here than with you. Thank you, sweetheart," he purrs.

"Shayla!" I yell.

He laughs. "Shay, give 'ol Foxy a kiss."

"Don't touch her!" I roar. I hear a kiss sound and I feel that I may throw up. "If you hurt one hair on her head, I'll kill you."

"Now, Ryan, that's no way to talk to the man who holds your would-be wife in his hands."

"What do you want?" I look over to Riley about the location of the call, but he can't pinpoint it.

"Ah, now we're getting somewhere. It's not me who wants

anything with Shayla. She wasn't my intended target. You ruined my plans for your son, but no matter. I think this works out better for me, even if I can't kill her."

"What do you mean?"

"I don't want to kill her, Ryan. I want her for … other things."

He laughs as he hangs up just as Tom Thorn walks in with my son, Tyler, and Faith.

"Go to your room and don't come out until you're thirty!" I scream. He pales but turns and walks right back out of the door, followed by his friends and grandfather.

"Ryan, talk to me, man. What's going on?" Marsh asks.

"We just got all the proof we need that Mathis has my girl."

"Did she talk to you?" I shake my head no. "Then we don't know. He could have been playing with you."

"He wasn't. That's not his style. He said he wanted her. He likes how she looks."

"She matches the description of all the women he's killed so far, of course he likes how she looks. She's what he looks for," Marsh reminds me.

"This is different. He's taken her from me. That's what he wants. He wants to make her his so he can brag about it to me. He made her kiss him."

"He could have had anyone do that. Until we hear Shayla's voice and know he has her without a shadow of a doubt, we need to assume he's lying and work like he's not."

"I hate you," I grumble. I really do. I hate that he's always so calm and rational.

He smiles. "I know. Now, go over there and make things right with your boy. I'll work on a plan for our next move."

He's right. I need to talk to Dylan. I just don't know what I'm supposed to say. The thought of him out there without me scares me so badly I can't think straight. I push open the side door and find Dylan, Tyler, Faith, and Tom all sitting at the table. He's gotten them food and drink, and is chastising them for running off.

Dylan sees me and pales. I hate that he has that reaction. "Can we talk?" I ask. He nods and stands. "Bring your food. You two stay put. I'll call your parents."

"Dad," Dylan starts, but I hold up my hand.

"I can't even begin to describe the sheer terror I felt when I learned you'd run off. I don't even want to talk about it right now. I just want you to know, I'm sorry. I should be including you in this search so you don't feel the need to run off. But I'll tell you this; you don't need to know it all. You need to trust me. I will and am doing everything I possibly can right now. Like it or not, I am your dad. I didn't have a chance to be there for you growing up. I didn't know you existed. I know I've made plenty of mistakes in my life, but you were not one of them. I refuse to let you go on thinking that I don't want you or that I don't need you in my life. This is serious, Dylan. I need you with me on this or I won't be able to find your mother. I can't worry about you and search for her. Do you understand that?" I ask, finally ending my scattered thoughts.

"I'm sorry. I shouldn't have left. I really thought they might be at the cabin we went to last summer."

"Well, after you eat and get cleaned up, you can tell me all about it. I'm taking you to school in the morning."

"What? Dad, no, I need to be here. I'm not safe at school."

"You will be. I'll be sending Paul with you."

He makes a disgruntled noise. "Yeah, that'll be terrific. A big military guy following me around all day. He won't be noticeable at all." He rolls his eyes.

"I don't care, Dylan. I don't care what it looks like. You don't need to get behind in class or miss practice. Being there will get your mind off of what's going on here, plus I won't have to worry about you all day."

"I swear; I won't run off again. Can't we just go get my books?"

I shake my head. My cell rings and I answer it holding up a finger for him to wait. "Hello?"

"Ryan?"

"Shayla!"

CHAPTER TWELVE
Shayla

The first thing I notice upon waking is not being able to move. My head hurts. I obviously have no clue how long I've been out, but at least I'm alive ... for now anyway. I try to open my eyes, moving as slowly as I can. Thankfully, it is pretty dark in the room and my eyes adjust easily. I can make out that the walls are aqua blue and the ceiling is white popcorn. I turn my head to the left and see a vanity and on my right is a dresser. Both look like something out of the nineteen-fifties. I look above my head to see my hands are cuffed to the metal frame of the bed. I'm trying to stay calm, but the urge to scream is growing by the second. After a few swift tugs, I know I won't be getting free without some serious pain. My legs are tied to the foot of the bed; it's when I look down that I realize I'm not wearing my clothes. I'm wearing a white night gown, one like I'd seen my grandma wear multiple times. Someone changed me. Someone changed my clothes! What did they do to me? Did they touch me, take pictures for themselves, or the very worst of all, did they rape me? I can't breathe. I know hyperventilating is not in my best interest. I try desperately to control my breathing. *Slow deep breaths, Shayla. Calm. Calm.* I do this over and over, but never feel one-hundred percent calm.

The door opens and a man stands, leaning against the frame with his arms crossed over his chest. He laughs. "Struggling won't get you anywhere, sweetheart." I can't see his face. The light behind him is too bright. "I have to say, this isn't really my style, but my cousin took a liking to you. If it were up to me, you'd be in a much ... different situation."

I still can't see him, but I know in my gut this is Jason Mathis. I also know I'm the type of woman he would normally seek out to kill. My only saving grace right now is this cousin he's mentioned. For some reason he wants me alive. I'm thankful for that small blessing.

Jason steps into the room, coming right up to me and staring down.

He looks different from his pictures. He's very handsome, but his blonde hair is now black and his skin is much tanner. It's so tan that it makes him look Hispanic. He seems to be wearing contacts, because his blue eyes are now brown. Even with all these changes, I know it's him. He reminds me of someone, but I can't think of who that it is. I don't really care who. I just want to go home.

"Please. Please, let me go home."

He chuckles, running the back of his hand down my face. "Oh, sweetheart. Don't beg. I like it too much." Tears roll down my cheek as I shake in fear. I wish I'd never seen those crime scene photos. I know what this man can do to a woman. I know the damage he can inflict. I'd suffer it to save Ryan or Dylan, though. I'd do anything for them.

He sits down in a chair beside the bed, resting his left ankle on his right knee. He rubs his beard as he stares at me. It's unnerving. "Let's start with introductions. I'm Jason, but you can call me Fox. That is what Ryan told you they called me, isn't it? On the account that I'm so sneaky." He laughs uproariously. That in itself is frightening. He's crazy. "Did he tell you about me?" I don't answer. I'm terrified. His eyes pinch together and his face grows red and angry. He leans towards me and in the most menacing voice I've ever heard says, "You will answer me. I don't like to be ignored." He grabs the chain wrapped around my ankle and jerks hard, causing me to cry out.

He then sits back, resuming his previous position. Steepling his fingers under his chin, he asks, "Did Ryan tell you all about me?

"Y ... yes," I stutter through my tears.

"I knew he would. I was his hardest case. He had me fooled too, but no one fools me and gets away with it. Did he tell you what he did for me?"

"No," I whisper.

He chuckles merrily. "Ah, well. He worked for me for two years. You see, my family is one of the biggest crime families on the East coast. My father is the boss, I guess you could say, but he was training me to take over. He doesn't approve of my little hobby, though, and threatened to give my rightful position to my stupid brother. I had Ryan kill him."

I gasp and he smiles happily. He's trying to rile me up. "I'm sure he just did what he had to do to survive."

He bobs his head. "I'm sure. I would have killed him if he hadn't complied, but I didn't make him go through women like they were candy."

I know my face pales. Ryan and I haven't talked about our pasts. I didn't want to know. I knew it was possible he was with other people, but I didn't want to think about that. "It doesn't matter. It was before."

"Yes, it was before. But you know, he used to talk about his high school sweetheart a lot, especially when he was drunk. She was the one that got away. He regretted giving her up, but her name wasn't Shayla, it was Gracie. Do you know who she is?" I nod. Gracie is me; Shayla Grace. He smiles. "I know you do. Did you know that's how I found you?" He continues to stare at me for several long moments. Tears pool in my eyes, but I try desperately to keep them at bay. "He wasn't very smart. It wasn't hard to find out who you were after the press revealed that Ryan Jacobs had posed as Lucas Marks to infiltrate the Mathis Mob Family. Did you know his personal tag was Marks always gets his mark? Cheesy, right? But true. He took out about twenty people. Some agents, others just because they annoyed me. Your boyfriend isn't as innocent as you may think. He fit into our lifestyle perfectly. He never showed a bit of remorse for his actions. Even I feel a bit bad for what I do, although not bad enough to stop."

He winks at me. My stomach rolls. I feel like I may be sick. I sob. I don't want to hear this. I don't want to know what he was forced to do as Lucas. He's not him. Ryan would never do anything to hurt innocent people. He's sweet and caring. He loves me and our son.

"Shut up. You don't know him," I say with as much muster and strength as I can manage.

He stares at me a few seconds before he laughs. "Oh, sweetheart. I admire your spunk, but your boy is dark. He doesn't deserve you, or your son. Not that my cousin does, but he's a good guy. He has a great job. He'll take care of you both, and as much as it pains me to admit it, you'll be protected by me and the family now that you're his." He stands, coming to sit on the bed beside me. I try to scoot over, but I can't move much. My breathing picks up again as my fear grows. "Soon you'll be the perfect little family. If Ryan hadn't messed up our first attempt, Dylan would already be here with you."

I jerk sharply as I yell, "You leave him alone!"

"Now, now. Settle yourself down. We don't want you bruised." He grabs me around the waist and pulls me back to the center of the bed, so my bindings aren't cutting into my skin. "Stay." He runs his fingers down my cheek again. I shudder with fear. My whole body is shaking. "It's such a shame. Your skin is so beautiful. I told Ryan he was a lucky man."

"I told you not to touch her," a very familiar voice says. "Why do you still have her tied? I said as soon as she woke to let her go so she could move around."

"You're a fool. She'll run or fight you," Mathis tells him.

He's still standing in the bright door way. I think I know who he is, but I don't want to admit it to myself. Why would he do something like this? My eyes squeeze shut. I'm so stupid. Of course it's him.

"You're not going to run are you, Shayla?" He walks over to me and I sob. I can't believe he's doing this. Ryan was so right about him. "You'll do everything I say or I'll find someone to take it out on those you love. Understand?" I nod my head. "Good." He leans over me, releasing my hands and then my feet. I lie as still as I can, as to not anger either of them. "See. She's good." He holds his hand out to help me up. I reluctantly take it and he pulls me slowly upright. He sits on the bed beside me. "I'm going to give you a quick exam. I want to be sure the chloroform hasn't affected you."

I sit very still as he looks at my eyes and listens to my chest. I breathe as he tells me to and I don't say a word.

"Leave us," he tells Mathis.

"You're an idiot," Mathis grumbles, but leaves.

"Why are you doing this, Trevor?" I ask, barely controlling my emotions.

"I told you. Perfect pairs are hard to find. I found mine. I'm not letting you go."

The notes! He sent the notes! I should have known. The possessive anger he showed towards me around Ryan. The off-handed things he'd say to me in passing. The way he touched me, never quite inappropriate, but not quite acceptable either.

"You sent the notes," I say, looking down at my hands.

He lifts my chin. "Of course I did. Detective Jacobs is clueless. He doesn't know how to treat a lady. But, I do. I'll protect you and keep you safe. You'll love it here. I built it for you, for us."

He gestures to the room. I look around. This room looks like it's straight out of the nineteen-fifties. It reminds me so much of my grandmother's home. She loved the fifties and never changed a thing as the years went by. Why would he think this is what I want? I'm not a housewife. I've never been one to care a ton about cooking, cleaning, or what my house looks like. I do all those things, but Dylan is my priority.

"Do you like it?"

"I don't understand. Why would you build this for me?"

"Because, this is where a woman should be. This is what will make her feel safe. You don't have to work anymore. You won't have to worry about anything. I'll take care of you. We'll have a wonderful life together."

He reaches out to stroke my face, but I jerk back and jump off the bed. I'm a little uneasy on my feet, but I go for the door. He grabs my arm, jerking me against his chest and then slams me into the door behind me. His face comes within millimeters of mine. His voice is low and angry.

"Don't misjudge my kindness for weakness. I don't want to hurt you, but if you do not obey me, there will be consequences. Am I clear?"

"Yes," I whisper.

My body vibrates in fear and quite possibly shock. He notices. I know he does. I can see the wheels of his physician brain turning, but he ignores my symptoms. He pulls me over to a door, a closet, where he picks out a dress and hands it to me.

"Put this on. There are undergarments in the drawers. Fix your hair. I'll be back to get you in ten minutes. You'll need to cook us dinner."

He slams the door closed and the lock clicks. I sink to my knees and sob, scream, and wail. I flat out lose myself in my sorrow and fear. Never in my life have I been this terrified. I have no clue what they will do to me. I know they want me alive and that might be more terrifying than death.

~*~

I have no clue what day or time it is. They could have kept me knocked out for hours. The windows are dark, but it's almost like they've been covered instead of a dark night. I feel disoriented. After I cry myself stupid, I find there is bathroom attached to the room. So I take advantage and shower quickly. I don't want to be exposed any longer than necessary, but it does help me feel better. Now, I stand in front of the mirror, dressed in the typical 1950's panties and bra. How in the world did my grandmother stand these ridiculously big panties or this stiff uncomfortable bra? I really want my own clothes back. I don't want to think about them changing me. I refuse to dwell on that now. After taking several deep calming breaths, I put on the dress I was given. It reminds me of the dresses I saw on *Leave it to Beaver*. It's a pretty blue one with small white flowers on it. It's a little tight through the waist and chest, but at least I'm fully clothed now. I comb through my hair, but leave it straight down. I'll wear the clothes, because I don't want to be naked, but I refuse to wear my hair a special way for him.

"Oh, good, you found the bathroom. Fix your hair, it's time for you to cook us our meal," Trevor tells me.

"No," I say, my voice holding more bravado than I feel.

He wheels around quickly, his face full of furry. "You will do what I say or you will be punished!"

"I like my hair down."

He steps forward and I step back until I'm pressed against the wall. He hasn't touched me, but he's barely an inch from me. "Put your hair up, in a bun or braid. Do it now or I'll take you across my lap and tan your hide. Am I clear?"

I blink a few times, trying to comprehend what he's saying. I snort. "You'll spank me? Like a child?"

I almost want to laugh. Sure, I've heard stories of couples being into that sort of thing, but I don't think this is sexual at all. I think he really would beat my butt if he thought it'd get me to do what he wants.

"Yes. Like a child. I don't want you bruised. I'm not abusive, but I will correct unwanted behavior. You're mine now. Do. As. You. Are. Told!" He says each word slowly, deliberately. I shiver. "Are you going to obey?"

"No."

He growls, grabs my arm and flings me to the bed. He immediately begins undoing his belt. I jump up and run for the closet, trying to shut the door before he reaches me, but it won't close all the way. There is something blocking the latch. I hold it to me as tightly as I can, but it doesn't work. He rips it out of my hands before I can try to think of another plan.

He throws me stomach down onto the bed, putting his knee on my back to hold me in place. I scream and cry out for him to stop, but it seems to make him only hit me harder. He wails on me over and over until I go limp from the pain. This isn't a spanking; it's a beating. He's hitting anything he can reach. My back, legs, and butt are all burning with pain. Finally, after what feels like hours, but is most likely only a minute or two. He stops. His breathing is ragged and heavy. He stands and straightens his white dress shirt and puts his belt back in place. I lie there as still as possible, sobbing.

"Fix your hair. Am I clear?" I just nod, covering my face. "Don't disobey me again." He slams the door.

I lie there for a few minutes to gain control of myself. I feel foolish, scared, lonely, and sad. I want Ryan. I need him so badly. I need to find a way out of here. I eventually get up and go to the bathroom. I haven't a clue how to fix my hair like it's the 1950's, so I put it up in a simple bun.

I go to the bedroom door and turn the nob. It's unlocked, surprisingly. There's a hallway before me. On my left is a small door, most likely a linen closet. On my right is a longer hallway leading to an opening, a foyer area. There are two open doorways off the foyer, both look like living room areas, but the larger room appears to be connected to a dining room, so I head that way. In the dining room, there's a door to a kitchen. Mathis and Trevor sit talking at the small kitchen table.

"Ah, good. You found your way. It's late, so I think sandwiches would be fine," Trevor tells me. I nod and head over to the fridge to gather the supplies. "I don't like mayonnaise. I'll take a turkey and cheese on wheat, with lettuce, tomatoes, and onion. Mustard is fine." He resumes talking to Mathis, but then speaks to me again, "Oh, toast the bread and I'll take potato salad. I bought some this time, but you'll make it from scratch the next time I want it." I just nod my head and set to work on his sandwich. Tears fill my eyes, but I try desperately to keep them at bay.

When I'm finished, I set it on the table in front of him. As I start to pull away, he grabs my wrist, making me flinch, but he simply presses a kiss to my flesh. "Thank you, sweetheart. Now ask Jason what he'd like to eat?" I turn to Mathis, who is smiling up at me.

"Would you like something to eat?"

He stares at me for a long moment, then says, "Yes, but I can't have what I want." I shiver in disgust. "I'll just have the same, but I like mayo."

I nod and turn back to the counter to fix his food. While I'm "cooking" he calls Ryan and torments him with news of me. Trevor punches him in the arm every time he says something about how I look, but when I set the plate in front of him, he asks me to kiss him. I look at Trevor and he touches his cheek. So with tears streaming down my face, I move to kiss Mathis' cheek, but at the last second he turns and kisses my lips. I hurry to the sink and wash my lips. Trevor punches a laughing Mathis in the face, making him drop his phone and end the call.

"I told you she's mine! You have no right kissing her," Trevor roars.

Mathis holds his hands up in defeat as he laughs. "Calm down, cousin. I won't do it again. You're just too easy to get a rise out of; I couldn't resist."

I'm still standing at the sink when I feel hands touch my shoulders. I jump. "Are you all right?" Trevor asks me softly. I nod, though I'm anything but all right. "He won't hurt you." He kisses my neck behind my ear. "You smell so good. I knew I'd love that soap." A small sob bursts through my lips. "Shh, I won't hurt you. I won't do anything against your will, but I know one day you'll love me. One day you'll want me as much as I want you."

"You're keeping me here against my will," I tell him. He inhales sharply. "I'm sorry," I add quickly, afraid he'll hit me again. My whole backside is throbbing in pain.

He rubs my arms softly. "I told you, I don't want to hurt you. I have issues with my temper, Shayla. I'm not a perfect man. My intentions are good. I don't want you unhappy. I know if you give it a chance, you'll like it here. Come, I'll show you."

He takes my hand and directs me to the door. He hands me my coat; I cling to it like a life line. It's mine, and as crazy as it might sound, I never want to take it off. I feel shielded. He opens the door and pulls me outside. I say pull because he's not casually holding my hand, he is pulling me along like an errant child.

Outside it's dark, but the moon is so bright you can clearly see for miles. I hold back my tears. We are in the middle of nowhere. All I see is open land and trees off in the distance. I'd never make it to them if I were being chased. There's nowhere to hide, nowhere to go. I'm truly trapped here without means of escape.

"Beautiful, isn't it?" Trevor asks happily. I nod. It is beautiful. "I figured you could plant a garden in the spring if you wanted. There's even a spot for a strawberry patch. I know how much you love strawberries." He leans towards me and I freeze. He pays me no attention as he presses a kiss to my neck again. "You miss your son?" he asks softly.

I turn to look at him. To someone who didn't know, they'd think he was a caring boyfriend. He looks at me like I'm the greatest love in his life. It's kind of sad that he couldn't have found someone who could feel the same about him. It makes no sense why a handsome, educated man couldn't find love with someone who could love him in return versus doing things because they want to avoid punishment. Believe me, I will avoid that as much as possible.

"I do," I answer.

"Not for long," he tells me, smiling brightly.

I look at him with wide horror filled eyes. "No, please don't bring him here."

"Why not? You miss him. I want you happy."

"I do miss him, but I had him for fifteen years. Ryan should have a turn." My explanation is lame, but hopefully it will be enough.

Anger fills his eyes. Before I can blink, he backhands me so hard that I cry out and fall to my knees. "Don't you ever say his name again, do you understand me?" I nod frantically as I hold my cool palm to my cheek.

"You shouldn't have to miss your son and that man doesn't deserve him, or you. He left you when you needed him most. I'll never leave you, Shayla." He helps me up and moves my hand from my face. He frowns as he looks at me. "I'm sorry. I didn't want to do that. You really need to watch what you say to me. It's so very hard to control my temper." He pulls me into a hug, pressing his cheek to mine. I can't stop the tears from falling. He's going to bring Dylan here. I know he will. I wish there was some way of warning Ryan. He holds me for a lot longer than I'm comfortable with, but I don't dare move. I don't want to anger him.

"I'm tired. May I go to bed?" I ask after he pulls away. He strokes my face softly.

"Of course, sweetheart. I'll be in soon." I must look as I feel, horrified, because his face softens. "I told you, I won't force myself on you. I want you to want me. I'll come say goodnight. Your room is yours."

"Okay."

I turn and walk away before he can change his mind or become angry. I hurry back into the house. No one is in the kitchen when I come through, but I see the cell phone Mathis used on the table. I grab it and call Ryan as quickly as I can. The phone rings a few times before I hear the best sound in the world.

"Hello?"

"Ryan!"

"Shayla!"

"Yes, I don't have much time. They're going to come for Dylan. Please keep him safe."

"Who?"

"Mathis and …"

"What do you think you're doing?" Trevor growls. He grabs the phone from my hand and smashes it to the wall.

"I'm sorry." I don't know if he can even understand me. My voice trembles with fear.

He grabs my upper arm and drags me to my room. I try to fight him off, but the more I do, the angrier he becomes and the rougher he is with me. He throws me into the room and I land on my hands and knees. He slams the door behind him. The lock clicking makes my stomach revolt and I dry heave. He pays me no attention as he grabs my arms again and throws me onto the bed. He takes his belt off.

"No, please. No. I swear I'll listen. I won't do anything else. I promise!" My pleading falls on deaf ears.

He glares at me. "You could have ruined everything! Why would you call him? He doesn't care about you. He left you for sixteen years. He left you when you needed him; when you were pregnant and alone! Did you forget that I knew you when Dylan was small? I saw the sadness, the fear you had. I've only ever wanted to take that away. I want to make you happy. Don't you see that?"

"Then let me go! I don't want to be here, Trevor. I want to go home. I want my family!" I yell at him.

That's a big mistake. His face grows beat red and a vein is popping out of his neck. I've seen Trevor angry plenty of times in the four months I've worked with him, but never anything close to this. He's livid.

"I'm the only family you need to worry about right now. You'll never see any of your so-called family again. Bend over the bed. You deserve this." His voice is eerily calm. I stare at him, which seems to anger him more because he yells, "Now!"

I jump, but still do not move. I refuse to willingly comply. He stomps over to me, jerks me up, then throws me back down to the bed on my stomach. He grabs my coat and rips it from me, pulling my arms at an odd angle, making me cry out. He doesn't seem to care as he starts to wail on my back, butt, and legs. I try to move away, scream for help, but nothing helps. He hits everything he can reach as I move. It's not until he hits my face that he stops. The change is immediate. He drops his belt to the floor and scoops me up into his arms.

"Why do you insist on defying me? It makes me crazy." He moves my fallen hair from my face, making me flinch, but he holds me tight. "I'm not going to hurt you. I want to see. I'm so sorry. I never meant to hurt your face. You have to be still, Shayla." He kisses the mark on my face. Then picks me up and carries me to the bathroom, sitting me on the counter top. "I'll get some cream for your face. Go ahead and start yourself a bath. I'll be back in a few minutes."

As soon as the door closes, I slump in relief, but I can't stand, I can't think, I can't cry. There's nothing left in me. The last thing I remember is slowly pitching forward towards the ground and hitting my head on the porcelain tub, too exhausted to even try and catch myself.

When I wake up again, I'm in the same room, but it's light outside. I'm not tied to the bed this time, but there is an IV in my arm. I look up to see a bag of saline dripping into the line.

"You gave him quite the scare. He was late to work."

I look over to the chair in the room and see Jason Mathis sitting there with a book on his lap. In a weird way, he seems very normal to me. Like an all-around nice guy, until I remember what he's done to his victims and know for a fact that he's not normal in the slightest. He's definitely not a nice guy.

"Yeah, well that happens when I've been beaten practically to death."

I don't even try to hide my sarcasm. For some unknown and obviously foolish reasons, I'm not afraid of Mathis anymore. I should be, but right now I'd rather see him than Trevor.

He laughs. "Oh, honey. That was not 'beat to death'. That wasn't even close. Too bad I can't show you."

I sigh. "To bad you can't just kill me and get it over with." This really makes him guffaw.

"There's more fun for me to keep you alive. I do love to torment your boyfriend."

"Why can't you just leave him alone?"

He seems to think about it for a while and then says, "I like revenge. It makes me feel extremely gratified to take from others, for what they've done to me. Lucas, or Ryan, took a year of my life and almost completely dismantled my business. I'm slowly rebuilding, but there's nothing I can do about the year I spent in prison. Keeping you here is a start, but for you to reject him and willingly go to my cousin … well, that will be the revenge I'll need. I don't even feel the need to harm you and that's really saying something."

"I'll never choose Trevor willingly."

He smiles. "Oh, I know. But you'll choose him because you want to save Ryan or Dylan. You know your son and his friends came looking for you. They got almost to the end of town. I could have taken them then, but it was too soon."

I gasp. My baby was looking for me. Why wasn't Ryan keeping an eye on him? The thought makes me angry. "Please don't bring him here. Just leave Dylan out of everything."

"I could, but I won't. Your son will be here by tomorrow evening. We're setting it up now. Although, your little phone call the other day messed things up a little. Now, they have proof you were taken and who took you. Not that they'll recognize me. I'm being hunted down like a common fox." He laughs at his pun. "Get it, a fox. They call me The Fox."

I roll my eyes. "Yes, Jason. I get it."

"You know. I like you. I can see why my cousin is so gone for you.

You're funny, clever, and pretty easy to talk to. I don't think I've talked to someone about much of anything since my wife died."

I sit up a little. I figure if I can get him to talk and form a bond, he might help me. I doubt it, but it's worth a try. "What happened to her?"

"I killed her," he says in a matter-of-fact tone. I'm taken aback. He laughs. "You thought I had a heart, didn't you?" he chuckles again and smiles at me. "You remind me of her."

"Why would you kill your wife?"

"She slept with your boyfriend," he tells me gleefully.

"No! Ryan wouldn't do that."

"He did. I caught them in the act." I just stare at him in shock. Why would Ryan do something like that? "If it makes you feel better, he didn't know she was married. It's the only reason I let him live. Turned out, he was a good employee and someone I used to consider a friend. Too bad he crossed me."

I say nothing. I don't know what to think. I don't know if he's trying to turn me against Ryan, or if he's being honest. But if he's being honest, does it matter to me what Ryan did undercover? I'm not sure. It's definitely not important right now.

"Do you know when Trevor will be back?" I ask. I don't care about him but I want to know how long I have because this IV needs to come out.

"Not until tonight. He was late this morning, because he was checking on you. He's very worried about you. He's called me four times already, and he's only been gone a few hours."

"His love for me is misguided. I need to take this out. Do you know if there is any gauze or band-aides?"

"Yep, he left it on the nightstand. He said if you weren't awake in an hour to call him, but if you were, you could do this yourself."

I nod and set to work. It only takes a couple of minutes to take it out and clean up. Once I'm done, I turn back to Mathis. "Do you mind if I have some time alone?"

"Sure thing, just knock on the door when you're finished. You can help yourself to the kitchen. You haven't eaten since you got here, you must be hungry."

"I am. Do you know where my clothes are?" I ask, hopeful. I really do not want to wear the June Cleaver garb.

"He threw them out. You're stuck playing his little fantasy." He laughs as he shuts and locks the door to the bedroom.

I'm still a little shaky on my feet, but I manage to check each window. They are all locked with thick black bars on the outside. I won't be getting out that way. Hopefully, if I can do as he wants today, I'll be able to find a way out. I need a plan and a shower. Yes, definitely a shower.

CHAPTER THIRTEEN

Ryan

"Shay!" I yell as I hear an angry voice shouting at her. The call is disconnected so abruptly, all I can do for several long moments is sit and stare at my phone. What's that psycho doing to her?

"Dad?" I look up into my son's worried eyes. "Is Mom okay?"

"She's alive, but she won't be okay until she's back here with us." I turn to my guys. "She said Mathis has her. There's someone else too. She didn't get to say the name before someone grabbed the phone."

"I'll run a search on anyone he could possibly know in this area. The map is complete so we can start searching. Unfortunately, you weren't on the phone long enough for me to trace the call," Riley explains. "We'll find her, Ryan."

I turn to Marsh. "Have we gotten the hair samples we sent off back yet?"

"Yeah, I just got off the phone with a lab. The sample I sent matches."

I close my eyes, trying to rein in my temper. He's been after her the whole time. How did he even know who she was? We weren't dating when that hair was found. How did he even get it? I breathe out slowly. It doesn't matter now. He has her, and I have to get her back. I slip into commander mode. I can't deal with my feelings right now. I won't survive if I think about what could happen to her in the clutches of that psycho.

"Marsh, plan out the search routes. Riley, keep searching for a link with Mathis. Jon, are you fit for duty?" He nods. "Good. I want you on Dylan. He doesn't leave your sight. Paul, weapons. I want everything we have in our arsenal locked and loaded. I'm not messing around with this guy. I want him dead."

The men disperse to their areas immediately, jumping to their tasks.

We work for hours. Planning areas to search, gathering extra bodies to help, and coming up with backup plans. We have everything covered several times over by the time we break to get some much-needed rest. I pour a glass of water for myself as Dylan and Jonathan enter into the kitchen from my side door.

"Hey, Dad. Uh, is it okay if I go to school? Coach really wants me to start at the game tonight."

I set my glass in the sink and then run both my hands through my hair. I look up at the ceiling, letting out a long breath. I haven't thought about my son once while I've been working. I put Jon on him and didn't give it a second thought. What kind of father am I? A lousy one, that's for sure.

"Dad?"

"I don't know, bud. I know I told you I wanted you to go to school, but things are so ..."

"I know. I know she's gone, but there's nothing I can do to help. I tried to follow what you guys were talking about last night, but I was lost. I can't read a map, or fire a gun, but I can play football. I need to do this. I can't sit around here all day wondering if they're hurting her, or if she's ..."

He can't finish his sentence as his voice becomes shaky, overcome with emotion. I pull him against my chest and hold him tightly. He doesn't cry, but he does hug me back for a long time.

"Okay. You can go, but Jon stays with you." I look over Dylan's head to Jonathan. "Eyes on him at all times. I don't care what you have to do to get in that school. I won't leave him unprotected."

"Yes, sir," Jon mutters.

The two of them leave and I head upstairs for a shower and a few hours of sleep. We're meeting at ten with some of the local cops and other agents Marsh called. As I lie in my bed staring at the ceiling, I do something I haven't done since I first left for the service, I pray. Coincidentally, back then it was for Shayla as well.

"God … Heavenly Father, I know I don't call on you much, but I haven't forgotten about you. I know even though I'm going through this tough time right now; that you haven't forgotten about me either. Please take care of my family. Watch over Shay. She's with a mad man and he won't think twice about hurting her. I need her safe. I can't live without her. She's given up so much in her life because of me, please don't let her lose her life because of me too. Keep Dylan safe today. He's such a good kid. Thank you for that. He's one of the best things to happen to me in a long time. I regret not getting to see him grow up, but God, please keep him safe so I can continue to see the man he's becoming." Tears roll down my face as I'm too overcome to continue. I don't know how long I lie there and cry, but I finish my prayer, though shakily. "Help me find her. Please help me find her. Thank you for loving me, for sending your son to die for me. Please, just please bring my Shay back to me. Amen."

~~*~~

The first wave of men arrives at ten as expected. They're a mix of veterans, cops, and FBI agents of various ages and skills, but the one thing they have in common with us, is they are willing to give their lives to catch the bad guy. Some have been through similar experiences as I'm going through right now. Frank "Linc" Lincoln's wife was abducted six years ago by a man he had tried, but failed, to catch. His wife was eventually rescued, but had gone through so much violence she took her own life six months later. He retired from the force and has been a hostage negotiator for the FBI since. He's saved over twenty victims to date.

Linc shakes my hand. "We'll find her, Ryan. I've brought my two best men with me. This is Howard and Smith." He points to the two men with him.

Howard looks like your stereotypical nerd, pocket protector and all. Smith is clearly the muscle in the group. He's about my height and looks like he stays in the gym more than necessary.

"Good to meet you all. Thanks for coming."

I shake everyone's hand, then stand before the six newcomers. The other two men and one woman are from local police stations who happen to be on their vacations. I feel honored they're using their time off to help us out.

"I'm going to let Marsh take things from here. I have some other matters to tend to."

I bow out. It's not that I really want to, but I can't talk about this anymore. I feel like every time I mention Shayla that my heart will explode. I grab my coat as I head to the door.

"Ryan?" I turn around to see Riley coming through the kitchen. "Where are you going?"

"I need to clear my head. If I hear this again or look at another map, or rescue scenario, I'll lose it. I need a breather."

"Got ya. I'll call you if we need you. We'll probably send out the first round of searchers in about thirty minutes. We don't want to wait too long. We're losing light."

I just nod my head. I need to get my act together. The love of my life is depending on me to save her and, as of right now, I don't think I can even say her name without breaking down or breaking something. I head straight through the backyard and past the tree house where I spent a good part of my childhood, along the creek that is almost frozen solid, and I keep walking until I come to a small clearing about half a mile at the top of a fairly steep hill. I haven't been to this spot much, but I remember once finding Shayla here, crying because a boy in her sixth grade class had made fun of her for having braces. She'd scared her parents to death that day, and me too. I looked for hours to find her.

I don't know what compels me to do it, but I dial her number. Just hearing her voice on the answering machine will have to be enough for now. It rings twice and someone answers. My heart starts racing, then I curse myself for not being home for the guys to trace the call.

"Ryan, what a nice surprise," Mathis answers joyfully.

"Where's Shayla?"

He chuckles. "You know, everyone always wants to know where she is, or how she's doing. I feel left out. I have feelings too, you know."

"Yeah, well I don't care what you feel, unless it's my Glock aimed at your forehead," I spit.

He tsks. "Now, Ryan, is that anyway to talk to the man who literally has your girl in his hands?" Bile rises up my throat.

"You better keep your hands off her."

"Ryan. Is that Ryan? Please let me talk to him, Jason. Please. I swear I won't say anything," Shayla begs. I close my eyes, trying hard to keep my emotions in check. The sound of her begging him for anything makes me sick.

"If you say anything, I'll get the belt." The belt? I'm going to kill every last one of these sickos.

"Ryan?" Her sweet, sweet voice sobs into the phone.

"I'm here. Are you okay?"

She sighs. "Yeah, I'm okay. Jason is keeping me company. I can see why you liked him so much."

My brows scrunch in confusion. I've never liked him, I barely tolerated him for my assignments. "Liked him? What are you talking about?"

"He's funny. He talks a lot about how I remind him of his wife." My stomach drops to my feet. He's telling her about my time with him. She may never forgive me. "He has a lot of things to say about his family. They're important to him, doesn't matter if its brothers, sisters, aunts, uncles, even cousins are important. He's not so bad, Ry. He's protecting me."

I run my hand through my hair. I really hope she's trying to tell me something that I'm just not getting at the moment. It would really suck if she has Stockholm syndrome already.

"Baby, how is Mathis protecting you? He kidnapped you to kill you."

"No, he didn't do that."

"He didn't?"

"No. He reads to me. That's weird, right?" She giggles. My eyes burn hot. *Oh, Shay.*

"Baby, I'm going to find you. Can you tell me where you are? Anything at all?" I wipe at my eyes roughly.

"Uh, no, I don't know." I hear movement and then she says. "It's far away."

"Shayla, that's long enough," I hear Mathis tell her.

"One more minute, please. He'll be back soon."

Come on, baby, tell me who *he* is.

"I know. Let me talk to Ryan."

She sighs. "I have to go. I love you so much."

"I love you too. Sit tight. I'll find you."

"I know. Can you do me a favor when you do?" she asks. I almost fear what she'll say. "Don't kill Jason."

I groan. "Shayla ..."

Mathis' wicked chuckle comes through the line. "She's good. I'll tell you that. She just told you everything you need to know to find her. And you know what? Come on. I'm done messing around."

"Look, I'll let you live if you just give her back to me unharmed and alive."

"It's not me you have to worry about, Ryan. She really does remind me of my wife. I understand now why you were so drawn to her. It's a real shame I had to put a bullet between those lovely hazel eyes. It'll be an even greater shame if I'm forced to do it again."

"Mathis, I swear …"

"Oh, calm down. I'm not hurting her. She's fine."

He hangs up. I throw my head back and scream, punching the closest tree. The pain brings me back to reality. I take off running back to my house. I'm going to find him and kill him. I don't care what Shayla wants; the man deserves to die! I barge into the house, startling my men, who promptly aim their guns my way, but holster them as soon as they realize it's me.

"Are you okay?" Marsh asks as he walks around me, inspecting outside before shutting the door. "What's going on?"

Panting, I answer, "I talked to Shayla. Her phone was on. Run a constant check on it, Riley." Tom hands me a bottle of water and I down it before continuing. "She's okay." I pause, shaking my head at our strange conversation. "I think she may have been trying to tell me something, but I'm not sure." I fill them in on the conversation and how she was acting.

"That's definitely out of character for Mathis. He would torment you. This other person has to be family," Marsh says.

"Okay, but why would his relative want Shayla?" Paul asks.

I shrug. That has me baffled as well. "Let's just look for anyone he could be related to. I don't care how distantly related they are. I still want the surrounding areas searched, but I'm pretty sure she's at least a couple hours away. She said she was far."

"Are you sure you can trust anything she said? I mean, you said she sounded off. Maybe she's being drugged," Marsh offers.

I run my hand through my hair in frustration. "I don't know. All I know is this has to end. We have to find her soon. Mathis could very well be messing with me. He says she's fine, but he knows I don't believe him. They don't call him The Fox for nothing. He's sneaky, he keeps you guessing. No crime was ever the same, other than the origami and they were all women. Each time the scene was different."

"Let's just concentrate on finding her. We'll broaden our search. We'll worry about everything else later. Okay?" I nod to Marsh, but offer nothing more on the subject.

I'm leaning over my dining room table, looking at the map and searching the areas within a 200-mile radius, when my son barges into my house. He throws his bag roughly across the room and plops down on my sofa with his arms crossed over his chest and a deep scowl on his face.

"What's going on?" I ask as Jon shuts the front door.

"I got escorted off the school property by a cop," Dylan answers.

Jon clears his throat. "If I may?" Dylan shrugs and I motion with my hand for him to tell me already. "The school was not happy with my presence. They let me follow Dylan around for a couple of periods, then the principal asked me to just wait in my car. I refused, as per your order, and offered to stand outside the classroom door, but that wasn't amenable for her. She asked us to leave."

"I refused. It's freaking insane. You're almost chief of this pathetic town; they should at least let you have some say in your kid's life!" Dylan is now pacing in his anger, reminding me so much of myself.

"So, you refused and they called the cops?" I ask for clarification.

Jon shakes his head. "No, she called the chief. The police didn't come barging in. The chief said he understood your concern, but he had to side with the principal. The school is a safe place and Dylan would be fine. I reminded him there was a threat to Dylan already, but he wouldn't budge."

Anger boils within me. It's all I can do to not pick up the closest thing to me and chuck it across the room. Why is this town against helping me find my wife! Okay, she's not my wife, but as soon as this mess is over she will be. I'm not wasting anymore time.

"I can't play tonight. Do you know how badly I want normal? This is so freaking insane! I hate this!" Dylan screams, storming towards the door.

"Where do you think you're going?"

He scoffs. "Why do you care?"

"I care because you're my son and I love you. I'll figure out a way for you to play."

"Don't worry about it. I'd be on the bench anyway." He throws the door open and runs out.

"I'll go," Jon says, grabbing his coat and heading out after him.

"He's just worried. I'm sure he knows you care."

Gail pats my arm. I had forgotten she was here. She has been constantly bringing us food and treats. She is just as worried as I am. Shayla may not be her blood, but she is her daughter, and the love that woman has for Shayla is unending. She'll do anything to help bring Shayla home. She'll also do anything for Dylan. For that, I'm thankful. I'm totally out of my element with being a parent, especially to a teenager.

"I know. I just don't know what to do. He's angry at me. I thought, at first, he was going to be okay, that we'd talked everything out and he knew I'd do what I could, but I think he blames me. I don't know how to fix it with him. This is all my fault."

"No, it's not your fault. It's the fault of the people who took her. That's all. Don't worry about Dylan. You just find Shayla. Bring my baby home, and I'll take care of my grandson. Tom and I will take him to our house and make sure he knows you aren't the bad guy here."

She hugs me with that motherly way she's always had, making me immediately feel better, even though it is short lived. I watch her and Tom leave and then turn back to my maps. I will find Shayla. I won't stop until I do.

CHAPTER FOURTEEN
Shayla

"You're something else. I underestimated you," Mathis chuckles as he stuffs my phone in his front pants pocket. "You gave him everything he needs to find you. Granted, probably not in time, but he may surprise me."

"I didn't tell him anything," I defend, praying he won't really get the belt. I'm so bruised and sore. I don't think I can handle anymore abuse.

He bops my nose with his fingertip. "You're cute. Now, be a good girl and go to your room so I can go get your son. I'm moving the time table up a bit. We don't want Ryan finding you too soon. I may not be able to do anything to you, but that son of yours is fair game."

I jump up. "No! No! Please leave him alone. I'll do anything you want. I swear. Just please leave Dylan out of this."

He stares at me with his head cocked to the side. "You mean that, don't you? You'd really do anything?"

"Yes! Yes, I'll do anything you want. Just leave my son alone."

His calculating glare makes my stomach turn but I don't care. I meant what I said. I would do anything for Dylan. If it'll keep my son safe, I'll do it.

"Prove it."

"How?" I ask.

He grabs my arm and pulls me to his chest, his grip is tight and painful. His other hand grips the back of my neck, pulling my hair until I'm straining to look up at him. My heart is pounding so hard in my chest, I'm afraid it might explode, and my breath comes in quick short pants, bordering on a panic attack. His face leans down, his lips almost touching mine.

"It doesn't matter what you do for me. I'll still kill your son. I'm not your friend, Shayla. I won't kill you, but that is only because my cousin is infatuated with you." He pushes me away roughly. I stumble back, hitting the table and falling to the floor with a startled scream. I don't bother getting up. I'm too afraid. He opens the side door, but pauses as he says, "Mark my words, Shayla. The moment my cousin is done with you, you will be mine and I will kill you in front of your beloved Ryan." The door slamming makes me jump.

Sobbing, I scramble to my feet and run to my room, shutting and locking the door. I know the lock won't stop anyone, but it makes me feel a modicum of safety. I grab the blanket from the bed, go to the closet, and curl up in the corner.

"Shayla?"

I startle awake as I hear Trevor calling for me, but I don't answer. I assume, if he's back, that I've been asleep most of the afternoon. I cover my head with the blanket and pray he doesn't find me.

"Shayla?"

The door to the closet opens. I hear him approach. The blanket is slowly pulled from over my head.

"What're you doing?" I don't respond. He's crouched down beside me. "Sweetheart, what happened?" He moves the hair out of my face. Gently, he wipes the tears from my face. "Please tell me what happened? Did Jason hurt you?"

I start to cry. The fact that I still have tears is amazing to me. I've done nothing but cry since I've been here. He pulls me into his lap, cradling me to him. He shushes me, promising me everything will be okay and Mathis will never touch me again.

"Tell me," he demands with more force than he has so far.

"He just scared me, is all."

"Scared you? How?"

I decide it isn't in my best interest to mention my call with Ryan or that Mathis wants to kill me in front of my boyfriend. Instead, I go with, "He said you'd get over me and then he'd have me."

Trevor growls, but his voice is tender. "No, I'll never get over you. Your hold on me is permanent. I'll do anything for you." He kisses my temple. "You're the most important person in my world."

We sit on the floor for what feels like hours, maybe it was, I don't know, but it's the first time since I've been here that Trevor hasn't scared me.

"Let's get some dinner. I'll help you cook." The offer surprises me.

I turn to look at him and see he's sporting a black eye. Instinctively, I reach to his face, barely touching him, but he leans into my palm. I try not to cringe. "What happened?"

He crocks a grin. "Your ex-boyfriend."

"He punched you?" I ignore the ex part. I know arguing with him will only make me hurt worse than I already am.

"He did, but some officers pulled him off me. He's convinced I have you."

Relief floods through me. Ryan did catch my meaning. I doubt he'll find me that quickly, but at least he's headed in the right direction.

"I'm sorry," I say lamely.

"Don't worry. I give as good as I get. Now, up. We need to eat."

My stomach drops and my lip quivers at the thought of Ryan hurt. I want to go home, so badly. If Trevor notices my response, he ignores it, for which I'm thankful. We head to the kitchen, his hand grasping mine tightly. He leads me over to the refrigerator.

"I wanted meatloaf for tonight, but since you're so upset, why don't we just have soup and sandwiches?"

"Sounds good," I tell him. Though really, the thought of food right now makes my stomach roil.

"This is my grandma's famous chicken noodle soup. She makes it when she comes to visit and freezes it for me. You'll love her. She's probably the sweetest woman alive." His face beams as he speaks of his grandmother.

"She sounds nice." I give him my fake smile, just to appease him.

"She is. Here, why don't you warm this, and I'll get the grilled cheese fixings."

I take the soup and reach for a pot. "Um, would it be okay if I just had the soup. I'm still a little shaken up from today. I'm not sure I can eat much."

He frowns and walks towards me; I flinch. "I'm not going to hurt you. I'm sorry my cousin wasn't as gentlemanly as he swore to me he would be. I'll talk to him."

He pulls me into a hug, then leans down and kisses me. I want to shove him away, scream, and hit any part of him that I can reach, but I don't. I let him kiss me and try to stifle my tears.

"I love you so much, Shayla." His voice is barely above a whisper.

He's so sincere. How can he be so delusional? Can't he see and tell that I don't want him? That I don't want to be here. I don't say it back. I just can't make myself give into him any more than I already have. I give him a forced smile and turn back to the stove to stir the soup. He strokes my hair like I'm a small child. Oh, how I hate him.

"You don't have to say it back. I know you don't love me yet, but you will. I know you will. I'll be so good to you." He leans down and kisses my shoulder before turning back to work on his sandwich.

~*~

The following morning, Trevor leaves for work around four a.m. From what I can tell, we must be at least two hours away because he's generally not scheduled until six. I try to think of what counties are those distances away, but I just don't know. I'm not familiar enough with the area to even venture a guess.

Mathis isn't here today, but he's left two of the men who tried to take Dylan to watch me. They mostly stay in the kitchen and play cards while I stay in my room. It's at least nine before I decide to venture from my quarters, and since I'm free to roam the house, I take advantage of their distraction and try to find a way out, or maybe gather some information on where I am.

I'm not sure who stays in each room, but I choose the one beside mine to explore first. It's like mine, as it's decorated with nineteen-fifty era furniture, but there's also a modern TV and computer. The computer is password protected and I yield no results in guessing. I leave it and move on to the dresser. There's a small jewelry box and when I open it, I see a watch, a bracelet, and several rings. Three of which look like an engagement ring and two wedding bands, one in a man's size. I hope those are hand-me-downs of Trevor's and not intended for me. I pull open one of the drawers on the box and gasp. There inside lies my necklace, the one that was stolen from my childhood bedroom.

"What are you doing?"

I jump, dropping the locket into the pocket of my dress and grab a piece of paper off the dresser, balling it into my hand, then I quickly turn around, finding Lester leaning against the door frame with his arms crossed over his chest.

"Nothing," I say immediately.

"Doesn't look like nothing. What's in your hand?"

He stalks over to me and I back up, looking frantically for a way around him, but there's nowhere to go. I'm literally backed into a corner. He grabs my hand and wrenches it forward so he can rip the balled up paper out of my hand. He smirks.

"Do you think this will help you out of here?" He flips it back at me. "We change the codes daily and now we'll do it a few times more." He winks. "Get out of here!" he barks as he leaves the room.

I obey and hurry back to my room, slamming the door closed. I plop down on the bed. I wonder if they have the rest of my things. I'll look for them if I get another chance. I don't know what I'm going to do about escaping. They're going to bring Dylan here. I have to warn Ryan; I have to do something. I need to get out of here. Maybe if I can escape, I can find a service station or someone who can help me.

I go to the closet and try to find something to wear outside. Most of the stuff in here are spring types of dresses. There's nothing I can wear that will be warm. I head to the dresser. I find a sweater that will work, but the only other thing I can find is a long poodle skirt and some long johns. It'll have to do. I get dressed as quickly as possible and casually wander into the kitchen.

"What're you doing?" Travis, Lester's brother, asks.

"I'm hungry. Trevor told me I could roam around as I liked. I thought after I had lunch that I might clean the house a little."

They smirk at me. "I think you're a little overdressed for cleaning. You planning on going somewhere?" Lester questions, giving his brother a look.

"No, I'm just cold."

"Umhm. I'm going to run a perimeter check. Keep a close watch on her. She's up to something."

Lester rises from his seat, grabbing his coat before heading to the back door, but as he passes me he reaches out and pinches my butt. I squeak and jump away from him.

"Don't you go causing any trouble?" He laughs, exiting the house.

"He don't mean no harm. He just likes to stir up trouble. He won't hurt ya," Travis says in his thick country drawl.

I decide to be nice, maybe if he trusts me, he'll let his guard down. "Would you like a sandwich?"

"Nah, I just ate. Thank you though. It's a little early for lunch, isn't it?"

I shrug my shoulders. Trevor had me up with him at three thirty, and made me make and eat breakfast with him. So I honestly wasn't hungry until now, around ten.

"This must be hard on you, being away from your loved ones." I nod but don't respond. "I didn't want to take you or your boy. I'm glad he got away. I didn't get into this to see anyone hurt."

I sit across from him at the table. "Then why not help me get out of here?"

He chuckles. "I can't do that. Nice try, though. I may not want to do this, but I'm being paid well enough not to care. That doctor of yours has deep pockets."

"He's not mine."

"No, but you're his now. Even if you tried to run off, we'd find you or you'd freeze to death. There's nothing around for at least ten miles."

My stomach drops. There goes my getting away plan, although it might still be worth trying. I finish my lunch, clean up in the kitchen, then head to the living room. It is decorated like the rest of the house, in the nineteen-fifty style. There's a small uncomfortable looking sofa, two chairs, and an old TV set. There's also a small corner fireplace and an old rotary phone. *Please work.* I check to be sure Travis is still occupied with his game, then hurry over to the phone and pick up the receiver. There's a dial tone! I quickly call Ryan's number.

"Hello?"

"Ryan, it's me. Listen, I don't have much time. Mathis left during the night. He's after Dylan. Don't let him take him."

"Okay, baby. Can you tell me where you are? Who is the other man who has you?"

"The guys who tried to take Dylan are here." I hear Lester come in.

It sounds like he's talking to Travis, but I don't want to risk it. "I've got to go. I love you."

I don't wait for him to reply before hanging up. I quickly hurry down the hall and into my room. It's almost dark. Trevor will probably be back soon. I'm not sure if it would be best to try to leave tonight or in the morning. Tonight, the darkness would give me some protection from being seen, but it will be warmer in the morning.

I don't want to wait. I'll do it tonight after everyone is asleep. Trevor hasn't locked me in since the second day. At least I think it was the second day. I'm not exactly sure how long it's been, but Trevor has gone to work four times and was here all day once. So I'm guessing five, possibly six days. I'm not sure how long I was out.

It's well past midnight when I finally get up the courage to try to leave. I tiptoe to the kitchen and find it empty. Trevor always hangs his coat by the back door so I grab it and his keys. If I can't get to his car, I can at least stop him from leaving. Carefully, I open the door and close it softly behind me. I take a few seconds to let my eyes adjust to the darkness. I have to admit it really is pretty out here. It's so far removed from the city that you can see every star in the sky. The natural light they provide is enough that I can see clearly for miles.

Carefully, I make my way around to the front of the house. There's no garage, so Trevor's car just sits in the driveway. It should be easy enough, but I'm not going to use the automatic buttons on the remote in case they make noises. The last thing I need is for one of them to come out here.

As I'm putting the key into the lock, I hear the gravel crunch. My heart sinks to my feet. There's nowhere for me to go. I know that, but I'm still going to try. I look behind me and see Travis and Trevor.

"What are you doing, love?" Trevor asks.

"Um, Trevor, I just really want to get some stuff from home. I'm uncomfortable not having my things. Can't I just run home?"

He smiles. "No, you can't just run home, it's midnight, Shayla. Your home is here now; I'll buy you anything you need. You don't need that life anymore."

He steps closer and I step back. My heart is pounding too quickly, but I don't let it stop me as I take off running from them. I'm so glad I started running with Ryan. My endurance is better than they expect. I turn to look as I run. They are a good thirty feet behind me, but Trevor is gaining on me. I scream. It's such a stupid response, but my fear and adrenaline are sky rocketing. I press on towards the trees.

The forest is about ten feet in front of me when I'm tackled to the ground. Trevor roughly turns me over on my back and pins me to the ground with my arms over my head and his legs pinning mine down. He's breathing just as hard as me. I expect him to be furious but he smiles at me.

"You know, chasing you is pretty exhilarating." I struggle to get away from him, but he holds me tightly. "You're not getting away, Shayla. I told you, you're mine."

"Let me go!" I yell. I shove and thrash around as much as I can, but he doesn't budge. His grip tightens painfully. "You're hurting me."

He laughs. "Stop struggling." I comply. He jumps up and pulls me with him, never letting go of my wrist. "Let's go." He jerks me hard, but I don't budge. He turns to glare at me. "You're making me angry, Shayla." He jerks me again, but I pull back away from him. His grip slips and I take off for the woods.

"Shayla!"

I can hear his heavy foot falls as he runs into the forest after me. I have no clue where I might be, but I can hear a stream to one side of me. I avoid the water, I can swim, but not well enough to get away if I had to, plus it's freezing out here. I run as fast as I can to my left. Praying it's the direction the road may be in.

"Shayla!" He's closer. I try to pick up my speed, but trip and fall. My skirt is caught on something. "I will find you." I tug but it won't come loose. I take it off. I have long johns on and it'll be easier to run without the big skirt in my way.

I run a little farther and stop, hiding behind a huge oak tree and listen. He hasn't taunted me in several minutes. Nothing. I hear nothing. Slowly, I move from my spot behind the tree to continue heading away from him. Only, I'm met with a white t-shirted chest as I step out into the open. How did I miss him? He grabs me roughly by the upper arms. I scream, kicking any part of him I can reach. His grip tightens on me as he growls menacingly in my ear.

"Stop fighting me or I'll let my cousin cut your son up in front of you."

"Dylan," I whisper as everything fades to black.

CHAPTER FIFTEEN

Ryan

There's a sense of relief knowing that Dylan is with the Thorns. Maybe that's not the way a parent should feel, but in a situation like this, it helps me focus on finding Shayla and not worrying about my son's whereabouts.

I pour myself a cup of coffee and head over to our makeshift work station. "Talk to me," I tell Riley as I sit across from him.

He scratches his head and scrunches up his face. A look I've seen him have a million times when he's got something, but unsure about it. "Well, there's not much in the way of extended family on the Mathis side, but his mother had a sister who had a few kids. I'm having some trouble finding one of their names. It's a little odd, but it does happen sometimes. If they are born out of state or a different country, they might be logged in differently, or if they have a different father. I'll find out though. I do know that the two kids are both girls, so they are less likely to be suspects. You heard a man's voice."

"Yeah, but that doesn't mean there's not a woman involved. Is there any other family?"

"He's got a second cousin, again on the mom's side. Her name is brought up a few times as Mathis' lawyer. I'm still checking on whether she had any children. It looks like her husband was also a lawyer, but passed away about fifteen years ago. I was able to go through his history, and as far as I can tell he never fathered any children and had no cases involving anyone in the Mathis family."

"If she's a second cousin, what happened to her parents?"

He clicks away for a few minutes. "The McAdams, that's the mother's maiden name, died in a car accident in Florida about thirty-eight years ago. They only had the one daughter, Rachel. It looks like she lived with the Mathis' until she went off to college. There's no other mention of her in any way until her name shows up as his lawyer."

"I'm sure she was his lawyer during sentencing?" I ask.

"Yep, she was. It was both she and her partner, Clinton Reyes."

"Who filed the paperwork to get Mathis released?" I'm not sure if there's an actual connection, but it's worth checking into.

"Um ... Reyes, but that doesn't mean she wasn't in on it. I'm sure she at least knew about it. They worked the case together."

"See if you can pull up McAdams' family records, maybe she had a kid before she got married. If she did, it's probably our best lead for now."

"On it," he replies and all I hear is clicking. He makes some sort of grunt before glancing up at me. "It looks like someone deliberately hid her family. It's an encrypted file. Probably the best job I've seen in a long time."

"You can break it though, right?"

He snorts. "Of course I can."

I can't help the grin that spreads on my face. Riley is the best computer guy I know. He was hacking into FBI mainframes in his spare time at fifteen. That's why he ended up going into the military. His family wanted to 'set him straight'. It worked to a point, now he just does everything legally. Well, for the most part.

"Ryan," Marsh says as he and Paul make their way into the room.

"Yeah?"

He motions for me to get up. "We have a lead. There's a warehouse about an hour from here. A body of a woman was found with an origami fox."

I'm on my feet, swinging my coat around my shoulders before he can even finish his sentence. I know it's not Shay, but it could lead to her.

It takes us about forty minutes to make it to the warehouse. The scene is much like the last one, cops and medical personnel everywhere, a body lying on the concrete. She looks to have been dropped from the top of the warehouse. Her legs and arms are at unnatural angles. She does match Shayla's description, blonde hair, about five-six, with blue eyes. We need to catch this guy before more innocent woman are murdered.

"Detective Jacobs?" A tiny pale woman more than a foot shorter than me with too large for her face glasses asks.

"Yes."

She sticks out her hand to shake mine. "I'm Medical Examiner Tracy Lipz. I understand you're investigating some similar cases?"

"Yes, we've found two other bodies in the surrounding areas."

"Right, well you should know that this girl wasn't killed here. She has trace evidence under her nails. It appears to be grass and some small pebbles. There's also some possible tissue under her nails. Most likely from where she scratched her assailant. I'll know more in a few hours. I've already sent it to my lab." She shoves her glasses up onto her nose, then hands me a card. "Here's my card. Can I get your number so I can call you with the results?"

"Yeah, of course." I grab one of my own cards, making sure to write my personal number on there as well.

We examine the scene for a good hour, taking our own pictures and samples. We also take the origami fox with us to examine. The sheriff here is much more accommodating than the chief was, thankfully. We wrap up with the local detective working the case before getting back into the SUV to head to my house; we have a lot to go over.

I stare at the stupid fox in the crime scene bag for a long time. He's toying with me, I know that. But this time, he's slipped up. He left DNA evidence. This could be exactly what we need to put him behind bars for good. That is if I don't kill him first. I'd much rather kill him. Carefully, without taking the fox out of the bag, I unfold the paper. I stare in disbelief as I unwrap it to reveal a photo of Shayla. She's sleeping. Her face is bruised and bloody. I growl squeezing the bag tightly in my hand.

"Hey, hey, let go before you destroy the evidence. What is it?" Paul asks, taking the evidence bag from me.

"It's her," I bark at him.

Paul is quiet for a few minutes. "This is good. I mean, obviously it's horrible she's hurt, but she's alive. There's a newspaper. It has today's date on it. The M.E. already told us that the woman was killed last night."

"I knew Shayla was alive. He won't kill her until I'm right there to watch."

"Then we have time. Time is a good thing."

"The longer she's there, the more chance there is that he'll go too far and kill her on accident."

"He won't do that," Paul assures me and then sets the bag back down. "Personally, I feel this other person that's working with him likely has something to do with Shayla."

"What makes you say that?" I ask.

"It's just a hunch." He notices my scowl and continues, "He's never worked with anyone before, for his killings anyway."

"I guess that's possible. We'll know once we figure out who the person is."

We continue searching for about an hour when Howard, one of Linc's men, yells, "I found it!"

I jump up from my chair and hurry across the room to where Howard has set up his station. "What's the name?" I ask

"Does the name Trevor Daniels mean anything to you?" he asks.

I stand there in stunned silence for several long moments before turning and picking up the chair beside me and flinging it as hard as I can into the closest wall, barely missing Smith.

"That bastard is going to die!" I growl before marching out to my SUV.

I ignore the yells coming from my men as I start the truck and speed my way to the hospital. I barely have my vehicle in park before jumping out and running into the building. I head straight for the nurses station in the O.R., figuring that's where he'll be.

"Where's Daniels?" I ask Julie.

She jumps as I startle her. She looks at me with wide shocked eyes before she points behind me. I turn to see him casually walking up the hallway without a care or worry. Well, that's about to change.

"Daniels!" He looks up. His eyes grow big for a second before he schools his features to mild curiosity.

He smiles. "Detective, what a pleasant surprise. What can I do for you?"

By the time he finishes talking, he's about a foot from me. I take a short step forward and deck him, hitting him as hard as I can in the face. In fact, I swear I can hear the bones in his nose crunch as my fist makes contact. He stumbles back, landing on the ground.

"What the hell was that for?" Trevor spits blood onto the white floor.

"Where is she?" I yell. I reach down, grab him by the collar, and slam him into the wall. "Tell me where Shayla is right now. I know you have her. I know Mathis is your cousin!"

"I don't know what you're talking about," he insists. I slam him hard into the wall again.

"Don't lie to me. I have proof. I know you're his cousin and I know you took her."

He looks behind me and smiles. "You're out of time," he says sinisterly right before I'm jerked back from him by Marsh and Smith.

I fight against their hold with all that I have, but once Paul and Riley join in, there's no way I can beat them. "Tell me where she is?" I demand.

"Doctor Daniels, are you okay?" I turn to see one of the hospital security guards.

Daniels adjusts his coat and picks up his fallen files. "I'm fine. Thank you. Detective Jacobs was just leaving."

I roughly shake the guys off me. I've calmed down marginally, but I will find answers. I say nothing as I turn and walk away from my men, though they follow me immediately. We walk out to the front of the hospital. I turn to Paul.

"Follow him." He nods.

"What's your plan, Ryan?" Marsh asks.

I stand there for a long moment, thinking. I don't know what my plan is. I just know that he has her and I will stop at nothing to get her back. He will be dead for this.

"To kill him," I say blandly, walking away.

They run to catch up with me. "That's not a plan and you know it. We need to think this through and have a set idea of what is going to happen. You can't let your emotions take over. The safety of Shayla is more important than your bloodlust." I turn towards Marsh, causing him to stop short to keep from running right into me.

"Fine. Here's your plan. You get your ass out of my sight and start looking for my girl. You do everything in your power to find her. You kill whoever gets in your way. You don't stop until she's back in my arms."

"Ryan!" he yells as I take off running down the road. I have no idea where my car has ended up, but right now I just need to blow off steam.

I run the ten miles back to my house and by the time I'm there, I've calmed down enough to know I've been irrational. The house is pretty quiet as I enter it; each person seems to be in his or her own little world. Riley and Howard are typing away on their laptops, Marsh and Linc are talking quietly over the maps. Smith and Paul are missing, hopefully tailing Daniels.

I run my hands through my hair as I address the room. "I'm sorry. I acted completely unprofessional and irrational. I should have never approached Trevor, and I'm sure I've compromised this mission and put Shay in even more danger." Saying the words aloud makes it so much more real. Tears well up in my eyes as I continue, "I can't seem to separate my personal feelings on this. Marsh, I need you to take lead."

"No one expects you to be infallible, Ryan. I'll take lead if that's what you really want, but don't doubt your detective skills. You can lead this team to a successful rescue, of that I am certain."

Linc clears his throat. "I've been where you are, Ryan. This isn't easy, but I think we have some good resources and two excellent IT guys over there. We can find her and bring her home safely."

"I agree," Riley pipes in. "I've been going through every bit of info I can find on Trevor and his family. His father was from an area up north, about two hours from here. Which fits in with the area we'd originally thought they might be hiding her. His great, great grandparents owned a huge area of land around the turn of last century. Each of the original children were deeded a piece of the land, which they in turn gave to their own children. So by the time Trevor's grandmother inherited her piece, there was roughly 300 acres left. It should be fairly easy to navigate that amount of space."

"Is there a house or anything?" I ask.

"Not according to any records, but we could get Jon to do a flyover. If we can find a house, it sure would make this a heck of a lot easier. I'm sure Mathis has surveillance of some sort as well. I should be able to hack just about any system they have and if I can't, this guy can. His skills surpass mine by a long shot." He thumbs behind himself to Howard.

"I don't know about surpass, but I will do my best for you, sir." Howard seems nervous as he pushes his glasses back up his nose.

I'm overwhelmed with the support of my team, but I really shouldn't be. They are dedicated to a fault. "Thanks. Let's get on this first thing in the morning. I don't want her there any longer than necessary."

I leave the men to work and head over to the Thorns to see Dylan. I barely knock before the door opens. "You look awful, is everything ...

Oh God, please don't tell me she's gone?" Gail's eyes begin to tear up. I reach out and clasp her arms, giving them a gentle squeeze.

"She's alive. We have a really good lead. We're heading out in the morning. I just wanted to see Dylan."

"Oh, your mom came and got him. I hope that was okay." She looks worried.

I shake my head. "Right. She sent me a text. I totally forgot. He's probably better off over there and away from all this mess. Maybe you guys should head out."

"Nonsense. We'll be just fine. I want to go with you when you go get my baby," Tom says. I look over to the couch where he's sitting, cleaning his gun. "Don't give me any crap about me being a civilian. You know I served this country longer than you did."

"I don't doubt your skills, Mr. Thorn. I just know if you get hurt, your daughter will kill me."

He laughs as he stands up and walks over to me. He slaps my shoulder, staring me straight in the eyes. "Son, I think it's time you started calling me Tom, and I don't care what Shayla wants, I'm going." I nod at him.

"Okay. I'll let you know what time we're heading out."

Gail pats my cheek. "You need to eat." She grabs my arm, pulls me to the kitchen, and gently pushes me down in the chair. "I made meatloaf."

I groan and rub my belly. "My favorite."

"I know." She kisses my forehead. She sets a big plate of food in front of me and smiles. "Eat."

About an hour later, I'm back over at my house going over maps and anything else we think might help with a plan to get Shayla back. It's already dark, so we've planned to do a flyover at daybreak. It'll make it less suspicious if they happen to see us. The land is located on a common flight route, though not many helicopters fly by.

The quiet hum of our working is abruptly interrupted with the phone ringing. "Marsh ... hold on." He put the phone on speaker. "Go ahead, he can hear you."

"We lost Daniels. He arrived at his apartment. Moved around for a while and then turned the lights off. We waited about fifteen minutes, then approached to put up some hidden surveillance cameras. We noticed his back door was open and a few potted plants were broken. It appears he climbed down the emergency ladder and headed into the woods. We've searched the house and planted a few bugs, just in case, but the trail ends at the road. It looks like he had a car parked off the road. The tire tracks are headed north."

I curse, grabbing my coat. Marsh grabs my arm. "Let go!"

"No. You're doing it again, Ryan. You're not thinking rationally. I know this is hard for you, but you can't go running off when something doesn't go our way. We will find him, but we need to be prepared."

I jerk my arm out of his grip. "Fine. Let's get this stuff nailed down and go."

"We will, but we need to wait for daybreak."

"Great. Hopefully they don't kill her tonight."

I turn and run up the stairs to my room. I know I'm being unreasonable. I just can't do this any longer. I decide to shower and get some rest. I'm obviously not helping the guys anyway. Sleep does not come easily or last long. I wake up a little before four. I head downstairs. No one is up yet and I'm fine with that. I grab a cup of coffee and sit out on my back porch in the cold. It's peaceful.

"I was wondering if you snuck off in the night."

I snort as I turn to look at Marsh. "You didn't check?"

"Nah, almost did though." He sits down in the chair beside me. "We have a plan."

"Lay it on me."

"Jon was able to secure a small plane from a neighboring farm. It's common for this guy to fly over that area several times a day. He gives flying lessons. They'll have no idea we know where they are. That is, if there's anything to find. Jon, the owner, Paul, and Riley are going up. They'll do four fly arounds, just like the lessons, and then if there's a need to go back up, they'll go at the next lesson time. That way, there's no suspicious activity, but I think once will be enough. Riley will chart everything while in flight."

"Sounds good. When will we move in?"

He takes a long sip of his coffee before answering me. "I know you want to bust in there and take them down, but we have to do this legally and safely. I talked to your chief, he's agreed to send his men with us and a couple of the surrounding towns are giving us a few men as well. We'll have enough to surround the house."

"Okay."

"That's it?" He looks at me in disbelief. I don't believe I'm conceding either.

"Yeah, I put you in charge of this. I can't get in the right headspace. I need you on this one. My future is in your hands."

He gives me a half smile and then slaps my leg. "You're gonna owe me big." He heads back inside. He's right, I will.

After everyone gets up and we have a huge Gail Thorn breakfast, the guys leave to do the flyover. It will take them about two hours to get to the farm, another two hours at least for the flyover, and then two hours back, so we're looking at them not getting back here until at least one this afternoon. Hopefully, we can head out of here to get Shayla by early evening. Until then, I'm stuck here waiting, which is killing me.

Around ten, my phone rings. It's a number I don't recognize.

"Hello?"

Shayla! Oh thank you, God! I listen as she tells me of the plan to get Dylan and the confirmation that Lester Harvey is definitely working for Mathis. Unfortunately, she doesn't confirm Trevor, but that's okay. I know he's in on it. His sneaking out of his apartment was confirmation enough for me. I hold the phone for a few seconds too long after her abrupt goodbye.

"What's going on?" Marsh asks.

"Dylan. They're after Dylan." I snap out of it, shaking my head. "Where is he?" I ask. Then remember he's at my mother's. "Is Jon with him?"

"No. He's headed to the flight center." I knew that.

"So, no one is guarding my mom's house?" I ask, getting angry.

"No, she's not been involved. Ryan, what's going on?" Marsh asks.

I shake my head and dial my mom's number. "Hello?"

"Where's Dylan?" I demand. I don't even attempt to hide my anger. Why didn't I make someone watch the house?

"What's wrong, Ryan. He's still in bed. He hasn't been sleeping well. He was so exhausted. I told him to sleep in as long as he wanted."

I take a few calming breaths. "Mom, please go check on him."

"Okay, sweetheart, hold on." I can hear her walking and the rattling of the bedroom door. "Dylan," she says softly as if she's trying not to wake him. "Oh, God! Ryan, he's gone!"

CHAPTER SIXTEEN

Shayla

A constant tugging on my wrist wakes me from my sleep. No, my unconsciousness, I'm pretty sure I was clubbed in the head by something hard. Blearily, I open my eyes. Trevor sits on the bed beside me, typing on his laptop, my wrist is handcuffed to his, jerking about as he types away.

I glance around the room without moving my body and notice that we aren't in my room. I'm pretty sure this is his room, though I'd thought it was Mathis' when I was snooping around. It too is done in a fifties style. It has much more masculine tones of navy and black, but the walls are painted a stark white. Framed black and white photos top his dark mahogany dresser while clothes are thrown on the back of a navy colored chair in the corner of the room. The only thing that is blatantly out of place is the very modern TV that sits on top of his matching mahogany chest of drawers. My eyes settle back to him to find him gazing down at me with a half-smile.

"How's the head?" he asks. His tone isn't angry like I imagined it would be.

"Hurts," I say, stopping to clear my throat. "What happened?"

He turns and sets his laptop on the nightstand, and then moves back to me with a pen light in his hand. He quickly flashes it in my eyes and then moves down in the bed so we are lying face to face. I want to jump out of the bed and away from him, but I know that won't get me anywhere because I'm cuffed to him. I'm sure that was his intention.

"Lester hit you on the head with a rock. I thought he'd killed you at first. There was so much blood, but head wounds are like that. Once, I got you inside and cleaned up, I knew you'd be fine. It wasn't that big of a cut."

He reaches towards me and I flinch, but he doesn't stop. He gently moves my hair back and runs his finger tip over the cut, making me wince.

"You'll be fine. It's already starting to heal."

"Why am I cuffed to you?"

He lets out a sardonic chuckle. "You think I'd risk letting you get away from me again? Shayla, I don't think you understand how much you mean to me. I can't lose you. If you were to have gotten away last night you would have frozen to death, or been mauled by a wild animal. These woods aren't safe. They're known for their vast population of wolves and coyote."

"I don't understand why you care so much. Why do you want to be with me when I can't return your love?"

He lifts my chin so that I'm looking him in the eye. "You will." He presses his lips to mine, but I don't kiss him back. Thankfully, he doesn't make it an issue. "Let's get you breakfast and I'll explain to you what's going to happen in the next few days."

He gives me little choice as he hauls me out of the bed. I stumble, but he helps me right myself until I'm able to walk on my own. I feel dizzy and sick to my stomach.

"I'm pretty sure I have a concussion," I tell him.

"Oh, I'm sure you do. You've been out for hours. I gave you fluids and kept a check on your vitals. Like I said, I knew you'd be fine."

"You should've taken me to a hospital, Trevor. You couldn't have known if there was swelling or internal bleeding. I could have died. Where would that have left your grand plan?"

He stops abruptly and turns to me. "Are you questioning my skills as a doctor?" I glare at him. "I do have basic lifesaving equipment here. I never would have done anything to jeopardize your life."

"You're jeopardizing my life right now by keeping me here!" I yell. I instantly regret it, as it makes my head throb. I clutch my head with my free hand.

He tsks at me. "You're only making things worse for yourself, Shayla. Please calm down. You'll be fine. I have some pain pills in the kitchen."

He pushes me to sit down at the table, then removes the cuff from his wrist and attaches it to the table leg. He moves over to the refrigerator and pulls out a carton of eggs and a tube of sausage. He goes to work, preparing my breakfast with his back to me as he talks.

"Mama is coming over to meet you tonight. I know you probably won't feel like cooking, but I want you to make a pot roast. You can start it after breakfast. It should have plenty of time to cook by suppertime."

"What makes you think I know how to cook?"

He snorts. "I know all about you, Shayla. I happen to know that you enjoy cooking, especially baking. Though, you do tend to stick to healthier, new age-y types of food."

"I do like to bake, but I don't really enjoying cooking."

I feel more satisfaction in correcting him than is probably sane. It just drives me crazy that he thinks he knows me so well. It bothers me even more knowing that he has so many things about me right.

"Well, either way you will fix a pot roast. I have my aunt's recipe, it's my mother's favorite."

He sets a plate of fried eggs and sausage in front of me and my stomach lurches. I gag. Seeing my reaction, he removes the food and replaces it with a plate of dry toast.

"How about some toast?"

I nod a minuscule amount and watch as he sets my plate on the counter before taking his seat beside me as if we were an old married couple. I nibble on my toast and sip the juice he's given me, wondering why on earth he's doing all of this. Surely I never gave him the impression that I would enjoy being his little housewife. After he finishes his food and cleans up his mess, he turns back to me.

"You won't be allowed to roam freely anymore. Someone will be with you at all times. Although, I'll give you privacy in the bathroom. Today, you will shower and make yourself presentable for my mother. I've laid your clothes out on your bed. You can put the roast together right now."

He lays a recipe card on the table in front of me and then releases the cuffs. I pick up the card and read it. It seems simple enough, but it's not something I want to do. None of this is. I lay the card back down.

"And if I say no?" I ask.

He narrows his eyes at me. "If you refuse, then I'll have to punish you."

I shove the card away. I'm so sick of him and his twisted delusions. I want to go home. I want my son. I want Ryan. I can't be here anymore and I will not play his ridiculous game any longer.

"Is that your refusal?" he asks.

I glare at him. He grabs my arm and hauls me out of the chair. He pulls me over to the counter top where he's left the ingredients out for me. He slaps the recipe down in front of me.

"Do it!" he commands.

"No."

He growls at me. "Do it now or I'll get the belt."

I turn calmly to him. "I'm not yours, Trevor, and I will never love you. I don't want to meet your mother. Although, now that I think about it, I'd really love to tell her all about how you kidnapped me and that you are forcing me to be here against my will. I'm sure she'd love to know how sick her son ..." I don't get to finish my thought as he backhands me hard across the face. I stumble into the countertop. My head throbs and I see stars as the dizziness comes back full force. I turn away from the counter and vomit all over Trevor. He curses and jumps back from me.

"I don't know why you insist on making me so angry. This is all your fault. If you'd just do as you're told I wouldn't lose my temper and you wouldn't be hurting right now. In spite of what you might think, I don't like to hurt you, Shayla."

"Sure you don't," I sass.

"Shayla! Stop this." He pulls me to my room, shoving me down on the bed. "Shower and change clothes. I'll be back in thirty minutes."

I sit there. I don't know for how long, but it feels like it could be thirty minutes. I don't move until the door knob turns and Trevor returns, freshly clothed and showered. He lets out a heavy sigh and releases the buckle on his belt, pulling the belt free.

"Why do you make me do this to you? I don't want to hurt you, but you won't listen. You give me no choice."

"You do have a choice. You can let me go. If you really loved me, you'd let me go."

He scoffs. "This isn't some fairytale. I won't let you go. I need you. Don't you understand that? I need you so much that I've changed my plans for you."

"How so?"

The very thought of him changing his plans sends my stomach to my feet. Nothing good will come of this. I just know it. He runs his hand through his hair and it reminds me of Ryan, which makes my eyes water and my chest ache.

"I wanted you to be here with me, meet my family and learn to love me. Then, I planned on marrying you and having children with you. We could have a good life together. But now ..." He shakes his head and my stomach revolts. "Now, I have to move things along faster. We'll be married tomorrow afternoon."

I stare at him dumbfounded. "No!" I say harshly, jumping up from the bed. "You promised you wouldn't force me."

He moves toward me and I back up, hitting the dresser. He pins me there with his hands on either side of me, his face inches from mine.

"I don't want to, but you're forcing my hand. Tomorrow you will marry me and tomorrow night we will consummate our love."

"I will never willingly do anything with you!" I yell in his face.

He smiles at me. It's unnerving. "Oh, you will." He turns. "Jason," he says slyly.

Mathis appears in the doorway with my son blindfolded and gagged with his hands bound in front of him.

"Dylan," I say, my voice breaking as tears start to pour unbidden from my eyes.

"Mom," Dylan mumbles through his gag, fighting to get away from Mathis.

Trevor nods to Mathis and he takes Dylan away. "No!" I yell, trying to move away from Trevor, but he holds me tightly.

"You will do what I say or I will let my cousin take your punishment out on your son."

"Fine! Fine! You win. Okay. Is that what you want?" I scream at him.

He grins. "It is. It's exactly what I want." I sag in defeat. He pulls me into his arms, hugging me. I hate him so much right now. He kisses my temple. "Now, shower and change. Mother will be here at six."

I just nod. All the fight in me is gone.

"And, I put the pot roast on for you," he says as he walks out the door.

I blow out a breath and then do as I was told. After my shower, I fix my make-up and hair just as Trevor has asked me to do. I dress in the clothes he's laid out for me, another June Cleaver dress, then go to the door and find that it's unlocked. I walk to the kitchen and see Dylan sitting at the table, still blindfolded and with his hands bound.

"Dylan," I say, rushing to him.

I pull the blindfold off and see that he has a black eye. "You hit him?" I turn to Mathis. He just shrugs but offers nothing. "Are you okay?" I ask Dylan, still checking him over.

"Yeah, I'm okay. I'm just tired."

"Are you hungry?"

He nods. "A little."

I jump up. "Where are you going?" Trevor asks.

"He's hungry. I want to fix him something."

Trevor shakes his head. "No, you do what you're told and be on your best behavior with my mother, and then I'll let you feed him." He turns to Lester and Travis. "Take him to the building."

"What? No! Please don't do this. I swear, I'll do whatever you want, Trevor. Just let him stay."

Trevor wraps his arm around my waist and pulls me to him. He kisses my forehead. "Prove it to me tonight and I'll let you tend to him."

"He's just a little boy," I say, tears pooling in my eyes and slipping down my cheeks as I watch them take Dylan away.

Trevor wipes my tears away. "If you don't obey, he'll be a dead little boy." I've never heard Trevor's voice so menacing. I shiver. "Mother will be here in forty minutes, get the table set and everything ready."

I nod my head, stepping into the kitchen. His mother arrives exactly forty minutes later. She isn't at all how I imagined her to be. I had envisioned the typical 1950's era woman, but she is dressed in a modern pants suit and talking on her cellphone. From the sound of it, she is possibly a lawyer. She promptly hangs up as she walks into the house.

"Trevor, what on earth is all this about? I have court in the morning." She looks around the house as if she's never been here before. Her eyes settle on me. "Who's this?"

Trevor wraps an arm around my waist. "This, Mama, is my fiancée Shayla. Shayla, this is my mother, Rachel McAdams."

She narrows her eyes at me. "Fiancée? I had no clue you were even dating."

"We went to college together and recently reconnected through work. She's given up her position so that we can be together. We didn't want to waste any more time, so we're getting married tomorrow."

She balks. "For heaven's sake, boy, she's probably after your money."

"That's not the case at all, Mother."

"We'll see." She sticks her hand out to shake mine. I slip mine into hers and she shakes it firmly. She squints her eyes at me and pulls me to her a little. "What happened to your face?"

Trevor pulls me back against his chest. "Mama," Trevor warns.

"She's a grown woman, Trevor. Let her answer for herself." She looks at me again. "What happened to your face?" I cup my cheek. I had forgotten about him slapping me. I stare at her for a moment too long. She nods her head. "I see. Trevor, a word." As she is pulling him away I swear she says, "You're just like your father."

She drags him into the living room. I can barely hear them.

"Did you hit that girl?"

"I'd never hurt her on purpose," Trevor responds. He sounds like a scared little boy.

"That's not what I asked you, Trevor. Did you hit her?"

There's a long pause. "Yes. She wouldn't listen and I got angry." I hear a loud smack.

"Sorry, I got angry," she says sarcastically, and walks back to me. "You don't have to put up with him hitting you. His father was the same way. I left him... then he died."

There's no remorse in her voice at all. She just stated it like it was a matter of fact. It makes me wonder if he died because of her family connections with the Mathis'.

I mumble, "Wish I could."

"What was that?" she asks.

I shake my head. "Nothing."

"Let's eat," Trevor offers quietly.

"Yes, fine," she states, not too impressed with him.

She takes a seat as dinner is served. It's very quiet, but every time I look up at Trevor, I have to fight back my smile. His mom hit him so hard there is still a faint hand-print on his cheek. I wonder what she'd do if she knew he beat me with a belt? I'm honestly so baffled at why he's like this. Obviously, his father was abusive, but did he want Rachel to be the epitome of the 1950's housewife? Was that why he hit her? His mom seems to be a very modern woman, not anything like this passive housewife Trevor wants me to portray. Is that why he wants me like this? He doesn't approve of his mother's chosen profession? She didn't nurture him enough? He seems almost submissive around her, like he's afraid of her. Maybe he is. An uneasy feeling creeps into my belly, things might be worse for me now than they were before. If she knows I'm here against my will, would she be willing to help me? She did say I didn't have to tolerate his abuse. I'm so confused and scared, especially now that they have Dylan.

Please hurry, Ryan!

CHAPTER SEVENTEEN

Ryan

"Mom, calm down. What do you mean he's gone?"

My mind is going through a thousand different scenarios. She takes a deep breath, but I can hear her sobbing.

"He's not here, Ryan. I checked on him last night around ten. He was sleeping. I made sure the windows were locked and left him be. I'm so sorry."

My heart sinks. They got him. I know they did.

"We're on our way, Mom." I numbly hang up the phone. The guys look at me for a long moment before I speak again. "They have Dylan."

Marsh responds, "We'll find him. Let's head over to your mom's. We may not get any evidence, but we can assess the scene." I nod, but make no move. "Ryan?"

I shake my head. "I can't do this anymore. I can't put my family in danger. What if they don't make it back? What if we aren't in time?"

"You can't think like that. The guys are up in the air. They'll have a plan. After we check out your mom's place, we'll head up to the airfield. We'll use that as our home-base. We'll be closer. We will save them."

Marsh puts so much bravado behind his words that I can't help but believe him. We pack up all of our gear in preparation to head to the airfield. Apparently, the guys found a house, a garage, and what looks like some underground bunkers. It was all built off-grid so there are no actual blueprints, but from what the guys could tell, it's solar powered with a backup generator. They spared no expense.

Tom comes out of his house as I'm locking mine. "Ready?" he asks.

"Yep."

I look behind him at Gail to see tears streaking down her face. She wipes them away quickly. She always tries to put on a tough face, but I know this is hard for her. I wrap her in a hug.

"I'll get them back, Gail. I swear."

"I know you will," she whispers against me.

"Will you reconsider going with my mom to my brother's?" I say as I look into her determined eyes.

"Oh, honey. I'll be fine. I'm going to my sister's, but as soon as Tom calls to say you're on the way home, I'm fixing everyone a big meal to celebrate."

I chuckle. "Of course you are. I love you." I give her a kiss and she squeezes me a little too tightly, but I don't mind.

"Love you too, Ryan. Bring my babies back to me."

"Will do, Mom."

I give her and Tom a few minutes alone as we load up the last bit of stuff. We wait for Gail to pull out of her driveway before we head off to my mom's. If I know my mother, she is stressed, upset, and likely blaming herself for this.

"Mom!" I call as I take the steps two at a time.

"Upstairs!" she calls back.

I take a left at the top and find her in my old bedroom, the one she's converted for Dylan. I scoop her up from the floor and sit her in the chair across from Dylan's bed. I kneel down in front of her, taking her hands in mine.

"I'll find him."

"I'm so sorry." She sobs.

I hug her to me. "Don't. This isn't your fault. I should have had your house watched. If anyone is to blame, it's me."

"I set the alarm on the house. I never heard anything," she says looking up at me. "You don't think he snuck out do you?"

"No, I really don't think so."

"Ryan." I turn to Marsh, he holds up a smashed origami fox. "It must have fallen when she was checking for Dylan. Found it under the pile on the floor." He points to the heap of blankets.

I curse and hold my hand out for it. He hands me a glove, then the fox. I carefully unfold the paper creature to find the word 'Soon'. I close my eyes to try and rein in my anger as well as my fear.

"What does that mean?" My mom asks.

I shake my head. "I guess he's ready to face me."

"There's nothing else to see here. We should get going," Marsh tells me.

I nod, but turn to my mom. "Nathan should be here soon. Will you be okay? I can wait for him."

"No, no. You go on. I'll be just fine. If they wanted me, they would have taken me as well. I'm so sorry, Ryan."

I hug her again. "I know, Mom. This isn't your fault. I'll get the ones responsible."

"Just be careful, please."

"I will."

As we load up in the car, my brother pulls up. I speak to him briefly, explaining the situation before leaving with my men. I'm confident that my brother won't let anything happen to our mom. He may travel a lot for work, but family always comes first for him. We've been on the road about twenty minutes when the chief calls me.

"Ryan, I don't know how to tell you this, but there was a body found out by the marina at Walnut Cove. It appears to be a teenage boy around fifteen. He matches your son's description."

"It's not Dylan," I say immediately. I know I'm probably in denial, but it can't be. Mathis would wait for me to be there, that's part of his game.

"I'd like you to come confirm that," the chief continues. "We found Dylan's backpack and his cell phone on the body."

"It's planted. I don't have time for this, Chief, do a DNA sample and you'll see it isn't Dylan."

Marsh hits mute. "I think we need to check it out. We're only about ten minutes from Walnut Cove."

"It's not him. This is a waste of time."

"Ryan, you put me in char …"

I glare at him. "Yeah and I'm revoking your title. We're not going!"

"Chief, I have a solid lead on Shayla. I'm certain Dylan is with her. Just run a DNA test. Dylan's results are already on file. The hard copy is in the filing cabinet in my office."

"Okay. If that's what you really want, but, Ryan, I've met Dylan and this kid looks just like him. We compared him to the picture in your office. I really think you need to come here."

My stomach drops and my heart beat picks up. I turn to Marsh. He must see the panic in my eyes.

"Chief, we'll be right there." Marsh disconnects the call. "Ryan, you know this isn't Dylan. You're right. He wouldn't take him to just kill him. He probably got someone who looked like Dylan.

"Marsh, the only kid I know who looks anything like my son, is my nephew, Danny. They could be brothers, it's so close."

"But your brother was just at your mom's."

I shake my head. "Danny is Paul's son. They live in Walnut Cove."

I stare at my phone, debating if I should call Paul or not. I decide to wait. I'll make sure before I stir up trouble. We arrive at the coroner's office less than fifteen minutes later. I hurry out of the car and jog up to the front door where the chief waits for me.

"Ryan, I want to warn you. This isn't a pretty sight. If you want to wait until he's cleaned up a bit I understand."

"No. I need to see him."

He nods solemnly and leads me into the building, down to the morgue. We walk over to the table where the body lies. I nod to let him know I'm ready. He pulls back the material and my heart falters. I know immediately that it's Danny.

"Oh, God!" I cry, shoving my fist in my mouth to stop myself from completely losing it.

I squat down on the floor, trying desperately to control myself. This may not be my son but this boy is my blood, my family. I watched him grow up, albeit mostly in photographs, but he is my blood nonetheless. He was such a great kid. He didn't deserve this. My brother and his wife don't deserve this.

"Ryan?" chief says. "Is this Dylan?"

I shake my head. I stand up and wipe my face. "It's Danny Jacobs, my nephew."

"I'm so sorry, Ryan." The chief pats my back. "There was one of those paper foxes left at the scene. Do you want it?"

I wipe at my eyes again and nod my head. I take the evidence bag containing the fox and hand it to Marsh. I can't deal with that right now. I have to tell my brother that his son is dead. I swallow thickly as I look towards Marsh.

"I need to call my brother."

"We'll give you a few minutes."

"Thank you."

Once they are out of the room, I stare blankly at my phone for a long while before I call my brother. I haven't talked to him in months. He answers on the first ring.

"Hey, baby bro."

I sniffle. "Paul, I need you to meet me downtown at the station."

His jovial tone changes immediately. "What's wrong?"

"It's Danny. Will you come down?"

"Of course I will, but what's wrong with him? Did he get into trouble? He went to a friend's house last night."

"He's not in trouble."

"I'm just down the block. I'm almost there."

"I'll meet you out front."

I head to the front door. We arrive at the same time.

"What's going on?" I can't hold back, tears fill my eyes and my lip quivers. He knows without me saying the words.

"No. No. Please no!"

"I'm so sorry."

"What happened? Where is he?"

I grip his shoulders and make him look at me. "I don't know what happened yet. They're investigating. They thought he was Dylan, so they called me.

He looks a little confused. "Was Dylan with him?"

"I'm not sure, but Dylan is missing. I have a lead, but we haven't found him yet."

"Danny is here?" he asks, his eyes filling with tears. "Can I see him?"

"Are you sure? He's ..." I trail off, not knowing what to say.

"I don't care. I need to see him."

I lead him to the room where Danny is. He stands there at first, just staring at the sheet covered body. After a long few minutes, he looks up at me with sadness in his eyes.

"Why did this happen?"

"Because of me," I tell him honestly.

"Why because of you?"

My heart flutters and my head hurts. I'm ruining my family. They'd all be better off without me in their lives. Because of my past, their futures are all at stake. My nephew, Dylan, and Shayla are proof that I'm a danger to those around me.

"Ryan, answer me!"

"When I was undercover in the FBI, I worked for a man named Mathis. I did a lot of things I'm not proud of to gain his trust, but I did them and I was able to take him down. He was in jail, but he escaped and now he is hell-bent on getting his revenge. He took Shayla with the help of his cousin, Trevor Daniels, and now they have Dylan as well," I say quickly.

"But you don't know for sure if this Mathis person has Dylan or if he actually did this to my Danny?"

"I know for a fact that Mathis has Dylan. He left his calling card."

"His calling card?"

"When he kills someone, he leaves an origami fox at the scene. It's kind of complicated." I pause, not wanting to give him too much information. The less he knows the better. "But ... I do know that it's him."

"But you don't know that he did this to Danny."

"No. I don't. It's not his MO at all; so this doesn't make any sense to me."

He sighs and runs his hand through his hair. "Ry, even if this Mathis guy is responsible, this isn't your fault. I want to blame you, I do, but you can't control what anyone does. I don't want this to be my son, but you didn't do this."

"But I feel responsible. Everyone around me is getting hurt," I say and then stop. This isn't really the time or place to hash out my feelings. I gesture to the body. "Do you want to see him?"

"No, not at all," he says looking away. "What I want is for him to be at his friend's house. I want to be picking him up in an hour." He turns to me and wipes his eyes. "I know you haven't been a dad for long, but you understand, don't you?"

"Yeah, I really do. I'd give anything right now to have Dylan with me and not in the clutches of that man."

"I hope that you find him before it's too late," he says solemnly.

"Me too."

Paul turns back to Danny and grabs the corner of the sheet. He slowly pulls it down, uncovering his son's beaten face. He says nothing, has no reaction, he just stares.

"Tell me this isn't real, Ryan" he says, his voice cracking. "Tell me that I don't have to call my wife and tell her that our baby is dead. Oh God, Danny, please, no, this can't be happening."

He leans over and kisses his son's forehead and starts sobbing uncontrollably. I don't know what to do when I can't even control my own tears. I wrap my arms around my brother and we cry together.

"Sorry to interrupt but we really need to head out," Marsh says, as he steps through the door.

"Go, Ryan. Find your son. I'll take care of mine."

"I'm so sorry, Paul." I give him another hug, run my hand over Danny's head and place a kiss to his forehead. "So sorry, Danny. I love you."

Marsh and I walk silently back to the SUV. Mathis will die for this. I don't care what I have to do. Even if I have to rot in jail for the rest of my life, he will pay for the heartache he has forced upon my family. He will not screw with my family any longer.

After about fifteen minutes on the road, Marsh says, "I talked to Jon. They've landed and the owner of the hangar has given them access to everything he has. Riley and Howard have been in communication and have some ideas on getting through the security system. We should be able to have everything ready to move no later than tomorrow night."

"Sounds good," I say distractedly. "Did you talk to the chief about Danny's case?"

"Yeah, there was a fox, as you know. When we opened it, there was a picture of Dylan. He was tied and blindfolded, but there were no background markings to determine where exactly he was. On the back it said 'he's next'."

Anger surges through me. "I don't care how, but Mathis is a dead man."

"Agreed."

About fifteen minutes later, we are pulling up to the hangar. It's small, but there's room for two small planes and a couple of tractors, and there's plenty of space for us to set up a command area. I thank the farmer, then head straight to Riley and Jon.

"Show me what you have."

"We went up there and found it in no time. The house and land are completely open for about five hundred feet encircling the house. That will really be the only obstacle, getting to the house unseen. It appears that there are six people on the compound as of right now. There is also some sort of underground area that we can't account for so we don't know if there are people inside, but as far as the house, there are three heat signatures, and then three in the building off to the side of the house. I believe they are holding Dylan in the outbuilding, keeping him separate from Shayla. We were able to get a visual confirmation that Trevor Daniels and Jason Mathis are on the compound. They were outside arguing for a while."

"Do you have any one else on visual?"

"No, we haven't seen any other movement. We were able to tap into their security systems, but there are only visuals of the outside."

Riley pulls up several screens on his computer, showing me the outside of the property. I really wish I could see Shayla and Dylan. I need to know they are okay.

"We were also able to go back and see when exactly he built the house and surrounding buildings. It looks like it began about twelve years ago. There's no documentation online to say if the underground bunkers were there or not, but my belief is that they were. I can't find anything to state that Daniels built them himself," Howard explains.

I sit heavily in the chair beside him. This means that Trevor has had this in the works since he met her.

"He's been building it for twelve years?" I ask Howard.

Howard nods and searches his computer for a moment. "This small outbuilding was the first thing he built. It's not on the property here." He points to a photo. "But it is here." He brings the two photographs up side by side. "It looks like we're looking at maybe a two month gap. So he built the outbuilding not long after inheriting the land."

"Ryan?" I turn to Marsh, who is walking up to us. "Mr. Hastings says that about three years ago, a man calling himself Michael

McAdams asked for permission to land a helicopter on his airstrip."

"You think Trevor built all this by flying it in and not using big contractors? Wouldn't he need tractors and equipment?" I ask.

"I think he probably did have equipment, but I think most of the build was done so slowly that no one would have even noticed. The property is so far off the main road that no one would have been around to see anything anyway."

"Have you found a road up to the property?" I turn to Riley and Howard.

Riley nods and plucks away at the computer before turning it to me. "Here is the only road in and out of this property. They have a gate and surveillance at the beginning of the driveway, and at the gate before you enter the open area. I'd say our best bet is to avoid that road until we need the ambulance and other service personnel, but that won't be until after we've remanded the suspects."

"I have several four-wheelers you can borrow. I won't have enough for everyone, but I can probably have my sons bring some out. They come out here often," Mr. Hastings offers.

"That would work. Thank you."

There really isn't a need for discretion, as we are about ten miles from where Trevor's property actually is. We'll have to leave them a mile or two away and go on foot, but it beats walking or running ten miles.

"No problem. I'm happy to help." Mr. Hastings says before leaving to call his sons.

The rest of the crew begins talking rapidly as we start to form our plan of attack. My cellphone rings and without checking the ID I answer.

"Hello."

"Ryan, how are you?" Mathis asks with a dark chuckle.

Anger surges through me. "You're a dead man, Mathis. Danny didn't deserve to die."

He guffaws. "Who does, but it was a nice surprise for me. I knew the minute I saw that picture what I needed to do."

"What picture?"

"The one in your room, of course."

My room? How and when was he in my room? "You were in my house?"

He huffs. "Of course, but that's beside the point. I have your boy."

"I know you do and you killed my nephew. Give Dylan and Shayla back alive right now and I might consider not killing you."

"You know I have nothing to do with Shayla."

"Give me Dylan then. I'll be dealing with Trevor as well."

He laughs. "You know it doesn't work that way. I was only calling as a courtesy to let you know he's safe."

"He won't be safe until I have him back. Let me speak to him."

"Fine," he says, and I hear movement over the phone. "Talk to your father, Dylan. Tell him all about the nice accommodations we have you in."

"Dad?"

"Dylan," I say as relief washes over me. "Are you hurt?"

"I'm okay. Dad, he killed Danny."

"I know. I'm sorry you had to go through that."

"It was awful, but listen, Dad. I saw Mom."

"Is she okay?" I ask.

I know there are a million things I should be asking him right now, but I know we'll be there soon and he'll be safe with me.

"Yeah. She has a bruise on her face, but she's okay. Doctor Daniels, he's the guy that took her."

"I know, buddy. I'll get you both soon." I hear Mathis in the background, laughing.

"I'm scared." Dylan sniffles.

My heart breaks. "I'm so sorry, son."

Dylan cries out in protest and Mathis laughs. "Times up. See, Ryan, he's fine."

"What do you want, Mathis?"

"For you to suffer. I want you to watch me rip apart your son. That would make my world perfect."

He hangs up. I stand there stewing. I'm so angry I can't think straight. All I can envision is me killing this man.

"Ry?" My eyes flash up to Marsh.

"He has to die, Marsh. I don't care who does it, but he can't be allowed to breathe another breath. He's killed my family and is holding the two people most precious to me hostage, threatening to kill them in front of me. I don't care what you have to do. Kill him!"

CHAPTER EIGHTEEN
Shayla

Trevor's mom leaves as soon as she's finished eating dinner. She doesn't seem concerned with anything he has to say to her. She actually holds her hand up to him at one point so he'll stop speaking and tells him he's being ridiculous. She seems very cold. Before she walks out the front door, she turns to me.

"Shayla, dinner was very good. You follow directions well."

I sputter; I don't know what to say, but I don't have to worry about it because Trevor interjects.

"I made dinner. Shayla wasn't feeling well this morning."

She looks me over for a few seconds, then moves her eyes back to her son. "Well, she might feel better if you'd keep your hands off her. I swear I did not raise you to be like him."

Trevor immediately bristles. "I'm nothing like my father."

She looks around and gestures. "Really, because this house, her clothes, all of it is just what he wanted. A woman to wait on him hand and foot and to slap around if she didn't obey. This is exactly why I left your father."

"What? He died, Mom. He left us."

She only smiles at him. He doesn't seem to understand that he died because of what he did to her. I won't be the one to enlighten him.

"Aunty Rach!" Mathis bellows from the back door.

She doesn't look surprised to see him. "Ah, you got out. I never followed up with Clint." She hugs him and kisses his cheek. She's much more affectionate with her nephew than her son.

He snorts. "You have your boy do your bidding but then don't check to be sure it was done?"

"Obviously he did his job. You should really be more discrete." She chastises him like he just ate the last piece of pie, not killed two people, maybe even more.

He laughs. "Now, that's no fun. Why rush off?"

"I have court. Make sure your cousin doesn't slap her around anymore."

"Of course, Trevor never did know how to treat a lady." He slugs Trevor in the arm hard. Trevor just glares, but says nothing.

"Well, I'd tell you two to behave, but I know that won't happen. Just try to keep yourselves out of jail."

She kisses them both on the cheek before exiting the house. I stand there staring at the floor, unsure of what I should do. I don't want to anger either of them, especially now that Dylan is here. Mathis and Trevor talk quietly for a few minutes. I can't hear them but do catch the words Ryan and close. I really hope that means Ryan will be here soon. Trevor moves away from Mathis and grabs my arm.

"Come."

He tugs me along, not giving me a chance to obey his order. He shoves me into my room and my heartbeat accelerates. What's he going to do to me? He stands before me with his hands on his hips, staring at me.

"In the closet, there's a white garment bag. It's a wedding dress. Clean up and put it on. We're doing this wedding now."

"What? No! No! I don't want to marry you!" I scream at him. He growls and lunges towards me. I see him coming so I'm able to dodge him. "I don't want you, Trevor."

We're running circles around the bed and other furniture, but he's too fast for me and catches me as I try to dart out of the door. He pulls me tightly against his chest and angrily huffs into my ear.

"You will do what I say or I will let Jason start cutting parts off your son. How do you think he'll play football with no hands?"

"Please, no. Leave him alone."

"Marry me."

"Fine. Fine! Whatever you want, just leave Dylan alone."

I sob. I hate him so much. He kisses my cheek and releases me.

"Good. There's one more thing I need you to do." He pulls a cellphone out of his pocket. "I want you to call Ryan and tell him."

I look at him confused. "Tell him what?"

"That you don't love him, you want me, and that we're getting married."

That's crazy. He'll know that I'm lying and I think Trevor knows that. I think he just wants me to say the words, to plant a seed of doubt in Ryan's mind. I don't want to do this, but I will in order to save Dylan.

"I'll do it, if you give me something in return."

He quirks an eyebrow at me. "I don't think you're in the position to make demands, but go on." He crosses his arms over his chest.

"Let Dylan come in the house. Let me keep him. Please." My eyes fill with tears. "Please."

"I'll consider it, but Jason probably won't go for that."

I wrap my arms around him. "Please."

I sob onto his chest. I don't care what I have to do to save my son. I'll do it. I'll do anything, even live with Trevor as his wife for the rest of my life if it means that Dylan is safe. Slowly his arms wrap around me. He sighs, kissing the top of my head.

"I'll talk to Jason."

"I'd like him to be at the wedding," I say quietly.

He pushes me away just enough to see my face. "You'll really marry me. No complaints?"

"Yes. I'll marry you. I'll … make love to you. Just please let me keep my son."

I lean up on my tiptoes and kiss him. I pour as much into it as I can, giving him what he wants in hopes that he'll give me what I want. He pulls back breathless and his eyes are heavy-lidded. Cupping my face, he smiles.

"I'll do what I can." He kisses me again. "Call him."

He hands me the cell. I take it, backing up to sit on the bed. I fight the tears burning my eyes. Taking several deep breaths, I dial his number.

"Hello?"

"Ryan?"

"Shayla! Oh, baby. It's so good to hear your voice. Can they hear me?"

"No."

"I'm close, baby. You just hang in there."

"I need to tell you something," I say, after Trevor glares.

"Of course. What is it? Is Dylan okay?"

"For now. Uh, listen. I was just calling to tell you that I've decided to marry Trevor, so you don't need to worry about me anymore."

"What? You don't mean that." He's obviously upset. I thought for sure he'd see through it.

"I do. I think you and I have grown too far apart over the years. Trevor and I have a lot in common, we're more compatible."

He laughs humorously. "He's making you do this. Okay, baby. Tell me whatever it is he wants you to say. We're coming to get you soon."

I blink back the tears. I know he won't believe me, but to say the words is going to kill me. I don't want the possible last words I say to him to be that I don't love him, even if he knows it's a lie, but there is no other way. I have to protect Dylan.

"I called to tell you that Trevor and I are getting married tonight. You don't need to find me. I'm where I want to be … I love him. I'm sorry, Ryan, but I … I don't love you anymore."

He blows out a long breath. "Married tonight?"

"Yes, we're getting married tonight and … starting our life together."

I'm not sure how to imply that Trevor plans to consummate the marriage. I just hope that Ryan will understand.

"What?" he says angrily. He's obviously picked up on my very subtle implication. "He's going to rape you?"

Trevor jerks the phone out of my hand. I'm not sure if he's heard him or not. He listens to whatever Ryan is saying, his posture becoming more tense and adversarial.

"I'm not raping her. She has agreed to marry me and all that comes along with being a wife." He hangs up.

He pulls me into his arms. I can't control my emotions. I'm bawling like a baby. "Shh. It'll be okay, Shayla. Take a shower, get ready, and I'll see that Dylan eats and gets to stay in the house." He kisses my forehead. "I love you, Shayla."

"I love you too." That's the absolute biggest lie that's ever come out of my mouth. Trevor smiles broadly.

"I know you don't mean that, but it's nice to hear all the same."

I flop down on the bed as soon as the door clicks shut. What am I going to do? I don't want to marry him. I don't want to have his babies. If he really makes me do this, it's a huge possibility. I'm not on birth control. My ex and I were trying to have a baby, but it hadn't happened before he decided to leave me. Maybe I can't have any more kids. I mean, we'd tried for over a year. But then again, we both worked a lot and we didn't really time or plan anything. Oh, please, God. Please, let Ryan get here before tonight. Tears flow freely down my face. There's nothing I can do to stop this. If I fight, they'll hurt Dylan. I can't let anything happen to him.

"Come on, Shayla, you can do this!"

Before I let too much time get away from me, I shower and prepare myself for the world's most unloving and unwanted wedding. I'm just putting the finishing touches on my makeup when Trevor comes back into the room.

"You know its bad luck to see the bride before the wedding," I tell him.

He just smiles at me. "I don't believe in luck. You look beautiful." He kisses my cheek.

The dress isn't terrible. It's a white tea length dress with a sweetheart neckline and is covered with a lace overlay. The lace comes to the bottom of my neck, the sleeves are short. Not exactly a winter dress, not that it matters. There's a long veil that I've attached to the top of my head. My hair is pinned back in a low bun, with curled tendrils hanging around my face. My make-up is a little bolder with a pink lip and blush, making my bruise look less prominent. I do look pretty, I just wish that it wasn't for him.

"Let me get your shoes." He smiles as he rushes to the closet, pulling a pair of simple white pumps off the top shelf of the closet.

"Thanks."

I put them on and follow him out of the room and into the living room. Nothing looks different. The only things in the room that have anything to do with a wedding are him and me. I almost expected more.

"Where's Dylan?" I ask.

Trevor frowns. He turns to Mathis with a raised eyebrow. "I didn't think you'd want to be married with a dirty kid giving your bride away. I sent him to change and shower."

"Right. Good idea." Trevor seems nervous.

"Mom?" I turn to see Dylan, standing in the foyer looking lost and sad, but he does look better having showered and changed out of his ratty pajamas. I rush to him, throwing my arms around him. "Please don't do this," he whispers.

I try to keep my tears back. "I have to. I can't let them hurt you."

"But Dad ..."

"He'll understand."

"Yes, your mother has already explained to Ryan that I'm who she chooses." The pride in Trevor's voice is sickening.

Dylan looks at me questioningly and I nod my head. "Why? Why do you want someone who is holding you against your will? Dad said you seemed strange on the phone that one time, but I never thought it was because you wanted to be here."

Oh, Dylan. You're too young to understand. I want so badly to tell him. To explain to him, that if I had the choice, I'd be running with him out of this place and away from these horrible men. But I've seen the horrible things Mathis can do, and I won't allow that to happen to my son. If this is what it takes to keep him safe then I'll do it willingly.

"Do you trust me?" I ask him.

"Of course I do." His reply is immediate, with no hesitation.

"Then trust me when I say, I know what I'm doing. That your father understands."

He seems to have a slight understanding as he looks at Trevor, then back to me. He hugs me again and whispers, "You don't want to."

We pull apart and I nod slightly. I don't think Trevor heard him, but I don't want to make any huge movements to tip him off either.

"Can we get on with this?" Trevor huffs impatiently.

I take Dylan's arm and we walk into the living room to stand before Trevor and Mathis.

Mathis smiles evilly as he says, "Who gives this woman to this man?" He looks at Dylan with a raised eyebrow.

"What? Me? No, no way. I'm not agreeing to give my mom to this psychopath!"

Trevor growls and backhands Dylan sending him staggering back.

"Dylan!" I cry, grabbing him and pulling him to me before he can fall.

Trevor grips my arm tightly. "He will do what he's told or he will be punished."

In a panic, I grab Dylan and make him look at me. "Please. Just say the words. You don't have to mean it, just say it. Please."

I see my own stubborn look on his face. His jaw is clinched as he says, "No, this isn't right."

Trevor looks around the room for a moment, before grabbing a belt he'd discarded one night after beating me with it. He's livid. I stand in front of Dylan with my arms wide.

"No, please. He'll do it. He'll say the words."

"No, I won't!" Dylan insists.

I glare at him. "Dylan James. Stop this. Just say it."

"Mom, you can't be serious?"

There's a loud snap as the belt swishes through the air and lands across Dylan's shoulders. Dylan cries out in pain as he looks to me in abject horror. He has never been hit a day in his life.

"Trevor, don't!"

I do my best to try and block my son, but Trevor's brandishing the belt as if it's some sort of whip. He's hitting anything he can reach, even me. I shove Dylan down and out of the way as I charge at Trevor.

"Stop! Leave him alone!" I scream, jumping on him and trying to wrestle the belt out of his grip.

Trevor shoves me off him, tossing me across the floor like a discarded doll before attacking Dylan again. Dylan screams, covering his face with his hands. I move to try and grab Trevor again, but Mathis wraps his arms around my waist and pulls me against his chest. His mouth presses by my ear as I struggle to get free.

"Stop fighting. You're not going to save him."

"Let me go, Jason. Let me go! He's going to kill him."

Mathis chuckles. "No, he's not. I won't let it go that far. I can't have my fun ruined."

I struggle more, kicking, hitting, and biting anything I can reach. It does me no good. Mathis is too strong. He simply laughs at my struggle while I watch Dylan cower on the floor, trying to protect himself from a mad man.

"Trevor! Please stop. I'll marry you; I'll even make love to you, just, stop hurting my son."

Trevor finally pulls back. He turns to me, breathing heavily, and throws the belt across the room. His eyes look wild and dark, like a caged animal ready to strike as soon as he's released. He grabs Dylan and hoists him up from the floor.

"Say the words." The growl in Trevor's voice is deadly.

"I do. I give her away." Dylan is crying and shaking with fear.

"Good. Now that that's settled, lets continue."

Mathis reads through the standard vows. I can't focus. I hear nothing, but speak when I'm told, and before long Trevor is smiling and kissing me. I don't respond, until he pinches my arm hard.

"Introducing Doctor and Mrs. Daniels," Mathis says with a flourish, even taking a bow to us like we're royalty.

He thinks this whole situation is hilarious. I wish I had a knife, I would kill him now. Him and Trevor both deserve to die. I turn just as Dylan collapses onto the floor.

"Dylan!"

I'm immediately in doctor mode as I check him over. I roll him onto his back and unbutton his shirt, making sure his airway isn't restricted. To my surprise, Trevor also goes into doctor mode. He pulls out his pen light and checks Dylan's eyes, then examines his chest, stomach and sides.

"I think he's fine. He's bruised, but nothing is broken."

"Internal bleeding," I say.

He rolls his eyes. "I didn't hit him hard enough for that and you know it."

"Will you help me get him to my room?" I plead but when he doesn't say anything I add, "You said that he could stay in the house."

"Fine."

Trevor bends and picks Dylan up. I can tell it's hard for him, Dylan isn't little and he's dead weight, but he manages to get him to the room and on the bed. I grab a rag from the bathroom and wipe his face and neck. There are big, red, angry welts covering his arms, face, chest, and probably his back and legs. Thankfully, his clothing helped to soften the blows so there's no bleeding or broken skin. I kiss his forehead.

"I'm so sorry." Trevor grabs my arm and pulls me away from him. "No, I want to stay with him."

"No, you're staying with me. I'm your husband now. This wedding will be legally binding as of tomorrow morning. Ryan will have no legal reason to break in here and rescue you."

I roll my eyes. "Do you really think he needs a legal reason? Besides, you kidnapped his son. That's reason enough, even if I chose to stay with you."

He looks as if he'd never thought about that. What a stupid fool. He's getting too cocky with his plan. He thinks he's invincible. I hate to break it to him, but he's not. Ryan will end him for what he's done.

"It doesn't matter. You're mine now, and even if he gets you back, I'll never divorce you. You'll never be able to be with him like you really want to be. You'll always be mine." The evil look in his eyes terrifies me.

"I'll never be yours," I mutter.

He squeezes my arm. "You already are."

With a quick, sharp jerk, he hauls me out of the room and across the hall to his. He shoves me inside and slams the door behind me, locking it. I grab the knob and pull on it but it doesn't budge.

"Where are you going? Let me out, Trevor. If I'm your wife, I should be able to roam around my own house!" I yell, banging on the door.

There's no reply. I rip the stupid veil off my head and throw it on the ground, and promptly stomp on it until it's a dirty tattered mess of organza and toile. I'm so angry. I take off my heels and throw them as hard as I can. I start to grab anything I can reach and throw it against the wall and window. I hate him and want him dead. I slowly slide down the door, letting go of all my emotions. My entire body shakes with the strength of my sobs. I want my baby. I want Ryan. I want to go home.

"Ryan, where are you?" I mumble through my tears.

I don't know how long I sit there. It's probably only been ten or fifteen minutes, but it definitely could be longer. I've lost all sense of time. The door suddenly pushes against me, but I don't move. I don't want him in here and I'd rather die than let him in voluntarily.

"Shayla, move away from the door."

"No."

He growls. "Shayla Daniels, move now."

"I'm keeping my maiden name."

I shove back, slamming the door shut. He shoves hard on the door, causing me to fall forward. I just lie there. Whatever is going to happen, I'm not going to make it easy for him.

"Get up." I don't move. He picks me up, walks over to the bed and drops me onto it. "You're being a petulant child." I say nothing. I continue to lie there like a lump. He sighs dramatically. "If I let you check on Dylan will you perk up?"

I look at him. "Yes."

He smiles at me. "Come on then."

He holds his hand out, and I take it without thought. He pulls me up from the bed, kisses me, and then tugs me along behind me. He unlocks the door to Dylan's room. He's sitting up in bed eating what looks like a cookie. I rush to him, throwing my arms around his neck.

"Are you okay?"

"Yeah, I'll be fine. He brought me milk and cookies. That's weird, right?"

"Yeah, it's weird."

Dylan wipes at my face. "Are you okay?"

"Yeah. I was just upset because he wouldn't let me stay with you."

"He didn't hurt you?"

I shake my head. "No, he didn't. But I'm more concerned about you."

Dylan looks back at the closed door, then to me. "How long do you think he'll let you stay in here?"

"I'm not sure."

"I wish Dad would hurry and find us."

"Me too, was he getting close to finding me?"

"Dad wasn't very close, last I heard. We got into a huge fight and I stayed at Grandma Penny's. That's where they got me."

"What were you and Dad fighting about?"

"It was dumb, Mom," he says looking down.

Hmm, not sure what's going on with the two of them, but I can't deal with that now. I don't say anything for a little bit, trying to rein in my worry and concern for not just Dylan and Ryan, but about all of Ryan's family. How far will Mathis go to hurt him?

"Was Grandma Penny okay?"

"She is, as far as I know, but Danny …" Dylan stops, tears begin to form in his eyes. I hug him to me.

"What happened to Danny?"

"That guy, the one who Dad called The Fox, killed him."

I gasp, Danny was just a kid, just like my Dylan. How could he hurt a young boy, someone who can't defend themselves against attack. This is crazy.

"Mom, he beat the crap out of him and then shot him in the head. He did it in front of me. I tried not to watch, but he made me. Every time I looked away, he'd hit me. I should have done more to help Danny."

I squeeze him tighter as he cries. "Oh, Dylan, none of this is your fault. You did everything you could. I'm so sorry you had to see that; that you had to lose your cousin like that."

"I don't know how he got there. I woke up and we were tied together, then the next thing I knew he was dead."

I hold my son as we both mourn for the loss of his cousin. This whole thing has gone way too far. I hope to God that Ryan ends him soon. The door to the room opens and my heart sinks.

"Times up."

I turn to see Trevor smiling and looking like he's won the lottery. My heart sinks to my stomach and I fight the urge to vomit.

"Now, Shayla, or I'll get Jason."

I stand and kiss Dylan's cheek. "Please do what they say." He nods, gripping my hand tightly. "I'll be okay, Dylan. I love you."

"I love you, too."

After one last kiss to his forehead, I follow Trevor out of the room to face my fate, but in the back of my mind, I'm praying that Ryan finds me in time.

CHAPTER NINETEEN
Ryan

We set to work forming our plan of attack. Jon is on the phone with one of the guys from his office, arranging to have his helicopter delivered. We probably won't need it until the rescue is about over, but I want it there in case Shay or Dylan have to be airlifted out of here, heaven forbid.

"I think we can do a recon at dusk. We want to be sure we know exactly what we're going into. There may be areas we aren't seeing clearly on the monitors."

Marsh doesn't look up from the computer as he speaks. He glances at Linc, pointing out something on the map, then finally turns to me. He can see the anger in my expression. I want to go now, the longer we wait, the longer my family is with those psychopaths!

"I'm sorry, Ryan. This is what we need to do. We have to keep our men safe. We can't rescue Dylan and Shayla if we go in halfcocked and end up dead. I know this is tough, but I'll do everything I can, just like they were my own family. I swear that to you, Ryan."

I know he's right, but hearing that Shayla and our son have to stay with these monsters for a moment longer than necessary makes my skin crawl. Who knows what Daniels is doing to her? He wants her, wants her as his girlfriend, that much I know. Would he stoop so low as to rape her? God, I hope not.

As far as Mathis is concerned, I'm not sure what he'll do to Dylan. His sole reason for taking him is to torture me by hurting him. Is he okay right now? That phone call didn't make it sound like he was okay, which I'm sure is exactly what Mathis wanted. I shove my hands in my pockets, needing to do something with them.

"I know you're doing what you think is best, but don't expect me to sit by and do nothing. I'm not a civilian. I know what I'm doing. I don't want us going in unprepared. Losing one of our men may cost my family their lives. Don't worry, my head is clear, Marsh."

"Good. Now, get to work. We need you on weapons. Go help Paul."

I salute him, earning me a salute that wasn't so nice, but it breaks some of the tension in the room.

"I've set up these tables for weapons. We've got an overload of guns, but depending on who they call in, we might just need them." Paul lays two shotguns on the table, then turns to pick up two more.

"I'm sure there are more people at the property than we know about. Those bunkers worry me," I say, lifting a big box full of ammo to the table to sort.

"Exactly, I think Marsh called in the local police. Plus, we have your officers and the neighboring counties are sending men. I think we'll have at least thirty by tomorrow."

"That should be plenty." We could be walking into an ambush. Mathis has hundreds of people under his control. I pick up another crate to unload. "Uh, I don't see the point of these." I hold up a taser.

Paul smirks. "You know, you don't have to go in with guns blazing to win the war."

I snort. "If you're doing it right, you do." He shakes his head at me.

"Ryan!" I turn towards Marsh. "We have movement."

I drop the taser back into the crate and run over to the monitors. On the screen are two men, dragging Dylan from the house into the storage building.

"Talk me down, man, because right now I want to bust in there and get my kid." My anger is boiling so close to the surface that I'm not sure I can contain it. Marsh grabs my arm.

"We'll get him. At least we now know that he's alive and walking. We'll move in soon. It's about an hour before dusk. Let's get ready to do some recon."

"Yeah, I need to do something. Suit up," I order, not really caring that Marsh is the one in charge.

By the time we're ready to move out, a car is pulling down the long driveway. It looks like your standard rental car, which I'm sure Riley can trace. Marsh walks over to both Riley and Howard and taps the monitor where the vehicle is moving.

"Find out who it is and keep us posted. If they leave, we'll stop them for questioning," Marsh instructs Riley and Howard, then turns to the rest of us. "Ryan, with me to the west. Paul and Jon, head east. Linc and Smith, north. Jessica and Matthew, head toward the driveway entrance. You're both in uniform so you can stop the occupant and bring them in. We won't be able to keep them long, but maybe we can get some information. Sound off."

"I'd like to go," Tom says.

"Not this time. I want you to stay here and guard these guys." Marsh thumbs over his shoulder to Riley and Howard.

Reluctantly, Tom agrees. I know he just wants to get to Shayla and Dylan, but we can't risk him getting overwhelmed with emotion and reacting instead of thinking with his head. I'm sure that's why Marsh put me with him. He doesn't trust me. Of course, I don't blame him.

We each sound off in our coms, and when we have confirmation that everything is working perfectly, we head over to the four wheelers and set off. We can only go about six of the ten miles between us and the compound just to be sure no one hears or sees us, but it's better than walking the whole ten. We stop near a small open area. There's enough tree and shrub coverage to cover the ATVs in case someone should come near here.

"Promise me, that even if you see Dylan or Shayla, you won't do anything. We need to be sure we go in prepared so we don't end up killing them or us."

"I'm not a civ ..."

"Yes, I know. You've said that enough times. It doesn't matter if you're a civilian or not, Ryan. These are two people you love, people you'd give your life for. That can make anyone react, instead of act. You know this."

"I'm good. I want them home safe."

Marsh nods in response and we start our walk, guns at the ready. Mathis knows we'll be coming. There's no telling how far he'll be sending his men out or how many he has employed. If he pulled from his family's resources, then he could have a hundred for all we know. A noise to our left causes us to pause and assume fighting stance.

"A deer," I breathe in relief.

Marsh chuckles. "I feel like an army is going to jump out at any minute. I'm having some serious flashbacks."

"I totally understand. The desert is almost easier than all these dead leaves and evergreens. There are more places to hide out here."

"Exactly. Ryan, over there, it looks like they have an electric fence about 30 yards up."

I look and see a bright yellow anchor attaching the wire to the almost invisible brown metal post. Marsh radios the others, and it looks like they've run into the fence as well.

"Eagle to base. Come in base."

"Reading you loud and clear, Eagle, go ahead," Riley answers.

"Looks like we have an electric fence around the perimeter about a mile out. Over."

"I read you, Eagle. Shutting power to fence in three, two, one. Proceed with caution. Over."

Marsh reaches out and touches the fence, confirming that it's dead. "Proceeding. Eagle, over and out."

"Confirm proceeding. Hawkeye, over and out."

Marsh snorts. Riley did this crap when we were in the desert. He signed off with different handles, trying to persuade us to call him something other than base.

"Eagle to base. This isn't MASH. Over and out."

We can hear Riley's laughter, but he doesn't respond. We carefully cross the fence and slowly make our way towards the compound. A few minutes later, Riley is buzzing us again.

"Base to Eagle, come in. Over."

Marsh and I stop and look at each other. "Base, this is Eagle. Over."

"We have confirmation on the driver. Over."

"Roger, base."

"It's Rachel McAdams. Over."

My face burns red. Of course it is. My mind is spinning with possibilities. What is Trevor up to that he brought his mother here? Is she in on this as well? Marsh looks at me and touches my shoulder. Squeezing it and trying his best to focus me on the task at hand.

"Copy that, base."

"Ryan, let's deal with what's going on right now. We'll address why McAdams is here when she's stopped, okay?"

I simply nod. "Come on, let's go. I need to find my son."

We continue to make our way towards the outbuilding. Up close, it doesn't look like much, just an average windowless fourteen by twenty wooden storage shed. It sits about five-hundred feet from the tree line, like everything else on the compound. On the map though, it's near one of the possible entrances to the underground bunker, but looking at it now, there's no sign of anything that could be a possible door.

"The light is on," I whisper to Marsh. We're still in the cover of the trees, but we have a clear view of the building.

He pulls out his heat seeking googles. "It looks like there are three people in there."

"That's where they're probably keeping Dylan, at least until Rachel leaves."

"Pres to Eagle. I have a visual on Doc," Linc reports.

I growl lowly. "Eagle to Pres, do you have a visual on Mama Doc? Over."

"Affirmative. Mama Doc appears alive and well. No sign of Cub. Over."

Marsh points to the left and we slowly make our way so we can see the front door of the outbuilding. Lester Harvey is sitting on a chair outside the open door.

"Can you see Dylan?" I ask Marsh.

He shakes his head, and hands me some binoculars. "There's another guy inside. Similar build to Harvey, he could be one of the guys who got away during Dylan's accident."

I continue looking around, but before I can see anything else, the door to the building slams shut and Lester takes off running through the yard.

"Eagle to all. Report!" We hear shots fired in the distance.

Paul comes back, sounding out of breath. "Chopper has been shot. I repeat, Chopper has been shot. On the move. Over."

Marsh curses. "Fall back. I repeat. Fall back."

We take off back to the base. I don't know what happened, but we are hightailing it on the ATV's. As soon as we are inside the hangar, there is a lot of commotion happening as Jon gets patched up. He's fine, with barely a scrape on his arm. Once Jon's good to go, we all gather around Marsh to discuss a revised plan to get in there and get my family back.

"All right, we know the property is minimally secured. When you two," Marsh says, pointing to Paul and Jon, "tripped the sensor near the gate, only Harvey responded. That doesn't mean they won't or haven't called some in, but we'll be able to spot them if they do. I think our best plan will be to move in before dawn. That way, if he has called for reinforcements, we'll at least know what we're facing. I've already spoken to several of the local police stations. All of them have volunteered their services and can be here in a few hours."

"Incoming!" Riley yells.

We all jump up and move over to the computers. Two SUVs pull into the compound and head behind the outbuilding. Eight dark figures get out of the vehicles and head into the place where they are keeping my son. Curses fly from everyone.

"McAdams is leaving." Riley picks up his walkie-talkie. "Base to Turner and Hooch, come in. Over."

"We copy, but I really don't like that name. Over," Jessica says.

"You're Turner, beautiful." Now is not the time for his flirting. I'm about to blow my top, when he continues on task. "Target on the move. I repeat, target on the move. ETA two minutes. Over."

"Roger that, base. Over."

My cellphone rings and I step away to answer it. "Hello?"

"Ryan?" Shayla's voice rushes over me. It fills me with both relief and dread.

"Shayla! Oh, baby. It's so good to hear your voice. Can they hear me?"

"No." She sounds close to tears. I want to tell her my whole plan, to reassure her we're coming, but I won't.

"I'm close, baby. You just hang in there."

She clears her throat. "I need to tell you something."

I swear she's crying. Her voice is shaky. I look over at Marsh. He points to the computer, mouthing they are recording the conversation. I give him a thumbs up, then go back to Shayla.

"Of course. What is it? Is Dylan okay?"

"For now." The cryptic tone in her voice gives me chills. "Uh, listen. I was just calling to tell you that I've decided to marry Trevor, so you don't need to worry about me anymore."

Not worry about her anymore? That's absurd! Wait a minute, did she say marry? She can't marry him. She won't marry him!

"What? You don't mean that." I feel as if my heart has been ripped out of my chest and trampled.

"I do. I think you and I have grown too far apart over the years. Trevor and I have a lot in common, we're more compatible."

She pauses several times, taking deep breaths. A light bulb clicks in my head. She's being forced to do this. I can't help the laugh that escapes me.

"He's making you do this. Okay, baby. Tell me whatever it is he wants you to say. We're coming to get you soon."

She inhales loudly, it's like a sigh of relief. Her voice trembles. "I called to tell you that Trevor and I are getting married tonight. You don't need to find me. I'm where I want to be ... I love him. I'm sorry, Ryan, but I ... I don't love you anymore."

That was a lot harder to hear than I thought it would be.

"Married tonight?"

"Yes, we're getting married tonight and ... starting our life together."

Starting their life together. Starting their life together. Suddenly, my heart stops for a moment as realization sets in. He's plaining to consummate their marriage? Over my dead, rotting corpse he will.

"What?"

I'm so angry. If it wouldn't risk hers or Dylan's life, I'd be on the ATV riding full speed to kill that sorry excuse for a man. I state the obvious for confirmation.

"He's going to rape you? Shayla, you are not to let that monster touch you. Do you understand me? He will not rape you."

"I'm not raping her. She has agreed to marry me and all that comes along with being a wife," Trevor shouts into the phone and then the line goes dead.

I turn to my men. "We need to move out ASAP."

Marsh holds his hands up. "I understand your need to act quickly, but it won't do us any good to run in there with guns blazing and no plan. We will rescue them, but we need to be together on this."

"We aren't waiting. He'll rape her!"

"We have a little time. Jessica and Matthew just brought McAdams to the local police station for questioning in Trevor's disappearance. The only thing she will say is that she had dinner with her son and his fiancée. She knows nothing about a kidnapping or that Trevor's involved. She won't tell us the fiancée's name. Of course, we know who it is."

"I'm going." I grab my coat and head for the door. Marsh grabs my arm.

"And do what?"

"I'm a cop. I'll question her."

"You're a cop without a badge. She knows who you are." I don't need Marsh's reminder. I didn't forget.

"It doesn't matter. I want to question her. If she knows when they're getting married, then we can plan our attack."

"Fine, but I'm going with you."

"Whatever."

I storm out and jump into the closest SUV. We make it to the station in fifteen minutes and we're led back to the holding room moments later. I don't take time for niceties. I'm done playing games. I get right in her face.

"Tell me when your son plans to marry my girlfriend."

She looks at me with her head cocked to the side as if she's trying to figure me out. "It seems to me you might be a bit delusional."

"I'm not delusional. Trevor kidnapped and beat Shayla, he's going to force her to marry him and then he'll rape her."

She laughs. I stiffen, ready to fight. Marsh lays a hand on my shoulder in warning. "As far as I could tell, Trevor's fiancée is over the moon for him and there of her own free will. Why would he invite me to dinner if he were hiding her?"

"Delusional, remember?"

"Well, the point is, you have no reason to be holding me, Mr. Jacobs. So, if you'll excuse me. I do need to be heading home. I have a very early morning." She stands and straightens her shirt.

"I know you have something to do with Mathis' release. You won't get away with your part in this," I warn.

She smiles sardonically. "I have no idea what you're talking about. I've not seen or talked to my nephew since his indictment."

She shoulders her purse and pushes forward to the door. Jessica allows her to pass after a nod from Marsh. Unable to contain my anger any longer, I punch the wall. Marsh grabs hold of me, pulling me back before I do any serious damage to the station or myself.

"Calm down. We need to get back to base. Who knows what damage this is going to cause for us. She'll probably be on the phone warning him."

"We should have just questioned her as if she were anyone else," Matthew says.

I look at him and glare. "That was what you were supposed to do. This is really on you." I push my finger in his chest and storm out of the station.

"Ryan!" Marsh yells.

I turn to see him running towards me. I've made it about five hundred feet down the road from the station; he grabs my arm and jerks me to a stop.

"This has to stop. You run off every time something doesn't go your way. This isn't helping the case. We have a plan. We have people. We will get them. We're leaving at four a.m. Pull yourself together or I'll chain you to the wheels of the plane and you'll stay behind."

"I'm not running away. I'm blowing off steam so I don't murder someone. I'll be fine on the mission. I won't let anything cloud my judgement where they are concerned."

"I hope not. Let's get back. Riley called. They had a visual on Dylan again."

I smack his chest. "Why didn't you say that in the first place? Was he okay?"

"He appeared to be, they walked him back into the house."

"Good. Let's hurry. I swear I'm fine."

"You better be. I mean it, Ryan; I'll chain you up if you give me any more problems."

"Yeah, yeah!"

CHAPTER TWENTY

Shayla

Trevor shuts and locks Dylan's door, then turns and smiles at me. He runs a finger down my cheek and I have to fight back the urge to be sick.

"You are so beautiful."

I try to smile at his compliment, but the worry and fear running through me is overwhelming. I feel like I'm shaking all over, as if I'll come out of my skin at any minute.

"Everything checked, boss." I jump, startled at the sound of Travis' voice; I turn to see him looking at Trevor.

"Good. Make sure one of you stays in here at all times. Jason will be back shortly. If something comes up, get him. Tonight is the honeymoon for me and my missus." I shiver in disgust. He mistakes my action for excitement and tugs me into his side as he kisses my forehead. "Patience, my dear."

He talks to Travis for a few more minutes, but I don't hear anything he says. The smell of sweat and his strong cologne clog my mind and make me feel nauseated. Trevor guides me across the hall to his bedroom, sweeping me up into his arms and carrying me across the threshold. He looks positively ecstatic. I want to bash the stupid smile off his face, but fear has me frozen. He sets me on my feet.

"I'm so happy, Shayla. You just don't understand what your cooperation has done for me. You've made me the happiest man alive."

He pulls me to him, kissing me. I can't respond. I want to, only so he doesn't hurt Dylan, but my body is too afraid, nervous, scared, and a whole slew of other emotions I can't describe. He stops and looks at me.

"Kiss me." His lips meet mine again, but I still can't respond. He growls, gripping my arms, digging his nails in. I cry out in pain. "Do what you are told. I'd hate to have to punish Dylan for your insolence."

"I'm sorry. I'm just nervous, and scared."

His expression changes from anger to understanding, almost caring. "Don't be afraid. I'm not going to hurt you. It's not like you're a virgin."

"It doesn't matter if I'm not a virgin, Trevor. This is all against my will. That's not okay."

The anger comes back full force. "You're my wife. I'll make love to you like any good husband would."

"But I don't want to make love to you." I know I should shut my mouth, but I don't. "None of this is what I want. This is what you're forcing me to do. Don't you see how wrong that is?" I'm being sincere. I want him to see this is wrong. I cup his face in my hand. "If you want me to do this willingly, you have to give me time."

His eyes soften slightly, fear setting in. "I don't have time, Shayla. Someone tried to break into our gate today. They're getting closer. I don't have time," he repeats again with desperation.

He runs his hand through his hair, tugging it harshly. My heart soars with joy at the thought of Ryan getting closer to me. Oh, please, God. Let him find us in time.

"Is that where Mathis is?"

"Yes, he's dealing with it right now. Luckily, we'd already called in reinforcements. We were able to get at least one of them, but I don't know anything else." My heart sinks.

"Killed them?" I can feel my eyes burning.

"No, wounded. Let's not worry about that now. I know you are just trying to distract me. I need you, Shayla. It's a deep-seated feeling that won't stop, it won't go away. I need you as my wife, my partner, and I honestly don't care how I get you. The need is too strong. I don't want to take you by force. I want you to do this with me willingly, but honestly, it's beyond the point of reason now. I will have you and I'll have you tonight, right now."

A loud commotion outside the door startles us both.

"Mom!" I hear Dylan scream.

I'm out the door before Trevor has a chance to stop me. "Dylan!"

Mathis has him by one arm and Lester the other. They're dragging him towards the back door. Dylan looks terrified as he thrashes against them, desperately trying to get away. Mathis on the other hand looks like he is enjoying himself immensely.

"Where are you taking him?" I grab at their hands, trying to free Dylan. Mathis smiles evilly at me and swats my arm away effortlessly.

"You're not going to win. Just give it up already." Mathis laughs. He looks behind me, then shoves me back hard. "Take care of your woman or I'll do it for you." His face morphs into a scowl of hatred.

"You will not touch her, Jason. You swore you wouldn't harm family. She's my wife and that makes her family." Trevor wraps his arms around my waist and pulls me against his chest.

Mathis rolls his eyes. "You're so dramatic. I'll leave her be for now, but if you can't control her, then I'll be forced to do it myself." He waggles his eyebrows.

"Touch her and die," Trevor seethes. His grip on my waist tightens.

"Calm down. I have to take care of him first." He jerks Dylan, making his head roll and causing him to cry out in pain.

"Don't hurt him!" I reach out for Dylan, but Trevor pulls me back. "Please, don't hurt him."

"Don't worry about him, Shayla. I'll make sure he's well taken care of … at least until Ryan shows up." Mathis cackles wickedly as he leaves with my screaming son.

"Dylan!" I yell as the backdoor slams shut. I turn quickly, grabbing Trevor's shirt in my hands. "Please, Trevor. You have to help him."

He snorts. "I think you overestimate the power I have. Jason is in control here. He's placating me at the moment, so don't think you're out of danger. Neither of us is."

He almost looks afraid. The sight sends ripples of fear through me so badly that I physically shiver. He rubs his hands up and down my arms. Even Trevor recognizes how dangerous Jason is. Ryan, where are you?

"We'll be okay. Don't worry."

"How can I not worry? He has my son. He's planning on hurting him, and he wants to hurt Ryan. He's taking pleasure from harming the ones I love."

Anger flares on Trevor's face. "I told you never to speak his name again. You are a married woman; you need to leave your childhood crush behind."

I jerk out of his grip. "Ryan's not a childhood crush. He's the love of my life and the father of my child. He didn't have to force me to love him. I wanted to. I was happy to have his child!" I step away from him and reach for one of the plates on the counter and hurl it at him. "I hate you!"

I grab another dish and throw it at him again. He dodges both, but his temper is on the rise and he's reaching for his belt. I grab another dish, but before I can throw it, he takes it from me and shoves me hard against the counter, pinning me there.

"You will not talk that way to me. You'll do what I say or you will face the consequences."

"So you'll beat me like your father beat your mother. I bet her family killed him. It serves him right," I grunt as I push back against him, trying to get free.

He bangs my head against the countertop. "Shut up! You don't know anything about my family."

"I know you're a bunch of psychopaths!" He slams my head again and everything goes black.

I come to with a groan. I don't know how much time has passed, but I'm so tired. It has to be well after midnight. The room is dark, but I'm pretty sure I'm in Trevor's bedroom. I'm not tied up and my clothes are still on, so that's a good sign.

"You're awake."

Trevor's monotone voice comes from the corner of the room. He walks into a beam of moonlight. He looks horrible. His hair is standing on end, his clothes are rumpled, and he has a fresh black eye to match the one Ryan blackened.

"What happened to you?" I ask.

"I tried to get Dylan." He sits on the bed beside me. "He's fine, but Jason has him hidden. I'm sorry, Shayla. I tried. I want to be a good husband. I really do."

He looks so sincere. When he's like this, it's hard for me to hate him, but then again, I know this isn't how he always is. He can be so sweet, and then so evil. I'm almost positive he's got some kind of bipolar disorder. He needs medical help for so many reasons.

"Thank you."

I don't know what else to say. He risked his life to try to help me, even if his motives are less than honorable.

"I do love you. I know you don't believe me, but I've loved you since I first set eyes on you in college. You were perfect. You were sitting alone in advanced chemistry; I walked by you and you smiled. No one does that. They ignore me. Never had anyone looked up from what they were doing to see me, but you did. You spoke kindly to me. Even when you wouldn't go out with me. I understood, you had a son and you didn't want to date. I got that. Then you did say yes. I didn't handle our date well; I should've taken it more slowly. I think you would have loved me. I've screwed everything up. This was the only answer." He gestures around the room. "I built this place slowly over the last twelve years. I finished it last year. I didn't think you'd ever be mine, because you were married by then, but I took care of that."

That raises a huge red flag for me. "Took care of what? Is Todd okay?"

He smiles. "Of course he's okay. I'm not a killer, Shayla. I just found out about his wife, that the divorce was never actually legal. His marriage to you wasn't legal. I also paid him a good chunk of money to leave you, not that I had to try very hard. He didn't love you enough. As soon as I mentioned money, he was on board."

I'm in shock. My marriage fell apart because of Trevor. Of course, I reconnected with Ryan because of him as well. All of this was his fault. I'm equal parts furious and happy. How dare he interfere with my life, but then if he hadn't I might still be in an unhappy marriage, trying to have a baby to fix it.

"Why would you do all this?"

"I told you. I love you."

I'm so overwhelmed. "Trevor, as well-meaning as you may have been, it's not right for you to manipulate my life like this. I should be able to choose what's best for me and my son. This isn't it, don't you see that? My son is in mortal danger because of what you've done."

"I'm sorry for that. I didn't anticipate what Jason would do. Believe it or not, the fact that he knew Ryan and had a vendetta against him was merely a convenient coincidence for me." He smiles happily at the thought.

"Did you help Mathis get out of prison?"

"No, but the timing was perfect."

"You know he's not only a mob boss, but a serial killer. He's called The Fox in the FBI. He kills women who look just like me."

He frowns. "I know. It seems the men in our family tend to go for the same type of woman. We called him Fox when he was a kid. He was always so sneaky."

"As a kid? How did the FBI not pick up on that?"

He smiles, then rubs his hand over his mouth to stifle a laugh. "I guess since you're my wife now and you'll never be able to say anything, I can tell you this. There's an FBI agent named Gregory Edwards. He grew up with Jason and me. He gave him the nickname. He also helped him get out of jail." I gasp. He laughs. "I don't think you understand how far the Mathis ties go.

"How are you related to him?" I figure if I keep him talking then maybe Ryan will get here before he has time to do anything.

"Cousins. My mom and his mom are sisters."

"Oh. But your mom's last name is McAdams?"

He stares at me for a second. "I know you're trying to distract me, but that's okay. I'll answer. My mom kept her maiden name; her mother was a Mathis and married a McAdams. My dad was a lawyer and it was easier to differentiate between the two that way."

"Oh, that makes sense. I should keep my maiden name, you know, so they don't confuse us at the hospital." I have no idea why I just said that.

He chuckles darkly. He stands and leans over me. "I think you misunderstand, Shayla. You aren't going back to the hospital. You'll be staying here and taking care of me. I want you barefoot and pregnant." He pushes me back down to the bed until he's lying on top of me. I try to push him away, but he doesn't budge. "Did you think I'd forget?" He leans down and kisses me. I have nowhere to go. I shove at him again and turn my head, but he just trails kisses down my neck.

I have to find some way to stall. "I need to use the bathroom, Trevor. Please."

He sighs and rolls away. "That's probably a good idea. Go freshen up for me, sweetheart."

I run to the bathroom, shutting and locking the door behind me. I look absolutely horrible. I'm still in the wedding dress, but it's torn and dirty from our fight in the kitchen. My hair has fallen out of the up-do and my makeup is smeared; black trails of mascara mark my face. A huge knot and bruise have bloomed on my forehead and cheek. I don't know how he can even find me attractive. I'd be disgusted with myself if I hurt someone I'm supposed to love like this. I guess that's part of his problem. He can't see the hurt he's causing me.

"Hurry up, Ryan. I don't know how long I can hold off the inevitable."

I take my time. I wash my face, use the toilet, comb my hair, and reapply my makeup. I don't want Ryan to see the bruises if he gets here in time, because God knows what he would do if he did. I close my eyes for a moment and pray that he gets here soon. When I have nothing left that I can possibly do to waste time, I open the door. Trevor is sitting on the bed reading something on his cellphone. He looks up to me and smiles.

"You look lovely. Sorry your dress is ruined." He jumps up and goes to the closet. He grabs a white silky nightgown and robe. "Here, put these on."

I take the items and hurry back to the bathroom, anything to eat up the minutes. I change and sit down on the side of the tub. I'm so sleepy. It has to be close to dawn by now. A bang on the door startles me and I realize that I have actually started to doze off sitting there. Standing, I make my way to the door and open it before he breaks it down.

"What's taking you so long?" He's angry.

"Just wanted to be sure I was perfect," I tell him, trying to keep my rolling stomach at bay.

He smiles and cups my face, his anger draining away as quickly as it arrived. "You already are perfect."

He pulls my chin up and kisses me. It's slow and tender. I close my eyes and try to pretend that it's Ryan, but it doesn't work. I know it's not him. I try to pull back, but Trevor wraps his arms around my waist and pulls me over to the bed.

"I love you so much, Shayla. You're my entire world."

Trevor's words are sweet, but he's not who I want to hear them from. I want Ryan so badly. He brushes my hair off my neck, kissing me there. His fingers then wrap around the strap of the nightgown and he pushes it down my arm. He taps my bra.

"You're not really supposed to wear this with a nightgown."

I shrug. It was on purpose, obviously, but Trevor looks irate now. He roughly grabs the other strap of the night-gown and pushes it down so that the top falls to my elbows.

"Take it off now."

"Please don't make me do this." I know begging will do nothing except make him angrier, but I won't give in that easily.

"It's your duty as my wife to consummate this marriage, now do what I say or I'll cut it off you." I gasp, but make no move. He reaches into his pants pocket and pulls out a pocket knife. "I'm serious, Shayla."

I back away. "So am I. I don't want to have sex with you."

He grabs me roughly. I try to fight against him, but I'm so tired and probably have a concussion from the earlier blows to the head that I'm not successful in my attempts. He throws my ripped up bra to the ground and then stands there breathing heavily. I quickly pull the nightgown up to cover myself. He drops the knife and reaches for me, but I take another step back, bumping into the dresser. He smiles.

"You can't get away from me this time. The door is locked."

Trevor grabs me and pulls me tightly to his chest, kissing me deeply. I gag, but it doesn't deter him. He rips the nightgown and robe off me, and throws me down onto the bed. He's kissing every part of me he can reach as I try to fight him off. He's not deterred in the slightest by my kicks and hits. Growling, he sits up, grabbing my hair and wrenching my head back as far as it will go. I feel like I might hyperventilate. I'm flailing about, trying to find purchase on something that will help me, but I can't find anything.

"If you don't cooperate and participate, I'll have Jason cut off your son's hand."

"No." I struggle to get loose again. I can barely breathe.

He lets go and I collapse onto the bed, taking huge gulps of air as I try to get my breathing regulated again.

"Are you going to cooperate?"

"Yes, just leave Dylan alone."

He pushes me down and lies on top of me. He cups my face gently. "Tell me you love me."

"I love you." My voice is monotone.

Trevor shakes his head. "Tell me like you mean it."

I close my eyes and picture Ryan. "I love you," I say softly, full of longing. It's not hard. I do love Ryan.

"Better," he murmurs as he leans in to kiss me.

He kisses and caresses me, then takes my hands and puts them on his back, making me move them up and down. Tears slip out of my eyes. I can't stop this and Ryan isn't going to get here in time.

"You are so perfect, Mrs. Daniels. I'm ready for you. I'm ready to make us a true couple."

I panic, looking around everywhere trying to find something to stop him. "Condom!" I blurt.

He laughs. "Why would I want to use a condom when I want you pregnant? If I've done my math correctly, you should be ovulating right around now."

I stare at him horrified. "You tracked my cycle?" I can't believe he did that. How could he have known?

"Isn't that what a good boyfriend or husband does?"

"No!"

He smiles. "Well, I did and I can't wait to see you swollen with my child." He looks down, palming my belly. I whimper in protest and try to move back on the bed away from him, but he grabs my leg and pulls me back down to him.

"No!"

This can't happen. Please, God, don't let this happen! A loud bang sounds in the air and something wet hits my face as Trevor's eyes grow huge, then he falls forward, pinning me to the bed. I scream and shove at him. He rolls off the side of the bed and I scream again, scrambling up the bed and grabbing at the blanket to cover myself.

"Shayla."

I don't know what to do. I can't see straight and the light streaming into the room is so bright. I don't understand what's happening. What's wrong with Trevor? What's on my face?

"Shayla." Someone touches me and I jerk back.

"Please no. I don't want this. I want to go home. Please don't make me. I want to go home. I want Dylan. I want Ryan," I mutter repeatedly.

Arms wrap around me and a scent that I recognize immediately wafts around me. Not sweat and cologne like Trevor. This smell is fresh like the outdoors, rustic, woodsy; the warm sun. He's everything pure, honest, and safe. So safe. It's a scent that I know belongs to the one I love. I cling to him tightly.

"I've got you, baby. I'm here."

I slowly look up, my eyes having finally adjusted to the bright light. "Ryan?"

"Yeah, baby. It's me. I've got you. He's not going to hurt you again."

"Ryan?" I ask again.

"I swear it's me, Shay. You're safe."

"Safe. I'm safe."

He presses a kiss to my forehead and I know he's right. I'm finally safe, wrapped in his arms. He made it in time. He saved me from the fate I was sure was mine and prevented something that would have surely haunted me throughout my life. I squeeze him even tighter, basking in the strength of his arms and the love I know he carries for me. A love that is mirrored in me for him. That's what Trevor didn't understand. He thought he could make me feel something that I didn't, but all I felt for him was anger and, to a lesser point, pity. I breathe in deeply, knowing that Ryan is here and that I'm protected in his embrace.

CHAPTER TWENTY-ONE

Ryan

Everyone is busy gathering supplies. Twelve men from two local precincts have joined us and ten from my own. It's not quite as many as we'd hoped for, but it'll get the job done. As far as we have been able to ascertain, there are only fifteen armed men on the compound. Another SUV with four men arrived about an hour ago. There may be more on the way, so we have to move fast. I turn to Tom. I want to be sure he's mentally prepared for this.

"If you want to stay here, that's fine. Shayla will kill me if anything happens to you."

"I'm going. My baby girl and my grandson have been through enough in their lives. Things I couldn't protect or save Shayla from. I'll be damned if I let that happen again. I'm going." He shoves his gun into his chest holster making it final.

"Good. Just remember to stick to the plan. We don't want to go running in shooting wildly. We need all our men to be safe so that we can get Shayla and Dylan out."

He looks at me for a long moment. "I may be a lot older than you, Ryan, but I was in the military for a long time. I know how to work a rescue mission. I've been on several in my time."

I hold up my hands in surrender. "You're right. I forgot. You've been an accountant for as long as I've known you."

He slaps my shoulder. "As far as you know, I was an accountant." He turns and walks over to the group, leaving me stunned. I follow, but I don't have a chance to ask him what he's talking about.

"If I can get everyone's attention," Marsh says, drawing everyone to him. "I have a few things to go over. First and foremost, thank you all for volunteering your time. I can't say that it will be easy and I can't guarantee you'll come back in one piece, but I think if we can all work together, we can keep the casualties at a minimum and bring

Shayla and Dylan home safely. Now, I've already divided you guys up into groups, with one team leader on each. For the sake of simplicity, if you need to contact the base, you'll be known as team 1, 2, 3 and so on. Stay with your team. We don't need a rogue hero. That's how people end up dead. Cover your team and work together. We're moving out in ten."

Marsh steps down off the chair that he was standing on and comes to me. He shakes my hand and puts the other hand on my shoulder, looking me in the eye.

"I know you've got your head on straight for this, but let me warn you now. If you do anything to endanger these men, yourself, or Shayla and Dylan, I'll be sure that you never walk again. Am I clear?"

"I'm good. Don't worry about me."

He nods. "Good. Now, I'm sure you want in that house. I'm putting you, Paul, Tom, and Linc together. You're team leader 2. Don't make me regret this, Ryan."

"Who's one?" I ask, bypassing his warnings. They're unnecessary. I've never been as levelheaded as I am right now.

He smiles and winks. "Me, of course." I snort, rolling my eyes.

"Marsh, I gave each team and leader their call number. We're all packed and loaded. Just waiting on your word," Jon tells him.

"Good. Let's move out!" Marsh calls.

My team is to head northwest. The house is about five-hundred feet from the forest's edge, but there's really no point around the entire compound that is closer, or covered. It's out in the open. We'll be able to hide around a few buildings or cars, but we'll be sitting ducks for the most part. We've also decided not to use the ATV's. There are simply too many of us for that to be feasible.

"You good?" I ask Tom. I worry about him running the ten miles to the compound, but he seems to be as much on task as the rest of us who are half his age.

"I'm not as weak as you think I am, Ryan."

"I know you're not weak. This is a long run." I'm panting. I assumed he would be too, but he looks barely out of breath.

He smiles. "I run ten miles every day. This is nothing. Now, shut up and get moving. I want my babies in my arms by daybreak."

He's surprising me more and more. We'll have to have a serious talk when we get home. As we draw closer to the compound, I hold my arm out and slow my men.

"Team Two to base. Do you copy?"

"Team Two copy. Over," Riley replies.

"Team Two is at the forest edge. Ready to move on your word, Team One. Over."

"Team One to Team Two, hold position. Over."

"Copy that, Team One. Over."

I pull out my binoculars, looking for anything to give me an idea where Shayla or Dylan could be, but the only thing I can see is a light on in one of the bedrooms. I turn to my team.

"Paul, you're with me. Linc and Tom, you have our backs. We'll secure the house and then move into the room with the light." They all nod.

"Team One, to all. Proceed with caution on my mark. Base, cut the external power in three, two, one." Once it goes dark, we hear, "Move in. over."

It's almost pitch-black, save for the small light shining in the one window. Seeing no one visible, we take off running low to the house. We stop behind a small outbuilding. I look to the left and right and see two men. One is making his way to the back of the house, grumbling about the power outage; the other is standing guard at the front door. I signal for Linc and Tom to get the guy headed for the back and Paul to follow me to the front.

We almost make it to the porch when the gunfire starts. The guy starts to draw his gun, but Paul beats him to it, shooting him in the chest. He drops to the ground hard. I grab his gun and we make our way into the house. It's almost too easy, but I know we aren't out of the woods yet. Quickly, we scan the house and find no one else present.

We creep to the door with the light on and I slowly turn the handle. Opening the door, I see Trevor poised over Shayla. She is fighting him and screaming no; it's all the confirmation I need. I pull the trigger and watch him go down. I hurry to her and shove him off. She's hysterical. I call her name over and over, but she doesn't respond. She keeps screaming. I don't want to slap her out of it, but I may have to. I try touching her shoulder.

"Shayla."

She jerks violently away from me as she mutters that she doesn't want this and wants to go home. She mutters my name several times and I do the only thing I can. I wrap her squirming body in my arms and promise her that she's okay. She's finally safe. Shayla seems to be in a daze, but she stops fighting against me. Nothing she says makes any sense. I think she's in shock. The only word I can understand is the word safe.

"Yeah, baby. You're safe. I've got you now." I squeeze her tightly to me.

Paul comes in the door. "The house is secured, but the others may need some help outside." I nod in understanding, but that's not my first priority right now.

"We need to do something with him," I point to Trevor. I think he's still alive, but barely. "And find her some clothes." Shayla clutches me tightly. "It's okay, Shay. I want to get you something to wear." I look back to Paul. "Look in that closet for something."

"No, please. I don't want his clothes." She looks up at me with such panic in her eyes, I can't deny her anything.

"What about my shirt?" She nods. "Okay, you'll have to let go for just a second. She loosens her grip and I take off my gun holster so I can pull off my long-sleeved t-shirt. It's a good thing I layered up for this mission. I help her get it on and then I get myself back together.

"She needs something on her legs, it's too cold outside to just have my shirt on. Let's go look in a different room."

I stand with her in my arms with the blanket still wrapped around her lower half. It's a little awkward navigating, but we make it to the room across from the one I found her in. I try to sit her down on the bed, but she grips me tightly.

"I'm not leaving you, but we need to get you dressed in more appropriate clothes. It's really cold outside. Can you sit here while I look?"

"I can find something. You won't leave?" She looks so lost.

"No, baby, I won't leave you. Never again." She smiles. She stands up and is a bit wobbly, but I help her steady herself. I fight the anger rising inside me at the sight of her. She's obviously hurt, that much is clear. She's bruised and too thin. She's suffered more than I wanted to believe. I honestly thought, hoped, that Trevor would at least care for her basic needs, given that he wanted her as his. I've been a fool. My attention returns to the room as Shayla speaks.

"This is the room he made for me. There are lots of clothes." She kneels down in front of a dresser and opens the bottom drawer. She pulls out a piece of black material. "There are no real pants or casual clothes here. But I found these leggings the other day. They'll be okay for now."

She sits there holding them for a long moment. I stand to go to her, but Paul interrupts. Shayla jumps, but settles quickly. I glare at him.

He looks apologetically. "I found these tennis shoes in the closet." He hands me a pair of white Keds and then leaves the room.

"Is he dead?" She looks up at me with tears in her eyes.

"I'm not sure. It wasn't a kill shot. It should've been though, I'm sorry I didn't get to you in time." I kneel down in front of her as she cups my face.

"You did. You got there just in time."

Relief floods me. "Yeah? He didn't ..."

"No, he was about to, but then ... you shot him." She touches her face. "I have his blood on me. That's what that was?"

I wipe at her cheek, there's really not much on her. "Yeah, let's get you cleaned up and we'll get out of here."

"Where's Dylan?"

"I'm sure someone found him."

I don't want to worry her, but so far there's been no sign of him. I heard Paul call in Shayla's rescue over the com, but no one has mentioned any sign of Dylan. I'm afraid Mathis may have run with him, but right now, I need to get Shayla out of here. After she has her clothes, socks, and shoes on, we head through the house. There's still gunfire sounding outside. Shayla clings to me.

I freeze, listening to the commotion sounding in my com; I hear my team cursing and then a voice, I'm not sure whose, say, "They're coming out of the bunkers. There must be a least twenty!" Moments later, I hear Marsh telling our guys to go after the newcomers.

"Are you okay?" Shayla asks me. I look down and smile.

"No problem. There are just a few more men here than we anticipated, but everything is okay. We need to get you out of here."

"We need to find Dylan."

I turn her towards me so she can understand. "Shayla, I know this is hard, but right now we need to get you to safety. Once I do that, I can look for him, but I can't risk losing you both. I need to get you to the base."

"No, I need to find my son." She tries to pull away from me, but my grip is too tight. She starts to breathe heavy.

"Shay, calm down, baby. We will find him, but you have to get to safety so we can."

"Listen to him, baby girl." Her head jerks towards the door and I let go so she can run into the arms of her father. I know he won't let her get out the door.

"Daddy!" He hugs her tightly.

"Let's get you to safety, honey. Let Ryan find Dylan." She nods. "I got her, you go on. We'll just stay put here until you get back."

"You said you wouldn't leave me." Shayla releases her father and comes back to me.

I cup her face in my hands. "I can't do both. I can't stay with you and find Dylan."

She nods. I think she's in some sort of shock or is, at the very least, confused. It's understandable though. "Right. Right, go find our baby."

"I'll find him." I press a kiss to her forehead and my stomach drops as I feel her flinch from me. Oh, my poor Shayla.

"What's going on out there?" I ask Tom, who'd been outside most of the time we'd been in the house. I don't release Shayla just yet. She's settled against me, clinging to me.

"They had some men hiding in the bunker, but they've about got them cleared out. Maybe about twelve or so left. No sign of Dylan or Mathis from what I could gather on the com, but some of the coms have gone down according to Riley."

"Right, I heard that part. Shay, I'm going to go get our boy. You stay here. Please, stay here."

She nods, but says nothing as I head outside. Paul and I creep around the house and head towards the outbuilding. I can see Marsh and a few others fighting in the field about midway between the house and a gazebo looking structure. It looks like they have it under control.

Paul and I are almost to the outbuilding when two shots are fired. I'm hit in the abdomen, knocking me on my back and Paul is hit in the arm. Luckily, I just get the wind knocked out of me because I'm wearing a bullet proof vest. It'll bruise, but I'll be fine. I manage to sit up, just in time to see the guy raising his gun again. I shoot him and a man behind him.

"You okay?"

Paul grumbles under his breath as he rips off part of his shirt, trying to make a tourniquet. I grab it and quickly tie it around his arm. "It's just a graze. I'll be fine. Let's go."

I help him up and we're off again. Unfortunately, the outbuilding is empty. It looks like any other storage shed with gardening tools and a lawnmower, but there is also a chair with a rope loosely draped around it. They must have tied Dylan there.

"Let's look for a door to the bunker. The entrance could be in the floor," I say, as I start to move things out of the way.

"Here!" Paul calls. He's in the back corner of the building and there's a trap door under a shelf. We move it out of the way easy enough, but there's a pad lock. "There might be a key or something we can use to cut through it." He starts to look around and I do the same.

"Got it," I tell him. I hold up a pair of wire cutters and snip right through the lock easily. Paul stands with his gun raised and ready as I open the hatch.

"Clear." We shine our lights down into the hole. There's a ladder, but its pitch black down there. "We going in?"

"Yeah, let's just see what's down there." He nods and slowly descends the ladder. It's nothing but a root cellar. "Well, that was anticlimactic. It doesn't look like there's another way out of here either.

"It's empty?" I ask.

"Not exactly. There are shelves lining all the walls. It's dirt except for the floor and part of one wall. There are old jars of food and some empty wooden boxes, but other than that, I don't see anything. There's nothing that would lead to a door or path to the bunker."

"All right. Let's get out of here."

A shout calls my attention outside. I see Paul clear the door and hurry out of the building to see what's happening. Shayla is running to the opposite side of the house near the garage and Tom is chasing after her. I follow.

"Shayla!" Tom shouts.

She stops almost to the edge of the garage. "I have to find him."

"Shay, baby. We'll find him." I've made it past Tom and I'm almost to her, when hands reach out and grab her. "Shayla!" I run after her. I skid to a stop as I round the corner. Mathis has her pressed to him with a gun to her head.

He smiles at me. "Perfect timing, Ryan."

"You promised not to hurt me. I'm family," Shayla tells him. I'm surprised by her bravado.

He laughs. "Well, your husband is delusional. Besides, the marriage license won't be filed until morning. And I do believe that Ryan foiled my cousin's plan to consummate, so you're not family yet."

"You know Trevor won't see it that way," she tells him.

He squeezes her tighter, making her squeak in pain. Tom, Paul, and I have our guns trained on him. One wrong move and he's dead. He'd be dead if Shayla wasn't in his arms right now.

"Let her go, Mathis. It's me you want." I'm hoping I can buy some time, or he will move just a few centimeters so I can have a clear shot and end this.

"No, it's her I want. I want her to pay for everything you've done to me. You've ruined my life, Ryan."

"You did that yourself."

He laughs. "No, you're the one who slept with my wife and wormed your way into my circle of trust. You're the one who took down my organization. But you know what? You didn't stop us. We still have plenty of people who are loyal. So loyal that they'll do anything I ask, no matter what the consequences are."

"Mom!"

The sound of my son's distraught voice makes me automatically turn my head. Dylan is being dragged away by four huge men. Where are my people?

"Dad!" I start to move to him, but I need to get Shayla.

By the time I look back to Mathis, he is dragging Shayla away. I aim and fire. It hits him in the thigh. I pray to God that he bleeds out. He falls, taking her down with him, but before I can reach them, he's up and firing at me. I duck behind a tree as a bullet whizzes by. I hesitate on firing back, afraid I'll hit Shayla. When I look again, he's gone. I call over my com, not worrying about procedure.

"Mathis has Shayla. I repeat, Mathis has Shayla. I'm going after them."

Marsh comes back. "They got away with Dylan. We couldn't get a clear shot without injuring him."

I curse and kick several trash cans over. I don't know what to do; go after my son or my girlfriend. Each would want me to get the other first, but I know Shayla would kill me if anything happened to Dylan because I was saving her. Growling, I take off running toward where my son was last seen.

"What happened?" I ask Marsh.

"We were able to subdue all targets except for the four who had Dylan. They made it around the outbuilding and disappeared. I've confirmed with Riley that no vehicles have left the property."

"So they went into the bunker. Paul and I searched all over and couldn't find a door."

Marsh claps a hand on my shoulder. "We'll find him. Let's go talk to Daniels and see if we can get answers."

Talking to that man is the last thing on earth I want to do, but to find my son, I'll do anything. Trevor is sitting in one of the chairs on the porch. It looks like they gave him pants and shoes, but he's shirtless and shivering. Good. Freeze, psycho.

"Where's the bunker entrance, Trevor?" I demand, punching him in the face. Marsh grabs my arm before I can land the second blow.

"I don't know what you're talking about." Trevor's head rolls around lazily. He looks close to death, but he's been patched up by the medic so it's most likely drugs.

"Yes, you do. You built this place. There's no way you wouldn't know there's a huge bunker under the ground." I try to punch him again, but Marsh and Linc restrain me.

"Oh, that. It's not a bunker. It's just the old foundation of the house that was here before. It was a basement." Trevor yawns and blinks his eyes widely, trying to stay alert.

"I don't care what you call it. How do you get to it?"

"You can't. It's sealed off." His head falls forward. He's passed out. I growl and punch him before anyone can stop me.

"He's lying. There has to be a way in. They didn't just disappear."

Tom and Paul come around the side of the house, panting. Tom is holding his arm as blood seeps out between his fingers. I run over to meet them.

"What happened?"

"Mathis shot me. I'll be fine, but I need to see the medic."

Paul and I help Tom over to the medic and once I make sure he's really okay, I turn to Paul

"Where's Shayla?"

"They went behind the garage, but disappeared. There has to be an entrance to the bunker somewhere close. People just don't disappear. "

"No, they don't. We have to find them soon."

I don't know what I'll do if I lose Shayla and Dylan. Especially, after having Shayla in my arms. I will find out where my family is and I will bring them home safely if it's the last thing I do.

CHAPTER TWENTY-TWO
Shayla

After Ryan leaves to find Dylan, I slump down into the kitchen chair. I'm so tired. I haven't slept in over twenty-four hours, which isn't an unusual thing for a doctor, but with all the trauma I've recently suffered, it has left me almost useless.

Tom pushes my hair back on my forehead gently. "Nasty bump you have there. Do you need me to find a medic?" He asks as he sits in the chair next to me.

"No, I'm pretty sure I have a concussion, but it's not that severe. I'm alert. I'll get checked out after this is all over. Right now, I just want to know Dylan is safe."

"I'm sure Ryan will find him, sweetheart."

He squeezes my hand; making the ring Trevor gave me dig slightly into my middle finger. I jerk my hand away and pull the offending piece of jewelry off, laying it on the table.

"He really forced you to marry him?"

My father's face is so sad. He's seen me go through so much. I wish I could tell him that I wasn't hurt and that everything was all right, but he'd obviously never believe it considering my current state.

"Yeah," I finally say sadly. "It was awful, Daddy. He beat Dylan so that I'd cooperate. He used the fear of him hurting Dylan so I'd do what he wanted. I know it's probably bad for me to say this, but I really hope he's dead." Anger flares in me. I'd love nothing more than to shoot him myself.

"I'm sorry you both went through this. Looks like I've failed to protect you once again."

"Oh, no." I grab his hand. "This isn't your fault. You've always done everything you could for us. Please don't feel like you've failed."

"I'm glad you're safe now. Your mother and I have worried non-stop. I was so limited in what I could do. I've been out of the game too long, everyone I know is dead or moved on to other things."

I smile. Ryan really is so much like my father. "Looks like you're back in now. I think Ryan will flip when he knows you are retired CIA." I giggle. It feels so good to laugh.

Tom smiles. "Yeah, I've dropped a few hints to him. He looked pretty desperate to ask me about it, but we had to go."

"You're so mean to him."

"I've gotta be. I didn't do a good enough job with Todd, so I'm putting up extra effort with Ryan."

"Dad," I admonish with an eye roll.

He laughs. "He's a good kid, sweetheart. I would have helped you both back then, if you'd told us."

I regret how I handled things, but back then I thought I was protecting our little family. I couldn't see a future where Ryan wasn't going to get carted away and thrown in jail for us loving each other.

"I wish I could go back and do things differently. We probably wouldn't be here right now if I had made choices other than the ones I did, but Ryan has done so many great things with his life and career, which might not have happened if I'd told him about Dylan when we were younger."

"Well, none of that matters now. Let's just focus on your future. I expect more grandbabies to spoil." He winks.

I can't even think about that right now. I know what Trevor has done will cause me to need therapy. I'm sure I'll have nightmares and who knows if I'll even be able to let Ryan kiss me, much less work on grandbabies. He must sense the change in my mood and touches me on my shoulder.

"Sorry, honey. I didn't mean to upset you. You take your time and get better."

"I know. I just don't know how all this is going to affect my relationship with Ryan. I don't think I'll be able to handle it if we can't work it out."

"You'll work it out, sweetheart. That man loves you like no other. He looks at you the way your father looked at your mother. The way I look at Gail. He loves you."

"I love him too. You know I miss my parents, but you and Gail are my parents too. I'm sorry it's taken me so long to truly see that."

"It's all in the past. I can get used to you calling me dad."

"That's what you are. You've never failed me. You've always taken wonderful care of Dylan and me."

I hug him tightly. He has always been my rock. If it hadn't been for him, Dylan and I probably wouldn't have made it through those early years. We sit in silence for a few minutes before curiosity gets the best of me.

"Where's Trevor?"

"He's tied up on the front porch. Linc put two police officers out there to guard him and the medic is patching him up. The bullet is lodged near his clavicle."

"Oh."

"You're safe. He can't get to you."

I nod. "I know. I was just thinking that I'd like to jab my finger into his wound."

Tom guffaws. "I'll take you out there if you want."

I shake my head no. I'm not ready to see him. A loud disturbance outside has me up and running to the back door. It looks like there are more of Mathis' men out there and they're fighting.

"Dylan!" I yell as I whip open the door and run out into the cold. He's being dragged away.

"Shayla!" I turn to my father.

"I have to help him."

Ryan is running towards me. Seeing him sends a surge of relief through me, but I still need to save my baby. I didn't see where the men went with Dylan.

"Shay, baby. We'll find him."

He's almost to me when I'm grabbed from behind and a gun is pressed to my temple. There is a chuckle in my ear and I know exactly who has me. Fear ripples through my body as I try to figure out what to do to get out of this mess.

"Just what I wanted," he says to me and then turns and shouts a bit louder. "Perfect timing, Ryan."

I'm not going to lie, I'm terrified, but he made a promise and I remind him of that. "You promised not to hurt me. I'm family."

He laughs. "Well, your husband is delusional. Besides, the marriage license won't be filed until morning. And I do believe that Ryan foiled my cousin's plan to consummate, so you're not family yet."

I have no idea how he knows that, but the thought makes me sick. His grip tightens and I cry out.

"Let her go, Mathis. It's me you want."

Ryan and Mathis go back and forth for a few minutes, but I barely hear them. My concern is for my son. I see him again; the same guys from before are now pulling him towards one of the outbuildings.

"Mom!"

I look at my son, unable to speak with Mathis holding me so tightly. Dylan looks so scared and lost. I fight against Mathis but his grip tightens. Ryan turns to our son and Mathis uses the distraction to pull us away from the group. His grip moves from around my shoulders to my arm, with the gun pointed at my back. I'm not sure how far we run when a gunshot sounds and Mathis screams, knocking us both to the ground.

"He shot me!" he says almost astounded.

He fires his gun back. I try to fight him, but he elbows me in the face, making me see stars yet again. He drags me up and behind the side of the garage.

"I'm so looking forward to killing him."

"Leave him and Dylan alone and I'll do whatever you want me to do."

Mathis fires his gun again. I squat down against the wall and hold my ears to protect them from the noise and pray that Ryan is okay. Mathis grabs my arm and jerks me up.

"Get up."

He pulls me along to the edge of the woods, right inside the cover of the trees. Why are we out here? I look around but don't see anything. He bends down, feeling along in the brush until he finds what he is looking for; he pulls open a door and then shoves me inside. I fall to the floor with a thud. It isn't a far drop, so I'm not hurt, thankfully, but I'm a little stunned.

"What is this place?"

"One of the hideouts I built."

"Does Trevor know about it?"

He snorts. "No. He's been too obsessed with his dream girl to notice anything I did around here. He thinks the bunker is the old foundation from the house that was here a hundred years ago. It took my dad years to complete it and then I added a few more hiding spots here and there. My family is prepared for everything."

"Is there another exit?"

I'm starting to feel panicky; it's so small in here. You can't stand and there's barely enough room for the both of us. It's also hard to see anything down here with only his cellphone flash light.

"No. I never got this one finished, that's where you come in. You're going to patch up my leg and help me escape."

"Please, let me go. I want to go home." I start to cry.

He huffs. "Shut up. I'll let you go if you help me, but one day when you least expect it, I'll come back for you."

"So why should I help you then?" I ask annoyed.

He grins. "Because you can't help yourself. You're a do-gooder. It's in your nature."

I roll my eyes. "Will you tell me where Dylan is?"

He stares at me for a moment. "Fine, I'll tell you where the kid is after you patch me up and help me get away unseen."

"All right, I'll help you."

He tosses me a backpack from behind him. "There's a first aid kit in there."

I open the bag and pull out a generic first aid kit mostly full of bandages and antibiotic creams, which might help, but the only thing I can use to dig a bullet out with is a pair of plastic tweezers. I do find needles and thread so at least I can sew the wound up, but there's no numbing agent. Of course, it might be a little satisfying being the one inflicting the pain for a change. I know that's probably unethical of me, but I don't care right now.

"This is going to hurt. There's nothing in the kit to numb the pain."

"Just do it." He grabs the discarded backpack and pulls out a bottle of whiskey and chugs it.

"Let me use some of that to sanitize the area." He rips open his pant leg and pours it on himself, grunting in pain. "It looks like the bullet went clean through. It's not close to your main artery either. You'll live."

"Oh joy. Shut up and fix me."

I huff. "You know I could just let you bleed to death."

"I can kill you and then your son will eventually starve to death because they'll never find him."

"You won't," I say stupidly. I don't know what it is about this man, but my mouth just flies off the handle when it's just us.

He laughs. "And why is that?"

I run the first stitch and he hisses in pain. I fight to hide my smile as I continue. "One, because you want to see Ryan suffer. If I'm dead, then he can mourn and move on. Two, I look like your wife. Admit it or not, you really did love her and you probably regret your hasty decision to kill her."

"Look and act like her, but it doesn't really matter. I'll do whatever I have to do to survive, even if that's killing you. Are you done yet?"

"Yes, I just have to wrap your thigh."

I hold up the gauze and tape. He motions for me to get on with it and I quickly finish up. I sit back against the wall with my knees up and yawn widely.

"Do you know what time it is?"

"It's almost six. We need to move soon, or the sun will be up." He stands testing his leg, then climbs up the short ladder, pushing the trapdoor open. "Get up here. You're going out first. If you try to run, I'll shoot you."

I climb up the ladder and out into the darkness. On the horizon, you can just see the red of dawn starting to rise. In the distance, I can hear voices, but I can't make out anything clearly.

"It's clear," I tell him.

He climbs out and looks around. "Okay, here's what's going to happen. You're going to go with me to the next bunker access point. As long as I can get there safely, I'll let you go."

"And tell me where Dylan is?"

"Yeah."

We start walking. He doesn't bother to aim his gun at me, he just holds onto my wrist and I follow behind him.

"Maybe they found the access to the bunker already."

He snorts. "They won't. It's so well hidden that my men had to have a map and verbal instructions to find them."

"Where does this access point lead?"

"I'm not telling you that, but let's just say that by the time they find it, even if you tell them where it is, I'll be long gone."

I stare at him for a moment. He's so sure of himself. I hope his overconfidence leads to his capture, or better yet, death. We continue to walk for what seems like, at the very least, a mile until finally he points in the distance.

"That's it."

We're so far in the woods that I can't see the house or hear any chatter. We are really isolated from everyone and I'm starting to worry that I won't be able to find my way back. The only sounds are the morning birds and insects. It's creepy. He stops, then bends down to a tree stump and pulls it up. He's used nature to cover his tracks so well that I'm not sure even a professional tracker could find them. He starts to climb inside and I panic.

"Wait! You have to tell me where to find Dylan and how to get back."

He stops, only his chest and head remain above ground. "How to get back wasn't part of the bargain."

"Jason, please."

"I do love to hear you beg." He smirks and I immediately glare at him. "Fine. He's in a bunker, one of the unfinished ones. It's 100 meters into the woods behind the outbuilding." He starts to climb back down.

"Wait!" I yell after him. I peer into the hole and see him on a small ladder built into the earth around him. "You said it was hard to find even with the map. What do I look for?"

He thinks for a few minutes then smiles. "Nope, not gonna give you that one. The house is that way." He points straight ahead and closes the door.

"Jason!" I try to open the hatch, but it won't budge.

I don't want to waste any more time so I take off running as fast as I can in the direction he pointed. It's getting brighter as the sun rises and I can almost see clearly. The field is flooded with light when I break through the trees. I'm at least seven or eight hundred feet away from the house. I can see people walking around, and as I get closer, I can hear Ryan screaming at someone. I run as fast as I can.

"Ryan!" I scream over and over until finally he hears me and takes off running to me. He gets to me quickly, scooping me up in his arms almost at the exact time that I begin to collapse from exhaustion.

"Shayla," he murmurs, burying his face in my neck.

I hug him as tightly as I can. He pulls back and looks down at me with such relief that it brings tears to my eyes.

"I've missed you."

He chuckles. "Oh, baby. You have no idea. The past hour has been worse than the two weeks you've been missing."

"Two weeks?" He nods. "Wow, I had no idea I was gone that long. Have you found Dylan?"

His eyes immediately fill with tears, and I shove away from him. "Don't you dare tell me that after all this he's dead?" I can't breathe.

He shakes his head and swallows. "I don't know. We can't find him anywhere. The men who took off with him won't talk. I've beat the crap out of them and they still won't mutter a word."

"I know where he is." I take off running, a renewed energy flowing through me.

"Shayla! Wait!" I don't stop. I can't. I have to find my son. Others join us, but I pay them no attention.

He catches up to me quickly. "Where are you going?"

"He told me where Dylan is."

We make it to the tree line behind the outbuilding. "Mathis told you where to find Dylan? Why would he do that?"

"Because his plan was messed up, but he'll be back when we least expect it."

"You say that like it's no big deal."

I stop and look around. "It is a big deal, but I can't think about that right now. We have to find our son."

"Right. Dylan!" We both yell repeatedly. I hear a faint muffled sound to my left and head there. There's nothing but dead leaves and twigs.

"The hideouts are covered in leaves and stuff. The one he escaped through used a stump to open it."

I start pulling on every small stump I can find, as I continue to call for Dylan. Ryan, who is doing the same and also scanning each tree for a possible lever, hasn't let me get very far from him, for which I'm actually grateful. We search everywhere and come up empty handed. Finally, after what seems like hours, I hear my dad call out for us.

"Here!"

I run towards the sound of my father's voice. It takes him and two others to pry the door open, but they finally break it open and pull a tied and gagged Dylan out of the ground. I wrap my arms around him tightly, not caring that he can't do the same. I cup his beaten face in my hands.

"I'm so happy to see you." I say as I pull the gag from his mouth as Ryan and my father untie him.

"Me too. Are you okay?" Dylan asks me as Ryan takes his turn hugging our son. He doesn't say much, but I can see the relief in his face at seeing Dylan alive.

"I'll be fine, baby. We need to get you checked out. Do you think you can walk?" I ask him.

He limps a little. "Yeah, I don't think anything is broken, but I twisted my ankle.

"Here." Ryan wraps one of Dylan's arms around his shoulders and his arm around Dylan's waist to help him walk. "Let's get you to the medic."

"Can we slow down?" Dylan asks.

Ryan comes to a stop. "What's wrong?"

Dylan shakes his head. "I'm just really tired."

Smith, one of Linc's men, comes up to us. "I can carry him."

Dylan shakes his head. "I just need to rest for a minute."

"Sweetie, I think you should let him help you."

I rub his back tenderly. He finally nods. Carefully, Smith lifts him up bridal style and carries him the rest of the way without seeming to have any trouble. Once the medic has checked both Dylan and I out, they load us both into the same ambulance. Ryan climbs in behind me, taking my hand and kissing the back of it. I lean my head against his shoulder and sigh in relief.

"Ryan?"

"Yeah, baby?"

"Is Trevor dead?"

"Yeah, he bled out."

"Good."

I can't believe we are finally going home. I didn't think it would really be happening. I didn't want to accept my fate with Trevor, but I would have if Ryan wouldn't have shown up. I would have done anything to keep Dylan safe.

The steady hum of the ambulance traveling down the road lulls me into a sleep like state. I can hear the soft chatter of the EMT's and Dylan's answers to their questions. I can hear Ryan's soothing words in my ear, but none of it completely registers to me as I fall deeper into sleep.

CHAPTER TWENTY-THREE
Ryan

Shayla doesn't stir as we arrive at the hospital, so I carry her inside. She had insisted that Dylan have the stretcher in the ambulance, which was a good call. He seemed to be in worse shape physically than she was, at least in appearance. I think she probably has had far more damage inflicted mentally.

The doctors at the hospital insist on separate rooms for Shayla and Dylan for the examinations. Of course, I understand the reasoning, but it's still hard to choose between them, but Gail and Tom offer to stay with Dylan; so I readily agree. I'm sitting beside the bed, holding Shayla's hand, when Julie, the nurse who helped Shayla and I when we first started investigating, comes into the room.

"Hi, Detective."

"Nurse Julie."

She gives me a warm but sad smile as she picks up her chart. "How's she doing?"

"She's okay, I guess. The doctor seems to think this is normal."

She nods as she reads a bit more. "Yeah, she's suffered a lot of trauma. Her body is healing. Sometimes that means shutting down and resting."

"That's what they tell me. Have you seen Dylan?"

"I'm actually his nurse today. He's doing well."

"I went to see him for a few minutes earlier. Is he awake?"

"I believe he's still sleeping."

Julie checks over Shayla's vitals and then leaves us. I rest my head on the bed, still clutching Shayla's hand. The past two weeks have been miserable, but the past twenty-four hours have been almost unbearable. After Shayla disappeared with Mathis, I went berserk. I beat Trevor to death, literally, trying to get answers on Shayla or Dylan's whereabouts. He didn't know anything. He was only a pawn to Mathis' masterplan, he just didn't know it. I close my eyes as I think back to what happened with Trevor.

"What now, Ryan?"

Marsh stands with his hands on his hips, glaring at me as I stand over Trevor's lifeless body. I know I should feel guilty about this but I don't. The man was crazy.

"I'll beat every one of them to death if it will help me find my family. I'm done playing games, Marsh. I won't lose them after getting this close."

"I understand."

I know he's trying to defuse my anger, but I can't calm down. I'm past that point.

"No, you don't! You've never had your family taken from you. You've never had to wonder if they were being hurt or abused, or if they were suffering, or dead. I'm done wasting time."

I move passed Marsh and over to two of the men who had taken off with Dylan earlier. I'm getting answers, one way or another.

"Tell me where you took my son!" I scream as I get in their faces.

The man who seems to be the leader, smirks at me. "There's nothing in it for us to tell you anything."

"What's in it for you if you don't? You're going to jail." They all laugh. I kick the guy in the face, knocking him unconscious.

"Ryan, let us handle this for a little while. Why don't you take a break?"

Tom takes my arm and leads me away from the group of men we've caught and tied up.

"Ryan."

The sweet sound of Shayla's voice floats in the air to me, and I look around confused. I can't find her anywhere but I swear that was her voice. That's when I see her.

"Shayla?"

I start to run, but no matter how fast I go, I seem to be staying in the same place. I see her in the distance and run faster, but I can't reach her.

"Shayla!"

"Ryan?" I jerk awake, sitting up with a start. I rub a hand over my face and look up to see Shayla watching me. "Baby! You're awake."

She reaches out her hand to me. "Yeah, I'm awake. I didn't mean to wake you, but my hand was numb. You had a death grip on it."

I blush. "Sorry. I didn't want to let go. I guess I fell asleep."

"It's okay. I'd like to get up though. I need the bathroom."

I nod, helping her stand and get the IV situated in the bathroom before leaving to give her some privacy.

"Do you know where my clothes are?" She looks around as she exits the bathroom. "Are we at my hospital?"

"Uh, I'm not sure you have any clean clothes, but yeah, we're at your hospital. Neither of you were in critical shape, so we came back here. I thought you'd want to be closer to home."

"That was nice of you. Would you care to get me some clothes from my locker then? I'll write the combo down for you. There should be some gym clothes and underwear on the top shelf."

"Of course. Whatever you need."

"Thanks. I just want a shower and to see Dylan. Is he doing okay?"

I help her sit back in the bed. "He's okay. He's pretty banged up; has a couple of fractured ribs and a sprained ankle, but the doctor said he'll be fine."

"That's a relief. I'd like to see him."

"We will, but let me get your doctor first. I think they had some questions for you. They asked me about a rape kit, but I told them it wasn't necessary. They are pretty insistent on doing it though."

She pales. "Did they examine me?"

"Not like that. I stayed with you the whole time. They just checked your vitals, took some x-rays, and a CT."

She stretches. "Okay. I'm still so tired. I haven't slept well in so long."

"You're safe, Shay. You can sleep." I kiss her hand.

She shakes her head. "No, I can't sleep until we're all home. I need my own bed."

"I'll get your doctor; maybe she can discharge you soon." I kiss her forehead and make my leave.

"Dr. Thorn is awake."

"Thanks. I'll let Doctor Gwinn know." The nurse walks away.

I check on Dylan and find him still asleep. Gail and Tom are still in the room with him, she is knitting and he's reading a hunting magazine. They look as if it's any other day, but I know they're just as worried as I am.

"I'm going to get a few things for Shayla. She's awake," I tell them. "The doctor will be in there soon."

"I'll go over with her. Thank you for watching out for her." Gail puts away her knitting and kisses my cheek before heading to Shayla's room.

I leave Tom in the room with my son and head to Shayla's locker. I find everything just where she said it would be, but what catches my eye is a piece of paper lying in the bottom. I pick it up to see what it is and if it's something important.

"Thanks for your help. I can't wait to see you again."

There's no signature on the note, but there's a little doodle of a fox in the corner. I crumple the note in my hand and angrily punch the locker closest to me.

"You will die, Mathis. Even if it's the last thing I do in this life, you will die." I shove the note in my pocket and head back to Shayla.

The doctor is still there when I arrive. I let all the anger I'm harboring drain away so I can focus on Shay. "Do you need me to wait outside?"

"No." Shayla holds her hand out to me. "I missed you."

I smile. I missed her too. "How's she doing, doc?"

"Oh, she's fine. I was just telling her that I'll discharge her after she finishes this last bag of fluids. I'd like Dylan to stay another night though."

"I don't want to leave him here." Shayla looks up at me.

"I'm sure your parents will stay, baby. But you need to go home and rest."

"I need to stay with him."

"Why don't we see how he's doing the next few hours and then decide. It'll take you a little while to finish this up anyway." The doctor compromises.

"We can take stuff home and I can look after him. I can bring whatever equipment we need back."

Dr. Gwinn nods. "That might be doable. But, Shayla, you really need to rest. I also want you to follow up with Dr. Martinson. You really need to talk about what happened and deal with this trauma. I'm recommending that you don't return to work until you've been cleared by her." She hands Shayla a prescription. "I'll check in later. Please rest."

I squeeze her arm. "Hey, it's going to be okay."

"Eventually. I'm more worried about how Dylan will react than how I will. Trevor did awful things, but he wasn't well. I don't think he would have done any of the things he did if he was getting help. He was a sick man."

I snort. "Why do you always see the best in people? The guy was a psycho. He stalked you for twelve years. He was sick, but there was no helping him."

"I don't want to talk about him. I just want to get back to my life. I don't want two weeks to ruin everything. I don't want to lose you."

"You aren't going to lose me, Shay. I'm in this for the long haul. I swear to you." She smiles softly. "I mean it."

"I know. I want that too. I just worry that I won't be able to be what you need."

I look at her confused. "What are you talking about? You're exactly what I need. Shayla, I'm head over heels for you. I couldn't imagine a better person for me than you. It's always been you."

"But what if I can't be what you need physically? Not a lot happened with Trevor, but I still have … this fear. I can't explain it."

I move so that I'm sitting across from her. "Baby, look at me." She does and I continue. "None of that matters. I just want you to be happy. I want you in my life no matter how it has to be. If you just want to be best friends who raise their son together, I'll take it. If you want to be my neighbor, mother of my teenage son, I'll take it. If you want to be my wife and have more babies, I'll take it. I just want you."

She starts to cry so I gently pull her to me and kiss her head. "I love you so much, Ryan."

"I love you too, Shayla. We'll work this out." She nods into my chest.

After a few minutes, she pulls back. "I want to shower and change. Will you help me get my arm covered?"

"Of course."

We wrap her arm in a plastic wrap that the nurse left us to keep her IV port from getting wet and then I help her into the shower, making sure she's settled before I pull the curtain closed.

"You need anything else?"

"No, but can you stand there until I get this gown off? In case I get dizzy."

"Sure. Is your head still hurting?"

"No, not really, I just feel woozy." She hands me the gown. "After I'm done, I want to go see Dylan."

"We can do that. Do you want me to sit in here with you?"

She sighs. "Is it silly that I do? I'm afraid to be alone."

I feel a deep-seated sadness for her. She should never have to feel that way, but I'd be lying if I said the thought of leaving her didn't cause me pain as well.

"No, of course not. Honestly, I don't want to leave you either. Going to your locker made me feel a little anxious."

"We probably all need therapy."

"Probably. I'll go if that's what you want."

"I don't want to, but I think it's necessary. I'm sure there will be nightmares."

"I worry about that too, but we'll work through it."

We talk the entire time she's in the shower, then I hand her the towel and her clothes as she asks for them. She stays behind the curtain, but I don't blame her. I want her as comfortable as she can possibly be. As soon as we are back in her room, she is ready to leave.

"Can we go see Dylan now?"

"How about I brush your hair for you, then we can go over there."

She reaches up to her hair. "Oh, yeah. I forgot about my hair. You really want to brush it?"

"I've noticed you wince when you reach up. Let me help you." She nods and hands me the brush.

"Do you remember when we were kids and you tried to put my hair in a ponytail for me?"

I chuckle. "Yeah. It was pretty awful, but I did it."

"You used a regular rubber band and it got stuck in my hair. My mom had to cut it out, but she was laughing so hard she accidentally clipped some of my hair. I had to get layers to fix it. My dad was so sad that my long hair was gone."

"That's why you cut your hair? I don't think I ever knew that. I can do a mean ponytail now, if you want one."

"How about a messy bun?"

"My favorite." She giggles. I absolutely love that sound. I'm so thankful to have her back with me so I can hear it often. "Done."

She looks into the mirror and nods. "Not bad. Let's go see our baby."

"Last I heard he was still asleep."

I help her get her IV situated and we head to Dylan's room. He is still asleep, but she presses a kiss to his forehead and sits beside him.

"The doctor was just in," Gail tells us. "She thinks he'll be able to go home this evening as long as he's awake and eats before then."

Shay nods. "Yeah, they'll want to be sure he's alert and functioning properly. I think I'll take a few bags of fluids and a pole home. Just to be sure. He wasn't there long, but he's pretty dehydrated and probably starving." Shayla flips through his chart quickly.

"Are you hungry?" Tom asks her after she sits staring at Dylan for a long time.

She shakes her head as if to clear her thoughts. "Yeah, I could eat, but I don't really want to eat here."

Tom is on his feet, ready to get her everything she needs. "I'll get you anything you want."

"Honestly, I'd really like a big fat cheeseburger with everything. I probably shouldn't eat something like that right now, but I haven't eaten much in a while. I'm just hungry."

We all chuckle. "You've got it. I'll go to that new burger restaurant you like." Her eyes grow wide in excitement. He kisses her head. "Anything else?"

"No bread and a salad."

"How is that bad for you? I thought you wanted a big burger with the works?" I tell her with a laugh. She's too healthy sometimes.

"Okay, fine. I want it on bread and a side of fries with a milkshake."

Tom bops her lightly on the chin. "That-a-girl."

We talk to Gail while we wait on Tom to come back. Shayla fills her in on as much as she's comfortable with sharing. She doesn't say anything about her sexual abuse and she skims over her physical abuse, but it's understandable. Her mom has worried for so long, and knowing the person Shayla is and how much she cares for her parents, it doesn't surprise me that she's trying to downplay her experience.

Tom comes back with everyone's food orders after about twenty minutes. Gail jumps up and clears off the rolling patient table for him to set the food on when Dylan stirs. We all look over expectantly and unanimously sigh in relief as my son opens his eyes.

"Smells good," Dylan mumbles.

"Dylan!" Shayla rushes to him and kisses him.

"Mom, I'm fine. Stop." He starts to laugh as Shayla peppers kisses all over his face.

"Sorry. I'm just so happy you're awake. Do you feel okay?" She flutters all around him. He grabs her wrist.

"Hey, I'm okay. I promise." She starts to cry. "Mom, please don't cry."

"I'm so sorry, Dylan. I didn't protect you."

"You did all you could. We're safe now, right?" He looks to me.

"Yeah, buddy. You are both safe." I grab his hand, my own tears springing to my eyes. I rub Shayla's back. "Baby." She turns and buries her face in my shirt. "Shay," I murmur. She is totally losing it.

Dylan sits up gingerly and wraps his arms around the both of us. "Mom, please. I'm okay. I'll heal. Please don't cry."

She pulls back and grabs a tissue from the bedside table. "I'm sorry. I'm just so thankful we're okay. I mean, it could've been so much worse."

"It could've been, but it wasn't."

I kiss her cheek and she doesn't flinch. It's a good sign, because earlier when I kissed her forehead she inhaled so sharply it startled me.

"Can we eat now?" Dylan asks, eyeing the food Tom and Gail are pulling out of the bag.

"Of course we can, baby. Pop got your favorite, triple burger with the works." Gail hands him his food and he digs in.

As I watch my family eat, I can't help but feel overwhelming love and thankfulness that they are finally safe. Things could have gone so differently. I could have lost one or both of them. I can't even begin to fathom how I would have dealt with that. I'm truly grateful that God has brought them home to me.

CHAPTER TWENTY-FOUR
Shayla

"How does that make you feel?"

I try to hide the smirk on my face. Ryan absolutely hates therapy and hates that question most of all.

"It makes me feel like I'm not going to come back if you ask me that question one more time." I squeeze his hand and he turns to look at me. "I can see you trying to stifle your smile, Shay. It's not funny." He is such a grump today.

We've been home for going on three weeks. We've all been in therapy two times a week since. Dylan has, surprisingly, adjusted the best out of the three of us. He said he was knocked out so much that he really doesn't remember what happened. Though, he has been a little clingy to me and worries constantly if we are apart and has had a few nightmares about Trevor beating him. He also freaked out when Ryan was the one to check on him during his nightmare. We've made mistakes and are learning how to cope with this horrible event in our lives. Things may never be as they were before, but things are getting better.

"Shayla?" I shake my head, having been lost in my own little world, something that seems to happen a lot for me nowadays.

"Sorry, what did you say?"

"I asked how you felt about Ryan's revelation." I stare at Doctor Martinson, blinking like a lost toddler. "You didn't hear what he said?"

"Sorry. I kind of zoned out."

She smiles. "It's okay. Ryan, do you want to repeat what you said?"

Ryan shifts in his seat so he's facing me and takes my hand. "I said that I'm tired of trying to fight what I feel for you. I know you need time. I'm willing to give that to you, but I hate going home alone at night. I hate being in my house period if you guys aren't there, I want us to be a proper family. I want to get married. I don't want to wait."

I blink rapidly, trying to keep my tears at bay. "You want to marry me?"

"Yes, like on Saturday. You know, if you're not busy."

I jump up and start to pace. "Shayla, tell me what you're thinking," Doctor Martinson requests.

I turn and look at her, running my hands through my hair. "He wants to marry me. I can't even kiss him, but he expects me to marry him ... and ... and, be his wife. I can't. I ... I...."

Ryan grabs my hand and slowly, as if I'm a frightened kitten, pulls me into his arms. "We don't have to do anything you're not ready for. I just can't stand the thought of being without you as my wife for another moment. I've loved you my whole life, Shayla."

"I love you too, Ryan, but I can't be someone's wife."

"Shayla, we've talked about what Trevor did, it didn't make you his wife. That paperwork was never filed. It was never legally, or spiritually, binding."

"I know, but every time I think of getting married, I see him beating my son. Plus, he left all that property to me. It feels like it was real."

"Yes, he left that to you in his will. He willed it to you, Shayla Thorn. Not to Mrs. Trevor Daniels. You can sell that property and be rid of him completely."

I stop my pacing. "You think it's that simple? I just sell the land and it'll all be over?"

"I didn't say it would be over, but it could help you move on. Give you some closure. Is there a reason why you can't sell it?"

I sit down with a plop. I have no idea why the thought of selling that property sets me off. I feel anxious and scared. I know I could never go back there.

"Babe." Ryan sits down beside me and offers me his hand; I take it without pause. "I'm here for you one-hundred percent. If you want to wait to get married, I'll do it. I just don't want him to be the one holding you back. I'm not him, baby. I'd never force you to do anything you were uncomfortable with. We can get twin beds, like those old TV sitcoms."

I can't help it, I burst out laughing. Ryan smiles at me, the same boyish smile that drew me in all those years ago. I don't know what makes me act, I don't think it's a conscious decision, but I lean forward and kiss him. It's a short sweet kiss, but a kiss nonetheless. Something I've not been able to do since he rescued me. We stare at each other in complete and total shock. He lifts his hand to my face, and even though the need to flinch is strong, I don't, because I know Ryan would never hurt me. I lean my head towards his palm and close my eyes, covering his hand with mine.

"Can I kiss you?" he whispers. I nod and he leans forward slowly, kissing my lips in a soft lingering kiss.

"I'll marry you." I open my eyes and look at him. "I want to be your wife."

The earth shattering smile that erupts on his bearded face is absolutely contagious. "Really?"

"Yes."

He pulls me to my feet and hugs me tightly to him, picking me up and spinning me around as we laugh together and steal a few more kisses.

"Well, I'd say we've had a breakthrough today."

I'd totally forgotten that we were in Doctor Martinson's office. She is smiling widely at us, so it obviously didn't bother her in the slightest.

"Thank you," I tell her.

"How about we end on that note?"

We both nod as she rises and walks out of her office towards the receptionist. We set our next appointment and leave holding hands.

"Wanna get some lunch?" Ryan asks.

"Yeah."

"How about we order from Rosie's and eat on the river bank?"

"Sounds perfect."

We sit on the emergency blanket I keep in my car. Our impromptu picnic is perfect and quiet as we listen to the cacophony of sounds from the animal and insect life around us. It's not an uncomfortable silence; it's just a companionable one. It's nice and refreshing after a long session, especially with such a huge breakthrough. The silence is broken with a small pop and a squeak from Ryan's side of the blanket. I turn from watching the water to see that Ryan has knelt down on one knee and is holding out a small ring box with a bright shining engagement ring. I gulp.

"Shayla, I've loved you almost my entire life. First as a friend, then later as a girlfriend, and most recently as the mother of my son, but the most important thing I've realized over the past month is that no matter what type of love I have for you, one thing remains the same, I never want it to end. I want you always. Will you be my wife?"

I blink and wipe at the tears in my eyes. This isn't like anything I've experienced. Not when Todd asked me to marry him and definitely not when Trevor forced me to marry him. This … this is what I've always wanted. I've always wanted to be Mrs. Ryan Jacobs, I just never thought it would be possible.

"Of course I will."

He takes my hand and gently slips on my ring. "It's beautiful."

The ring is stunning in an understated beauty, a princess cut emerald wrapped in a ring of small diamonds on a platinum band.

"I'm glad you like it. I wanted something simple but different."

"It's perfect. I love you so much, Ryan."

I launch myself at him, knocking us both to the ground. He laughs as he wraps his arms around me.

"Glad you like it. What're you doing next Saturday?"

He brushes the hair back from my face and looks at me with so much love that I feel like I'll burst with happiness. This is the look I've always dreamt of and haven't had since we were together as kids.

"Nothing that I know of, why?"

"Let's get married in our back yard, under the tree house."

Maybe the thought of getting married so soon after a proposal should scare me, but after what I've lived through the past couple of months, I just don't see why waiting would be necessary. I trust this man completely.

"I swear I won't pressure you to do a single thing. You're in the lead here."

"Sounds perfect. I love you."

We kiss for a few minutes, then remember we are in a park and need to keep it more G rated, so we gather our things and head back home. It seems like things are happening so quickly, but really I've been waiting for this my entire life. I love Ryan like I've loved no other. He's always held my heart. I know this is the right choice. Our life may not be perfect, and we'll have things to work through, but we'll be just fine. We'll do whatever it takes to make our marriage work.

~*~

A week later, I'm standing in front of my bedroom mirror, adjusting my wedding dress when there's a knock on my door. I crack it open, then smile, and open it fully.

"Hey, baby." I hug my son.

"You look beautiful, Mom."

"Thanks."

I go back to the mirror and fidget with my dress again. Dylan comes over with me, but after a few minutes, he squeezes my hand, making me stop my ministrations.

"Are you okay?"

"Yes, sorry. I'm just really nervous. I shouldn't be; this is what I've wanted since before you were born."

"You're getting your wish. We all are. I know I didn't know about Dad for a long time, but even when I didn't, I always dreamed of being a real family one day. This isn't like with Todd, I could tell back then you didn't really want to marry him. Then … yeah, that other thing was just messed up. This is your dream wedding."

I smile at my very intuitive son. "It is. Everything looked so pretty last night. I can't wait to go out there."

"Then why are you so nervous?"

I think for a few long moments. "I guess because of what happened with Trevor." Dylan winces and I rub his upper arm. I don't want to think about it, but I feel it needs addressing. "I'm worried he'll show up. I know that's impossible, but we both know Jason is still out there. I have this overwhelming fear he'll show up and ruin everything."

"Dad said the last report he got was from Interpol saying that he was seen in Europe. I think you're safe today, we all are. Try not to worry about it. Dad has this whole place on lockdown. I think every FBI and CIA person he and Pop knows is here. The whole police force would be here too if they didn't have other duties."

I giggle. "You're right. Everything will be fine. I think it's just pre-wedding jitters. It's normal."

"Yeah, totally normal. I should get back out there. Dad needs his best man." He turns to leave, but stops. "Oh, I forgot to tell you, I had sex with Faith."

I stare open-mouthed at my son for a few minutes. "You did what?"

He throws his head back and guffaws. "Just kidding, I asked her to be my promise partner."

Now I look at him confused. "What?"

"At church, we had an abstinence pledge night and they said if you had a girlfriend that you felt strongly for that you should give them a token of your love as a pledge to be each other's promise partner. You know, to agree to wait for each other until marriage."

A huge smile crosses my face and I hug my son. "I'm so proud of you. I had no idea the two of you were that serious."

"Yeah, it wasn't until the accident, but I realized when I thought I'd never see her again that I regretted not telling her I loved her. I don't want to have any more regrets. I really like Grammy's church and I really think the promise pledge is awesome. I mean, I'm telling Faith that she's worth waiting for. That's honoring her, isn't it?"

I cup his sweet, sweet face. "Oh, baby. That is such an honor for you and her. I really am proud of you. That's one of the best gifts I've received today. You've really turned into a strong young man. I love that you want to go to church and that it has inspired you in this way."

"I do. I might want to be in the ministry one day. It would be awesome if we could go as a family."

"You bet, sweetheart. I'd love to go with you."

"Great! I'll see you out there." He turns again. "Oh, one more thing, I asked Dad if I could change my last name. I think we should all be Jacobs."

He kisses my cheek and hurries out of the room. I start to cry. I can't help it. My son is just too much for me to handle sometimes. I don't know what I did to deserve such an awesome child, but I'll thank God every day for allowing me to be the one he calls mom.

"Oh, why the tears?" My mom bursts through the door, looking worried.

I wave her off. "Just an overly sweet son."

She grins. "He told you about the name change?"

I take the proffered tissue. "Yes, and about the promise pledge."

"That's wonderful, isn't it?" I nod, but say nothing. I'm so overwhelmed with joy. "It's time to get out there. Are you ready?"

"Yeah, let me touch up my makeup."

It takes me a few minutes, and then she leads me down the hallway to my father. He wraps his arm around one of mine while my mom is on the other as we start our descent down the stairs and to the yard where Ryan waits for me. The joy on his face is enough to knock me down, it's beaming so brightly. He looks fantastic in his black suit with white shirt, his hair is pulled back in a bun and his face is neatly groomed. I was against the beard for a while, but it's honestly grown on me. He looks like a sharp polished businessman, with a fun playful side. Now that I think about it, that is very indicative of his personality, serious and hardworking, but fun and loving with those he cares about.

On the right of Ryan stands the preacher of the church Dylan attends, First Baptist of Oak Grove. To Ryan's left is Dylan, Marsh, Jon, Riley, and Paul; his team and best friends. They went above and beyond what any of us could have asked for. They are truly part of our family now. On my side stands less people, but they are still important to me, Jessica, Julie, and Laney. Jessica was relentless in her search for Dylan and I. Julie has been there for me since I started at the hospital, but really stepped up to the plate when we were recovering. And Laney, my very soon to be sister-in-law, has never wavered in her love and support of our little family. These women have been a huge help and blessing to me.

As we reach the end of the aisle and the pastor asks who gives this woman, my parents both proudly state that they do. All the while, I can't take my teary eyes off of Ryan and his equally teary ones. He takes my hand and I know that no matter what happens to us from this point forward that we will face it together as a team. The wish I made long ago on my birthday has finally come true. Choices, some my own, and some out of my control, led us the long way around, but we're here now and nothing can stop us.

EPILOGUE

Ryan

Eighteen months later:

"So how does it feel to officially be a senior?" I ask my son as he climbs in my car after his last official day of his eleventh year of school.

Dylan's smile lights up the world. "So good. I can't wait to get this next year over with."

"Don't rush it. Enjoy your youth while you can."

"I'm not trying to rush my life away. I just want to start my career. I've already completed four college courses. I'm taking a couple this summer too."

Ah, my son the overachiever, not that it's a bad thing. He's very focused on what he wants. It's what he wants that gives pause. His plan is to go to college for Criminal Justice, then go through the police academy, and then on to Quantico. I have no reason to stop or discourage him. It's actually an honor that he wants to follow in my footsteps; I just worry about his safety. That worry seems to have gotten worse over the past nine months.

"You'll do great. I have faith in you."

"I know you do. Speaking of Faith, she's coming for dinner so you and Mom can go out."

I grin. "You two spoil her."

"No way. She's perfect."

"I agree."

We arrive at our house a few minutes later and Dylan sprints inside. Once Shayla and I married, I went to work merging our houses. My house was on such a good corner lot and combined with her childhood home, I couldn't resist. Oh, when I say merge, I really mean that. Our houses were about fifteen feet apart, so we built an extension between the two and made it one large forty-five hundred square foot house. We took out my kitchen and turned it into a huge family area, but we left everything else the same for now. So we now have a five bedroom house, which we plan to fill with children.

"Hannah!" Dylan calls as he enters the family room.

She immediately starts babbling. Hannah's our honeymoon baby. Whatever hang-ups Shayla had were gone by the second night of our short honeymoon. Then, three weeks later, we found out that we were going to be parents again. Going through everything with her this time was absolutely amazing.

We were a little hesitant in telling Dylan, but we shouldn't have been. He was over the moon happy to have a sibling. It didn't bother him one bit that she was almost seventeen years younger than him. Watching him with her sometimes reminds me that I would have been about his age when he was a baby. I hate that I missed those days, but so glad I can have this now with Hannah and Dylan.

Hannah is named after Shayla's biological mom, and rightfully so, as she looked just like her grandmother and, in turn, just like her mother, with bright blue eyes and gorgeous blonde hair. Having a daughter has been life changing. The first time I laid eyes on her, I was a goner. There was nothing in this world that could come at us that I wouldn't stop. There was nothing I wouldn't do for this little bundle of screaming joy. It also triggered my need for more guns. I now have a locked room set aside on my old side of the house that's pretty much full of every weapon I could get my hands on. Extreme to some, namely my wife, but to me it will never be enough until every person like Mathis is out of our lives for good.

Mathis is still a thorn in my side. We've kept tabs on sightings of him over the past nineteen months, but for the past five, he's been off radar. I haven't mentioned it to Shayla, there's no need for her to worry, but Tom and I have spent hours locked away in my office, planning and searching. His CIA contacts have truly come in handy. I was floored when Tom shared his past with me. It explained so much that I didn't understand when I first started coming around Shayla.

"Tell Daddy bye-bye, Hannah."

I look up to see my son waving his sister's chubby arm as she laughs and drools all over the place. He is really the best brother and an excellent babysitter, if I do say so myself.

"Can't I at least say hello to my daughter before you kick me out of my own house?" I ask indignantly.

"Suit yourself, but if you're late picking Mom up, you have no one to blame but yourself."

"It's worth her anger." I scoop up my daughter and cover her face in kisses, making her squeal in delight. "Are you sure you and Faith don't mind watching her? I'm sure Gail and Tom, or even my mom would keep her. You should celebrate your last day of school."

"Maw's had her all day and Gran is all the way across town. It's fine, honest. Faith and I are going to play with her, feed her, and then put her to bed. We'll get our courses lined up for this summer and watch a movie. I swear things will be fine."

"I know I've said it a thousand times, but please try to pace yourself. I don't want you burning out before you've even gotten out of high school."

"I'm not, Dad. This is what I want. I want to be a cop. I want to help, to make a difference, just like you've done."

"I'm proud of you for that, but you're still a kid. It's not your job to babysit your sister every Friday."

"It's not every Friday. Next week, I'll take Faith out."

"Your mom is on vacation next week. You're off Hannah duty all week. Go get Faith and go to the beach or something. Just make it a point to do some fun things."

"I will. We're planning on volunteering at church with the Shepard program so we'll be busy with that during the days most of the summer. You can't be against that. It'll look great on college applications."

"I'm not against you helping inner city kids. I just want you to have the childhood that your mom and I never did. I don't want you to have regrets."

"I won't. I swear."

"All right, I'm going to get your mom. Love you both."

I kiss my baby girl on the cheek before handing her back to her big brother, whom she absolutely adores. Shayla and I hit the jackpot with those two. They are both more than I could have ever hoped or dreamed. I'm so ridiculously happy that I can't help but to grin like a fool as I make my way through town to pick up my wife.

Shayla hurries over to my car and jumps in. "You're late."

"Last minute baby snuggles and chat with the oldest."

"Ah, I miss my baby snuggles. What chat?"

I tell her briefly about our talk. I know she agrees, but she rarely mentions it to him. She feels like he's capable of making his own decisions. I do too, but I also like to give my opinion, needed or not.

"So, where are you taking me?"

"Date night tonight will be bowling and greasy food."

"Yum. I can't remember the last time I bowled."

Shayla and I make it a point to set aside one night a week for just us. We need the break and the reconnection that it provides. Sometimes we do an activity she enjoys, others that I like, but each time it is something that helps bring us closer. Our relationship is more solid now than it has ever been. Our past is behind us and nothing has held either of us back when it comes to each other. We are the happiest we've ever been, we're a strong unbreakable team.

We spend the night laughing, talking, flirting, and even poking fun of each other's game. It's the perfect night which ends with us kissing on our front steps, like most date nights, but tonight is slightly different. When we finish climbing the stairs, we notice a package sitting by the front door. Thinking nothing of it, I pick it up and carry it into our kitchen. I set it on the table before heading to the refrigerator for a drink. I'm about to ask Shayla what she wants when I notice her staring at the box.

"Honey, what's wrong."

Her head turns slowly to me, her eyes wide. "I recognize that handwriting."

I hurry over to her and pull the envelope attached to the box. I open it, taking out the unsigned letter.

You have a lovely family, Ryan. Your son seems so enthralled with his sister. Almost like he's the father, maybe he'll be the one to raise her someday.

I've so missed the chase, Ryan. I ache for it. The thrill of holding a life in my hands, knowing I'm the one who decides if they live or die. It's exhilarating.

Shayla looks well. I can't wait to make her mine. Have no doubt, Ryan. She will be mine. Maybe not tomorrow or the next day or even three months from now, but one day soon, she will be with me again. I'll be the one holding her life in my hands. Will she live or die? That's up to you.

I throw the letter down and rip open the box. We stare in horror, frozen in our places, at the small innocent looking folded paper in the shape of a fox.

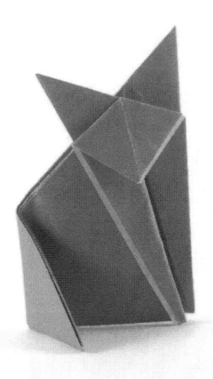

AUTHOR NOTE

Thank you so much for reading Vengeance. It has definitely been a great learning experience, one that I'll cherish for a long time. You know how you don't know if you can do something until you actually do it? Yes, I found out that with a little blood, sweat, and a few tears that I could write this novel.

Vengeance, however, is just the beginning for the Oak Grove Suspense Series. There is so much more to come. I do hope that you fell in love with Ryan, Shayla, and Dylan as much as I have, and don't worry; you'll get to hear from them again soon. The next book in the series, Penance, is already in the works and should be out by spring 2017.

As with most things, the second time around is so much smoother and I find that writing Penance is coming along quicker than anticipated. In Penance, we will continue to follow our favorite detective, Ryan Jacobs, and we'll also get to meet a new character by the name of Judson Hardenbergh. We'll learn a little about Judson's backstory and what ties he has to Oak Grove, as well as to Ryan, when a murder takes place on his property. You might be wondering how Mathis, aka The Fox, fits in to all of this. Well, guess you'll just have to read the book to find out, but I'm sure he's up to no good.

Thanks again for reading my book. I really appreciate it and am honored you took time for me.

Until next time …

Reese

ABOUT THE AUTHOR

Reese Stephens was born in the Appalachian Mountains, but was raised all over the East Coast. Since getting married Reese has settled back into her Appalachian roots, and currently lives on a small farm with her husband and three children. She has a Bachelor's of Science degree in Education, and is currently homeschooling her two school aged children. She considers herself a naturalist. She loves learning about and using natural remedies and essential oils to keep her family and herself healthy.

Writing was something Reese never thought much of, until she and her family went through several traumatic events. A friend advised her to keep a journal, but she just couldn't put into words how she felt, so she turned to the world of creative writing. It didn't take long for her to discover her passion there.

Reese is currently working on publishing the first book in her Oak Grove Suspense series, Vengeance which will be out this fall. The second in the series, Penance, is expected to be released spring 2017. In addition to writing crime suspense she also writes paranormal romance. Her first story in this genre is called The Reluctant Prince, expected release is late 2017. You can, however, read the first few chapters of it on Wattpad or her Website for FREE.

Social Media Contacts:
Facebook: https://www.facebook.com/ReeseAStephens/
Twitter: https://twitter.com/ReeseAStephens
Instagram: https://www.instagram.com/reeseastephens/
Wattpad: https://www.wattpad.com/user/ReeseStephens
Website: https://reeseastephens.com/

WINYAN
PRESS LLC

CONTACT INFORMATION

Email: WinyanPress@gmail.com
Facebook: https://www.facebook.com/WinyanPress/
Twitter: https://twitter.com/WinyanPressLLC
Website: http://winyanpressllc.org/
YouTube:https://www.youtube.com/channel/UCXDbnx5FNpduMnDHlu5eWiw

Winyan Press Mailing Lists

Young Adult Fiction Listserv

On this mailing list you will receive updates on new works of Young Adult fiction by Winyan Press authors as well as receive special incentives exclusive to members on the listserv. Titles in this genre include The Ceaseless Trilogy, The Diakrisis Tales and Thirty Eight. Join HERE: http://eepurl.com/bJB8Iv

Adult Romance Fiction Listserv

On this mailing list you will receive updates on new works of Adult Romance fiction by Winyan Press authors as well as receive special incentives exclusive to members on the listserv. Titles in this section will be adult in nature and may include graphic language and situations not suitable for younger audiences. Titles in this genre include The Helios Chronicles. Join HERE: http://eepurl.com/bJB7cj

Crime/Suspense Fiction Listserv

On this mailing list you will receive updates on new works of Crime/Suspense fiction by Winyan Press authors as well as receive special incentives exclusive to members on the listserv. Titles in this genre include The Talionic Files and the Oak Grove Suspense Series. Join HERE: http://eepurl.com/bKoAFv

Paranormal Fiction Listserv

On this mailing list you will receive updates on new works of Paranormal fiction by Winyan Press authors as well as receive special incentives exclusive to members on the listserv. Titles in this genre include The Rune Scrolls, The Diakrisis Tales and The Reluctant Prince. Join HERE: http://eepurl.com/b9ddWD

NOW FOR A SNEAK PEEK AT

BOOK 2 IN THE OAK GROVE SUSPENSE SERIES

PENANCE:
AN OAK GROVE SUSPENSE

SNEAK PEEK

"Ryan, you can't let them take him. He didn't do this," Laney says as she runs toward Judson. She puts her hands on his chest.

"Laney, please stop," he begs her.

Jessica looks over at me for help. I stride to my sister and wrap my arm around her shoulder. "We have to do our job. He'll be fine, but if you cause problems, I'll be forced to take you in with him."

"Me? I didn't do anything. Would you seriously arrest your own sister?" I smirk at her and she slaps me. Well, that was a surprise, but before I can respond, she starts speaking again. "I'm being serious. You know he didn't do this. Why do you need to cuff him?"

"Laney, just let them do their job. You don't have to save me," Judson tells her softly.

Laney throws her hands up in the air, obviously frustrated with the situation. "If I don't, who will?"

"Hey, just let me handle this," I interject. "If he didn't do this then there's nothing to worry about."

She looks up at me with so much sadness in her blue eyes that it breaks my heart. I didn't realize how much she cared about Judson. I pull her into a hug as tears start to run down her cheeks. I brush her fiery red hair back from her face and kiss her head. I can't stand to see my baby sister cry, and it's even worse because there's nothing I can do to fix this, at least right now.

Judson looks up to the sky with a frustrated groan. "I'm fine, Laney. Please, stop crying."

She looks at him. "You're not fine. You didn't do this."

"And they'll figure that out. Let your brother and these fine officers do their job."

"But..." Laney starts, until Judson interrupts.

"Stop, Alaina." His voice is stern, but not angry. "I'm serious. This is none of your business. I'm none of your concern. Just leave. Please."

I can see by his expression that it hurts him to brush her off like this, but at the same time, I can see a deep-seated resolve in him. He doesn't want her involved. He probably doesn't think he deserves her. I understand that because I felt the same way about Shayla. And even after I got over my anger with the situation, it still took me months to contact her. I just hope, for his and Laney's sake, that he really is innocent. And if Laney is the one then he better open his eyes before it destroys them both.

I watch as Jessica leads him to the squad car and helps him inside. Laney turns back into my chest, sobbing. I pull her over to my car and help her sit in the passenger's seat, taking her hands in mine.

"Laney, what's going on?"

She looks up at me with indignation. "What do you mean, 'What's going on?' You're taking an innocent man to jail for a crime he didn't commit."

"There's more to it than that, and we're taking him in for questioning and will hold him until we can rule him out as a suspect. Personally, I'm not convinced he did this, but I have to follow the law."

"But you know him. He was one of your best friends. Why do you have to treat him like a criminal?" I wipe the tears from my sister's face and hand her my handkerchief. She huffs out a dry laugh. "PawPaw used to carry these."

I smile at her. "I know; he gave me his before he passed."

I know that I could technically stop this right here and move on with my day, and even though I need to get to the station and investigate around these premises, I decide my sister is worth the extra time. She needs me right now.

"Laney, you know I'm not treating him like a common criminal. I can't pull favors just because I know someone. Even if it was you who was found with a dead body and near the suspected murder weapon, I'd still have to follow procedures. Please, don't fight me on this."

"He's just been through so much."

"I know, and you feel sorry for him."

She shakes her head. "No, it's more than that. I've always..." she pauses and takes a deep breath. "I've always had a thing for him. I gave up when he got married and had the kids, but when he moved back here, my feelings for him only grew stronger. He needs me. He just won't stop wallowing in his guilt long enough to see that."

"Okay, I get it, but you can't be his hero right now. Just be his friend. I'll call you, even though I really shouldn't, when he's released. You can stop by and get him. For now, though, please stay away from the station."

"All right, I'll go home. Ryan, even if he tells you not to call me, please let me know. I don't want him walking home."

"I'll do my best. Can you drive yourself home?"

"Yeah." I help her to her car and watch as she drives away.

"Pete, tell me whatcha got."

He motions with his head for me to follow him. I trail behind him to the back of the house and down a path, which looks to have been recently cleared. We walk about five-hundred yards and then veer off the path into the woods about 100 feet.

"How did Judson say he came upon the body?"

"He said he was out for his morning run and saw something odd; it was the body."

I shake my head. "Stay here."

I turn and walk back to the path, run down a bit, then turn and run back up, imagining that I'm Judson on his morning run. There are several people standing around or investigating the crime scene, who glance and look at me. I just don't see how he'd notice the body from the path. I know it's not impossible, but it is unlikely. I'll need to get his side of the story. I jog back over to the group.

"Is there anything that points to anyone other than Judson?"

"There's some debris under Mr. Clark's nails. It's very apparent that the victim fought his attacker. We'll look at the particulates and test them against Judson. It should only take about twenty-four hours before we have something concrete. We'll also test the weapon against the injuries and see if there is a match."

"Get back to me as fast as you can," I tell the M.E. Then I turn to my men. "Take pictures of everything and bag anything that's even remotely suspicious. I'm heading back to the station."

It takes me about twenty minutes to get back. I don't waste any time heading inside and go straight to the interrogation rooms. I don't bother talking to Jessica. I know Judson will tell me everything I need to know. He looks up when I open the door. I pull out the seat in front of him, but pause before I sit so I can get into my pocket for my keys and un-cuff him. I know we don't need them.

"Tell me everything from the beginning."

He rubs his wrists for a few seconds, then looks up at me. "I woke up this morning hung over from the night before. I felt awful, but I had work I needed to do so I went for a run to shake it off." I nod in understanding. "I run the same way every morning. I start up the right path to the pond and then go down the left path. I was on my way back when I saw something glinting in the sun. I stopped and ran back a bit to see if I could see it again, and I could. I stood there for a few minutes trying to figure out what it was, but I just couldn't tell, so I went into the woods and that's when I saw the body."

"What was glinting? Did you know it was Ralph Clark?" I ask.

He shakes his head. "Not at first. I felt for a pulse, but I knew there wouldn't be one, he looked cold and stiff. I flipped him over and saw it was him. I guess it was his watch I saw, but I didn't really pay attention once I realized it was a person."

"Did you touch anything else on the body?"

"No. I pulled my cellphone out, but I didn't have service so I left the body and ran back to the house. I called as soon as I got there."

"What did you do after you placed the call?"

He runs his hand through his hair. "I sat on the porch and waited for the cops to show. I told them where I found him, and then your officer talked to me until you got there."

I sit there for a few minutes, staring at him as he looks down to the floor. I know my next question will be incriminating, but it has to be asked. "Judson, can you tell me where you were last night?"

"You know where I was, Ryan."

"I need you to tell me."

He exhales a breath and meets my eyes. "I was at Mooney's. I had a few drinks, and then went home."

"That's it?"

He looks at me pleadingly. "You know what happened."

Of course I know. I was there. I broke up the fight between them but I need him to say it. "Judson, I do know and, from where I'm sitting, it gives you a motive."

"I didn't kill him, Ryan. I swear to you. I've never thought about killing anyone. I moved up here to get away from people so I could live the rest of my miserable life alone. I can't say that I liked Ralph because I didn't. He caused me a lot of issues in my business and in my personal life, but I didn't kill him."

"Did you go anywhere, see, or talk to anyone after my sister dropped you off at your house?"

"No. I found some rum and drank myself into oblivion. I don't remember what time I passed out, but I woke up strangely early this morning, maybe four-thirty."

"What woke you up?"

"I don't know; I just woke up suddenly. I couldn't get back to sleep so I eventually went out for a run."

"I'm going to have to keep you here, at least for a little while longer."

"I figured as much. Do you think you can talk Laney into leaving me alone?"

I can't help but laugh. I stand and clap him on the back. "You're on your own with that one, but if it helps, I think she's good for you."

"Nope, doesn't help at all."

"You know that she won't give up."

He sighs. "I know."

"Come on, I'll take you to a cell and get you something to eat."

Even though it's procedure, I don't re-cuff him. He's not going anywhere, and I know there's no way he did this. I just need to prove that without a shadow of a doubt. He walks into the cell and looks at the cot, then back up to me.

"Homey."

I grin. "Hey, I've gotten some good sleep on these cots," I tease. Then more seriously, I add, "I'll figure this out. It won't be long." He nods but says nothing.

I lock up and start to walk away. "Ryan," Jud calls. I turn around. "Um, I'm sure my parents are going to find out about this, but could you tell them I can't have visitors or something? I don't want them seeing me like this." He gestures to himself. I'm guessing he means behind bars, but maybe it's his rough appearance.

"Yeah, man. No problem." He nods and mumbles his thanks before sitting down on the cot.

Made in the USA
Lexington, KY
27 November 2019